BOOK ONE OF THE CIRCUIT FAE
GENEVIEVE ISEULT ELDREDGE

Monster
House
Books

First Published by Monster House Books, LLC in 2017
Monster House Books, LLC
34 Chandler Place Newton, MA 02464
www.monsterhousebooks.com

ISBN 9781945723117

For all you sleeper-princesses out there.

CHAPTER ONE

SYL

Can you see them—the fair ones, the dark ones?
Lurking just beyond the edge of light
They are there, waiting for you
Waiting, waiting for you to Awaken
- Glamma's Grimm

If dreams are supposed to be prophetic, then I must be destined to be a track star. I'm always running in this dream, running through the wet city streets after the crash. My leg is bleeding, a piece of iron shrapnel sticking out, glinting in the streetlights. The shadows warp. There are...*things* chasing me. Dark and terrible things.

And among them, *her*.

I've never seen her face, only a flash of sapphire-blue eyes ringed in gold. She's not human—because, of course she's not. Goodness knows, I can't have normal dreams—but I'm drawn to her, the deepest part of what makes me *me* tugged and stretched and pulled inside out until I'm aching.

Until my heart is an arrow pointing straight at her.

Also, she's chasing me, but also she's helping me escape.

Also also? I think I'm totally crushing on her. And her on me.

How can I tell? Because dreams are officially dumb.

Apparently, so am I, because for the first time ever in my dream, I stop running. I turn, waiting for her to come out of the night, my huntress, my savior. Her shadow moves in the darkness, closer, closer...

I'm just about to glimpse her—

Clink! Clank! I jolt awake to the clatter of dishes ten minutes before my alarm. *Ugh. I was so close.* Not to mention, today is not the day I want to wake up early.

I roll over, tucking the covers up over my head. It doesn't help. *Clank! Clatter!*

Mondays are Mom's day off—Mondays and Saturdays. The rest of the week, she's up before the street sweepers and gone hours before I even think of rolling out of bed. She's a business of one, cleaning the schools before anyone is even in them. I guess it's good she's a morning person.

Right now, I wish I were. Because I'm so not.

I lie there in my makeshift blanket fort, straining to get back to my dream, to where I was just about to see...*her.*

But nope.

In trying to be quiet, Mom's louder than ever. Every *clink* and *chink* is followed by an "oops" or sigh or the frenzied sounds of someone trying to quiet their actions while somehow managing to make even more noise. I love my mom, but of all days—

Clank! Claaaaaaaaaaank!

Seriously? I shove my beat-up e-reader off the bed and stuff my pillow over my head. I'm regretting my poor life choices in staying up till one a.m. to finish "just one more chapter." Maybe that's why I'm having crazy dreams. Too much Irish folklore. I've been obsessed ever since Ms Duffy assigned that "personal heritage" project freshman year. Whatever. That e-reader's been my best friend this entire summer.

Ever since Fiann started ditching me. Right after the accident.

I was dead for like two minutes, or so the doctors say.

Fiann was supposed to be my best friend, but hers was the only face that seemed unhappy when I awoke, when I recovered, when I came back to school for the last few weeks before summer break…

We're not friends anymore. Not really.

Our "break up" has been brewing for a while now. Ever since midway through my freshman year. My dad's checks stopped coming, which meant less money, which meant fewer extracurriculars. Which meant…I couldn't keep up with Fiann and the rest of my friends.

She started treating me different right away—ignoring me, excluding me, ditching me…

The night of the crash was the final nail in the coffin of our friendship.

All summer, I've been a regular hermit. A pariah.

"Syl!" Mom's voice echoes down the hall of our shotgun apartment.

Gah! "Just ten more minutes." I am so not a morning person. Even the idea of opening my eyes is painful.

My alarm goes off. It's clearly a conspiracy. I give up on sleep, on my dream, on seeing *her*. "Fine! I'm up."

"You don't want to be late," Mom calls from the kitchen like some cheerfully disembodied Jiminy Cricket. "Not on your first day as a sophomore."

Don't I? Dreams are scary and all, but it's reality I've been dreading. The idea of having to face Fiann and all the girls who I'd thought were my friends sucks the life out of me. Big-time. That, along with having to explain how I—we, Fiann and me—survived a train wreck. Now she's a local hero, and I'm just the weird "girl who lived."

It sounds all Harry Potter cool, but it's not. Not by a long shot.

Aside from my weird dreams, I don't even remember anything about that night. It's all a blare of blinding white—heat and burning flame.

Apparently, Fiann dragged me from the train, a huge spike of iron shrapnel sticking out of my leg. She saved my life, and now she won't even talk to me? It doesn't make any sense. I heave a sigh. *When you're going through hell, just keep going.* That's what my Glamma always says.

Said, I remind myself. Glamma died four months ago in May. I was in the hospital, in surgery to remove the shrapnel from my thigh, when it happened. Her heart just stopped. Mom still won't talk about it. She always got this scary, haunted look in her eyes whenever I asked what happened, so I stopped asking.

Anyway, Glamma didn't tolerate anyone being whiny-pants, as she called it. She was Irish through and through, straight off the boat. And even though she had some weird ideas, like fairies actually being real and needing to keep her own book of Fae lore—her Grimm, she called it—her lamb stew was the best I ever tasted, and she was one tough cookie. The whole time I was in physical therapy for my leg, I tried to imagine myself half as tough as her. And well…

Glamma wouldn't be caught dead being whiny-pants about Fiann, and neither will I.

I drag my butt out of bed, limping a little. My leg is always stiff and sore in the mornings until I work out the kinks. My red hair is so tangled it looks like it aspires to one day be a rat's nest, but totally can't be bothered.

My alarm goes off again, and I resist the urge to punt it across the room. It's so old it'd probably smash into a thousand pieces, and then where would I be?

Not being able to listen to Euphoria, that's where.

I turn the dial, hoping WCKD will come in. It's a nearby college station out of Richmond VCU, specializing in local bands. Their frequency is iffy at best. I guess hearing college kids fiddly-farting around on the radio isn't high on anyone's list of priorities, but they do play a lot of Euphoria. This morning, right on cue, darkwave synths and electric violin fill my room.

Euphoria's voice cuts in, sweet and dark.

A flash of my dream comes to me—those sapphire-blue eyes ringed in gold. Somehow, Euphoria always reminds me of *her*. The girl in my dreams. Not that I'd be so lucky.

No more dreams. It's time to face reality, Syl.

But when I listen to Euphoria, I feel like I belong. At least somewhere.

I'm sure Fiann'll have all kinds of cool stories about seeing Euphoria's secret shows at the Nanci over the summer. Fiann's a regular celebrity now. A pang of regret stabs me.

I miss my high school hangout. I miss my friends.

Last year, there wasn't a day I didn't take the trolley to the Nanci and meet up with Fiann and Lennon. Pizza, video games, we'd try our hand at pool, though we all sucked. I'd bring my camera and take fake glamor shots of Lennon beating all the boys at the fighting games and Fiann flirting with the ones brave enough to put their quarter up for next round.

But that was before Dad's checks stopped coming. Out of the corner of my eye, I catch my Elephant Thai takeout polo on the back of my chair. It smells like satay sauce and girl-sweat.

Mom needs help with the bills, so I do what I can.

Rubbing my eyes, I pad down the hall to the bathroom. A quick, lukewarm shower and tooth brushing later, a pick dragged hastily through my hair to deal with the worst of the knots, and I deem myself school-ready.

I'm not exactly what you'd call a debutante.

Nothing can hide my wild, curly red hair and grey eyes, or the dusting of freckles across my nose and cheekbones. I'm too pale for most makeup. It's like my Irish heritage wants me to be a misfit or something.

I should probably prepare for the usual leprechaun and Lucky Charms jokes. Fiann used to protect me from all that, ever since sixth grade, but…

Not anymore.

"Morning, bug." Mom looks up from her coffee and toast. Her hands are careworn, raw and chafed even though she uses gloves. But her eyes are bright, and her strawberry-blonde hair is barely touched with grey. She's looked tired lately—ever since my accident—and I feel like I have to constantly tell her I'm okay.

"Morning." My vision blurs for a sec, then slips into that weird second sight I've had ever since I died and came back. It comes and goes without rhyme or reason, but it lets me see people's moods and emotions as a cloak of colors—their auras.

Glamma would've called it "Fae-sight." At least, according to her Grimm, which…I might have snuck a peek-see at once or twice when I was younger.

Before Glamma died and the Grimm vanished.

But honestly, I hit my head pretty hard in the crash. I'm sure my "Fae-sight" is just some weird woojy-woo leftover from that. Despite my fascination with Irish folklore, I don't really believe in magic or fairies.

I mean, not *really* really.

I've gotta admit, though, Mom's aura looks tired, coloring the air around her like a personal gloom-cloud.

She works too hard. Vowing to pick up extra shifts at Elephant Thai, I shake my head to dispel my Fae-sight and squeeze her arm as I slip past her into the kitchen nook.

The hazelnut coffee smells delicious—flavored coffee is one of Mom's few indulgences—but this morning I go for tea. My small stash of caramel crème brûlée hides in the back behind the toaster pops and the coffee filters. I put the kettle on and slump against the scarred countertop.

I am so not a morning person. And I am so not looking forward to this morning.

"School today." Mom says it gently. She gestures at the pan of scrambled eggs and toast she's left on the counter.

"Yeah." I smile, but it goes sideways.

She sees it but only sips her coffee, looking at me over the rim. "I haven't seen much of Fiann around lately."

I sigh inwardly. It was inevitable that she'd ask. When the checks stopped coming and we had to move out of the sprawls of the Fan and into the narrow tenements of Jackson Ward, everything changed. She blames herself for me losing my friends.

I don't. I blame them.

"It's all right, Mom." I shrug. What can I say? That they don't hang out with me because I have a takeout delivery job and a crappy pay-as-you-go track phone, because my jeans have holes in them, and not the cool, factory-distressed kind? That Fiann only deigns to talk to me because I'm the school paper's photographer and she wants to make sure I get her good side during her cheering competitions? Or that she's barely looked my way since the accident? That I've heard her say not-so-nice stuff about me behind my back?

"Well," Mom says.

Other kids would have to worry about a Mom-ism at this point—an "It's their loss" or some other motivational poster response.

My mom only pins me with those bright eyes. What is it about moms? Seriously, do they learn interrogation techniques in secret mom school? I shift and squirm, but she's a pro. She keeps staring.

The kettle goes off, the broken nozzle wheezing where it should whistle. Like a train. I shudder. After the accident, I'd torn the whistle part out. I dream about the crash every night. I don't need any more reminders.

I busy myself pouring the hot water through the strainer, watching the leaves float and then sink to steep. The rich, dark scent of caramel is heavenly—the only thing other than reading, photography, and Euphoria's music that really calms me—and I take a deep whiff, aware that Mom. Is. Still. Staring.

"It's not a big deal," I finally say, turning with my combo tea steeper/mug and a slice of toast. I take a bite, but my throat's dried up over my lie. I chew for what feels like forever before I swallow.

Her aura bleeds from grey to a light blue that means she's concerned. She holds my gaze a moment longer before releasing me. "All right, then." She never argues, never fights. She sags a little in her chair, looking for all the world like holding that coffee cup is the only thing keeping her up. I lean over the counter and kiss her temple.

"Want me to make you a bento?" I pull my own battered *Kiki's Delivery Service* bento box from the drawer. Lennon's the one who got me into bento. For her, it's fun and artful and cute. For me it's a way to make our meager food last longer and look not so terrible. I've gotten pretty good at hot dog octopi and panda-face rice balls.

7

Mom says it always cheers her up to see those smiling faces. I know it does. I've seen the flashes of pink in her aura.

"Won't it make you late?" Aaaaand…she's studying me again. She's kept that shrewd eye on me ever since the accident. I remember it, lying in the hospital bed, my knee and thigh bound up in bandages. The doctors couldn't get the shrapnel out. They didn't know if I'd walk again.

But I didn't cry until Mom came in crying. It wasn't until I saw what losing me would have done to her that I felt it—all the guilt.

I'm all she has. "Nah." I grab the small stained pan from the cupboard and the packet of sticky rice from the bottom cabinet. I take her coffee mug and pour her another cup. "Why don't you go grab a shower? I left the hot water for you this morning." Most mornings she doesn't shower so I can.

She smiles, and her aura lights up in pink and lavender. "What's this, a shower coffee?"

A smile cracks my face. I remember that morning when I was ten and so excited I brought her a coffee in the shower. Of course, I spilled it everywhere, but she just laughed, even though the rug was stained forever after that.

She ruffles my red hair and kisses my cheek.

Making her bento is totally going to make me late. Whatever. It's worth it.

I can handle getting into a little trouble to see Mom happy. After all, I did walk again, and without a limp. Some days, I can be as tough as Glamma. And I'm determined to leave the train, the accident, and everything about it behind me.

Where it belongs.

CHAPTER TWO
ROUEN

The Wild Hunt is coming
Over road, river, and rail
The dark Fae sluagh have your blood-scent, sleeper-princess
And there is no escape
For either of us
- Euphoria, "The Wild Hunt"

I plunge out of the busy club and into the night, onto the rain-soaked streets of Prague's Old City. With a shrug, I hitch my violin case higher on my shoulder, the club's neon sign flashing on my face, advertising Euphoria. Advertising me. A pang of wistfulness strikes me.

How I wish I could escape into my Euphoria stage persona forever.

But the show's over, and it's time to leave Euphoria behind and become who I really am.

Rouen Rivoche. Dark Fae. *Sluagh*, outcast.

I am a Huntress, and it's time for the Hunt.

Even now, I feel the Huntsman's command burning in my blood, compelling my obedience. I turn the corner into the cobblestone alley, and there he is.

The Huntsman. He's waiting for me.

"Hello, Rouen." He leans against the wall, every line of his leather-clad, muscular body brooding and coiled as if to strike. He looks up through a curtain of stark-white hair, his eyes as soulless as a shark's, though I know he postures for my benefit.

In the hopes I might find him attractive.

Gross.

"Agravaine." I try to keep it short and sweet. *Just the facts, Roue.* "I've fulfilled your Command. I made first contact with our prey."

Agravaine's eyes dilate darker, and I smell the hunger on him— the need for the Hunt, the chase, the capture, the fear of our prey— noxious as burning rubber. "And she swallowed the bait?"

"Yes." She was down in the pit, at the front of the stage, the power of my music drawing her in, lulling her into thinking I am harmless, alluring, available. Lulling her into thinking I am the prey and she the huntress.

"She'll follow you?" His doubt is as fake as the rest of his emotions.

Dark Fae magic is strong, and I am one of the strongest.

I hate this part, but once the Hunt is engaged, I have no control over it. I shrug one shoulder like it's nothing to me. "They always do."

His smile is sharp as knives as he laces his voice with power. "Then reel her in, dear Rouen."

His Command slams into me, stealing my free will. Strong as I am, I'm a puppet made to dance on strings. *His* strings, Agravaine, the Huntsman who enslaves me.

For now.

I nod stiffly and pull up my hood. Glad to leave him behind, I head deeper into Old City, looking for the best place to lay my trap.

Some nights are born to nightmare and dream, dark yet achingly beautiful. Tonight, Prague is awash in ethereal fog and the light from a misty moon. Sounds muffle on the cobblestone streets, and people move like ghosts in a mythical place—Avalon, from the time of King Arthur, or the Celtic land of the dead, Tír Na nÓg.

Nightmare and dream, so beautiful it can cut you.

Crap. I'm going all emo again.

Pulling my hood down tighter, I prowl the hazy, wet streets of Old City, my battered, sticker-laden violin case bumping gently against my shoulder. The end-of-summer rain is passing, and fog curls in sheets on the riverside. It rolls in, filling the labyrinth of alleyways with mist and misdirection. It's what the Fae, both fair and dark, call a "tule fog," thick and good for cloaking mischief.

I know because I have called it. Rain and fog from the western sky, enough to mask my passage through the mortal realm.

It's a thousand-percent emo to say so, but tonight feels made of nightmare and dream. A glimmering moment stamped on the fabric of time. That night on the train tracks was like that.

The night I saw her. The true sleeper-princess.

I saw her and I let her get away.

I've always been a sucker for a pretty face. At least…that's my official excuse, as far as Agravaine's concerned. I didn't get a good look at her at all.

It wasn't her face that drew me. Unlike the others, this girl fought—and not just for herself, but for her friend, unconscious at her feet. She was everything brave and courageous. She burned so brightly in the night.

A sleeper-princess of the fair Fae, enemy of my people.

As a dark Fae, I should have dealt her a swift death. But no part of me wanted that. Even knowing I was disobeying Father and all the arch-Eld. Again. Yes, siding with the sleeper-princesses cost me. Dearly.

I flex my right hand, but all I feel is the low thrumming hum of black circuitry twisting and pulling, spliced into my flesh.

The Moribund. Dark, disgusting magic. It was the second of my punishments.

The first came when Father and the arch-Eld chose Agravaine's plan to save our world over mine. A naïve princess, I was unprepared for the consequences of speaking out against it.

But not for long.

I was stripped of my royal birthright and given to the Huntsman, the very man who convinced my father that killing all sleeper-princesses was the answer, even though my plan to team up with them was better.

It was Agravaine who learned of my plan to contact the sleeper-princesses of the fair Fae. It was he who turned me in.

So he could further enslave me to him.

I clench my hand into a fist, and all the black circuits spliced into it whine. Ever since I can remember, Agravaine's wanted to be my mate.

Fat chance, buddy-boy. You're so not my type.

I'm his Huntress, but I will never be his mate.

My motorcycle boots splash through a puddle, scattering my true reflection—pointed ears and fangs, high cheekbones, eyes that glimmer blue ringed in gold. Over my dark Faeness I wear a Glamoury, an illusion that cloaks me. The mortals will see passing shadows, ghosts on their periphery. A few rare and sensitive mortals, those we call the Wakeful, might see the face of a loved one long past. Perhaps it will bring them terror. Perhaps it will bring them peace.

Peace! I have been restless since that moment—the moment I touched her hand—and now she haunts my dreams.

You're really rocking that tortured Goth-star thing, aren't you, Roue?

Her hair like white flame, her eyes burning in my mind like fiery embers. Even though I can never see her face, not even in dreams or memories, I've gotta admit, it does make for good lyrics.

I hitch my violin case up and tuck my hood down even though there's no danger of me being recognized here. This place is gorgeous, but it's not exactly cutting edge. No one listens to Euphoria in the Czech Republic. Besides, my personal Glamoury is strong.

There's no danger here.

At least, not to me.

I can't say the same for my prey.

Even now, my black-handled sickle blades weigh heavily on my belt. I pull my longcoat closed to make sure they're covered. Sleeper-princesses are unpredictable, all of them in various stages of Awakening. Some of them can see through a Glamoury—even one as powerful as mine.

And some of them can touch you, deep inside.

She burned so bright.

Forget about her. Focus on this one.

I don't want this one to see me coming. It's the only mercy I can give.

Mercy, ha! I glance down at my right hand. I wear a glove over it now. The dark-magic circuitry pains me—black circuits of the Moribund spliced into my flesh, my fingers, my palm, the back of my hand. This fell circuitry magic is from my people's past. It should have stayed dead and buried, but it's part of Agravaine's dark plan.

We are the first Circuit Fae.

I am part machine, no longer whole.

No one gave me any mercy.

This is my punishment for wanting to team up with the sleeper-princesses, losing my hand to the Moribund. As if being bound to Agravaine in a Contract of Bone and Blood wasn't punishment enough.

I am no longer a princess, only a Huntress. A dark Circuit Fae, infected with Moribund, able to harness the killing magic in technology.

That is what I am. Until all the sleeper-princesses are dead. Only then can I be free—free of the Moribund, free of Agravaine.

Restless energy stirs inside me, aching. I want to play it to life on my violin and hear the bittersweet strains shatter the night.

But I'm not here to play. I'm here to hunt.

Tonight, I am not Euphoria, glam-Goth singer. Tonight, I am Rouen Rivoche, dark Fae and Huntress.

And sure as the mortal hells are hot, there's no room for mercy in the Hunt. I am the Huntress, the advance guard of the Wild

Hunt. A sluagh, worst of the worst, dead to my own people until I fulfill the Contract that binds me to Agravaine.

I must bring him seven sleeper-princesses. This one will be my sixth.

I raise my head to the passing rain and scent the air. Sweet vanilla and musky, resinous opoponax.

She's close.

After her, only one more. The girl with the burning eyes. *You won't be able to let her go the next time.*

Watch me, that quiet part of me whispers. I sigh. Why does all my self-control go out the window when I so much as think of her?

I turn the corner. I'm back at the club now. Clearly, I want to torture myself by getting one more glimpse of sleeper-princess #6 before luring her in.

She stands at the curb, looking out into the night. She's nowhere near as bright and burning as that last sleeper-princess, but the raindrops shine like jewels in her hair. I should not regret what I must do. Father would say it's unbefitting of a dark Fae.

At least…he'd say that if he were speaking to me.

I do regret it, but I have no choice.

Our world is sick, and only the sleeper-princesses can cure it.

Stuck in their ancient ways, my father and the arch-Eld sided with Agravaine. They wouldn't hear of my plan to team up with the sleeper-princess, so now, this girl's life is forfeit. She'll die, a battery to power the dying hearthstone at the center of our kingdom. With her blood, we should be able to eke out a few more months before our world goes entirely into the Harrowing darkness, into nothingness.

I have no choice. Bound by the Contract, I must obey.

I pull my right-hand glove on tighter. The dark circuits of the Moribund glitter brightly, sinister even through the leather. It's hungry.

With a thought, I summon my fairy wind. It swirls around me, speeding me through the city faster than any human can see—to the metro station, and down into the dark tunnels where I will lie in wait.

I unsling my violin case, unzip, take out my instrument. The clear, polished surface glistens like glass in the dim subway lighting. I bring it to my chin and poise the bow, waiting.

I'm a spider in her glittering web. *Come into my parlor, little princess. Let me make this painless for you.*

The nearness of the train prickles discomfort along my skin. My powers are always weaker here, surrounded by so much old-world iron, but this is where Agravaine wants it done.

Besides, the sleeper-princesses are immune to dark Fae gramarye, our personal magics. Mine manifests through music—my voice and violin. Using those as my focus, I can weave a euphoric spell over a crowd, or even a single person. They become spellbound. Faestruck. That's what gave me my stage name, Euphoria.

Agravaine's gramarye once manifested through smithing and metalwork. A talented dark Fae blacksmith, he held great renown, was respected.

That was why the arch-Eld sided with him.

Now we're both infected with Moribund, and our personal gramarye has taken a darker turn. Mine has become even more destructive, my voice and violin turned into ruinous violet lightning. His now manifests through machinery—cars, motorcycles, and the like. He can craft them, control them, suck the life-force from their riders.

Agravaine... He knew I'd be weaker here. *Jerk.* I flex my right hand. After the Moribund fouled my sense of touch, I had to learn how to play all over again.

I hear soft footfalls as she comes down the stairs. The sleeper-princess. There is no one else here at this time of night. Only her and me. I step closer to my violin case, feeling my rebellion rise within me like a storm.

Don't get stupid now, Rouen. I can't afford another slip-up. I only have one more hand.

How brightly that last girl shone, that night by the tracks. Her hair like white flame, her eyes burning, embers in the night. She'd been so alive, the thought of Agravaine draining her, infecting her

with Moribund circuitry and then blowing the fuses, killing her...
I couldn't bear it in that moment.

Just like I can't bear it every time it happens.

Even now, as my fingers tense on the bow, I hesitate.

"Do it." Agravaine's quiet voice rumbles in my ear as he steps from the shadows. Most people would be unnerved, but I've seen this trick like a thousand times. "Distract her."

"Aww, it's like you don't trust me."

"Do it now." He laces his voice with Command, and it burns in my blood.

The Moribund lifts my hand, lifts my bow to the strings.

The sleeper-princess glances up. Agravaine is cloaked in his Glamoury, so she doesn't see him—six feet of muscle and masculinity, his white hair and skin making him a ghost in this dark place—but she sees me. She dismisses me as another street musician begging for coin.

It's her last mistake.

In that moment, Agravaine's Command rules my body. The Moribund burns with it, lacing my bones and blood with fire. I have to obey the Command, the Contract.

I play. The sweet strains of violin strike the air, bringing feelings of bliss to everyone who hears.

They don't call me Euphoria for nothing.

She wavers, nearly goes under, and then shakes off my gramarye. A normal girl would already be unconscious, but sleeper-princesses can shake off dark Fae gramarye, even Circuit Fae gramarye, like a duck shakes off a shower. *Here it comes.* I brace myself for Agravaine's strike. He'll grab her, sharp fingernails piercing her skin as he levers open the glimmering black box—the phylactery—that contains the Moribund. He'll make the Moribund infect her.

Stay still, Rouen. Don't interfere. Don't—

But I'm already moving, getting between him and her. She sees me, her face opening up in shock and fear.

I feel Agravaine behind me, his rage a palpable thing. "Rouen!"

Screw you. I won't just let her die.

"Stop." His voice is calm—we've done this every time; he treats it like a game, smiling as his Command slams into me.

Or maybe I will let her die. Enslaved by the Moribund circuitry, my body stops, and I stand there, screaming inside as he seizes her, a wolf seizing a sheep.

He touches the phylactery, and with a liquid-smooth *clink, clink, clink* all its cogs and wheels and locks open.

No, no, no!

In a chittering black wave, the Moribund circuits teem from the blackness of the box and leap upon her like a swarm of scarabs.

In mortal peril, her body reacts, Awakening to the sleeping power within her. White light flares from her hands, encasing her in blinding radiance. But the blackness of thousands of Moribund circuits engulfs it, eating the light, sapping her strength, infecting her…

Taking her down into unconsciousness.

Smirking back at me, he hoists her limp body, circuits and all, onto his shoulder. He enjoys this little game of ours. He forces me to lure her; I try to save her. And fail.

It makes him feel powerful, in control—of his world, of me.

One day, I'll be free. And then… *Watch out, buddy-boy.*

Agravaine's smile is shark-sharp. "Good work."

But I don't feel good. Not good at all.

The thing about hunting is, you have to go to where they prey is. One night I'm in Prague, and the next I find myself back in Richmond, Virginia, thousands of miles from where we took the sixth sleeper-princess. The last time I was here, four months ago, we crashed a commuter rail.

The last time we were here, I let a sleeper-princess go.

That explains why we're back, why I'm standing with Agravaine in the dark, empty gymnasium of a high school in the middle of the night.

Then again, Agravaine did always remind me of that guy who peaked in high school. Maybe he's trying to relive his glory days?

I smirk, but it fades fast. We have to find the last sleeper-princess, and the clock is ticking.

Even now, I can feel the hearthstone weakening. As the dark Fae princess, I've always has a unique link to it, and that's remained even despite my punishment. Even though it's a realm away, at the center of my kingdom, the dark Fae land of UnderHollow, it rumbles in my chest like a second heartbeat, but sluggish, diseased and failing. The blood from that sixth princess isn't enough to sustain it. It's like downing an energy drink when you've had two hours of sleep. You're just kidding yourself.

And you're going to crash hard.

Only, when the hearthstone crashes, it's going to bring all of UnderHollow, the world of the dark Fae, crashing down, sucked into the Harrowing. We'll cease to exist.

My plan would have worked. We could have teamed up with the fair Fae and the sleeper-princesses. We could have put an end to the dark Fae/fair Fae war.

No one else would have to die.

But Agravaine has plans of his own.

Speak of the devil... Agravaine sidesteps from the shadows. He likes using that trick, stepping through the Snickleways, a dangerous tangle of passageways that connects UnderHollow to the mortal realm. His Glamoury shimmers a moment before it settles into place, pale skin and shark-black eyes morphing into deep bronze and warm brown like melted chocolate. He dresses himself in a Glamoury that matches mine.

As if.

"What are we doing here?" I'm sassier than the other hunters, and I can get away with it. I used to be royalty, after all. And after the seventh and last sleeper-princess goes into the darkness, I'll be royalty again.

And there's nothing Agravaine, Master of the Wild Hunt, can do about it.

"Isn't it obvious?" His curved knife is red and slick with blood. My bond with the hearthstone gives a little lurch inside my chest. The blood of the sixth sleeper-princess. He'll use it to pinpoint the seventh and last. Blood calls to blood.

She must be close by, the girl with hair like white flame.

I don't know how to feel about that, but I'm smart enough to mask my jumbled-up emotions. "If it were obvious, would I have asked?"

He paces, his hobnails tack-tacking on the polished floor, his shadow chasing him. Droplets of blood drip, drip, drip from the tip of the knife.

I watch the blood so I don't have to look at him. I hate seeing the way he stares at me.

Drip, drip, drip.

It's then that I notice the map in his other hand. He slaps it down on the gym floor. A map of the city. Red lines slash through the railways we destroyed—that night four months ago, the train, the accident, all those deaths—all to break the circle of iron that kept us from finding her, the last sleeper-princess.

That night, I didn't fail. That night, I saved her.

He points with the tip of the knife, and the blood drips off. Three drips, splat, splat, splat... Then four, five... Six... One for every sleeper-princess I've helped him capture. They run together, crossing the map to converge.

On the high school.

"This is where we'll find her." He stands, spreading out his arms to encompass the gym, the school banners proclaiming *Go, Spiders!* and I want to slap the grin off his face. "Welcome to high school, Rouen."

My look sours. He's been doing his homework. "If you already knew she was going to be here"—I gesture at the map and the blood—"then why all the drama?"

"Isn't high school all about drama?" His shark-black eyes glitter. "Come on, Rouen. Where's your school spirit?"

One thing's for sure. If I could find it, I'd shove it down his throat.

CHAPTER THREE
SYL

Once there were hundreds
Of sleeper-princesses
But the dark Fae slaughtered them
- Glamma's Grimm

My lungs are burning, my legs are burning, and as I pedal harder into the parking lot of Richmond Elite High, the train-wreck injury flares up and my right thigh, all the way down to my knee, becomes a screaming knot of white-hot pain. *Girl on fire, right here, people.* I'm going to spontaneously combust on school grounds. On my first day back. I'm sure of it.

Just as sure as I'm still late.

Ignoring the old injury, I crank down on the pedals, my lateness making this weird mantra in my head. *Late, late, late.* Four miles—my biking commute has doubled since we moved from the suburbs of the Fan—but the buses from Richmond E don't exactly come into the slums of Jackson Ward.

And Mom busts her bottom to make sure I can go to a school with a cutting edge art and photography program. She's kind of awesome that way—none of that nonsense about getting a "real job" when I grow up. She believes in me and knows that art is just as real as the next career.

I half dismount, standing on one pedal while coasting my bike to the rack.

Maybe I'll get lucky and Principal Fee won't be watching from the office window. I mean, it's only the first day. The old buzzard's gotta have better things to do than watch for truancy.

Besides, if I were really a truant, I'd already be at Nanci Raygun's on the bonus level of *Dragon's Lair*.

My right leg aches as I bend to chain up my bike. I try not to imagine the iron shard in there, moving around. Gross. My backpack slips off my shoulder and fwaps me in the face as if to tell me I'm stalling.

I am. It's been nearly three months since I've seen Fiann.

Although, I guess "see" is the right term since it's not like we talked at the end of the school year in June. The last time we actually spoke was mid-May. After that night at the tracks, she came to visit me at the hospital. Once. To show me all the papers hailing her as *Heroic Teen Saves Friends* and *Real-Life Supergirl!* I guess she did save me. But why can't I remember?

My memories are all white flame and heat. So hot I thought I *was* going to spontaneously combust. That's all I remember.

That, and my weird dreams about *her*. But why would she be chasing me? Did she cause the crash? Who is she?

Ugh. So frustrating!

The doctors say it's normal, that maybe I saw something horrible and blocked it out, but I don't feel normal. I should remember Fiann dragging me away like she said, carrying me from the wreckage, that shard of railroad-tie metal sticking out of my thigh, the train tracks torn up like the broken ribs of some massive butchered creature—

Quit it, Syl.

21

An ache jabs deep into me, stretching my chest with a weird, wistful feeling like I'm on the verge of discovering something powerful, life-changing, but then it slips away. Like smoke. Poof. Suddenly, I wish I was at the Nanci playing *Dragon's Lair*. That's the thing with video games—eventually you reach the level where you get the treasure, become the hero, understand the story.

Life has no such guarantees.

Syl, seriously. My inner cynic slaps me upside the head. I've been literally chaining up my bike for like ten minutes. *Stop stalling.*

Fine. I can't put off this reunion forever. Might as well walk in with my head held high.

I straighten and look up at the massive brick building. Forget Fiann. Forget Principal Fee—did I mention he's her father? Yeah, rad—I'm doing this.

But I'll do it my way. Like a freakin' ninja.

Breaking into a jog, I cut across the lawn toward the side door. The library opens up into a small rose garden, and if I'm in luck, the door will be open. Miss Jardin, the librarian, likes roses and she likes me. She'll probably let me duck through and into my second class.

Oh, she'll give me the stink eye and that raised eyebrow, but she's a redhead like me, and we kind of have this secret pact. All redheads do.

I slink to the side door. It's cracked. *Yes!* I do a little happy dance as I slip inside. The cool central air washes over me, making me shiver. I'm all sweaty from my stupidly long bike commute. I make a mental note to keep some deodorant in my locker this year.

That won't help me today, but whatever. A little girl-sweat never hurt anyone.

I slip into the stacks, channeling my inner ninja, using the giant shelves as a shield to check out the library. As usual, no one's here. According to the giant clock, it's just about the end of first period.

Maybe I won't even have to trouble Miss Jardin, just sneak into the halls and find my way to my second class. Bio 2 with Miss Mack. Ugh. She smells all cinnamony like those spice-sticks you put in your apple cider in autumn.

"Hi, Syl."

I jump like a mile. "Miss Jardin!" So much for my ninja-ness.

The librarian stands behind me, one red eyebrow raised. She's supposed to look strict, but I can totally see the smile twitching her lips. Plus, according to my Fae-sight, her aura's bright pink. She's one of the youngest teachers here, and she's super-cool to me. Plus, she always smells fresh, like the roses she grows. She used to let Lennon and me talk when no one else was in the library—back when Lennon and I still hung out.

I swallow my bitterness. "Hi, Miss Jardin."

"You had a good summer?" She has this way of turning every statement into a question. It's weirdly quaint.

Before I can answer, the double doors bang open. Fiann and her new posse barge in, Lennon trailing behind like some kind of secretary. "Miss Jardin, we need to find books on—"

Fiann stops, her gaze fixing on me. Suddenly, I wish I had super-powers. Invisibility would be rad right now. Or phasing. I could just phase back into the wall and poof! Bye, Fiann. Instead, I sway from foot to foot, my oxblood Docs making unhelpful squeaky noises on the floor.

"Syl..." Fiann's voice is syrup and spite. She comes my way and puts an arm around me. "How are you?"

I stiffen. It's been months since she last spoke to me. Is she messing with me? I don't even need to read her aura. The glint in her eye and the way her friends giggle tells me that yes, yes she is.

Fine. But I'm not backing down.

"Fiann." I give her half a stink eye 'cause she doesn't really deserve a full one. "Anything interesting happen this summer?"

She was probably expecting me to cop to her recent celebrity status, so my casual question hits hard. There's a flash of shock and anger in her eyes before she waves it off. "Well, you know, the life of a celebrity. I was so busy, what with news reporters and papers. Did you know *Vanity Fair* actually wanted to do a spread on me?" She simpers, preening for her popular-girl friends.

I recognize them—Danette Silver, captain of the girls basketball team; Maggie Xiao, varsity cheerleader and all-around fashionista;

Jazz Martinez, head of the anime club; and Lennon Van, student-body treasurer. Lennon hangs back shyly, tugging at her uniform skirt. She doesn't like confrontation. Fiann and her new friends thrive on it.

"Yeah, *Vanity Fair*." I roll my eyes. "My Glamma's bridge club loved that mag."

Lennon stifles a giggle, and Fiann nearly turns purple. I think she's going to swallow her tongue or something.

She falls back on her usual bullying tactics. "Where's your hall pass?"

"Who are you—my mom?"

The other girls twitter, but they shut up fast when Fiann glares back at them. She primps her perfect blonde hair. "Miss Jardin, you know Syl can't be in here without a pass."

Miss Jardin draws herself up, suddenly seeming a lot taller than her five-foot-one stature, and I get a weird whiff of something spicy beneath her usual rose scent. She pushes her chunky black spectacles up on her nose. "Well, that's between me and Syl now, isn't it?"

"She doesn't have pass, does she?" Fiann's shrewd. She doesn't miss anything. "You should probably give her detention."

"I'll take that under advisement, Miss Fee." Unlike the other teachers at Richmond Elite, Miss Jardin isn't threatened by Fiann. "Where are *your* passes, Miss Fee?"

Ohhhh…that's cold. I can't resist smirking as Miss Jardin nails them to the proverbial wall.

Fiann sniffs and tosses her blonde ponytail over her shoulder. "Come on, girls." She pins me with a glare. "But don't think this is over."

I shrug one shoulder. I don't even know what *this* is, but whatever. "If you say so."

She flounces out like some villain on *Buffy*, her friends flouncing with her—all except Lennon who looks back and mouths, *Sorry*. I smile at her, but I know it turns sad. Can't help it. Lennon's a good person in a bad crowd.

I turn back to Miss Jardin, and I swear, not five seconds later…

"Miss Syl Skye." The speaker on the wall statics to life. "Please come to the principal's office. Immediately."

I sigh. So much for sneaking in.

The bell to end first class rings, and the sounds of students pouring into the hallways breaks the library's silence.

Darn it. So much for sneaking anywhere.

Saluting Miss Jardin in thanks, I drag my butt from the library and into the busy hall. I'm a super-massive introvert, so dodging and ducking is something I do well. I turn the corner from the library and enter the gigantic atrium. The central hub is wall-to-wall with students. Jocks, popular girls, nerds, geeks, freaks—everyone's buzzing about the first day of school. Freshman freaking out, seniors flexing their social muscle.

It's enough to make a girl's anxiety go through the roof. Not to mention, so many people, so many emotions—it makes my Fae-sight freak out. Too bright, too many colors. It's like a flight of unicorns threw up in here. I duck my head and skirt the fringes, hitching my backpack higher.

Snickers and laughs chase me as I turn down the hall toward Principal Fee's office. Fiann and her posse are conveniently stationed nearby. She gives me that simpering smile—"Good luck, Syl"—and all her friends laugh on cue.

Ha-ha. I'm turning to tell her where to stuff her luck when the office door swings open. Mrs. Hawklin stands there, her tiny bird eyes pinning me like a bug to a card. What is she, psychic? I didn't even have the chance to knock.

"He's waiting," is all she says, ushering me in all cloak-and-dagger, like she's about to give me a top-secret briefing.

"Um, okay." I get ushered.

Out in the hall, the bell for second period rings. *Ugh.* They're probably choosing lab partners in Bio, and now I'll be stuck with Minecraft Mike, the kid who's always playing videogames on his school laptop. *A for effort, but seriously?*

"Miss Skye." Principal Fee stands up as I enter, placing his hands on his lacquered cherry wood desk. The sour look on his face is what Glamma always called a "puss." She'd stand there, hands on hamhock hips, and say, *"Wipe that puss off your face, young lady."* I totally get it now. I bet if you cut him open, it'd be all sticky Sour Patch Kids and rotten lemons.

He tries for a smile, but his aura is gross yellow, telling me he's not exactly sincere. "Let's not start this year off on a wrong foot, shall we?"

I give him my best stink eye. *I won't if you won't.*

He sighs, running a hand over his balding head. "Miss Skye…"

I'm bracing myself for a lame, let's-all-get-along speech when Mrs. Hawklin knocks on the frosted glass. "Your special guest is here, sir."

Principal Fee goes the color of cafeteria milk, and his demeanor changes from sourpuss authoritarian to freaking out ten-year-old. "I…I'll be right there." He tries to pick up a pen and pad and knocks them both onto the floor. After scrambling around under his desk, he grabs them and heads for the door.

"Um, hello? Remember me?"

"Syl…uh…"

Dang, someone sure does have his panties in a bunch.

"She could show me around." From the darkened far corner of the room comes a feminine voice as sultry as silk sliding over steel.

Shivers rake my spine, my skin prickling with awareness. Flashes of my dream erupt—the train crash, the night, those sapphire-blue eyes ringed in gold. *My dream girl. She'd sound just like this.* Suddenly, my heart is cardio-kickboxing my ribs.

Am I about to see *her*?

I turn slowly, and my breath goes out in a painful gasp.

She's not *my* dream girl, but whoa… She's *a* dream girl, that's for sure.

She's tall, *statuesque* even, and glamorously beautiful, like a movie star stepped out of the silver screen into my high school. Raven-dark hair cascades in thick waves over her shoulders. Her bronze skin and high cheekbones give her an exotic look, and her eyes! They're not the sapphire-blue of my dream girl, but a bright electric blue. I could lose myself in them. In her.

A warm, pleasant shock jolts through my body. I know her. Not from my dreams, exactly, though I do have about a million of her concert posters.

Her name comes, a breathy gasp, from my lips. "Euphoria."

CHAPTER FOUR
ROUEN

Her eyes, so innocent, so fierce
They burn me
Hotter than the sun in the Summer Court
Sleeper-princess, when will you Awaken?
- "Awaken," Euphoria

Crap. She sees me—the real me.

The moment the petite redhead walked in the door, I recognized her from the newspapers. She was on the train that night—one of two survivors—but since the other girl, Fiann, was hailed the hero, I'm pretty sure it's Fiann and not this girl who's our sleeper-princess.

Then again, she's seen through the first layer of my Glamoury. Somehow.

Four months ago, that night on the tracks, I'd been sloppy, forgetting to layer my Glamoury. It was after a show, and I'd gone there as Euphoria, destroyed the tracks as Euphoria. Like Agravaine Commanded me to.

But today… I'd layered my Glamoury—Euphoria's humanity over the dark Faeness of my pointed ears and fangs and luminous eyes, then a less glam version of a human girl over Euphoria. Layered like frosting over cake.

But apparently the pretty redhead isn't into frosting.

"Euphoria," she breathes again.

I smirk. She likes cake, though. At least the first layer. She doesn't seem to remember that night—or notice that an actual dark Fae is sitting in her principal's office. I mean, she's not running away, screaming in terror, so that's good. The second layer of my Glamoury's holding. The Euphoria layer.

Call me twice lucky.

Agravaine's not going to like that she's seen Euphoria-me, but he'll have to deal. It doesn't really change our plans.

I wave Fee away, and he slinks out like a scolded dog, tail between his legs. He's meeting with Agravaine, who's posing as some rich Norwegian prince looking for an American education. Agravaine's going all-in on our entry into the school. I don't get it, but whatever. As soon as I find the last sleeper-princess, I'm out of here.

She saw through your Glamoury, Roue.

That doesn't mean she's definitely the sleeper-princess, but I wonder… I fix Miss Redhead I Can See Through Your Glamoury with a shrewd look. *What if it is her?*

Hair like white flames, eyes like burning embers. That's likely just her power signature. In reality, she could have any hair color, but this girl seems too…nice, too soft to have the burning passion I saw that night four months ago.

Besides, if it really was her, I'd be able to smell the sleeper-princess power on her like vanilla and sweet sunshine.

It's not her, Roue.

Not the girl who stood up to me and protected her friend, not the girl who lit up with blaring white light and flame.

I remember the pain of it blasting me back. I flex my Moribund hand. It must've been the other girl. Fiann Fee.

"You are her, aren't you?" The redhead steps closer to me. I see it in her eyes; she's second-guessing herself. She can see through one layer of my Glamoury, but it's more of a web than a cake—sticky threads that catch you and bind you. Clearly a part of it catches her, tells her what she should be seeing. She fights against it.

I wait, crossing my arms. Maybe my Glamoury will win.

She squints. "It is you."

Then again, maybe it won't.

I sigh. *Blast and bloody bones.* There are a few people in this world who can see through a Glamoury. It doesn't make them a sleeper-princess, only one of the Wakeful. Just my luck, I've found one. *Awesome.* I've been here two seconds, and I'm about to have my cover blown. "You can't tell anyone."

"What do you mean?" She looks at me like I've got ten hydra heads. "How is anyone not going to notice?"

I waffle for a sec. *Tell her the truth,* that rebellious part of me whispers, and I resist the urge to smack that voice out of my head. I can't tell her the truth. *Yeah, we're here to find one of your little friends and spill her summer blood so our dark Fae realm—which, by the way, is totes real—can survive the Faerie Apocalypse.*

Yeah. I'm so not saying that.

"It'll be fine. Most people don't really know what I look like."

She looks at me skeptically, one corner of her mouth lifted in a wry grin. By the Hunt, she's cute. She arches an eyebrow. Cute—and she's not buying my story. Oooookay.

I love a challenge, and I've been sitting in Fee's stuffy, mothball-smelling office for a freaking eternity. Also, I'm a bit obsessed by mortal culture. I've read a million books, watched a ton of TV, and I'm curious as all get-out about this whole high school thing. Besides, if I can fool Miss Smarty here, I'll be golden. "I've got Bio 2 for my second class." I grab my backpack and gesture at the door. "Show me how to get there?"

"Um." She bites her lip and fumbles a schedule out of her own backpack. A blush scalds her cheeks. I feel my body responding, sending a flush across my own skin. Normally, my Glamoury would shift to cover it, but of course she sees right through that too.

It's only a matter of time before she sees through it to the real me—pointed ears, bronze skin, luminous blue eyes ringed in gold, and the fangs. *She'll probably think you're a vampire, Roue. No one sees fangs and thinks: Faerie!*

I catch her staring, and she looks back at her schedule.

Finally, she caves. "I'm in Bio too."

"Well." I look around at the empty office. "It looks like you're off the hook, so...shall we?"

Her pretty face breaks into a smile so bright it could power a thousand hearthstones. *She's not the sleeper-princess, Roue.* Whatever. Doesn't mean I can't flirt with her a little.

There's no rule in the Winter Court that says I can't flirt with mortals. Only fair Fae.

She gestures. "It's this way."

I follow her out the door and into the empty hall.

She's lithe, with a dancer's build, and she moves with an easy grace. I bet she can really run, and in that moment, I'm glad she's not the sleeper-princess. I'd hate to have to chase her down, to see that smile turn into fear.

Stop it, Roue. This is just the kind of thinking that made me let that sleeper-princess go. Will I even recognize her when I see her? *No one has white-flame hair, Rouen.*

This girl's hair is red—like real, actual flame.

The sixth princess's hair was blonde. The one before that was brunette. The one before that had black hair like mine. And in the end, they all turned as white as the hottest part of the sun. When they Awakened.

Yup. It's a power signature, all right.

Meaning: hair color will be zero help.

I reach out with my Huntress senses and take a deeper sniff, dowsing for magic. Nope, nothing. No vanilla, no musk. She smells clean, like shampoo and a light sweat, heady, intoxicating... I'm leaning in, and she's blushing hotter.

I straighten.

"What's your real name?" Her shy question takes me off guard.

"My..."

"You're not going by Euphoria here." She turns the corner and we head down a hall lined with lockers. "I mean, not if you want to stay incognito." She still looks dubious about that.

"It's Rouen Rivoche. Roue," I correct myself.

"Roue." She tries it out, and I like the sound of it on her lips.

I catch myself sneaking peeks at her as we walk. Among my people, beauty is nothing. Every single dark Fae in UnderHollow is achingly beautiful, but she is something more. There's a spark of life in her as bright as...

A white flame.

Please don't let her be the sleeper-princess.

I shake off the mercy that's trying to take root inside me. I clench my right hand and feel only the pull on numb flesh, the sinister thrum of dark circuitry.

This, Rouen, this is what mercy buys you.

I realize I haven't asked her name. *Good,* the callous part of me, the Huntress part, whispers.

"Come on." The redhead tugs my sleeve, and her innocent way of touching me strikes me to the core. I'm a Circuit Fae, one of the outcast sluagh, dead to my own people. No one touches me.

Yet here is this teenage girl dragging me down a high school hall. Me, the Huntress, dark Fae princess of the Winter Court turned Circuit Fae sluagh. It's scary how easily, how casually she touches me.

It's scary how easily I respond.

When she takes her hand away, I feel its loss. A sense of longing kindles in my heart, and I do my best to stamp it out. She opens the door to a classroom.

Twenty-five pairs of eyes come to rest on us.

No one freaks out, though, so I assume she's unique in seeing through my Glamoury.

The instructor, a tall lady dressed all in black, gives us a withering stare. She smells weirdly like cinnamon and nutmeg, but nothing like what I'm looking for. She smacks her lips. "So nice of you to join us, Miss Skye."

Syl toes the floor. "Yeah. About that…"

I cock my cockiest grin, leaning against the door. "We got lost."

Giggles ripple through the classroom.

Miss Mack—I see her name written on the board—gestures sweepingly, like she's casting a magic spell from Harry Potter. "Take those seats in the back. We've already picked lab partners. You two can be paired up."

I shrug like I don't care, but inwardly I'm jazzed to spend a little more time with the cute redhead. "What's your first name?" I whisper as we thread our way to the back, everyone still staring.

"She's Syl Skye," Miss Mack says. "I can hear you, you know."

Of course she can.

"Teacher hearing." Syl pitches her voice beneath the open laughter now.

Miss Mack throws the gauntlet. "And you are?"

I turn to face her. "Rouen." I look around, willing my Glamoury to hold. "Rouen Rivoche."

No one looks twice. Score! No, wait… A blonde girl in the back of the room is staring at me. She's surrounded by a bunch of pretty girls. Popular girls. I can tell by their designer shoes and Prada backpacks, their perfectly made-up faces. Not sure why clothes and makeup makes them popular, but whatever. These are mortal rules, not mine.

And yeah, this girl definitely sees through layer one of my Glamoury.

What, is everyone around here one of the Wakeful?

Then it dawns on me. She was the second girl at the tracks that night. Blonde hair, green eyes. She looks like the fairytale heroine the papers made her out to be. *Real-Life Supergirl!*

But is she one of the Wakeful, or is she the last sleeper-princess? There's a big difference, kind of like the difference between being Force Sensitive and being a full-blown Jedi knight. And I can't tell just by looking. I'll need to see a demonstration of her real power—her white flame power.

But she just sits there, staring at me, a calculating look on her face.

Imagining that blonde hair like white flame is easy enough, but her eyes...

They're much too cold to ever burn like the embers I saw that night at the tracks.

That night... How the two girls held each other, hands upraised. They were so close, and the white flame was so bright, blaring, blotting out their faces... Even now, I can't tell which one summoned it.

I can't tell which of them is my white-flame princess.

My...what? *You're losing it, Roue.*

I sigh. I'll have to tell Agravaine.

We have two. Two girls who could possibly be the last sleeper-princess. Syl Skye and Fiann Fee. Neither one registers as Awakened to me. Weirdly, impossibly, despite all the power she pushed that night at the tracks, the last sleeper-princess seems to have gone dormant again.

I'll have to lure them both in to find out which one's the real deal.

As soon as the bell to end second period rings, I'm gone. It's a Fae trick. One minute you see me, the next you're distracted by that glint of sun or dust mote or random noise, and I'm gone. Poof! Just like that.

I feel a slight pang of guilt for ditching Syl—she's really very nice—but if I have to sit through one more boring lecture, I'm going to lose my mind.

Besides, I don't want to have to answer a bunch of uncomfortable questions in front of half a dozen students. I trust Syl to keep my secret, but that other girl—Fiann? Miss Oh So Popular?

I don't trust her as far as I could donkey-toss her. Which, actually...is pretty far, but whatever. Agravaine's here. I kept getting whiffs of his asphalt and burning rubber smell the whole time Miss Mack was discussing the finer points of frog guts and wielding a scalpel with deadly efficiency.

It's one of the drawbacks of Huntress senses—I practically have smell-o-vision.

I slip down the halls, threading my way through the throngs of students pouring out of classrooms on either side. The library. I look over my shoulder, but no one else seems able to penetrate my Glamoury. They just see a nerdy, dark-haired girl going into the library.

Perfect.

I open the door.

It looks empty at first, but I know all of Agravaine's tricks.

In the blink of an eye, he steps snickleways and is standing in front of me. I lounge against the librarian's desk, displaying my lack of give-a-damn.

"Well?" He hates having to ask. I can tell by the testiness of his tone.

"There are two potentials. The ones we saw that night."

He snorts. "You still can't tell which one is the true princess, even up close?"

"It's not that easy." I arch an eyebrow at him. "She's not Awakened. At least, not anymore."

"That doesn't make sense." He paces. "The power we saw... It nearly..." He touches his left shoulder. It nearly melted all his Moribund circuits, and that, my friend, would have *really* ruined his day. "She'd have to be Awakened to be pushing that much power."

"I'm telling you, she's not."

"She's hiding. Somehow..." His bottom lip curls, turning his beauty into a mulish mess. "We have to draw her out, make her use her power, put her in fear for her life." He fixes me with his shark-black stare. "You. You have to draw her out."

I hate the very idea of it. Syl's kind, generous, funny... I don't want to hurt her. It goes against every natural instinct in my body. It's probably jerky of me to hope that Fiann's the sleeper-princess, but yeah, I do.

Agravaine sees the rebellion in my posture. "Rouen..." The warning tone in his voice tells me I can't defy him directly.

Crap, crap, crap... I'm literally biting my fingernails, and then... Lightbulb! I can't defy him, but I can stall him. I put on my most bored expression. "Fine, fine." I wave a hand. "I'll play their Homecoming and draw her out." Whew, sometimes it pays to eavesdrop on seniors. "It's in a month, and they'll all be there, the whole student body." I meet his gaze, willing him to swallow the bait, shark that he is. "The sleeper-princess is immune to my gramarye. My powers won't affect her, so it'll be easy to pick her out of the crowd. She'll be the only one not entranced."

I wait, my heart rabbiting against my rib cage. *Good shark, nice shark.*

He smiles at the bait and swallows it. "Good. That'll give me... time."

Time? I give him my patented *what the hell are you taking about* look, but he ignores it. Something sinister moves behind that smile. He's planning something.

Worry rises in me, worry for Syl. "What if she doesn't show?"

"You're a princess of the dark Fae. She's a princess of the fair Fae. Blood calls to blood, Rouen, the way summer calls to winter. She'll come."

CHAPTER FIVE
SYL

The sleeper-princess
Able to read auras
And see through Glamoury
- Glamma's Grimm

"You lucky bee-yotch." Fiann's voice rings down the crowded hall, over the hundreds of other voices, the slamming of lockers, and the hoots and hollers of the student body relieved that their first day is finally over. "Syl!"

Darn it. I'd managed to avoid Fiann since second period. Since Euphoria vanished. I thought we'd hit it off, but then again... *Maybe she doesn't like me.* It wouldn't be the first time a girl's faked friendship only to start ignoring me.

Euphoria's nothing like Fiann. At least, I hope she's not.

Fiann's making her way against the tide of kids toward me, her princess posse right behind her. "Out of the way, losers," she says, and people move away from her in droves.

She could've just yelled, *I'm gonna puke!* It'd have the same effect. Ugh. Why do people just roll over and play dead at her command?

She can tease and taunt me all day long. I'll never be one of her little minions.

Speaking of minions... I spot Lennon in the crowd, long black hair shiny, all *kawaii*-adorable even in the school uniform. She pulls off her cat-ear headphones and gives an apologetic shrug. I'm sorry too. She and Fiann used to be my BFFs. But now...

Now, Fiann gets right into my personal space. "I can't believe *Euphoria's* your lab partner."

"Keep your voice down or—" And then I notice that Danette, Maggie, Jazz, even Lennon are giving Fiann a super-nervous side-eye. It's like they didn't recognize Euphoria, and whoa, that is wizard-level weird.

"Or what?" Fiann leans in so her nose is almost touching mine.

"Nothing." I back up. I'm not going to let her bully me, but we're still on school grounds. Getting expelled on day one is not on my agenda.

I won't fight her. I'll just use her princess posse against her. "Who says that's Euphoria? It doesn't even look like her."

It's a wild stab, but it strikes the target. The primpy princesses are all fidgeting, glancing at Fiann, their auras shifting wildly from the reds and oranges of fear to the greenish-yellows of nervousness.

I pour on the melodrama. "What are you, a crazy stalker or something? Just because she looks like Euphoria, you're stalking her—stalking a *girl*?" I hammer that last word home.

Fiann's one of those girls who's always touching other girl's butts and then shouting, *No homo!* Like it even matters. Some girls like girls. Who cares?

Fiann does. Image is everything to her. Normally once she's on me, she's a dog with a bone, but she lets this one go. It's got too much gay on it, maybe. She sniffs. "Hmph. Maybe it isn't her. There's no way a cool girl like Euphoria would hang out with a poser like you."

The princess posse, clearly relieved that their fearless leader is no longer talking crazypants, laughs and throws shade at me.

"Seriously!"

"Good one, Fiann!"

"Yeah, Euphoria hanging out with *her*. Hi-*larious*."

Only Lennon stays quiet, twisting her hands in her uniform skirt, looking down at her cute Pusheen Mary Janes.

I walk away, their jeers ringing in my head. Maybe I'm the one that's crazy. I haven't seen Euphoria—I can't bring myself to call her by her real name—since second period. The day's almost done, and nothing. Not a whisper, not a glimpse.

It's like she vanished. *Or like she doesn't actually go here,* the suspicious part of me whispers.

Oh my God, stop. She said it was a publicity stunt, something her manager put her up to. I mean, why would anyone go to high school if they didn't have to? I glance back at Fiann and her gaggle. Especially Richmond E. I reach my locker and drag my books out of it into my backpack. I stuff my Elephant Thai polo down deeper so no one can see it. Work, then home, then homework.

Oh, the glamorous life of me!

I shoulder my pack and head out the door with the thousand other students. We pile out onto the lawn. The bike rack is thronged, so I stand back to wait. Through the gap in all the other kids, I spy my bike.

And the nail sticking out of my front tire.

Ugh. I push my way through—"Excuse me, sorry!"—and check the damage to my poor bike. I swear, I feel Fiann's eyes on me a second before her shrill voice breaks the air.

"Too bad, Syl! Nails happen." She's leaning against the shiny-new silver Porsche her daddy bought for her, smirking like she's Jennifer freaking Lawrence or something.

I want to put my fist through her car window. Just barely, I resist. My face is scalding hot, and I know it shows. Being Irish and pale, I wear any kind of blush like a brand.

Laughing, she flounces off to the driver's side, the rest of her princess posse climbing into Dani's F1 Cruiser. They're probably heading over to Nanci Raygun's.

A pang of homesickness hits me in the heart. I'm left standing there while everyone else grabs their bikes and takes off.

The buses are pulling out, and all the commuter kids are leaving in their shiny cars. I could run for the bus, but it won't drop me anywhere near home or work, which is where I really need to be.

I grab the nail and yank it out. The tire deflates as I do.

"Heyla."

I jerk my head up. *Euphoria!*

She's dressed all in Gothy black—leather pants and tank top, leather jacket, boots with shiny chrome accents. Even cooler, she's sitting on a sleek black Harley with violet lightning painted on the gas tank and fenders. Something about the lightning strikes me weird—*the train, that night...was there a lightning storm?*—but I yank my thoughts back to my real-life flat tire.

Besides, how did she ride up on me like that? Was I that focused on plotting Fiann's demise?

Now I notice all the kids that are left crowding around her and another guy—a guy in a black leather jacket with white anime hair, on an even bigger motorcycle. I want to kick myself for being whiny-pants.

Sorry, Glamma. I draw myself up. "My bike has a flat." I feel like a giant dork, but whatever. I'm nerdy. So what? I own it.

The corner of Euphoria's mouth lifts in a smile-smirk, and I want to kick myself for thinking how soft her lips look. She gestures, so super-cool I'm sure my heart's going to explode. "You want a ride?"

I keep my voice even. "Is this a trick question?"

Her serious face breaks into a smile for real. My stomach does a lazy barrel roll. Smiling looks good on her. "Well, come on."

My mom will probably kill me. But then again...if I'm late and I lose my job, she'll *totally* kill me. I'd rather be probably dead than totally dead. Besides, something about that wicked grin Euphoria is giving me makes my insides flip-flop like nervous butterflies on a roller coaster.

So this is what hormones are for. Who knew?

I guess the Harley explains all the leather she's wearing. And gloves. Seriously? Who wears gloves in Richmond in the fall? It's eighty degrees today. *Stop standing here like a dork, Syl.*

I leave my bike and hitch my pack up. She hands me her helmet. I look around, but she doesn't have a spare. "What about you?"

"Ah, my head's pretty hard."

She took off her helmet...for me. It's got the same violet lightning motif on it, and it feels surreal to even be holding it. Holy cats, I *am* the world's biggest dork. And...my cheeks are burning again. *Darn it.* But Euphoria only smiles, laughing gently. I laugh with her, and it's all okay. She's looking at me with those electric-blue eyes. We're so close I can smell the leather of her jacket and bike oil.

Oh yeah, I'm so dead. And not just because Mom will probably catch me.

In that moment, I don't care. I put the helmet on. I just want to be close to Euphoria. *Now who's the creepy stalker, Syl?*

I get on the bike and wrap my arms around her waist. At least the helmet hides my shameless blushing. She guns the throttle, and we're off. Of course she drives like a bat out of hell. Does anyone actually own a motorcycle to act responsible?

Spoiler alert: no. No, they don't.

She peels out, just short of a wheelie, and I'm embarrassed by the girly squeak that escapes me. Laughing, she tears across the parking lot, cutting in front of Fiann's Porsche.

Euphoria waves at Fiann. I wave at Fiann.

I laugh wickedly.

Oh yes, I like my new lab partner.

Hours later, sweaty and stinking of peanut sauce, spices, and satay, I step into the back alley of Elephant Thai for my "smoke break." I don't actually smoke, but when I noticed smokers got twice the number of breaks, I jumped on that bandwagon faster than you can say, *I'm a dirty Liar McLiarface.*

Whatever. Fair is fair.

I take a deep breath, trying not to smell the rancid Dumpster, and lean against the grungy wall. Today has been crazy-bananapants. First Fiann all up in my ladybusiness and then Euphoria, and no one knows it's her? And then she gives me a motorcycle ride—*the* Euphoria, glam-Goth rock star. I didn't even know she was my age. She seems so much older, and yet, I saw her schedule. She's definitely in my grade.

Aaaaaaand…attending high school for some publicity stunt? It makes a weird sort of sense. I mean, she could be doing research for a new album or even a movie role.

All I know for sure is it's all super-surreal, like I'm the one who's stepped into a movie where the ordinary dorky girl discovers she's not so ordinary. I mean, seriously, what is going on?

I wipe my sweaty hands on my apron. I should get back inside.

The crunch of a soda can.

I spin around, staring into the dark alleyway. The streetlight barely penetrates the far side of it, casting thin light in slats all the way down to where I'm standing. Anything could be lurking there.

Quit it, Syl. It's probably a homeless guy.

They do hang out here on Mondays to raid the Dumpster. I usually triple-bag the leftover food and set it on top with smiley faces on it. The restaurant only throws it away anyway.

A bottle *tink, tink, tinks*…and comes spinning out of the alley.

I stop it with my foot.

A dark shadow stretches and hunches against the alley walls. Panic prickles the hairs at the back of my neck, and a fresh layer of sweat breaks out all over me.

I can't see what it is, but my body knows enough to be afraid. From the alleyway, a low growl rumbles. A jolt of fright spears me. Two glowing-green eyes wink open in the pitchy-dark, then two more, and two more…

Daaaaaannnnnnnggg… I back up fast and fetch against something solid.

A hand lands on my shoulder. My scream echoes down the alley. "Syl!"

I jump and turn, looking up into Euphoria's face. "Euph—"

"Nope," she cuts me off, but her gaze is on the alley. Does she see the freaky eyes? "Off-stage, I'm just Roue."

Apparently not.

"Roue." Cautiously, I peer into the alleyway, but the shadows and glowing eyes are gone. I'm panting now, leaning over, hands on my thighs. The fear still having its way with me. "Wh-what are you doing here?"

"I came to pick you up." She shrugs a shoulder and manages to look both sheepish and super-cool all at once. "I know you left your bike at school."

"Yeesssss…" I drag the word out while I wait for reality to kick in. There's no way I'm standing in a dirty alleyway outside my take-out job, talking to *Euphoria*. And there's certainly no way on Gaea's green Earth she's here to *pick me up*.

I mean, seriously. I'm just ordinary Syl Skye, geek, nerd, the weird "girl who lived."

"Um, I can leave." She jerks a thumb at her Harley sitting there not ten feet from the door I came out. I swear, only Santa Claus is better at sneaking in and out of places.

Say something. She's going to leave, dummy! My brain finally kicks in. "Oh! No… I mean, yes. I mean…" *Good going.* I take a breath. "What I mean is that I still have half an hour left."

"Okay, sure." She nods. "I'll just wait here for you."

Holy—! She's going to wait for me. "You can come inside if you want. The kanom jeeb and stuffed chicken wings are pretty boss."

She smiles almost shyly as she shakes her head no, and my heart seizes.

"All right. I'll be back in a half hour. Don't…" I swallow my uncertainty. "Don't disappear on me."

A soft, rolling laugh. "I won't."

"Okay." I stand there, drinking in the sight of her leaning against her sleek black Harley. I could look at her for hours. *You're staring, Syl.* I yank myself away and head back to the door.

"See you soon," she calls.

I go back in, my heart soaring like maybe I am in that movie, after all.

CHAPTER SIX
ROUEN

Your face, your lips
So tempting
Transfixed, I'm tempted
I should run away
Transfixed, I stay
- Euphoria, "Transfixed"

Please don't let her be the sleeper-princess, I pray as I watch Syl slip back into the Thai takeout place. *Please let it be that other girl. What's-her-name. Fiann.*

I lean against the Harley, the glinting of Moribund circuitry in its engine winking at me. It's one of Agravaine's dark machines, this motorcycle, meant to infect the rider.

Joke's on him. I'm already infected. The only thing that can make the Moribund worse is me.

As if in answer, my right arm aches to the elbow with phantom pain. *Case in point.* I grit my teeth, sweat beading on my brow. *It's not real, Roue. The pain, it's not real.* I'm like a soldier who's lost a limb. Difference is, my dead arm is still attached, glittering with dark-magic circuitry. The Moribund's spread farther up my arm since the sixth sleeper-princess.

Since I used my power against her. Since I failed to save her.

There is no saving them, Roue. Agravaine won't allow it. *And face it, without them, your people are as good as dead.*

Please, I pray, looking at the closed screen door where Syl vanished. *Don't let it be her.* I don't think I could take it. Seeing the Moribund swarm over her, watching the light drain from her eyes. Giving her over to Agravaine...

"Daydreaming?" Agravaine's deep voice rolls out of the darkness like sinister smoke.

Speak of the devil.

He steps snickleways into the alley—or should I say, *drives* snickleways? His huge Ducati emerges with him as he peels back the shadows like a shroud. He's a pro at traveling like that, tapping into the mortal realm's natural ley lines to speed his way through the winding Snickleways of UnderHollow and through the gates that link both worlds.

And not only did he bring the motorcycle, he brought...

Dinner, my mind unhelpfully supplies as I eye the semiconscious pair on the back. A blond boy and a brown-haired girl. I remember them from the group hanging out near Agravaine in the parking lot. They were talkative, full of life. Now they're on the back of Agravaine's motorcycle, blissed-out, sweating, and holloweyed, holding each other up.

Drunk on dark Fae Glamoury and faestruck.

He's going to infect them with Moribund, blow the fuses, devour them.

Fury rises inside me. "It's against the rules, bringing them through the Snickleways. Dark Fae do not truck with mortals."

"What?" A sly smile slides over his face. "I only gave them the ride they asked for."

That stops me cold. In days past, it was not uncommon for mortals to ask favors of the Fae. So long as they paid the price. If they knowingly asked for this, then there's nothing I can do. It's one of our oldest rules: *Consent, once given, is consent taken.*

Still…Glamoury ravages mortals. They could die if they don't get medical attention. I take a threatening step forward.

Agravaine heaves a sigh. "Very well." He snaps his fingers before the boy's face, and when the boy wakes, Agravaine hits him with another Glamoury. "You're quite dehydrated and possibly going into shock. You will take your friend and you will seek medical attention. You will not remember anything that happened."

I watch, my stomach rolling sickly as the boy goes glassy-eyed, repeats Agravaine's words, picks up his girlfriend, and totters off down the alley. I feel only slightly better once they've vanished into the darkness.

I turn to Agravaine and size him up. Glamouring mortals is easy. It's taking machinery betwixt and between that's hard. Normally, only flesh and blood and bone can pass—and he's riddled with the Moribund, dark circuitry running up his arm and shoulder, across his chest.

A spike of dread bolts up my spine. *He's growing more powerful.*

He grins, parking his bike next to mine. Smug jerk.

"Stepping snickle with machinery now?" I pretend to consider. "What's your secret? You drinking milk?"

"What does milk have to do with it?" He seems amused, though the joke passes him by. He loathes the human things as much as I am drawn to them. "Rouen…" He looks at me, those shark-black eyes placid. For now. Good. There's something we need to get straight. But he can't know I care as much as I do.

He only wants me to care about him.

Like I said, joke's on him. I'm not wired that way.

I lean back on my Harley, tracing the violet lightning on the gas tank. I am a Huntress, and I must lure him in. "Is this a social call, or did you actually want something of me?"

He shrugs, and even the slight movement makes the dark circuitry on his left arm and shoulder ripple with indigo lightning. I know what he wants—for me to be his mate.

I'd rather gargle with Moribund circuits.

And I know what else he's been doing tonight. I saw those glowing eyes in the darkness, watching Syl, stalking her. But I play the game with him. It's always a game with him. "Stalking teenage girls now?" I ask.

What he doesn't know is, this time, I'm going to win.

"Just checking up on our little sleeper-princess." He looks to the back of the Elephant Thai building, narrowing his eyes. He doesn't like the rich, spicy smell of human food. The more his body takes on the Moribund, the more it becomes machine over man, the more he detests things of the physical world.

Whatever. More stuffed chicken wings for me.

"You sent the *cú sluagh*." I say it calmly, but I can't quite keep the accusation from my voice. I'm the advance scout, the Huntress—not those mangy hounds. After all, isn't that why he betrayed me, so I'd become the Huntress? And now he's undermining me?

No way, buddy-boy.

He fixes me with that shark stare, as if trying to discern whether or not I'll start my rebellion early this time. "You're not able to sniff her out, so…the *cú sluagh*."

I give him my best glare. That's not how the Wild Hunt works, and he knows it. The Huntress tracks down the prey; the hounds chase it to the ends of the earth.

It's my job to flush out the sleeper-princess.

We both know it, but I have to be careful calling him on it. Even now, he senses my uncanny attraction to this girl. And it's not like my previous track record of trying to free every single sleeper-princess is any help.

I shrug. "Whatever. The hounds can take the girl's scent all they want. She's not the one."

"We'll see," he says slowly, watching my every movement.

I still my restlessness, throwing up an air of casual calm as I look into his eyes. "We certainly will." *About a lot of things, pal.*

He leans back on his bike, tracing the Moribund circuits running up from the engine, threading indigo veins across the gas tank and handlebars. The humans will only see the tribal decaling that is Agravaine's signature. This is his gramarye, his personal magic. Even before he was a Circuit Fae, he had an affinity for machinery.

47

It makes sense that he'd be the one to want to revive the ancient forbidden magic in the Moribund. It was Agravaine who first put forth the idea. At first, the arch-Eld denounced him as insane, but as the hearthstone began to go black and dead, as parts of our world crumbled, collapsing like brittle, sugar-coated spiderwebs, they started to listen.

They agreed to let him infect himself, and then me, with Moribund. We became Circuit Fae, capable of harnessing the killing machine in technology, capable of infecting other living creatures with the Moribund and then blowing their fuses to consume their life-force.

We're no better than parasites.

I want a better way for my people. One that doesn't turn us into dark, soulless machinery.

I think of the hounds of the Hunt, their bodies riddled with Moribund, living flesh spliced with circuits. They are no more than dark machines, expendable. Agravaine can blow their circuits and devour their energy at any time.

That is the true danger of the Moribund—becoming nothing more than a dark battery, soul-stripped and consumed.

His low, rumbling chuckle breaks my reverie. "Daydreaming about a girl, Rouen?"

His jab strikes close to my heart, and I volley back before thinking. "Maybe. She is awfully cute. It's too bad she's not the sleeper-princess. The blonde is. You should go stalk her. That's your style."

His answering growl tells me I probably shouldn't remind him that he's a creepy stalker, that rarely do I get a few hours without his intrusion. Checking up on his premiere Huntress, he says. In reality, he's worried that I'll find a way to break the Contract, that his will isn't enough to keep me prisoner.

I'm supposed to be his Huntress, his fated mate, but not even a Contract of Bone and Blood can force love.

And he knows it. The rules of the Winter Court are absolute. Consent given, and all that.

His eyes burn with black fire. Indigo lightning purls off the Moribund circuits infecting him. "You like girls so much." He spits the words like venom as he reaches into his jacket. "Here." He tosses me something.

Instinctively, I catch it. It's a microphone. What the—?

"Toss it to a girl at the end of your next show."

Oooookay. I flick the switch. A dark hum lights up the mic in my hand, and my right hand prickles with pins and needles.

The Moribund.

He wants me to infect my fans. What for? "We're supposed to be here for the sleeper-princess." I flash my fangs. "What makes you think I'm going to infect a bunch of innocent kids?"

A glimmer in his shark eyes is the only warning I get. Then he's on me in a flash of black leather. He slams me back into the wall, crushing the bricks beneath me. My breath goes out in a whoosh. His hand is around my throat. I glare at him, my eyes burning with fire. I raise my right hand and breathe a single note. Licks of violet lightning ignite the air around us.

"Shall I sing you a song?"

He recognizes my threat, and his hand tightens painfully. "I could rip your throat out."

"Before I tear your body apart with one note?" I smile wickedly.

"Heh." He does the math—my Circuit Fae gramarye is more powerful than his, more outwardly destructive—and relents, letting me down. "Why is it always so hard with you, Rouen?" Sighing, he laces his voice with Command. "Throw the mic to a girl at the end of your next show."

A jolt shoots through my bones and blood. I have no choice. The Contract will make me obey him. The next time I play, I'll throw that mic to a girl as surely as I live and breathe. Anger pulses up inside me. I want to launch at him, but with one word, he could stop me cold. And he would.

Agravaine doesn't brook what he calls "insolence."

I call it calling him on his BS.

"Fine, I'll do it." I kick one leg over the other and lean back, pretending I have a choice. "The next time I play. Don't know when that is, though."

"It's tomorrow night."

I glare at him.

"I booked you for the entire month at the Nanci Raygun. It's the local high school hangout. Don't worry, Euphoria, I'm sure you're still popular with all the girls." He hides his bitterness by viciously kick-starting his bike and roars out of the alleyway in a full-throttle-fueled display of aggressive bro-dudeness.

Rock on with your bad self, Agravaine. It's like the air gets lighter when he leaves.

I look down at the mic in my hand. He wants to infect the students for some larger plot he's got cooking in that twisted mind of his. But what's he up to?

And then there's Syl.

Guilt seizes me. I should leave, run away from her before she gets drawn in, or worse, infected with the Moribund. I clench my fist, and in that moment, I feel the truth in my bones, in my very blood. Command or not, I'll never let that happen to Syl. Tossing a mic off the stage, letting a stranger become infected—that's bad enough. But Syl...?

No. Just no.

Hating myself, I kick one leg over my Harley, one hand on the ignition switch, the other on the clutch. I feel bad about leaving her like this. *You're a huge jerk, Roue.* But what's jerkier? Leaving now and keeping her safe or staying and putting her in the worst danger of her life?

She's safer with you, Roue. But is she? I have to do Agravaine's bidding. *Then make sure he doesn't find out.*

"I'm done."

Her bright voice and bright smile snare me.

She's done, and I'm so done.

"Heyla." Instead of pushing her away, I beckon her in.

She puts a huge, triple-wrapped bag on the Dumpster and then comes to me shyly, that adorable blush on her face. We have an awkward moment or two navigating the bike, her height, her backpack and the small bag of leftovers in her hand...and then her slight weight settles on the back.

She's shier than back at the school. "Should I?" She pantomimes wrapping her arms around me, and a thrill goes through my body.

I keep my voice steady, casual. "Sure."

She scooches up on the seat and puts her arms around my waist. The slight press of her body against mine feels good, natural, and I find myself relaxing, all my muscles unknotting. It's as though I've been weary to the bone, tense and cramped up for years, and now, with her, I finally know what comfort is like. As though her touch is healing me.

Healing.

No, she's not the sleeper-princess. She can't be.

I pull out of the alleyway with her clinging to me.

My mind tells me she's not. My heart knows differently.

CHAPTER SEVEN
SYL

The downfall of the sleeper-princess:
She is always drawn to darkness
- Glamma's Grimm

I cling to Euphoria on the back of her bike, the nighttime streets passing us in a blur of asphalt and city lights. She's given me her helmet again, and the wind lashes her raven-black hair against the faceplate, the muffled *tack-tack-tack* of it like fingers knocking on the doors to my soul.

Too late. I've already let her in.

She turns onto my street. With Fiann or any of the other girls, I'd be ashamed for them to see the tenements I live in, but with Euphoria… My cheeks flame hot and my heart races. What will she think? That I'm poor? I am. That I'm a loser? I lift my chin. Mom and Glamma didn't raise a loser. After Fiann's fake friendship, I suddenly decide that I want Euphoria to know who I am. Who I really am.

She doesn't bat an eyelash when she pulls up in front of the rundown tenement. Just throws the kickstand down and shifts forward to let me clamber off the seat. She pulls her gloves off while I tug the helmet from my head, bemoaning my helmet hair.

Whatever. I smell like peanut sauce and fryolator grease. Helmet hair is probably the least of my worries. "Thanks." My breath goes out of me when her eyes meet mine. Those blue eyes darken, almost sapphire and…glowing gold?

Like the girl from my dream.

Could it be her?

I study her hard. I've seen partway through her disguise, but my Fae-sight blurs, freaked out by whatever personal woojy-woo she's got going on. There's something I'm *not* seeing—something *beneath* her Euphoria-ness.

Something she's hiding.

That doesn't mean she's your dream girl, Syl.

Whoever—whatever—she is, I suddenly want to reassure her. She doesn't have to hide from me. Clearly, she's not normal, but I like that. I have Fae-sight. She can disguise herself. Maybe she was in a deadly accident once too.

We make a good pair. "Euphoria?"

She turns to me, her face open and honest. "Hm?"

I step in and touch the back of her hand. It's a monumental effort for me to reach out like that. I'm brave enough, but I'm not bold by nature. At least not when it comes to matters of the heart.

Matters of the heart? *Get a grip, Syl. You just met her. Today.*

Ugh. Fiann would say that's so stereotypical gay-girl, but there's no way to explain what's going on. I feel connected, suddenly, deeply, with Euphoria—a connection that burns like fire, like there was an ember smoldering inside me all these years, and suddenly… Suddenly, she's fanning it into flames.

My breath goes out as I see it reflected back in her blue eyes. She feels it too.

In the face of that, what do I care what Fiann would think, what anyone would?

Go for it, Syl. What do you have to lose?

My pride, my dignity, any future chance I have of ever asking another girl out. Ever.

"Are you all right?" Euphoria's so tall that, even sitting, she has to bend to look me in the eye.

I exhale shakily. "Look, I just want to say…" The rest of it catches in my throat. *Say what?* "You don't have to hide from me."

Shock shivers through her eyes, and they darken from brilliant blue to sapphire. "What do you mean?"

I look down at the helmet, at my reflection in it. Will she think I'm crazy? "I can see your…your aura. I know you're hiding what you really look like, but it's okay." I rush on before she thinks I'm body-shaming her or whatever. "I don't care. I—"

"Syl Skye."

That voice hits me like a hammer to the bones. *Mom.*

I sigh. Did she have to pick now to display her Supermom powers? I'd hoped she'd be in bed when I got home. She usually is. I look back to make sure she's real and not some figment of my angsty teen mind…

Oh yeah, she's really there, and she looks mad. Mad enough to spit iron nails, Glamma would say.

"Syl Skye, you come here this instant."

I freeze, caught between my mom and Euphoria and all the things I want to say to her. But the moment's passed. And there's no way I can say anything gushy in front of my mom. Nope. No way. I'm red to the tips of my ears as I hand the helmet back to Euphoria.

"Sorry," I manage, feeling like the world's biggest dork.

"It's okay." She hands me my leftovers. That super-cool-sexy smirk tilts her lips, but her posture is stiff. "I had a mom once too." Our fingers brush, and a spark jumps between us.

"Now, Syl." Mom is trembling. With rage, maybe? I've never seen her so angry, and yet… Her aura cloaks her in a deep crimson shot through with yellow, with…fear? What is she afraid of?

It must be something. She's got an iron poker in her hand.

What is happening? This is like my dad coming to the door with a shotgun on prom night. Surreal. Seriously, is my interest in Euphoria that obvious? Or is it just the shock of seeing me on the

54

back of a Harley that's freaking my mom out? Whatever it is, she steps in and grabs me, yanking me away from Euphoria.

Euphoria, for her part, seems a bit freaked out too, looking at my mom like she's something out of *The Twilight Zone.*

And then the moment breaks.

Mom waves the poker. "Leave this instant or I'll call the police."

Euphoria fixes my mom with a death glare, her irises practically glowing a dangerous dark blue.

I step between them, feeling like a teeny ref between two beefy football players. "She was just bringing me home, Mom."

"I know what she was doing."

From the look on Mom's face, she knows I'm crushing hard on Euphoria. *Warning, warning!* Desperate, I try to pull back from DEFCON 1. "My bike got a flat and—"

"Inside." I know that tone. Mom is done talking.

I look back at Euphoria. "Good night."

"Goodbye, Syl."

It sounds like she's saying *goodbye* goodbye. I want to turn back, but my mom corrals me inside and slams the door. When I turn back, Euphoria is gone. I scrunch my face to the window, looking both ways, but only an empty street meets my searching gaze.

"Come upstairs." Mom's voice is gentler now that Euphoria's gone, but her hand is still white-knuckled on the poker. She ushers me upstairs. Every footfall is like doom and dread. Halfway up, on the landing near our neighbor's door, I turn, but Mom only points. "Upstairs, Syl."

Huffing out a breath, I keep going, catching the flash of initials on the door—J.J.—painted in sprawly script with weird symbols around it. Bizarre. Still, part of me hopes the noise we're making might draw attention. *Look! A wild neighbor appears!* But no. The door stays closed, and I stay firmly on the hook.

Mom's hook. I already know what she's going to say.

She drops the bomb as we enter our apartment. "You're grounded, Syl."

"What? Mom, come o—"

"For a month."

"A month! But Homecoming is mid-October and—"

"Shall we make it two months?"

That shuts me up fast.

"And I don't want you going near that girl. Do you understand me?"

No. I don't, but Mom has that breathless rage thing going on, and underneath it, I sense her fear. It stains the air around her a bright canary yellow. "Yeah. I understand." But I don't. Not one bit.

Is she upset that I'm interested in a girl? A pang of hurt stabs me, but Glamma's sensible voice rises in my mind, *Don't flying-frog leap to conclusions, Syl.*

One thing's for certain, I won't be getting any answers out of Mom.

She points to my room. "Get some sleep. You've got a long walk to school tomorrow."

Ugh. She's right. Over a mile and no bike means I'll have to get up at least thirty minutes early. I schlep off to bed. I'll talk to her later when she's more reasonable.

She doesn't get more reasonable. A week goes by and then two. I go to school—my bike is an easy fix, so at least there's that—and then I come home right after. No hanging out, no afterschool anything, not even my assignments for the school paper. I have to give Suzie Chang all my editorials. Aside from work, I don't see the outside of our tiny apartment.

And though I pretty much throw myself on the mercy of the Court of Mom, she's stalwart as a Spartan. The first time I try, she listens and then tells me no. The second time, she cuts me off with the threat of more grounding.

Man, she does not like Euphoria.

So I'm stuck. Days go by—school, work, school, work…

I see Euphoria in bio class, and apparently everyone else does too. Whatever woojy-woo weirdness she had is no longer disguising her. Everyone sees her for who she is—Euphoria, glam-Goth star—and she's mobbed by fangirls and fanboys wherever she goes. Social media blows up, but try as they might, no one can get a good pic of Euphoria.

I figure it's got something to do with the woojy-woo. Some kind of side effect that messes with machinery. I read about it in Glamma's Grimm once—that machinery didn't work right in the presence of certain supernatural creatures, like ghosts or vampires or faeries. Well, I know Euphoria's not a ghost since I touched her more than once. There's no way she's a vampire because I've seen her in daylight. And, no. She didn't burn up or sparkle or anything.

So clearly she's a faerie.

And clearly I've been grounded for too long and I'm going stir-crazy because that is the most insane conclusion ever. *You're losing it, Syl.*

Whatever. I know she's hiding something, but I can't even get close to her.

Worse, Miss Mack moves her to be Fiann's partner. I smell a rat. A giant, principal-shaped rat. I don't have any other classes with her since I'm in AP everything, and I only see her in passing—sometimes in the hall between classes and sometimes in the parking lot. She meets my gaze, and I meet hers.

Every time, the longing between us ignites and scorches me, threatening to light me up. I'm a moth dancing on a flame, ever burning, burning, burning…

She feels it too. I can tell by the way her eyes darken, both of us burning, aching, the connection a fiery thread between us, wrapped around both our hearts.

But she doesn't talk to me beyond a "Heyla, Syl."

Now *I* feel like I'm in *The Twilight Zone*. One minute I thought we had a connection; the next I get grounded, and she's all over Fiann. Well…that last isn't true.

It's Fiann that's all over Euphoria; not in a "gay way"—or so she claims—but I see the way she looks at Euphoria. It hurts my heart to think they might get together, start dating, that Fiann might take my place on the back of Euphoria's bike.

But for all Euphoria's avoiding me, she doesn't seem interested in Fiann. Not like *interested*-interested. According to Lennon, who takes pity on me and keeps me informed, Euphoria's busy playing the Nanci Raygun and tossing mics off stage to fangirls. As much as I wouldn't mind being one of those fangirls, it's nice that Lennon is my new lab partner. We get to spend some time awkwardly doing silly experiments. Sometimes it feels like old times, and then the bell rings and she goes trailing after Fiann again.

Fiann.

Every day, she smirks at me from across the room. *Ugh.* And as the days draw closer to Homecoming, the posters go up. *Real Life Supergirl! Heroic Teen Saves Friend!* And the stories come back out. Stories of the night I cannot remember.

The night that's nothing more than a blur of white light and heat.

And a girl with sapphire-blue eyes ringed in gold.

The more I dream of her, the more intense my connection with Euphoria gets. Like what I see in my dreams becomes what I crave in real life.

Just a glance of E's intense blue eyes, and I'm a goner all over again. Burning, burning, burning... But whenever I try to talk to her, Fiann's there, getting in the way. I want to tell her to step off, but I don't have any claim to Euphoria. Not really.

I'm sure tons of girls have dream fantasies about her.

Meanwhile, everyone at school is acting weird—possessed or something. My Fae-sight keeps showing me a deep indigo aura hanging over them like shrouds. I have no idea what it means. I've never seen anything like it.

Except that one guy.

The Norwegian exchange student, Agravaine what's-his-bucket. He's dirty with dark indigo; it follows him like a cloud of squid ink. When I get too close, the feeling slides over my skin all sinister, slimy, like turning over a log to find squirming, black beetles beneath. Gross. He's all up in Fiann's new Euphoria-based crew too, her manager maybe? Rumor has it some of the juniors and seniors are buying some weird designer drug from him and ending up in the hospital, all hollow-eyed and dehydrated.

Meanwhile, Fiann is eating up all the attention from pre-Homecoming, from being Euphoria's supposed BFF, from everything... She's taken to catcalling me in the hall and encouraging her princess posse to booby trap my locker.

I take it for as long as I can.

Two days before Homecoming, I finally snap. It's the shaving cream incident that's the final straw.

I open my locker after lunch, and shaving cream pours out. Like...a ton of it. It's all caked in my books, my notebooks, *my DSL camera.* I just stand there while it poops out of my locker and splats onto the floor.

"Hey, Syl. You should shave at home, you know."

Fiann leans against her own locker halfway down the hall, the princess posse laughing all around her.

"Didn't you know, Fi?" Dani says, all exaggerated with a garbage-eating grin. "Lezzies don't shave."

I see red.

The next thing I know, I'm marching toward Fiann, and kids are getting the heck out of my way, like, fast. Like I'm a bull with steam coming out of my nose and ears.

"What's wrong, Syl? You—"

I grab Fiann and slam her against the locker. "What is your problem?"

Her face gets red, and all of a sudden, she's shaking, pale yellow bleeding all over her aura. "Get your hands off me." She whispers it in a how-dare-you tone, and then when I don't, she screams it. "Get her off me!"

Danette is the bravest. She grabs me. I shove her away, but she and Maggie haul me off. Fiann is sweaty-faced and puffing. She doesn't look so pretty now.

"You'll pay for this! You'll have detention forever!"

"Go ahead," I fire back, "and I'll show the admins my locker. I'm betting they'll recognize your handiwork."

Now she pales. Like a lot girls in Richmond E, Fiann's pretty-girl deception depends on her being utterly fake. Her father really does think she's some kind of angel. Well, this'd put a big, glaring black mark on her shiny halo.

We're locked in a tense standoff until suddenly Danette and Maggie let me go. A gentle hand on my shoulder turns me. "Syl." I look up into Euphoria's bright blue eyes. Concern lines her face, and her touch is soft. Her presence soothes me even as it sets me on fire.

Burning again. *Katniss Everdeen, you got nothing on me.*

"Syl..." The look on her face tells me she realizes I've been pushed too far.

I want to lean in to her strength, her comfort. *I volunteer as tribute!* But I don't.

I push her away. "Leave me alone."

"Syl!" She chases me down the hall. I double-time it, but she's tall and lanky and way more athletic than I am.

Heads turn as we pass, but then again, she always makes heads turn.

I'll bet half of them have dreams about her, just like mine.

"Syl, stop, please."

"Why do you care?" Tears burn hot on my lashes, and I dash them away, angrier than I've ever been at myself. I want to be by her side, even after all she's put me through these past weeks. "Fiann's your BFF now, so whatever."

"Who told you that?"

"I see the way she hangs all over you, and you don't even"—crap, my voice is breaking—"talk to me anymore."

"Syl." Euphoria takes my shoulders gently, her expression open and earnest. "I'm so sorry. I'll explain everything after the Homecoming concert."

"I want to go." I'm just blurting crap out now, my breath hitching over my sobs. "To Homecoming." I'm losing my cool, and I don't even care. Glamma always said if someone's important to you, be straightforward. "I'm grounded, but I don't care. I want to come, to see you."

Thunderclouds darken her face. *She's going to tell me to get lost, that she's into Fiann.* But then she softens. "Are you…asking me to Homecoming?"

Shock hits me like a Mack truck. Am I? *No…yes…no!* Ugh. My heart's gone all arseways and beyont, as Glamma would say. Not really sure what-all that means, but I take a sec to get my head on straight at least, squaring my shoulders and looking Euphoria right in the eye.

"Yes. Yes, I am." Should I kneel or bow or something? I've never asked a girl out. But darn it, I forge on ahead. "Euphoria, I'd be pleased if you'd accompany me to the Homecoming dance."

My heart is freaking out, trying to punch through my rib cage like Ronda Rousey, and the minute that passes is the longest in my entire life.

Euphoria's intense blue gaze is on mine, and the world goes away as I burn and burn and burn. She touches my hand. Her skin on mine is hot, feverish. She's burning too. "I'd love to." Her voice is sultry, like silk over steel. "Let me pick you up and bring you home."

I hesitate for, like, a fraction of a second. "Yes." I'll have to sneak out. Mom'll be furious, but seriously? I just got up the courage to ask out the girl of my dreams. Yeah, I'll *so* be sneaking out.

I look up into Euphoria's eyes. I'm lost. I'll be there. I'll so be there.

CHAPTER EIGHT
ROUEN

Sleeper-princess, only you see me
Only you see the true me
Can we break Winter's hatred for Summer?
Can we break the chain of blood and death?
- "Chains of Blood," Euphoria

Syl's the seventh and last sleeper-princess. I can feel it in my bones, in my blood. But most of all, I feel it in my heart—the truth of her. Not to mention she can see through Glamouries *and* she can read my aura.

She's the last sleeper-princess all right—sweet, innocent, pure. A beacon of white flame against the crushing darkness.

I am that darkness. And I should not be anywhere near her.

Famous last words, Roue. I couldn't stay away from her if all of UnderHollow depended on it.

Come to think of it, it probably does.

But Agravaine's plan is garbage. Infecting the previous six sleeper-princesses with Moribund, blowing their fuses and draining them of their life-forces, even their blood.

All that, and the hearthstone is no more healed than when we began.

Without it, my world is doomed.

It might be emo, but I fight with myself anyway as I head down the hall, away from Syl, dodging students and trying not to look back over my shoulder. *I'm taking her to Homecoming.* And on the heels of that, *The exact opposite of staying away from her.* Plus, it's a bad idea for her to be at the Homecoming concert, in the audience, under Agravaine's scrutiny.

But back there, looking into those stormy grey eyes, I was captivated. That spark that flares between her and me whenever we touch... It burns me too.

I couldn't deny her anything.

Truth is, I've missed her. The way the long winter misses the summer.

Okay, that was *definitely* emo.

I go to my locker. Fiann tries to meet me halfway, but one look at my grim-dark glare, and she finds something else to occupy her attention. *Good girl.* I thumb open my locker. I never use the padlock. No one would dare put shaving cream all over my stuff.

All over her camera and everything. I just don't get it. Dark Fae and fair Fae might want to kill one another, but we never stoop to such petty bullying. And while I like a lot of things about humans, the mean-girling is not one of them. I'm glad Syl's not like that.

Syl...

A pang of guilt seizes me. I didn't realize keeping my distance would be so hard on her. Time passes differently for Faekind in UnderHollow. In the blink of my eye, a hundred years might pass in the mortal realm. I was trying to protect her. *By hurting her? Good going, Roue.*

Gah! I grab my trig book. I'm so torn. Stay away from her or keep her close?

It was only one day that we spent together. One day. Why do I feel so connected to her? And her to me?

Because one second, one minute, one day can change your life.

It changed mine.

And that's what decides me. Right here and now, standing in a high school hallway, I decide. I failed to protect the six sleeper-princesses.

Now I vow to protect the seventh.

As much as I don't want to admit she is the seventh, her words come thundering back. *"I can see your aura."* I slam my locker overly hard. Why did it have to be her? *Because you always fall for the wrong girl, Roue.* In my heart, from the very beginning, I've known who she is—what she is.

The same way I know what I am. Her Huntress, her executioner. *No. Not this time.*

This time, I'll save her. This time, I'll be smart. I won't wait 'til the end, and I won't defy Agravaine directly. If I do, he'll only use the Contract to order me to hurt Syl.

I won't give him the chance. Not this time.

Besides, it's time I tried out my plan. Forget Agravaine's.

I join the crush of students moving through the halls. Fiann pulls away from her group and trails after me. She's already berating one of her girlfriends—Lennon, I think.

By the unholy Hunt, does she ever give it a rest?

And people say dark Fae are awful.

At least we're loyal to our friends and loved ones. That's why I've been distancing myself from Syl this past month, staying close to Fiann. All to throw the Huntsman off Syl's scent. Besides, Agravaine favors Fiann as the sleeper-princess. According to local legend, she's the one who saved herself and Syl from the train crash.

I remember the two of them clinging together, the wreckage all around them, their hands upraised. And then the burning sheet of white fire that scythed into my body, a brilliant agony stealing my consciousness.

After spending two seconds with Fiann, I knew she'd never have the strength or will to pull that off. But Syl? Definitely. *Syl, Syl, Syl.* My heart beats it like a mantra, a brand on my soul.

I will do anything to protect her. Even if it means throwing Fiann to the wolves. Oh, it's callous and so dark Fae of me that

Father would be proud, but after about three weeks of watching Fiann backstab the girls she calls friends, after her constant bullying and how she wants to use me to get to Syl…

Well, let's just say I'm a lot less sympathetic.

Fiann could use a little mauling by wolves. And Agravaine won't kill her—not once he finds out she's a fake.

Plus, dark Fae or not, I'd trade ten Fianns for one Syl. Any day.

That's why I've stayed away.

I turn the corner and catch a flash of Agravaine's white hair as he slips into the hall to cut class. Instantly, he spots me. He always does. He tips a wink at me, fangs glinting beneath his arrogant smirk. He's surrounded by jocks and all the pretty, popular boys. They mill about him the same way the girls throng to me.

Between the two of us, we rule the school. He's always been obsessed with being royalty, and now he's king of the school. Unlike him, I don't want power or popularity. I just want to save my people.

Agravaine uses the crowd of students to mask himself as he goes to a side door and shoves it open. All his bro-dudes pile out while he covers their escape with Glamoury. He's up to something, all right.

Infecting the guys with Moribund circuits while I infect the girls.

I start after him, and he pins me with those shark-black eyes. "Enjoy class." It's a taunt, but it's also a Command.

Seriously?

He gives me a jaunty wave before he slips out into the parking lot. Meanwhile, my limbs are busily disobeying me, carrying me to my trigonometry class, a dopey smile plastered on my face. *I hate him.*

At least he can't really make me enjoy class. Not even the Contract of Bone and Blood can control my feelings. That's why he's never tried to get me to date him. He knows his Command would fail and he'd crash and burn. Hard.

I slump in my seat and ignore Fiann as she slides into the desk next to mine.

65

Agravaine's got something sinister up his sleeve. It has to do with all the Moribund microphones I'm tossing off the stage, all the high school boys he's roped into his motorcycle-racing club, all the shimmering black circuitry I see the students unknowingly sporting in the school halls.

He's infecting the student body with the Moribund, but why?

His plan involves ferreting out the last sleeper-princess, infecting her, taking her to UnderHollow to use her. He's smart enough to realize that once we're gone, the Moribund lairing in the bodies of mortals will die off. It's Circuit Fae magic. It needs our presence to sustain it.

So why infect them at all? What's his master plan?

Mr Barney limps over to the board with his cane, his glasses flashing in the fluorescents, and begins writing trig stuff. Fiann passes me a note. Grudgingly, I open it.

Can't wait for Homecoming! Too bad you can't be my Homecoming king!

I snap my pencil. Girl has no shame.

"Miss Rivoche." Mr Barney's voice booms over the squeaky two-step his chalk is doing on the board. He doesn't even stop writing. "Will you kindly stop distracting the class?"

Someone's got to. This class is the cure for insomnia. Swallowing my smart-ass answers, I stand up and fling the broken halves of my pencil at the trash can at the front of the room. They give plaintive little *pangs* as they hit the rim and fall inside. Two points. Or is it four? I admit, I don't get the mortals' preoccupation with sportsball.

"Sure thing, Mr Barney." I sit to the snickering of the class.

He fixes me with an *I'm warning you* look, but I pull out another pencil and diligently get to work. Or at least, I fake it. The Command makes me.

At least it means I can avoid answering Fiann's note. Homecoming king? Oh, hells no. I glance at Fiann, all blonde-haired, green-eyed perfection. I don't want to be lab partners with her, never mind fake high school "royalty."

She slides a piece of paper to the edge of her desk. *It'd be great for our popularity!*

Maybe it was a mistake letting down my Glamoury.

Fiann wasn't one bit interested in me when I was just plain Rouen Rivoche, new sophomore at Richmond E. In fact, no one was interested in me. Only Syl.

I sigh as I copy the trig assignment, the Contract binding me to stay in class. *Damn Agravaine to the Harrowing darkness!* I could have remained anonymous, but distancing myself from Syl was so much easier with a billion fans around me creating a buffer.

I thought I was keeping Syl safe. But I can't stay away, even though I can feel all of us eventually colliding: Agravaine, Fiann, Syl's mom…

Georgina… I shake my head. Seeing her again is a kick in the face, but there's no way I'll give her the satisfaction of knowing I'm rattled.

I'm sure she feels the same about me. That iron poker left zero room for interpretation. I'm probably lucky she didn't try to brain me with it. If she knew the danger her daughter would be in, in just two nights, she probably would have.

Homecoming.

Rumor is Fiann's used her "pull" with me to get me to play. The truth is, Agravaine's orchestrated the whole thing to flush out the sleeper-princess. He knows the seventh is here. And the sixth's blood confirmed it. Blood calls to blood. Just the way something inside me calls to Syl.

On Homecoming night, in front of the entire student body, I'll play and use my gramarye. The one girl who's immune, who doesn't fall under my Euphoria power—she'll be revealed as the sleeper-princess.

I blow out a heavy breath. It's going to be intense. But there's no keeping Syl from Homecoming, with or without me.

It'll take every trick up my sleeve, but I vow to protect my girl from Agravaine. *My girl?* A second pencil creaks as I squeeze it. *When did she become my girl?*

My heart gives a painful tug. The idea of Syl in danger is awful in a way that's completely foreign to me. I shouldn't care. She's fair Fae, princess of the Summer Court—at least, she will be when she Awakens. I am dark Fae of the Winter Court, a sluagh even, the worst of the worst.

I shouldn't care. But I do. And I don't know why.

All I know is, I'm going to enjoy at least one dance with her at Homecoming before it all goes to hell and Harrowing.

CHAPTER NINE
SYL

And by her fascination
With the darkness
Will the sleeper-princess
Be revealed
- Glamma's Grimm

I pace my room, fully dressed to the nines and chomping at the bit. Only an hour before Homecoming, before I see Euphoria. *Before I dance with her.* In public. In full view of everyone— students, teachers, Fiann. My stomach does a lazy barrel roll, but I steel myself.

I'm ready for this. Ready to dance with another girl in front of God and everyone.

I glance in my full-length mirror. A cute black A-line skirt and an emerald-sequined bodice make up my semi-formal mock two-piece, and I keep it real by pairing it with sheer black stockings and my black Docs. My red hair is still unruly, but I've managed to tame it up into a twist with pretty little tendrils falling around my cheeks. I keep my makeup minimal and classy, just some shadow, liner, and lip gloss. I can't hide the freckles on my cheeks and shoulders, but whatever. The gem-tone of the bodice suits my coloring.

Spinning in the mirror, I deem myself ready and way too adorable for mortal man.

But what about mortal woman?

If Euphoria can even be called that. Wait, what? I shake those thoughts away even though they nag me. *Your Fae-sight, Syl. Her aura... There's something off about her.*

Ugh. Now is not the time for me to be putting stock in Glamma's old fairytales. I loved Glamma to the moon and back, but I never did believe all her tales of faeries and bogies. So what if I see other people's auras? There are about a dozen psychics in town who can do that. And so what if Euphoria has some kind of woojy-woo? That's what makes tonight awesome. We can be odd together.

But I'm in a holding pattern until Mom leaves.

Through my closed door, I hear her getting ready for work. She's got a late shift over at Richmond Public High. Their Homecoming was last night, and apparently, the kids trashed the auditorium the way rock stars trash hotel rooms. I'm kind of thanking my lucky stars for that. It's good for Mom to make a little more money. And it's good for me.

For my sneaking-out purposes.

"Syl, I'm leaving!" she calls tentatively.

These past few weeks have put a bit of strain on our relationship, so she's being cautious now. I regret that. I really do. I love my mom, but a month? For riding a motorcycle?

It's kind of overkill.

Still... "Bento's in the fridge!" I call back. I made one special for her. Okay, so some of it was fueled by my guilt for sneaking out, but mostly I want her to eat. Her shift is 'til one a.m. Where else is she going to find decent food at that hour?

"Thanks. Lock up behind me, okay?" A soft knock at my door.

Oh, crap. I grab my bathrobe and toss it over my dress as I scramble for the door before she opens it. I crack it open just a bit. "Hi, Mom." My heart is hammering so loud I feel it in my temples. If she sees me dressed up, she'll know in a heartbeat—but I don't want her to think I hate her or anything. "I…uh…I'll lock up." I give her what I hope is a convincing mopey face.

She looks for a sec at my makeup but doesn't say anything. She probably decides I'm so bored I've taken to giving myself makeovers in desperation. She reaches through the cracked-open door and touches my cheek. "Love you, bug."

Normally I cringe a little at the pet name, but tonight there's something sad and plaintive in her eyes, and this feels absurdly like one of those times where, if I don't say it, I'll regret not saying it. "Love you too, Mom."

And that's it. She takes her hand away, and I close the door. A moment later, I hear the door to the apartment open and then *click* closed. Heart still pounding, I wait, counting out sixty long, agonizing seconds. Then I cross the room, gown swishing, to lock up all the deadbolts.

I won't be going out the door anyway. Hence, the short A-line.

I head back to my room to wait by my window. Okay, so I preen a little more in the mirror, smoothing down my gown. It's cute, but it's way more elegant than anything I've ever worn. I got it cheap—I'm kind of an eBay shark—and I know it's less fancy than the other girls' dresses will be, but it's got emerald rhinestones on it and it glitters prettily, so score. It's cool in my book. And I think Euphoria will like it too.

What if she doesn't?

A jolt of fear goes through me, but I shake it off. I know what I saw. The fire in Euphoria's eyes that matches mine. My knees want to buckle even thinking about it. And speaking of knees… My right leg throbs all the way to my knee tonight. It's been acting up something fierce. I rub it to work out the kinks, imagining I can feel the iron spike wedged there.

Ugh, gross.

Sighing, I twist a stray red curl around my finger. *She'll like it.* I check my brown eyeliner and the dusting of gold shadow on my lids. The combination brings out the grey of my eyes, like a storm at sea. I leave my cheeks alone. Foundation makes me look like a scary clown, and there's nothing I can do to cover up all my freckles anyway.

If you got 'em, flaunt 'em, Glamma used to always say.

And I so mean to flaunt—my freckles, my dress, *Euphoria…*

I check my clock. 7:05pm. *She's late.*

She's not coming. Oh my God, she STOOD ME U—

The purr and roar of a motorcycle cuts through my doubt. The relief that pours into me makes me sit down on my bed, hard. *You got it bad, Syl.*

I do.

Peering down into the alley outside my window, I feel my heart give a leap as Euphoria pulls up. She's all sleek and cool in her black leather pants and jacket, a black lace and mesh long-sleeve shirt, the metal on her New Rock boots glinting. She puts down the kickstand. With held breath, I wait for her to look up.

The seconds spiral away, and then she does.

Her gaze meets mine, holds mine, and the fire ignites between us, a raging bonfire rushing heat through my whole body. My stomach clenches, and my knees turn to Jell-O. It seems surreal that, in a few moments, I'll head down the fire escape—in a ball gown, yikes!—and have my arms wrapped around her.

Me. Syl Skye, geeky school-paper photographer and nerd extraordinaire. It's seriously impossible to believe.

She cocks her head to the side, a questioning smirk tilting her lips up as if to say, *What's wrong?*

Nothing. Nothing is wrong. Belief is overrated.

I slip one leg over the windowsill and duck out. My knee throbs as I manage my dress and clamber down the fire escape. In moments, I'm standing before Euphoria, ready to storm Homecoming like a boss.

"You look…" She seems to be trying hard to catch her breath. Her eyes are that dark, intense sapphire blue, glowing, almost molten like…gold? "You look beautiful."

"So do you," I say shyly, shaking off the spell. Stupid Fae-sight. Nothing is wrong. In fact, everything is perfect.

The Homecoming dance is at the Nanci Raygun. I can hear the house music thumping from a block away. Our football team won, so the place is packed, people spilling out into the streets.

Euphoria guns it, and we roar past a bunch of juniors and seniors drinking mocktails on the makeshift sidewalk patio. They all turn to look. Smirking back at me, she pulls into the rear parking lot near the band's entrance, and cuts the engine. With her easy grace, she puts down the kickstand and helps me off the bike.

Taking off the helmet, I smooth my hair back and cock a shy smile at her. "How do I look?"

Her eyes never leave mine. "Syl, you're…" She blows out a breath, and holy cats, is that Euphoria blushing? "You're gorgeous."

My face feels as red-hot as my hair, and I have some trouble speaking. "You…you too." I enjoy the excuse to look her up and down, from the tips of her New Rock boots to the tight leather pants with slits and stitches up the sides to the artfully torn long-sleeved black top and motorcycle jacket. She's totally rocking the Goth-chic semiformal look. Her raven-dark hair cascades over her shoulders, and those eyes…

In the falling twilight, they're a brilliant electric blue.

They pierce my soul.

"You might not be the girl *from* my dreams, but you're definitely the girl *of* my dreams." *And holy cats…DID I JUST SAY THAT OUT LOUD?* Hashtag: whatiswrongwithme.

She chuckles softly, fondly, and takes my hand. "Shall we sneak in the back or"—a mischievous smirk curls her lip—"are you brave enough to walk right in the front?"

She's challenging me, the little minx.

While the idea of being surrounded by so many people, all of them staring at me, has my heart trying to Bruce Lee its way out of my chest, there's no way I'm losing this challenge, not even to Euphoria.

I fold my hand into hers. "Come on." My heart doesn't stop kung-fu kicking me, but I stride through the back parking lot and toward the crowded front entrance, head held high. I meet her challenge head-on. "How's this for brave?"

"Not bad," she says, teasing with good nature. "But the night is young."

"Challenge me again at your peril," I retort playfully. She cocks a cheeky eyebrow in response, and I know she will. Later. The anticipation thrills through me. I can't wait.

Euphoria and I walk in like we own the place. In a way, we do.

The instant we step foot into the club, the throbbing, bassy hum envelopes us, vibrating through the soles of my Docs and thrumming in my chest. We stop just inside the door. My eyes need time to adjust to the strobing light and darkness, and Euphoria seems to sense this. She waits patiently, though for some reason I'm sure she has no trouble seeing.

Soon enough, Euphoria tugs gently on my hand. My eyes still aren't fully there, but she smiles gently. *Trust me,* that look seems to say.

I do. I trust her with my life.

Hand in hand, we enter the main room of the club. More than half the school is already here, milling about, sitting at tables, dancing. Banners and streamers cascade from the ceiling, and disco balls cast a parade of lights on a dance floor crammed with bodies.

My introvert instincts freak out. Too many voices, too much scent and sight and sound. The flashing lights—violet lightning, the disco ball—white flame.

White flame...like on the train tracks. My heartbeat ratchets up about a thousand notches. *What's wrong with me?*

I feel faint, but Euphoria takes my arm.

Heads turn, people whisper, rumors fly.

"She's with Euphoria."

"What's Euphoria doing with *her*?"

My face is so hot I feel like I'm going to burst into flame. *White flame.* I shake my head hard as Euphoria leads me through the crowd, shielding me from the worst of her personal paparazzi.

Get your act together, Syl. I raise my chin. At least the flashing lights keep my Fae-sight or whatever it is from going into overdrive. All these people...so much emotion. I shudder at the thought. Sometimes all the colors give me blinding headaches.

"Syl!" Lennon threads her way like a cat through the crowd, her Goth Lolita frimps and lace bobbing. She's super-cute in a cocktail dress with skeletal animals all over it. She checks out my gown and squeals in glee. "You look amazing!"

"So do you." I mean it too. Lennon is pretty, her long black hair perfectly straight and shining, her almond-shaped eyes fringed with long lashes and the perfect color of shadow.

We smile at each other, and then I introduce Euphoria.

Lennon nearly faints, all fangirl-like. "I know who you are."

"We all do." Fiann's voice breaks in.

Ugh. Seriously? She keeps popping up like the killer in a cheesy slasher flick.

"Hi, Euphoria." Fiann prowls up next to her, preening like a swan, her burgundy-red dress accentuating her fair skin and blonde updo. She displays herself like an alley cat in heat.

"Fiann." Euphoria nods politely but doesn't give her a second glance.

When we try to move past, Fiann's princess posse flounces up in their stupidly expensive prom dresses. They tower over me, all MAC cosmetics, perfect updos, and high heels.

"Nice dress, Syl." Jazz gives me a snotty once-over, pursing her lips.

"Nice duck face," I shoot back. "Make sure they get a picture of that for the yearbook. It's a winner."

Red-faced, Jazz steps in, but Fiann stops her. Clearly Jazz's hurt feelings aren't Fiann's main concern. She gets in Lennon's face, using her height to bully. "Did you get lost on your way to hand those out?"

Now I notice that Lennon has a stack of photocopies. *Fiann for Homecoming Queen!* blares gaudily off the top one. I nearly choke. Campaigning for Homecoming queen is the height of lame.

"Something wrong, Syl?" Fiann's really warming up the nasty now. "Oh, aren't you supposed to be grounded?" She takes out her iPhone 1000 or whatever the newest model is. "Maybe I should text your mom a pic of you?"

Crap. If she tells my mom I went AWOL, there'll be a citywide manhunt for me. I mentally scramble for a comeback.

Euphoria saves my bacon. "Come on, Fiann, that's not cool."

Fiann makes a show of thinking about it, but the cold steel in Euphoria's eyes backs her down. "Whatever. If I call your mom and have your sorry butt hauled out of here, then you won't witness me winning Homecoming queen." She steps out of way and gestures.

I groan inwardly as I finally notice what's on the banners— *Heroic Teen Saves Friend! Real Life Supergirl! Local Girl Hero!*— all of them blown-up pictures of the newspaper articles from last summer. And every one of them smeared with Fiann's smiling face.

She saved me.

That night...on the tracks...

Or did she? Violet lightning and white flame light up the darkness in my mind's eye. A shiver runs through me.

Fiann's looking me up and down, expecting some kind of retort. Normally I have one, but... The train screeching, derailing, the two of us pitched out the window, train cars arcing up over us like a massive steel caterpillar, the smashing of metal and glass...

Sitting up, my leg screaming in pain, and then...

White flames bursting from my hands, from deep inside me.

"Whatever." Fiann looks at me like I have ten heads. She reaches out and tugs at Euphoria's hand. "Dance with me?"

Over my cold, dead body. I come out of my trance fast as a bullet train, but Euphoria politely pulls away.

"I'm here with Syl."

She just said it aloud. *With Syl.* My poor heart!

Fiann looks like she's just bitten into the sourest lemon on the planet. She purses her lips and pouts. I'm sure that works with her boy toys, but Euphoria only looks at her, one eyebrow raised.

Something dark moves behind Fiann's eyes, and suddenly, the air is filled with tension, electric and wild and dangerous. I'm still fever-hot from whatever waking dream/nightmare I'm having, and I smell and taste burning iron. My gaze meets hers, and the truth is suddenly there between us. She sees it in my eyes, and I see it in hers.

That night on the tracks.

My mind flashes with half-remembered memories— violet lightning and dark figures hunting us, the train crashing, trying to run, agony slicing through my leg, the dark hunters closing in, and then my whole body burning up in fear and power and purpose.

White flame bursting from my hands.

And Fiann lying in the wreckage at my feet. Fiann. Unconscious. *I saved her.*

The truth hits me like a bucket of cold water in my face.

She's been lying all this time. The shrapnel in my leg aches.

Fiann smiles, but it's twisted, wrong. She knows I know. "Fine, then." She plays it off, but even her words sound forced, wooden. "'Don't forget to watch me win." She flounces away, her princess posse trailing her.

Euphoria puts a gentle hand on my arm. "Are you all right?"

"Euphoria, it's time."

From my periphery steps a massive guy, all masculine beauty and white hair. Agravaine. Rumor has it, he's Norwegian royalty. Already the most popular guy in school, he's got some kind of testosterone-fueled motorcycle fight club going on. I think he's part of her crew, maybe even her manager. Whatever he is, the guys who hang out with him usually end up in the hospital, or worse—missing altogether.

He's looking at Euphoria like she's on the menu. He touches her hip, keeping his hand there even when she tries to move away.

Ummm…no means no, dude.

His gaze turns to me, his eyes dead black like a shark's. Something about that look stops me cold. *Violet lightning…the train heaving up, the boom of his voice. "Find her. Find the sleeper-princess."*

What in holy hell is happening to me?

Euphoria's touch breaks my trance. "Syl, I have to play now. Are you okay?"

"Y-yeah…" I choke out. I don't really want her to go, and she seems to sense it.

She hesitates, but Mr Impatient snaps, "Now."

Her spine goes rigid, and a weird look comes over her face. "Stay back here, okay?" she says so low only I can hear. "Stay back, and when the crowd starts swaying, sway with them."

Wait, what?

And then she's gone, vanishing in the crowd, and I'm left standing there, the sudden knowledge that Fiann's been lying, that *I'm* the teen Supergirl, the hero, swimming in my mind.

What is going on?

But the lights go down, and I'm in darkness.

CHAPTER TEN
ROUEN

Run from me, my princess
Run far, far away
Where the music takes you
No magic can reach you
- Euphoria, "Run, Princess, Run"

I walk away from Syl without looking back. If I do, Agravaine will see. He'll know I warned her. He'll know my interest in her isn't your standard dark Fae princess's interest in the sleeper-princess of the fair Fae.

And he'll force me to take her.

That's his plan—for me to capture Syl while he captures Fiann. Two of them, two of us. That's his logic. He's been the Master of the Wild Hunt for a long time. He's smart enough to cover all our bases.

But he's not smart enough to suspect I'm already betraying him. I need to use that to maximum advantage. For my own sake, but primarily for Syl's.

Syl. My footsteps are heavy with dread. Seeing those blasted posters made her memory jolt. I should be happy that she'll eventually get that missing part of herself back—but it will only cause her pain.

If only Fiann were the sleeper-princess. But she's not. No matter how much I want her to be.

One thing's for sure, though—somehow Syl Awoke to her powers that night on the tracks and then went right back to sleep.

A blip of power on our dark Fae radar, only to vanish.

It makes no sense... No one Awakens and then goes back to sleep. Once you're Awake, you stay Awake. And since it takes some kind of trauma for a sleeper-princess to Awaken to her powers, it doesn't make sense.

I mean, she'd have to forget—

A chill rakes up my spine. *Syl doesn't remember what happened that night. Not yet.*

"Rouen." Agravaine's cool facade is broken by his annoyance. It's past time I was on stage, and I'm testing his patience.

Get used to it, buddy-boy. The night is young.

He seems to sense I'm full of snark and shade. He stares with those shark-black eyes. *Don't forget your place,* his look says. I catch his meaning. I'm here to play, to flush out the true sleeper-princess. Nothing more.

I bow my head. Let him think I'm subservient. I won't hurt Syl. No power on Earth or UnderHollow can make me.

Except the Contract, that unhelpful part of me whispers. My heart is in my throat as I take the stage under the hot, flashing lights.

The crowd's shouts and cheers swell and then die down as Fiann steps to the mic to introduce me. Her hair looks like white flame under the stage lights, and I seize that one wild shred of hope that I've been wrong about Syl all this time, that Fiann is really the sleeper-princess.

"Hey, everyone! I'm Fiann Fee, running for Homecoming queen, but you all know that."

Ugh. Is she seriously using this as a campaign platform?

"My good friend Euphoria is here to play for you, as a favor to me. When I told her you were all going to make me your queen, she got really excited…"

I roll my eyes. Apparently yes, yes, she is.

The dull roar of my blood muffles the rest of her little speech. When she's done, I take the mic from her, set it back on its stand. The Nanci's house band moves into place from the shadows, helpfully Glamouried by Agravaine. The Huntsman himself poises at the end of the stage, dressed all in black like one of the roadies. His posture is predatory as he studies the crowd, watching every little move.

If I know him—and I do—he'll have the hounds of the Hunt, the *cú sluagh*, waiting in the wings. Or maybe in the alleyway. To make sure the sleeper-princess doesn't escape.

I have my work cut out for me. *Syl…*

I see her in the crowd, in the way back like I asked. Good. Let's hope she stays away. Let's hope she sways with the crowd when they fall under the spell of my gramarye.

Seizing my frustration, I launch into the first song with passion, belting the lyrics, my voice soaring above the synth and blare of instruments. I'm just warming up. I haven't loosed the full force of my gramarye yet. For that I need both my voice and my violin.

Agravaine indulges me. He lets me have my one song. After this, he'll want me to weave my spell, the spiderweb gramarye that captures mortals and bewitches them with euphoria. The last time I cast such a wide web was…that night on the tracks. Everyone on the train that night died in peace. It was the one gift I could give them.

You could give the sleeper-princess that gift.

No.

Think of your people. The hearthstone needs her blood.

No! I won't allow her to be harmed. There is another way to save my people.

The realization hits me like a thunderbolt. I just have to tell her…everything.

Even if I lose her.

The first song ends in cheering and clapping, the student body going crazy. I glimpse Syl. *Bloody bones.*

Our connection has drawn her to the front of the stage. She looks up at me, her face so open, so vulnerable it's a blade across my heart. She's beautiful, standing in the light, her red hair a halo, her grey eyes burning with passion as she loses herself in my music.

We never even got to dance. Regret washes over me as I pick up my violin and lift it to my chin. If I close my eyes, I can imagine the feel of my arms around her, her breath on my cheek as she leans in…

Why, in the midst of all this, am I thinking about kissing her?

A wry smile twists my lips. It might not be the best battle strategy, but hey, a girl needs something to fight for. *Sway with them, Syl. Please.*

"Do it." Agravaine pitches his voice low in the lull of cheers and shouts.

His Command blazes through me, blood and bone, lacing my limbs with obedience. The Moribund circuitry in my right hand throbs with phantom pain. I bear down, bow on strings.

The first note is discordant, but I turn it right away and it becomes sweet. The sweet strains of my violin thread the air and fall on the crowd, entwining them, weaving them into my spell. The ones at the front are captured immediately. Their faces go slack with bliss, with euphoria. My strings hum with violet light, the Moribund spliced through my flesh throbbing in time with the music.

Agravaine's gaze is on me. He watches my every move, every sweep of the bow on strings, every strand of my gramarye as it wends its way, capturing the students in its glittering web. One by one, they fall to my dark spell and begin to sway gently until the crowd is nothing more than an undulating wave of bodies.

Faestruck, all of them.

I scan their dazed faces. They are fresh and young, vibrant in their youth. But none of them shine as brightly as her.

Syl.

I feel her more than see her. Standing at the front of the stage, unmoving. She looks around. She wonders what's happening.

Of all of them, she's the only one who knows she's caught in a trap.

The only one immune to my gramarye.

My heart aches as the last shreds of my hope go up in flames. *Syl, why did it have to be you?*

She's staring at me as though seeing me for the first time. Does she? Does she see the real me, in all my dark Fae glory—fangs and pointed ears and high cheekbones, sapphire eyes ringed in Fae gold? Could she ever truly like me...*for me?*

Stop staring at her, Roue. You'll blow your cover, and hers.

I want to stare at her, to drink her in, but that would be her death. Agravaine would notice. I jerk my gaze away and scan past her. Did he notice?

Not yet. Syl is short, and she's blocked from his view by a massive deck of amps. Agravaine gestures for me to play on, and I do.

I pour more of myself into the spellbinding music. The circuits in my hands pull and stretch, working with my gramarye to bind the crowd tighter and tighter. I can feel my arm moving, but I cannot feel my fingers on the bow.

The crowd undulates in time, caught up in my dark spell, a waking sleep. I step the edge of the stage and sway with them, meeting Syl's gaze, willing her to move with me. *Dance with me, sway with me. Syl...*

A pang of guilt spears me as I come to the end of the song. From the moment I entered her life, I have caused her nothing but pain. The accident, the train—violet lightning lashing from my bow, ripping up the tracks, hurtling train cars up into the air like a child's toy and then smashing them down. Broken glass and twisted metal and lost lives.

And two girls huddled in the midst of it, protected by the sleeper-princess's power. I know now that it was Syl and not—

"Get her."

Agravaine's Command comes harsh, cutting through the final soft notes and the hush of the crowd as they wait for the end.

He's spotted her! My heart seizes painfully. I cannot breathe. The Contract laces my blood and bone with fire, compelling me.

And as the crowd breaks into cheers, my body jerks forward. I fight it, and agony lances through my Moribund hand, up my arm, through my chest, leaving me gasping.

I grit my teeth. *Bloody bones.*

Agravaine fixes me with a warning glare, but he knows the Contract will win and I'll do his bidding. Confident, he slips from the stage into the crowd, slicing through their ranks like a shark through water.

Fiann. He's going after Fiann.

I see her now, struggling against my gramarye. She's one of the Wakeful, but she's no sleeper-princess. She's a deer in the headlights, and she knows it. I feel a pang of pity for her. She's just a foolish girl.

A fresh wave of agony slices through me. If I don't do as he says, the Moribund will devour me from the inside out. No thanks. I'd rather die young and stay pretty.

He said *get her.* Not *kill her* or *destroy her* or anything permanent sounding. Maybe I can twist his words. Dark Fae are good at that.

Leaning down into the crowd, I reach for Syl. A dozen hands reach for mine, their faces entranced. They want to get closer to me; they gravitate toward me, toward the euphoria flooding their veins.

The spotlights flash over the crowd, blinding me, and then a small hand slips into mine. I know from the heat of her. She burns my soul. *Syl.*

I pull her up on the stage.

Her face is lined with concern. "Euphoria, what's happening?"

She says something else, but the Command screams in my mind, *Get her, get her, get her.*

Agravaine watches, his gaze shrewd, while I pull Syl in against my side. Behind me, the band picks up my lapse, synths and bass and drums pounding. They don't need me anymore. My gramarye is cast.

"Euphoria…" Syl touches my face.

Her touch is like a lick of flame, igniting my every nerve ending. Her heartbeat is a rabbit kicking beneath my hand. My own heart is racing. At the closeness of her, her small body pressed up against me, at the scent of her. I am burning up with desire, my entire body responding to her.

I smell it now—the barest hint of vanilla and sweet sunshine.

She is Awakening.

And I am drawn to her, a winter moth to a scorching summer flame.

"Syl."

Get her, get her, get her!

She looks up at me, her expression dazed, but not from my spell. Her eyes, fiery and fierce, lock onto mine. Her breath is warm on my face. She burns me hotter than the fire from resisting Agravaine's Command.

My hand falters. I drop my violin with a clang, the bow with a clatter. Syl is so close. The Command jolts through me again, bringing agony like burning blades. *I'll get her, all right.*

I sweep her up into my arms. *I'll get her…out of here.*

I'm completely disobeying. And one hundred percent not caring about the consequences.

I turn to run—

A rough hand on my jacket yanks me back viciously. I push Syl away, staggering then falling beside my violin. Agravaine hulks over me, his face flushed in anger, Fiann cowering behind him. He wants to be the one in my arms. Not her.

He stands between us, glaring at us both. "That's not what I meant."

Way to interrupt a moment, jerk. "Maybe you should word your Commands better."

Rage turns his pale skin an interesting shade of purple.

He opens his mouth to issue another Command.

That's when I kick my bow into my hand and drag it across the violin. A flare of violet lightning lashes from the strings. It strikes him in the chest, knocking him sprawling onto his back.

Awww, did the big bad Huntsman fall down, go boom?

Grinning like a madwoman, I leap to my feet, bow and violin in hand. Syl is staring at me, breathing hard, her eyes wide in fear.

"Run," I say as I turn and start flicking switches—house music, amps, volume, loud, loud, louder!

The club fills up with noise as feedback spirals through the speakers, house music cutting in over the band, instruments blaring, mics backlashing a wall of sound.

Agravaine is shouting at me.

I smirk at him. "I'm sorry. Are you trying to Command me? Can't hear you, buddy-boy!"

He can't hear me either, but he gets the gist of my mutiny. Already, he is gaining his feet, the rage on his face propelling him toward me, toward Syl.

I step between them.

Syl grabs me, but I shove her toward the stage door. "Run!" The noise swallows my scream, but she gets it.

She looks at me, betrayal and hurt and confusion swimming in her grey eyes. It tears at my heart. "Please, Syl, please run!"

She runs.

Relief washes over me just as Agravaine's fist crashes into my cheek.

CHAPTER ELEVEN
SYL

A sleeper-princess can only Awaken
In times of great stress
And even then, perhaps not fully
- Glamma's Grimm

"Run!" Euphoria shoves me one last time, and I go stumbling. The music is blaring, the feedback loop screaming through the amps. My heartbeat ramps up, jack-knifing me in two. That night, the tracks, the accident, the train whistle that went on and on and on... My brain struggles to remember details, but looking at her, looking at Agravaine, only fear comes, bright and stabbing.

Panic lights up my limbs. I'm at the stage's edge before I look back.

Agravaine stands over Euphoria, his face black with rage. He grabs her, lifts her off her feet with one hand. One hand. *Holy--!* I'm stunned by the unreality of it—like I'm watching two actors do a Hollywood stunt.

One hand is bunched in her leather jacket. With his other, he viciously yanks the main power cord. Sparks fly, the music cuts off, and a whole bank of stage lights go out, all the blues and greens winking out until we are bathed in red like blood.

Red lights. Emergency lights. That night on the train, our train car pitching over the side of the viaduct, the James River a black abyss below us, Fiann's screams in my ear, her fingernails digging into my arm.

She stands behind Agravaine now, a look of sick triumph stamped on her face.

It's the look of someone who's totally lost their grip on reality. Her loopy grin is movie-villain creepy. She walks over to the pulpit the Homecoming committee's erected and grabs the crown. She puts it on her head.

Homecoming queen. I'd like to brain her with the royal scepter, but I've got bigger problems.

Agravaine lifts Euphoria up by the throat. Pain lines her face, her hands tensing on his as she struggles to escape. He leans in, whispers something I don't hear, and the gloomy-dark indigo aura that surrounds him waves over her. She stops fighting.

I have to help her!

I run, but I don't flee.

My hand touches the fire alarm. "Hey!" I shout my challenge over the dazed crowd, but their collective aura stays all violet. They're still under whatever spell Euphoria cast. They won't be any help. I'm on my own. "Hey, jerkface!"

Agravaine whips around to look at me, his white hair flying anime-style, those shark-black eyes eating into my soul...that indigo aura rippling off him. I feel its gross, sticky heat lapping at my skin.

"Ugh. No wonder you're single." That, and he clearly doesn't know how to treat a lady. "Let her go."

"Sleeper-princess." He growls it so deep it reverberates in my bones. "Sleeper-princess." He growls it like my name, and it fits. Like a glove. I don't know what-all he's talking about, but some part of me deep down feels the truth.

I *am* the sleeper-princess. Whatever that means. I can worry about it later. Right now, my give-a-damn is totally broken. I only care about Euphoria.

I make like I'm going to pull the alarm. "Let her go. Now!"

He only smiles while Euphoria fights his dark Command, fear for me in her eyes.

"Go ahead, sleeper-princess." He squeezes her throat tighter, calling my bluff.

I should be shaking in my Docs. Euphoria's badass, and if she's afraid, I should be running my butt off, but Glamma always said, "*Wear your big-girl panties to the ball.*"

Well, I'm at the ball, all right. I pull the fire alarm. *Your funeral, pal.*

The glass breaks, and a howling wail fills the club. It shatters whatever woojy-woo Euphoria's got going on. People scream and grab their ears. The violet-funk aura over everyone dissipates like mist in a high wind. Yay!

And then the panic starts.

Not yay.

Like thunder, the stampede begins, students pushing and shoving to get out, a panicked mosh-pit of bodies crushing toward the small doors. Glaring at me, Agravaine yanks Euphoria close and whispers in her ear. Whatever weird power he has over her stains the air dark, like ink dropped into milk.

She turns to me, her face pale, her eyes swimming with misery.

"*Bring her to me.*" Agravaine says it again—I read it on his lips— but all sound is lost in the blaring alarm and thundering riot.

She fights it. Her limbs jerk and her fists clench and unclench. Like a marionette, she walks stiffly to her violin and picks it up, picks her bow up too. A lick of violet lightning leaps from her right hand.

Violet…lightning. I jolt, memory rushing back…

That night at the tracks, violet lightning flashing right before the train went off the rails.

No… It can't be.

Euphoria's looking at me as Agravaine's power, that gross, icky, indigo-darkness, overtakes her. Her luminous eyes burn as she meets my gaze, intense, predatory. My heart leaps against my rib cage, and my fight-or-flight instinct kicks into overdrive.

Yeah, it's time for some *Jurassic Park*-level running the heck away.

Besides, maybe if I can lure her away from him...maybe I can talk some sense into her. Maybe?

I bolt off the stage and into the crowd. They're in a blind panic now, pushing, shoving, the wailing alarm muffling their screams and cries. A girl goes down under the barrage, and I grab her arm, hauling her up. "Run!" I shout at her, and she takes off.

My way is totally blocked.

The front entrances are jammed with people trying to get out, their ball gowns and tuxes washed red in the emergency lights. Like that night on the train. The screams, the train pitching and shaking, thrown up into the air...

Panic shoots through me, but I force it down. *Get a grip, Syl. Right. Now.*

There's no way out here. I loop back around toward the backstage area, expecting Euphoria or Agravaine to roll up any second.

But they don't. In fact, I don't see either of them. Or Fiann.

Whatever. I think I'll run first and dazzle everyone with my logic later.

I hit the backstage door, burst out into the alleyway behind the Nanci, and run like a girl—which, as it turns out, is pretty darn fast.

If I survive this, I should totally go out for track. I'd crush the fifty-yard dash.

Even in a ball gown and Docs, I'm eating up the distance to the alley's opening, my legs churning. Not even that piece of shrapnel in my leg is bothering me.

What is happening to me?

And Euphoria. What is her deal? And how is she related to Agravaine? And why does he have some kind of wonky control over her? And the violet lightning. Was she at the tracks that night? Is she really the girl from my dreams? A thousand questions drum in my mind as my feet drum the pavement.

That's why I don't see the punch.

It blasts me in the shoulder and takes my feet out from under me, laying me out flat. I land hard on the concrete, the breath whooshing out of me.

Not my finest moment.

A flash of black; my instincts scream a warning. I roll just as a motorcycle boot Hulk-smashes into the asphalt, sending chunks of broken blacktop flying.

Whoa! That was almost my head.

I spring to my feet easy-breezy, like I've practiced it a hundred times. I haven't. It seems like my body is ready for a fight whether my mind wants to catch up or not.

And then she steps out of the shadows. Euphoria.

"Syl…" Her voice is pained even as she strides toward me.

I back up. How can I save her? How can I save myself?

She throws a punch, and my body *reacts*. I sidestep faster than I can blink. Her hand crushes the brick behind me. *Holy—!*

"Whoa, take it easy, Supergirl!"

"Syl, please." Her face is contorted in agony.

There's a trickle of blood coming from her nose, thin but bright scarlet against her bronze skin.

And that's when my Fae-sight kicks in.

My vision doubles. I see Euphoria, and then I see *beneath* Euphoria, beneath her faerie Glamour. Raven-dark hair. Her ears long and pointed, her skin a glowing bronze, cheekbones high, sharp, her fangs glinting.

Sapphire-blue eyes ringed in gold.

My breath goes out in a painful gasp. Euphoria is the girl from my dreams.

They're both from my dreams. Her and Agravaine.

That night… They came after me, shadowy silhouettes hunting me, attacking the train. All pointed ears and fangs. Dark Fae, Glamma called them.

Holy cats! Glamma was right. The dark Fae are real, and they're out to get me.

And all those fairy tales she told me… Are they all real too?

I shake my head. It's crazy, ridiculous, impossible. But here's Euphoria, standing right in front of me. In all her dark Fae glory.

And she's been ordered to capture me, to bring me back... to him.

"Syl..." Her face is fierce with that Command, but beneath that fierceness, there is a softness to her, a glowing burn that ignites my soul and lures me in.

Just like in my dream.

But this is way too real.

All I wanted was a date, a dance, maybe a goodnight kiss.

And now...now my heart aches like it's being torn out. Who is she? Has she been lying all this time, just to get close to me? Hurt wells up in my chest and spills over. "Did you attack the train that night?"

My question stops her dead. Another trickle of blood rolls from her nose. She's resisting Agravaine's Command. "Yes," she says.

My mind flashes me back—violet lightning in the sky, the train rattling and rolling, and then the sudden, terrible lurch. We're in free-fall, tossed into the air, backpacks and coffees, laptops and books and purses. And the people...the look of glazed-over bliss on their faces.

Just like tonight.

She cast some dark spell on them.

I step back and back and back until I fetch up against the wall. "You...you killed all those people." I stare at her, trying to see the monster beneath her Glamour. Glamma always said the dark Fae were evil to the core, that they'd steal your soul right from inside your skin.

But when I look at Euphoria, none of that is right.

The hurt in her eyes, the pain...

"Syl..." She steps forward, reaching for me, reaching for my hand.

Her touch is fire and ice, wonderful and terrible and amazing, and my emotions tangle up inside me, squeezing into a tight ball in my chest.

And then her body jerks as though someone's pulling invisible strings. Agravaine. The effort of resisting his Command rocks through her, twisting her face in agony.

She wipes dark red blood from her nose. "Syl...I can't fight it much longer."

I feel for her, but I slap her hand away. The smack hurts me inside, a spear to my heart. "You don't get it, do you? Ever since that night... Fiann doesn't talk to me. My life is a nightmare. And what about all those people on the train? All those *people!*"

She crumples inward, sagging. She's powerful and badass, but in this moment, I could push her over with a feather.

I don't want to. I just want to hold her, to comfort her.

"It wasn't me... Agravaine..." She jerks. Her body lurches forward, her hand pistoning out. The bricks behind me shatter, and I'm covered in dust. She grabs me, her hand tightening like she's going to crush my arm, but she only pushes me away. "Go. Toward the train tracks. You'll be safer there. Go!"

I look back at the building. Everyone's pouring out the front. Everyone is safe, but I'm not.

Euphoria loses the battle.

Her eyes dilate black with the force of Agravaine's command, and in my Fae-sight, the dark shroud of his power falls over her. "Run, Syl." Her voice rasps like she's gargling razor blades.

I reach out to her, to help her—

Wild howling fills the back of the alley. The shadows there light up with glowing green eyes—two, then four, six, eight... My guts go slick with dread.

"The hounds of the Hunt..." Euphoria rasps. "They're here for you."

Crap. I decide the better part of valor is running my butt off.

The growling breaks into snarls, and I hear them behind me, their great paws thudding on asphalt, their hot breath snuffling. They're fast! I hurdle a spilled trash can and dodge behind a Dumpster as one leaps at me.

What is going on? My body is like an Olympic athlete's all of a sudden.

And then the hound hits the Dumpster and the Dumpster hits me. "Oof!" I fall on my butt.

Better not start counting those gold medals yet, Syl.

I scramble to my feet and duck into a narrow side alley as the lead hound misses me and smashes into the bricks. A glimpse over my shoulder tells me all I need to know.

Euphoria is after me.

"Toward the train tracks," she said. Can I trust her?

The sounds of an oncoming train blare through the night. That night, violet lightning and dark figures chasing me. What choice do I have?

I feel like I'm running toward my past, but my present is trying to kill me.

So I run.

CHAPTER TWELVE
ROUEN

Sleeper-princess
Why can't you remember?
How brightly you burned
My white-flame sleeper-princess
- Euphoria, "That Night by the Tracks"

I hold back as long as I can, Agravaine's Command—"*Go after her, Rouen. And bring her back.*"—pounding in my head, threatening to split my skull in two. The blood that began with a trickle from my nose now gushes. With every moment I fight the Command, the agony grows worse.

But I have to give her this head start. She has to make the train tracks.

It's her only chance—our only chance.

The iron will weaken me.

I wait as long as I can, and then I hear them... The *cú sluagh*, the hounds of the Hunt. They have joined the chase now. They flash past me, all bristling black teeth and claws and glowing green eyes. I have to catch her first.

I let the Command take me, my limbs propelling me forward.

I race after her. The night flashes past me, velvety-dark just like that night on the train tracks. We didn't know who she was. We only knew where. We only knew that the sleeper-princess was on that train.

I never imagined it would be *her*.

The girl I met five months ago in the bathroom of the Nanci Raygun.

I was going in, and she was coming out, her face flushed—I heard the heated argument but not the words—and smack! She ran right into me. Pretty girl, curly red hair and grey eyes, the most adorable smattering of freckles on her nose.

She'd held my gaze for a moment. The sleeper-princess, right in front of me.

But somehow, I only saw *her*.

My heart… For the first time, it was truly beating, making me a creature of flesh and blood instead of Moribund and magic. Truly beating…for her. But I'd ignored it. She was mortal and me, Fae-kind. And Faekind do not truck with mortals.

It's especially bad for dark Fae. For us, draining a mortal's life force is as easy as blinking.

I brushed it off, brushed her off, so tense and worried about the idea of wrecking the train that I failed to recognize her for what she was. And later, when her white-flame power blasted out into the night, it blinded me, it burned me. I never saw her face.

And now, flash-forward five months, and she's all I can think about.

Too bad I'm chasing her through a parking lot behind the Nanci Raygun. It's not exactly awesome first-date material.

We leave the streetlights behind as we crest the hill, flashing over broken pavement and around the few cars still left here. She's fast. It's her fair Fae blood Awakening, the stress pounding through her, lighting her veins like the first rays of summer, her body stretching to find its limit. She's got more strength and stamina than ever, but she has no training.

In the end, I'll catch her.

No!

I shake that off. That's Agravaine's Command talking. I don't want to hurt Syl. I won't. *Not even to save the hearthstone?* a dark part of me whispers accusingly.

No. There is another way.

I have to get to her before the hounds. I'm ahead of them…for now, but once they have the scent of their prey, the *cú sluagh* are relentless, tireless, ruthless.

I call upon my fairy wind for the last push to catch her. It swirls around me, a blast of wintry wind speeding me through the night. The parking lot flashes by.

I'm ten steps behind, then five, our boots pounding broken pavement, then whispering through grass at the edge of the tracks. Three steps, two…

And then I am standing before her.

She pulls up short to keep from colliding with me.

The Command slams into me. *"Go after her, Rouen. And bring her back."*

I grit my fangs and shore up my resistance. I pay for it in agony. My Moribund hand ignites in scorching pain, the fire of my rebellion racing through my limbs, my head pounding as if it'll split open like a too-ripe melon.

Screw you, Agravaine.

If I take her to him, he will kill her, infect her with the Moribund and blow the circuits, channeling her raw power into the hearthstone. But she is more than that.

More than just a battery.

She is the last sleeper-princess of the fair Fae. If she dies, there will never be another.

She crouches before me, eyes like grey smoke piercing my soul. With every drop of my royal blood, I want to stop myself, to stop the Command that drives me to subdue her for Agravaine. But like a nightmare, it rises within me, controlling me. I will bring her back to him like a faithful Huntress.

I see it on her face—she's not hiding like Agravaine thinks. She has no idea the power that slumbers inside her.

If only I could teach her.

That thought rises like blasphemy. I could.

But I step in, the Command ruling me.

Syl looks up. Her face is tear-stained, fresh tears tracking down her cheeks. "Why? Why did you lie to me? Don't you…?" She swallows hard and then sicks up the words. "I thought you liked me. I thought you were my friend!"

The anguish in her voice cuts me to the quick. "I…" But what can I say? *Yes, I do like you. I really do.* "I…I'm sorry." *Ugh. So lame, Roue.*

She backs away, puts her face in her hands, and sobs.

I only stare at her, my pain forgotten. I know what to do with a girl who wants to kick my butt. But a crying girl? *Hells and Harrowing…* I scuff my motorcycle boot in the dust, kicking small pebbles onto the tracks. "I have to bring you back."

That's the understatement of the century. My head's about to blow clean off my shoulders.

"Because he tells you to." Misery swamps her every word.

She knows. She knows I'm his servant, his slave, his Huntress. I nod slowly, pulling my hood up to cover my face.

You can't hide from the shame, Roue.

But I do. I want to hide it from her—all my shame and pain and regret. Once, she looked at me and smiled, her eyes full of hope and promise. I want to sing for her, to play for her and bring her joy. Instead, I am here, fighting with her over foul iron and steel.

"I…" I reach out to her.

Howling echoes up over the hill and chills my blood. The *cú sluagh.*

I want to scream at her to run, but the Hunt is already upon us—all spiky black fur and bristling hackles, teeth flecked with foam.

They line up behind me. *I'm not with them,* I want to say, but that would be a dirty lie. I am with them. Huntress and hell-hounds.

They growl, hackles raised, creeping toward her, bellies low to the ground.

"Euphoria…" Her voice shakes with terror.

"Get inside the tracks." My pain flares, splitting through my head, leaving me gasping. Blood runs down my face, coppery and slick.

She steps back into the cradle of train tracks. I taste iron on the air.

In this moment, I remember everything—bumping into her in the bathroom at the club, the flare of white flame as she struck me and Agravaine, meeting her in Principal Fee's office, the bike ride, picking her up at work, seeing her in that gown for the first time tonight...

My heart pulses, awakening to her, my body igniting. Even now my hands remember the touch of her.

The very thought of hurting her makes me ill.

The ache inside me stretches deep in my gut, turning over, rolling and expanding, filling me up.

The first hell-hound leaps.

Screw it.

I go full-on rebellion, lunging to meet the *cú sluagh* like a linebacker, fouling its leap, crushing it from the air. Jaws snap, scraping across my forehead. My vision is suddenly all water and crimson. My head reels, the hound is on me, all teeth and scrabbling claws and heat and fur. I punch, hear a yelp, kick out, and see foam fly.

And then white teeth flecked with blood is all I see, and the furnacing green glow of its eyes. It dips its head almost casually to tear out my throat.

"Down, boy!" I smack it with my violin, get some space between us, and bear down on the strings.

Violet lightning burns the air, static and alive, humming, and with a great volt, it lashes into the *cú sluagh*. Its growl turns to a yelp, and the stench of burning fur and Moribund circuitry fills the air. The thing buckles and breaks apart, scattering dying circuitry, its body more machine than mammal. I push it off, rising to my feet.

I'm a bloody mess, but I don't care.

I whip my hood off. Let them see me. Let them all see me for who I am—the dark Fae princess who will protect the last sleeper-princess of the fair Fae.

Winter fighting for Summer.

This is what rebellion looks like. Bring it on.

I stand between the hounds and Syl. I bare my fangs at them. "Come on!" I lift my violin, my bow. "Come on, you filthy beasts!"

As one, they leap at me, and the air is filled with snarls and guttural growls.

I bear down on the bow, and the world lights up in violet.

CHAPTER THIRTEEN
SYL

Once the Wild Hunt has
The scent of its prey
It is relentless
It will never stop
Until the prey is dead
- Glamma's Grimm

I should run, or like Glamma said, "leg it," which basically means both arms, both legs, no waiting. Just get the heck outta Dodge and never look back.

But Euphoria...

Euphoria's in a tense standoff against the...*hell-hounds*, my mind unhelpfully supplies. I guess all those years of geeking out over D&D's *Monster Manual* have finally paid off—that and sneaking peeks at Glamma's Grimmoire. Hey, just because I don't believe in faeries and magic doesn't mean I don't find that stuff interesting.

At least...I did. Until it ruined my date, not to mention my dress.

But I've got bigger problems than fashion.

With those slavering jaws, those eerie fiery-green eyes, hackles raised like black spikes, they creep forward, hemming Euphoria in against the tracks. Oh yeah, they're hell-hounds, all right, come to life right off the pages of Glamma's Grimm.

Now I know why Fiann cracked back there. Seeing your childhood nightmares come to life right before your very eyes? That's definitely gonna require therapy.

I fidget inside the circle of train tracks. Wait, what was their weakness again? Glamma told me... Kryptonite? The color yellow? A fluffy kitten? Gah!

Run, the logical part of me whispers. But I don't. I stand in the crossing of train tracks, my heart hammering as the hell-hounds corral Euphoria.

She stays between me and them, my protector.

She's beautiful and super-cool—a shadow made flesh, her raven-dark hair flowing like molten night, her bronze skin glowing, those startling blue eyes ringed in gold fixed on her enemies. She's not human—I can see that with my Fae-sight—but in this moment, I'm glad because these things are so not kidding around.

They're here to kill me.

Her right hand bristles with violet lightning, tiny arcs that zap across the bow and onto the strings of her violin. They dance there like electric fireflies.

She's fierce, but even Euphoria has her limits.

I see it, just like I can see through her Glamour. I see how tired she is—exhausted and bloody from fighting the hell-hounds, from fighting Agravaine's power over her.

The closer she gets to the tracks, the more she stumbles, the weaker she looks.

Run, the logical part of me whispers, but *Help her!* the totally illogical I'm-crushing-hard-on-her part of me urges.

What can I do? I'm no lover, and I'm sure as heck not a fighter. Not even with the weird super-strength flowing through my body.

The hell-hounds snarl; they crouch low to the ground, those green eyes searing through the night. The biggest one inches forward, waiting…waiting…

My heart slams against my ribs. I want to beg her to run with me, but what if she loses control again? Whatever. I have to risk it. "Euphoria—"

"Stay still."

"Euphoria!"

She turns. "Stay—"

With a chilling snarl, the biggest hell-hound leaps. It crashes into her, and they fall back onto the tracks at my feet, the hound on top of her, all snapping teeth and slavering jaws. Euphoria's swearing, her teeth bared back at the hound as she holds it off. She's got her violin, but she can't get the bow to the strings.

With monumental effort, she throws the hell-hound off. It lands among its pack, and now they all start to howl, their baying sending chills crawling up and down my spine. Bow and violin in hand, Euphoria drags herself to her feet. She looks dazed, pained. She staggers.

It's the iron in the tracks, I realize. That's why she told me to run here. She was protecting me, even then.

As one, the hell-hounds creep closer, muscles bunched beneath coal-black bristles, and now I see it with my Fae-sight. Weird black circuitry teems across every bristling hair, and an inky-indigo aura wafts off them like smoke. They're infected with…with whatever Agravaine's infecting the student body with.

Rad.

They try to circle Euphoria, growling, snapping.

Any second, they'll close that circle and surround her. Any second, they'll attack.

A rush of panic floods me—*Help her!*—and on the heels of it comes power, thrumming up from the core of my being. She saved me. I have to save her in turn.

The power coils in my chest, hot as the sun, threatening to burn me from the inside out.

In the next moment, I'm pressing my back to hers as they surround us on the tracks. She is warm and solid and strong, and my brain does a little freak-out at the feel of her against me. The heat inside me blasts hotter, fiercer. I want to lean in to her, but the hellhounds attack.

Way to ruin a moment. Jerks.

My newfound strength sings through me. I kick a hound aside, a lucky blow to its head that has it shaking and snarling, its green eyes burning like poisonous furnaces.

Euphoria steps in, all super-cool sexy, sawing down on her violin. Violet lightning leaps from the bow and zaps my hell-hound and then another one, the night lit up with bright purple lashes. She staggers against me. "Damn it…"

I steady her. "Euphoria!"

"The tracks." Her nose is gushing now. She dashes the blood away, droplets of red flying, and saws at her violin. A violet storm lashes out, lightning snapping like whips into the pack, singeing them, scattering them.

I'm terrified. I'm impressed. Holy cats, I'm so into her.

"Your power…" she grits out, her entire body trembling.

"My what?"

"Your power. The white flame. Use your power, sleeper-princess!"

"Sleeper-what?" In this moment, I can't decide if I'm more confused or annoyed because she sounds a tad *accusing*, like I'm not pulling my weight in this fight. I give her the stink eye, though she's right. "I…" Even now, I feel the power, the heat, building up inside me, painful, stretching my rib cage, my lungs, my everything. I'm hot. I'm cold. I'm everything in between.

The power is there, but it's stuck fast. I can't get it out.

Seriously?

"Let's go, sleeper-princess!" Euphoria lightning-lashes a hell-hound back and kicks another in the face.

Okay, clearly she means me. "I'm trying!"

"Try harder."

Damn her for being so effortlessly cool and badass. *Okay, Syl.* My mind kicks into overdrive. Whatever a sleeper-princess is, I can figure it out. How hard can it be? I thrust a hand out. Nothing. Not even a fizzle. "What, do I just have to believe or something?"

She glances back at me. "Are you serious?"

"Are you? Look out!" A hell-hound leaps for her throat, and I hammer-fist it with both hands, swinging for the fences. The thing yelps, crashing to the tracks. I shake my stinging hands. Blood on my knuckles. *Urggggg…*

"You're not going to faint, are you, princess?" She says it all snarky, but there's real concern behind her teasing. She sidesteps a hound, smacking it with her bow and then slashing it with a stroke of lightning. Its snarl turns to a howl, the lightning boring through it, hot knives through butter.

It shatters like burned-out coal, circuits skittering.

I get my act together. "No, I'm not going to faint. Jerk." But something about our teasing banter is riling me up, and not in a let's-fight-hell-hounds way.

She's smirking and so darn sexy—all effortless power and acrobatic fighty moves. "Blasted iron." She grits her teeth, tries to step out of the circle of tracks, but the hell-hounds leap and snap, their teeth snapping shut.

She dances back. "I can't defeat them all. Not standing on iron tracks." She gives me a grin that is part teasing, part cocky. "It's all you, sleeper-princess."

All…me? It can't be. She's the badass dark Fae. I'm just Syl. Syl Skye, high school photographer, mathlete, geek.

"Any time now, princess."

"Hold your horses, Miss Impatient!" Fine. I'll try, but I don't really believe it.

I thrust my hand out. It looks like this in every TV show—the heroine making some silly hand gesture no matter how complex the spell or power.

Now I know why those shows drive me nuts.

The power fizzles inside me, refuses to come out.

It's because silly hand gestures are lame.

One of the last hell-hounds darts in, all snapping teeth and burning eyes. It latches on to her violin, teeth scraping the glassy surface, trying to tear the instrument from her grip.

I want to help her. If I'm this sleeper-princess, that should mean power, but how do I use it? I think back to that night on the tracks, being chased, hunted, sun-hot fire bursting up from within me, white and blaring. If only I can tap into that again…

The hell-hound growls, yanking hard on Euphoria's violin. She lets go, dragging the bow across the strings. The hound comes away with the violin in its teeth and a burst of lightning in its face. It falls, a smoking heap.

Euphoria kicks her violin back up into her hands.

Gah, she is so cool!

A shadow falls on her from behind.

"Euphoria!" I scream, throwing my hand up to ward off the last hell-hound leaping for her neck. The burning in my body swells, my hand cramps and twists like I'm throwing a curve ball, and with a sudden burst, the power pushes painfully past the blockage inside, rushing up and out of me.

That's it!

A jolt of white flame pulses from my hand. It strikes the hell-hound. For a moment, its fur ripples as though caught in a high wind, and then it burns away like birch bark and paper, leaving only cinders behind. No fur, no bones, no circuits.

Euphoria and I are alone once more.

Whoa… I stare at the blackened ground for a half sec, and then, "Awww, yes! In your *face!*" I fist-pump, giving Euphoria the cheekiest grin in the history of ever. "How's that for sleeper-princess awesomeness?"

Euphoria limps away from the tracks. "Finally." She quirks an eyebrow at me. "Took you long enough."

The look she gives me sends warmth and butterflies warring inside me. "You know me," I joke. "Maximum drama." Far off, I hear the sirens. "Come on, we have to get out of here."

"Rouen!"

His voice rings out over the tracks, making them vibrate. Agravaine.

Ugh, guy has the worst timing.

We both turn to see Mr Stompy-Pants stomping up the slope. His face is twisted with anger and his fist clenches. "How many times do I have to order you, Huntress?" He points at me, right at my face.

Rude much?

"Bring her to me. Now."

Euphoria fights his Command. Her jaw clenches, her muscles lock. She refuses, holds one hand over her nose even as it gushes like a faucet. "Screw you, Agravaine." She's playing all cool, but I see the dark circles beneath her blue eyes.

"Seriously." I step to her defense. "No means no, dude."

His shark-black eyes glitter. "Does it now?" He cracks his knuckles, and this time, when his voice rings out, it's oddly hollow, striking like a bell, clear and loud. *"Rouen Rivoche, bring me the last sleeper-princess."*

There is something different about this Command.

Euphoria turns to me, her face sick like she's going to hurl. "Run, Syl. I can't… My true-name…"

True-names. Glamma always said that it was the ultimate power over a Faekind.

And he just used it against Euphoria…to get her to capture me.

She steps toward me, and I stumble back into the safety of the tracks. If I run, she'll just chase me down. I'm fast, but I'm not dark-Fae-on-steroids fast like she is.

Maybe I can wait her out. Even now, I hear the police sirens wailing. *The fire alarm.* I pat myself on the back for that one.

But my luck and cleverness is about to run out.

While I'm pretty sure the cops saw the Lady Gaga-level light show we've all been putting on, they're still miles away.

Euphoria will get to me first.

"Syl." She sets down her bow and violin, and tugs at the glove on her right hand. Fear slices through me. My Fae-sight sees the air warp and weft around her hand—the same inky indigo ick that's infected the rest of the students.

Crap.

"Syl, run."

I should. I should be running my butt off, but I'm not. Apparently, being a sleeper-princess comes with a giant pulsating martyr complex. I decide to own it. "And leave you to him? No way."

"You don't understand." She leaps for me, and I barely dodge. "I can't stop. I can't!"

"Then I'll just have to stop you." My words are brave, but my heart thrashes like a trapped bird in my chest. Can I do it without killing her? Without hurting her?

She lunges for me.

I lift my hand, flex my fingers. *Just a little.* The power in me swells like a solar flare, and a pulse of white flame jolts from my fingertips.

It strikes her in the chest, knocking her a dozen feet into the air. She crashes down on the train tracks with a bone-crunching shudder.

She tries to rise, violet lightning licking over her hand. "Syl." Her eyes roll back into her head, and she collapses, but there's that snarky-sexy grin on her face.

I did it! Holy cats! I look around, but of course. It's Murphy's law. That one time you do something über-cool, there's no one around to see it.

"So...you are Awakened, little princess." Agravaine takes a step toward me, eying the white flames around my hand.

I shake them off, and they snuff out in a super-cool plume of white smoke. "You bet your sorry patootie, pal." Not that I know what-all being "Awakened" means...

He chuckles, runs a hand through his white hair. "You wish to try yourself against me?" He shrugs his jacket off. "Very well."

The leather jacket hits the broken asphalt, and I see it. Hundreds, thousands of black circuits meshed into his flesh. Like a disease, they eat up the left side of his body, all the way up his shoulder and arm and biceps.

And it all glows with deep indigo lightning, warping the air around it.

The power a thousand times stronger than Euphoria's.

Thanks, Fae-sight. I really needed to know that. Crap. I've bitten off more than I can chew… But I take a step to Euphoria's side. "You're not taking me—or her."

Glamma always said when you bite off more than you can chew, just spit some out.

I square off against Agravaine. I'll spit him out all right.

We stand there like in the movies, both of us sizing the other one up. Why doesn't he just rush me? Even now, the air is black and warping around him, and me… My white flame seems so small, so weak in comparison.

Down below on the road, I see the blues and reds. The police are here. They'll be looking for me.

They won't arrive in time.

Agravaine steps in, and I summon up my power to take him down a peg—or a head.

Nothing. Fizzles.

"Come on! I'm doing the hand gesture right!"

"You don't get it, do you?" His smile is sharp as a shark's. "Sleeper-princess power has to be trained." He lifts his arm, and the black circuits swarm down his biceps to his forearm then fingertips, threatening to leap off his skin at me.

That's when the night splits with the sound of a car horn. Someone's really leaning on it.

Headlights slice the darkness, and an SUV tears up, tires squealing and spitting gravel. Tiny pebbles roll off my Docs. *And why does that car look so familiar?*

The window rolls down.

"Mom?"

Not only is it my mom, but she's got a ginormous gun.

Correction: that thing's a hand cannon.

She pulls the trigger—*blam! blam! blam!*—and Agravaine goes tuckus over teakettle. A few circuits fall from his fingers and squirm toward me.

"Holy—! *Mom?*" Seriously? *This* is the woman who grounded me for riding a motorcycle? She's wearing a leather jacket and toting a gun like freakin' Clint Eastwood.

She gets out of the car and rushes toward me, crushing the circuits under her— Wait. Is my mom wearing Docs?

"Mom, what the—?"

"Get in the car, Syl." She holsters the gun in a move that would make ol' Clint green with envy. "He won't stay down for long, and I don't have any iron bullets." She fixes me with her best Mom stare. "Get in the car. And bring that damned dark Fae with you." She points at Euphoria.

I'm too freaked out to do anything but obey her.

I grab Euphoria. She looks like she's all leg, but dang, girl is *heavy.* I sling her non-infected hand over my shoulder, carefully not to touch the other one, and hoist her up.

My knee screams in alarm. Appears my sleeper-princess superstrength has gone the way of the dodo. At least for now.

And then my mom is there helping me.

Who *is* this woman? And seriously, who needs an absentee father when I've got Supermom. Together, we carry Euphoria to the car and load her into the back seat. She's so tall, her legs are bent up over my seat.

I don't care. I like being near her. Also, I kind of can't wait to tease her about this a little. *You mean flirt with her.* Flirting, teasing—same diff.

My mom gets behind the wheel and pulls out, all pedal to the metal and *Fast and Furious.* My heart is in my throat, and I'm grabbing the oh-crap handle for all I'm worth.

The whole time, I'm glancing between her and Euphoria and the blue flashing lights receding out the back window.

"Mom?"

"What is it?" Her voice is all business, but I hear a tired note in it.

A million things rise up in me. I want to ask her what the heck is going on—with her, with Euphoria, with *me*... But the farther we get from the Nanci, the more unreal everything becomes. I make a stupid excuse. "I... It's not what it looks like."

She turns to me—one of those moments you have as a kid when you want to tell your parents to keep their eyes on the darn road. "It's exactly what it looks like. And so are you."

Whoa. That's not what I was expecting. "What do you—?"

"You're a sleeper-princess, Syl."

Shock rolls through me. "Wait, what?" She knew? She *knows*? "How do you…?" This entire thing hurts my brainmeats.

"I know," she says, her eyes severe on mine, "because I was once a sleeper-princess too.".

CHAPTER FOURTEEN
ROUEN

My heart
Tied to the hearthstone
I can never be free
- Euphoria, "Heart & Hearthstone"

The last thing I feel is the scorching white flame of Syl's power. It strikes me in the chest, pulsing against my heartbeat. I curl in on myself, instinctively protecting the hearthstone as her sleeper-princess power takes me under. My consciousness slides away from me, and as my eyes close, I reach out for something, anything to slow my descent into darkness.

There! A glimmer, a shimmer. A ley line.

Perfect. I can use this. As the last dark Fae princess, I can use the ley line and my bond with the hearthstone to pull my consciousness away from my body and into dark Faerie. For a time. It's called obtruding, and it's dangerous as hell, especially with the hearthstone dying, but I risk it.

I need to check on my people, on the hearthstone. And it's not like I can regain consciousness in the real world—at least not until my body recovers from Syl's blast.

I reach for the ley line.

It makes sense it's so close to the tracks. When mortalkind first discovered us, this was their way of corralling us, controlling us. Iron railways mapping the surface of the world, carving up Earth's natural magic—its ley lines—into manageable sections, severely limiting our access to all that power.

I can't do much with the ley line here, but even the weakest ley line is a natural gate to Faerie, and my bond with the hearthstone strengthens the way, keeping me from getting lost in the labyrinthine Snickleways that connect the realms.

The moment I lose consciousness, I tap into the ley line and obtrude into UnderHollow.

The velvety black Shroud peels back, and I step from the realm of the mortals and into the realm of the dark Fae—at least, my mind does. Normally I'd have the choice whether or not to take my body, but it's currently lying there on the train tracks.

Looking pretty darn good, I might add.

Separated from my body, I can still travel here…for a time.

UnderHollow opens up before me. My vision of the mortal realm begins to fade as all the pieces of dark Faerie click into place like a puzzle built before my very eyes. A broody-black castle on a wintry hill, the misty moors, shadowy crag mountains slagged with ice—one by one, the pieces slam down, shutters that block my view of the mortal world.

My last view of the train tracks is of Syl and Agravaine.

Run, Syl, I beg her from the other side. My heart seizes when she faces him, and pride surges inside me as she stands up against him.

That's my sleeper-princess. I knew she had it in her and—

When, exactly, did she become my *sleeper-princess?* Now my heart is beating crazy-fast, and it's not only because I'm afraid for her.

By the bloody Hunt, she's beautiful, strong, brave.

And she's not alone. Agravaine takes a step, then a car screeches up, and Syl's mom gets out.

My old enemy.

And of course, I'm lying on the train tracks…unconscious. Not my finest moment.

Georgina Gentry was a sleeper-princess before I was a Huntress—and way before she became Georgina Skye. She was a sleeper-princes when there were dozens of them, perhaps even hundreds.

Before the fair Fae poisoned our hearthstone and started our downward spiral into the Harrowing void.

Georgina's changed. She's gotten older, but she's no slouch. She's a dead shot with that gun of hers. She plugs Agravaine four good ones in the chest. Those aren't iron bullets, but I'm relieved. Georgina is resourceful. She always was. Even after—

UnderHollow finishes *becoming* around me, ice and snow and biting wind, and the mortal world fades away.

Syl will get away. Relief burns in my breast. *Good.*

When my mind returns to my body and I wake to Agravaine's anger, his punishment, it'll all be worth it.

For now…it's just me and UnderHollow.

The halls of the royal palace are deserted, abandoned. Loneliness echoes with my every footstep. Everyone has gone into Winter's Sleep to avoid being a drain on the hearthstone. Entire families, highborn and low, the arch-Eld, my father…

Only Agravaine and I are left.

The Horde slumbers, and only the Hunt remains. Agravaine, me, and his hounds, such as they are—more Moribund machine than dark Fae.

Your emo is showing, Roue.

I shake it off. It is what it is.

Such was the decree. Before they succumbed to Winter's Sleep, strands of dreamlike filaments binding them into a never-waking dream, the circle of seven arch-Eld put our fate in Agravaine's hands.

The sleeper-princesses, he whispered to them. *Killing the sleeper-princesses will save us.*

And they believed him. My own father.

I never got to say goodbye. *Father...* But then, my crime in wanting to team up with the sleeper-princess was glaring, and I was disgraced. My penance: to be infected with Moribund, bound even tighter to the Contract of Blood and Bone, a Contract that made me a Huntress of the sluagh and their Wild Hunt. Agravaine was all too happy to have me.

After all, he's always wanted me.

Fat chance, buddy-boy.

He had no chance when he was a lowly Huntsman and I a princess. Now I am less than royalty. My name and title stripped from me.

And now...unless I give him Syl, I'll never be free of the Contract that binds me to him.

Fatter chance.

I'll never give him Syl.

She's the key to saving my people. Besides, I...like her.

Like-like, Rouen?

Tamping down on that thought, I close my eyes and *dowse,* stretching my senses toward the hearthstone at the center of the castle, the heart of the Winter Court. There...

I feel it weakening in the darkness. Even though it's devoured six sleeper-princesses. Even though Agravaine wanted to give it Syl.

My realm is dying. And there's nothing emo about it.

I walk the cold, dark corridors, a prodigal daughter come home to find her realm in ruin. But we are not done yet. We stand on the brink of destruction, but I can pull us back.

I can and I will.

I must.

I have no choice.

A princess does the impossible for her people.

I will do the impossible, and I will do it without harming Syl.

Brave words, Rouen.

When I wake up, Agravaine will Command me back after her, and this time he won't slip up. All those times I twisted his words. This time, he'll make sure to give me explicit instructions.

He's overconfident, but he's not stupid. He knows I played him. He knows I'm into Syl.

I'm not, the double-talking side of me insists.

You are, my heart whispers back.

The hearthstone pulses harder for a second, the thoughts of Syl rushing through me, strengthening my resolve, my will, pouring liquid strength into my limbs.

Syl, Syl, Syl, the hearthstone seems to beat.

Does it want her blood?

At the idea of harming her, the pulse fades.

Ooookay...

I try again, letting my thoughts of Syl run wild—the feel of her in my arms, warm and soft, dancing with her on the stage, so close we nearly breathed the same breath, right before things went to holy hell and high water.

In answer, the hearthstone pulses, hard and fast.

No. No way.

The hearthstone doesn't like the idea of me harming her. But it does like... I think of her in my arms, dancing, her body against mine, safe and sound...

The hearthstone pulses again. It beckons me, and I follow the dying pulse into the darkest recesses of the castle. Deep, gloomy caverns we have carved out to keep our secrets and the core of my people's power.

If it dies, all of UnderHollow will perish.

I let out a breath and it echoes, the vaults soaring up high above me on all sides as I enter the dark cathedral of the hearthstone. Gloom shrouds the dark vaults, the stained glass of the hearthstone chamber filmy with dust and decay, rimed with ice.

The chamber opens up before me, and there is the hearthstone, a dark heart riddled with brilliant faults and cracks. It's clasped in obsidian claws, like a gem in a setting, the size of a dragon's heart, pulsing pitch-black. Shining white veins riddle its surface. One bright fissure runs right through the center of it.

If it cracks fully, if that dark heart lets out the punishing light within, the ensuing explosion will obliterate UnderHollow.

I step forward, drawn by its dying thrum. I reach out to touch it with my good hand.

I don't see the remnants of Syl's power until it's too late.

Wisps of white flame purl off my sleeve and lick the hearthstone like fiery tongues. *No!* I lurch forward to grab them back, but of course, my fingers snag only air.

Bloody bones! I brace for the howling hunger of the hearthstone, insatiable and furious, to crack it further, deeper, destruction rippling out across its surface—like it has after every sleeper-princess was devoured.

After all, light like theirs is its weakness, our weakness.

The tongues vanish, sucked into the hearthstone's dark facets.

Wait for it. I shield my eyes with my arm.

The hearthstone thrums, and then brilliant white light shoots from its facets, washing the walls. The hearthstone pulsates once, hard, rocking the entire castle on its foundation. The cracks and fissures heal, running backward like water to its source, and the hearthstone sits in its setting, whole and hale.

Slowly, all around me, the walls of the chamber run like watercolors in rain, showing me an illusion of what was. And what could be again.

UnderHollow, brilliant and dark and returned to its former glory. High flying buttresses and obsidian-veined vaults, windows and leaping arches glittering with wintersteel, and the people come alive beneath them—dark Fae of all kinds: sluagh, bogies, maorbh—all the Unseelie of the Winter Court caught up in glimmering celebration.

Just as quickly as it comes, the Glamoury vanishes.

The wisps of white flame gutter out, and the hearthstone fades to black once more. Cracks and fissures riddle through it, and it stands dark and dying once more.

As for me…I have never felt more alive and full of hope.

Syl… We need her. But not her blood.

Her blood would only crack the hearthstone. Her touch can heal it.

My heart leaps with hope long unfelt.

And fury. Agravaine… He knew. He knew that killing the sleeper-princesses, bathing the hearthstone in their blood… He knew that it would hasten the bright poison within the heart of our people.

He knew it would destroy UnderHollow.

He wants to destroy UnderHollow.

But why? I cannot fathom it, not in a thousand years and a day. No matter. Whatever his reason, I will stop him.

A heavy breath pulses out of me. *It's time to return.* Bracing myself, I push my consciousness back into the mortal realm, obtruding from UnderHollow back into my body. Back into the mortal realm.

Agravaine will answer to me.

And Syl… There has to be a way to use her powers to heal my realm permanently.

There is, the hearthstone whispers. And I know that Syl and I must find it together.

CHAPTER FIFTEEN
SYL

To keep a dark Fae
From your home
Nail an iron horseshoe
Over the front door
- Glamma's Grimm

Mom's words ring in my ears long after we peel away from the train tracks and hit the interstate. *"I was once a sleeper-princess too."* I can't wrap my brain around it. Mom? A sleeper-princess? And what is that, even?

Agravaine called me that. And though I can't stand the guy, I felt the truth of it down to my toes and the roots of my red hair.

Sleeper-princess.

Mom guides the SUV down the interstate, the headlights cutting the darkness. She's nervous. I see it in the way her hand trembles on the wheel. I see it in the way she glances behind us in the rearview. The way she steals glances at Euphoria, as if the glam-Goth singer is going to pop up like some evil jack-in-the-box.

I want to tell her that it's fine, that Euphoria wouldn't hurt me, but…my shoulder still aches from where she laid me out, and I can't deny that Agravaine has some weird power over her.

Besides, Glamma always said the only good dark Fae was a dead dark Fae.

Glamma, everything you told me was true. I'm totally reeling. I sigh heavily, glancing back at Euphoria. *Well, maybe not everything.* Euphoria did save me. She fought those hell-hounds for me, and in the end, she told Agravaine to go pound sand.

That counts for something in my book.

Not so my mom's, if the way she's giving Euphoria the stink eye is any indication. Did she have a different experience with dark Fae when she was a sleeper-princess?

My mom…a sleeper-princess. Like me.

I am still staring at her by the time we get home. She pulls into the tiny alleyway between our building and the next. We're not supposed to park here, but I doubt anyone will care. Mostly people keep to themselves in Jackson Ward. It's safer that way.

Mom flicks off the headlights, and darkness swallows us. We sit there for a moment, both of us catching our breath. I don't know what to say, and I think she doesn't either.

I peer up at our apartment building. This side is almost completely in darkness, the height of the building blocking the streetlights. Plus, there are mostly retirees on this side. As long as we're quiet, we should be able to sneak in unseen.

So no one will see that I've basically kidnapped a Goth rock star. Good times.

Mom nods as me, and we open our doors quietly. I'm having serious teen culture shock here. It's totally next-level weird that the first time I'm sneaking back in from a wild night, it's *with* my mom. Seriously, how many people can say that?

Not many, I tell you.

Also, not many people have moms as badass as mine.

Mom gets out of the car and opens the back door. "Come on, Lady Gaga," she says, grabbing Euphoria's boot-clad legs.

Whoa, did she seriously just throw shade at Euphoria? I stare at her. "Who *are* you?"

Mom's lips quirk like she's going to smile, but she keeps her Mom-drill-sergeant tone with me. "Grab her arms. Hurry up now." And when I stand there frozen by her cool, she gives me the mom glare. "Stop staring at me, young lady, and do as I say."

Her tone is steel, and after seeing her in action against Agravaine... Yeah, I'm not about to disobey.

Together we haul Euphoria out of the car, to the building, and into the back hallway. The cruddy yellow light bathes us as we huff and puff up the stairs. My arms ache, my right leg is a screaming knot of agony, and my breath is a panting mess.

Holy cats! For a tall chick, Euphoria is not a petite flower.

We hustle and jostle our way through the tenement, taking the long way around. I stop to rest against the neighbor's landing, the sprawling initials J.J. on the door looking like two hatchets to my tired mind.

"Ready?" Mom asks, and I nod. We continue, huffing and puffing, and haul Euphoria up the last landing.

I'm careful not to knock her head against the wall.

Could knock some sense into her, if you ask me.

I mean, she could've just told me about Agravaine. But I'll wait 'til she's awake. After all, fair is fair.

Mom juggles Euphoria's boots and the apartment key and gets the door open like a champ. We pile inside and put Euphoria down on our beat-up couch.

Her legs dangle off the edge, she's so tall. It looks like I've decided to redecorate. A few throw pillows, a glam-Goth star... She looks beautiful, her raven-dark hair spread out on the lumpy pillow, her face peaceful even despite the blood—now that she's not under Agravaine's Command.

Mom goes into the kitchen and bustles around. She puts the kettle on. "Wetting the tea," Glamma always called it. I know the drill. There won't be any talking until there's a steaming-hot cup of Assam with cream and sugar in front of each of us. I sit on the love seat, prop my foot on the coffee table to rest my aching leg, and wait.

I have nothing to do except study Euphoria.

Yeah, total bummer.

I settle in to do some first-rate ogling. My heart rate jacks up about a thousand notches, and guilt floods my cheeks with a hot blush. Euphoria's been kind of an obsession for me ever since I first heard her that night in DC—the night of the train crash.

I remember her standing on stage, all lanky and gorgeous and grave, the way she played the electric violin, sawing at it all fierce, like her parents made her take years of lessons and this was finally her rebellion.

I remember bumping into her coming out of the bathroom.

It seems like a lifetime ago.

And now she's here, lying on my couch, and we're all tangled up together. Tangled up. The image those words put into my brain—me and Euphoria kissing and—oh, my! Suddenly, I'm red to the ears. Wow. Oh...wow. *I think this is more than a girl crush, Syl.*

"Penny for your thoughts?" Mom sets my cup down.

I shove my hormonal thoughts away and grab the cup to have something to do with my hands. Glamma always used to joke, *"Why is it a penny for your thoughts, but you put your two cents in? I mean, where does that extra penny go?"*

But I'm not in the mood for jokes. In fact, I'm pretty darn furious. My mom's secretly been a gun-toting vigilante all along? Euphoria's a dark Fae, and I'm... What the heck am I? I clear my throat and glare at Mom like I'm the parent and she's the kid. "When were you going to tell me?"

"When the time was right."

"That's super lame." My anger flares, and I realize the ceramic teacup is groaning between my hands. I let up before I break it with my newfound strength.

"I did what I had to do. To protect you." She's unapologetic for keeping this from me. I want to be angry, but I know my mom. She doesn't do anything without reason.

I take a deep breath, resigning myself to giving her the benefit of the doubt. For now.

I look at her over the steaming tea. "Tell me," is all I say. I want desperately to make sense of this night—of the last five months of my life. Everything from the train crash on has seemed a hazy dream, and me some kind of sleepwalking marionette. I rub my leg, thinking I can feel the bit of iron lodged there.

She takes a sip of her tea and winces, maybe at the heat. "I was a sleeper-princess, like you." She looks at me, her usually bright eyes dulled by sadness. "Both sides tried to drag me into their war."

"Both sides of what?"

"The Fae."

I set my cup down before I drop it. "Fairies?" I think of Glamma and her stories, her Grimm, all the tales I've read in Irish folklore, and my suspicions about Euphoria. Well, she's got fangs, but she's no vampire.

She's a Fae. A dark Fae, just like in Glamma's Grimm. And she kept it from me, even when she knew I kinda knew.

Part of me wants to lean in real close and whisper, *I don't believe in fairies,* just to see if Euphoria keels over.

It would serve her right. The big dummy.

And as for my mom… I fix her with a darn good impression of her own mom-glare. "Tell me everything."

Mom sighs and pushes her silvery-red hair from her face. "All right. You deserve to know the truth. Both sides, the fair Fae and the dark Fae, wanted me for different reasons, but mainly for the power slumbering within me. *Sleeper*-princess, get it?"

I do. Agravaine said something about me Awakening, so it makes sense. Sort of. "But…I'm a girl, a regular girl. And so are you. Well…you *were*. Once, when dinosaurs roamed the earth." I tease her a little so she knows I don't hate her or anything.

Her lips twist wryly at our in-joke. "I have Fae blood running through my veins. So did Glamma, and"—she pins me with those bright eyes—"so do you."

Fae blood? All those times Glamma told me, I'd thought her eccentric—you know, *old.* It just doesn't make sense. "But…then why did the dark Fae wait so long? Why not get me when I was little?"

Mom sips her tea, and the steam curls around her, making her look like some kind of carny fortune-teller. "They would have, but Glamma and I brought you here just after you were born. To keep you hidden from them."

I glance at Euphoria. With all her power, I can't imagine anything escaping her—or Agravaine. Dude is terrifying. I cock an eyebrow at my mom. "Seriously?"

"All right, Doubting Thomasina." She rifles through the coffee table magazines and comes up with one. *Richmond Mayor Green-Lights Trolley Reconstruction*, the cover says. She opens it to a map of the city. Red and blue and purple lines cross the map. Train tracks. "See?" She traces them to the center of Richmond, around the Fan and Shockoe Bottom, where they make a rough circle, the tracks crossing and crisscrossing one another. "A circle of iron to protect you."

A shiver claws my spine as I look at the map. A circle of iron.

"Now look." She grabs a marker and draws lines through the circle, cutting it open. "These are the tracks after the train crash. That"—she stabs the map with her index finger—"is how they found you."

My heart goes cold. The accident, the train... They broke the circle of iron so they could find me, hunt me.

My leg aches, and I rub it. Iron tracks, iron in my— "My leg!" I look at Mom all wide eyed and wild now. "You said the doctors couldn't get the iron shard out."

She blows out a breath, and the steam puffs away from her cup. "That...wasn't exactly the truth."

Chills flood me. I can't even feel the heat of the teacup in my hands. My lips feel numb as I ask, "What is the truth, then?" That night, the accident, the iron shrapnel in my leg. Even though I remember the white flame, the aftermath is still foggy—flashing lights, an ambulance, and then the brightness of a hospital room, and Mom and Glamma leaning over me.

Glamma's voice comes like it's plucked out of my memories. *"The iron shard will have to stay. It's the only way to put her powers back to sleep."*

Mom sees it all on my face. She knows I'm remembering, and she's calculating what to tell me.

I probably look as freaked out as I am, but I straighten up. I can handle it. I need to hear it. "Glamma was there that night? The night she…" My throat closes up over the word *died*.

"Yes," Mom says gravely, holding the cup in both hands. "Your power had Awakened, Syl. During the crash. That's why you and Fiann survived. Because you Awakened. And your grandmother…"

"She protected me. Somehow." A rush of guilt floods me. I know what Mom's going to say next.

"It cost her her life."

My hands tremble, and I barely get my teacup down on the table before I drop it. Tea sloshes all over. *Glamma. It's all my fault.* I put my face in my hands so Mom won't see the tears burning on my lashes. *Damn it all!*

I feel her hand on my shoulder. "Syl…"

I look up at her.

Mom's face is pale, but her eyes are steel and seriousness. "Your grandmother died to protect you. She knew the dark Fae would sense you once you Awakened. She cast a powerful spell—a Grimmacle—to lock your power down and put it back to sleep. But it was her decision, and she would not want you to blame yourself. Glamma's Fae blood was strong. She knew what she was doing. And she knew the cost."

"The cost? You make it sound so simple!"

Mom folds her hands. "It is simple. People were after her grand-daughter, and she gave up her life to protect you. It's what you do when you love someone."

She says it in that tone that brooks no argument and rings a thousand-percent true. Glamma was Irish, stoic, and stalwart as the Cliffs of Moher. She was a Gentry, a warrioress in her own right, and I… With a jolt, I realize I'm totally being whiny-pants.

Glamma died to protect me. She was a tough cookie and whip-smart. She wouldn't have done that without a darn good reason.

I take a deep breath and straighten up. "So what now?"

"Now your mom should tell you the truth about why you're being hunted."

I give a start as Euphoria sits up, wiping away the dried blood, her electric-blue eyes luminous even in the cruddy 60-watt glow of our living room lights. She lounges on the couch, one long leg thrown over the ratty arm like she owns the place. Her presence is intense, captivating and menacing.

I'm not sure if I want to run to her or away from her. Maybe a little of both.

Tingles race across my skin, and my heart kicks into overdrive. I've never felt so alive as I do when I'm with her, and... A blush scalds my cheeks. And my mom is *right here*.

Aw, hell. My entire face burns like a brand, and I silently curse my Irish heritage, just a wee bit.

"Rouen."

"Georgina."

Glaring, my mom and Euphoria exchange one-word greetings like they'd rather choke each other than occupy the same space.

Wait, what? "You two *know* each other?"

They're still glaring warily, and the weirdness of having my leather-clad mom and a dark Fae giving each other the stink eye *in my living room* is not lost on me.

I wave my hand. "Hello... Earth to Mom."

"I heard you, Syl." My mom doesn't look away from Euphoria. It's the look you'd give a spider you find in the shower—that *I'm watching you so don't you dare try anything* look. "And yes, we know each other."

"That's not an answer," I say, feeling like I'm the only person in the room that doesn't get the joke. Only, no one is laughing. "How? How do you know each other?"

Euphoria crosses her arms and raises her chin. Her blue eyes glint dangerously. "Do you want to tell her, Georgie, or should I?"

My mom's glare could peel paint, but then her gaze softens as she looks at me. Resolve settles her face into grim lines, and a spike of fear shoots through me.

Maybe I don't want to know.

"I poisoned the dark Fae hearthstone."

Whoa, yeah...I so did not want to know that.

CHAPTER SIXTEEN
ROUEN

A childhood destroyed
By white flame poison
My world crashing down
At the hands of the enemy
- Euphoria, "Destroyed"

I'm still a little out of it from obtruding back to the mortal realm only to find I'm not with Agravaine but with Syl. My entire body aches. I pumped out a ton of energy with my gramarye, the iron tracks sapping my strength as I fought the hell-hounds. One of them hit me like a Mack truck, and that's how I feel—run over and hung out to dry. But Syl's nearness, her kindness, the blazing heat between us...

She brought me with her. That fact warms me to the tips of my toes.

My sleeper-princess has a heart of gold.

I'm determined to protect her.

But this next part will be hard. Georgina Gentry is my enemy, an enemy of my people. I was only a child when she poisoned the hearthstone.

She's my personal boogieman—er…boogie*woman*?

And now here she sits, not ten feet from me. My good hand itches for my knives, but I grip my leather-clad knee instead. She's still Syl's mom.

But I'm not letting her off the hook that easy.

"Say it again." My words come out deadly and low.

She turns to me, those bright eyes level and serious. "I poisoned the dark Fae hearthstone."

Once, long ago, I'd dreamed of the joy it would bring me to see her admit her crime in front of her daughter. But now, when I see the look on Syl's face—destroyed, disbelieving—a spear of pain lances my own heart.

It gives me no pleasure at all.

But it is the truth.

And the sooner Syl accepts the truth—that her mother caused all of this and that she herself is the sleeper-princess—the better.

I hate that it hurts her, but growth is often hurtful. Especially for the Fae.

"What?" Syl whispers, her pretty face distraught as she looks at her mother. "How…? But you're mortal."

"She is now." My glare doesn't waver. "But she wasn't always."

Georgina gives me her mom stare, and it almost works. I catch myself fidgeting on the beat-up couch and stop myself. *Damn, even mortal, the woman is scary.*

"Rouen's ri—"

"Euphoria," I snap. Names have power, and I'm determined she'll have none over me. "You don't get to use my real name."

She sighs and sets down her teacup. "*Euphoria* is right. I wasn't always a mortal. I was once a sleeper-princess. Like you."

I lean back, crossing my arms to make myself look more intimidating—hey, it works—and listen as she tells Syl.

Georgina Gentry, sleeper-princess, sneaked into UnderHollow, entered the Winter Court and touched our hearthstone, the source of all our power. She simply laid a finger on it, but that was all it took. Her very touch infused the hearthstone with the foulest Faerie poison, the white-flame power of the sleeper-princess. Unable to draw in dark and shadow, unable to harness the power of magic in the wintry darkness around us, the hearthstone began to die.

It's her fault.

I want to hate her, and I do, but for Syl's sake I can't *completely* hate her.

Syl sits there, rocked. She doesn't believe—I see it on her face.

"It's true." The words come out as the memories assail me, the chaos of that night, the castle trembling on its foundation, the hearthstone filling up with foul white light, cracking, sending shockwaves through UnderHollow. Several of our elderly died instantly from the shock as it rolled over our land and all that was darkness was revealed in blinding, burning light. Countless more were wounded.

And Mother... She died when the vaults collapsed.

No wonder my father was so upset when I stood up for the sleeper-princesses.

No wonder he punished me like this.

I clench my Moribund hand so tight my glove creaks and look at Syl's mom. "Go on. Explain it to her."

Georgina glares, but this time, I steel myself against her mom power. I remember glimpsing her in the dark hallway as she made her way to the hearthstone chamber. I didn't think anything of it.

I should've known. But how could I?

I was a child.

But not anymore. I'm sixteen now, almost an adult in my world.

For me, it's been twelve years, though here, in the mortal realm, it's been many more—long enough for Georgina to get married, have Syl, and for Syl to grow up.

We're about the same age, Syl and I.

I don't have the heart to belabor the point—that her mother's brought this dark fate down upon her.

Syl looks at me, then at her mom. I don't want to come between them, but the truth should be told. Then Syl can make her own decision.

But Georgina's glaring at me, and I'm glaring back. Great. We're locked in a juvenile schoolyard staring contest. *Weren't you just saying that you're almost an adult?* the snarky part of me prods.

Whatever.

Georgina Gentry was my enemy.

She might still be.

I mean, she did show up at the front door with an iron poker to chase me away. *That's because you were macking on her daughter, Roue.* I raise an eyebrow at her. Maybe it was, and maybe it wasn't.

Who can tell with a fair Fae? Except...Syl's mom is no longer a fair Fae.

I snarl and curl my fingers into the torn couch cushions.

"—some tea?"

With a start, I come back to myself and the room. Syl's standing, an uneasy smile on her face. She's got two teacups in her hands, and she's moving to the kitchen to refresh them. "Would you like some tea?" she asks me again.

The look in her eyes is pleading. I can tell she needs a moment alone.

Who wouldn't after all that's gone down tonight? I totally get it. I am literally the poster child for introverts—well, except when I'm on stage.

I give her a vague shrug-nod because I haven't decided yet. Sharing food is a big deal among the Fae. There's ritual and ceremony to it. You don't just break bread with anyone.

And certainly not with enemies.

Time to hash this out—at least between me and ol' Georgie.

Syl leaves the room, and Georgina leans forward. "I regret what I did, you know," she says softly, trying to look me in the eye.

I meet her gaze. I'm not afraid of any used-to-be sleeper-princess. "Do you regret all the death and destruction you've caused?" I won't tell her how the hearthstone is breathing its last gasps. That it's only months, perhaps weeks or even days away from snuffing out completely, that our world is inches from collapsing, a guttering flame in the darkness. Even now, I feel it like a second heartbeat failing inside my chest.

I won't tell her that. I won't give her the satisfaction. "Do you?"

"I do," she says, and I hear the sincerity in her voice. She glances over at the kitchen nook where Syl is bustling over tea and making snacks.

"Umm..." Syl clears her throat, adorably awkward. "You guys are playing nice, right?"

"Yes," we both say in unison, narrowing our eyes at each other.

Oh, I'll play nice all right.

"So you regret poisoning half of Faerie and then running away from it. Are you still working for them?" I look around and glimpse the iron horseshoe over the front door, the iron nails cleverly woven into the curtain ties at the windows, the iron poker, though they don't have a fireplace.

In the kitchen, Syl loudly tears open a package, probably to mask the sound of our raised voices.

"No," Georgina says gravely, "I stopped any contact with the Summer Court after that night. After..."

"My mom died." The words feel funny twisting out of my mouth.

She winces. "Yes. You have to believe me. If I had known—"

My anger rises, gets the better of me, and my voice becomes a guttural snarl. "My mother thought there was another way, other than war between the fair Fae and the dark Fae." My eyes fairly burn with anger as I glare at Georgina. "You were the one who ended that. She's dead. Because of you. Those other sleeper-princesses are dead. Because of you. And your daughter is hunted—"

"I get it." Her voice edges in steel. "Because of me."

Syl comes back then.

Blast it. I didn't mean to lose my cool.

Now I've upset her. She looks back and forth between me and her mom, but resolve settles in her grey eyes. "Let's have some tea." Her tone is commanding, and her gaze is shrewd on both of us— like she's the mom and we're two unruly kids. "All right?"

Georgina and I both give grudging nods, and I add a dash of *this isn't over yet* to mine.

"Good." Satisfied we'll behave, Syl sets the tea tray down. Three cups of steaming hot tea, traditional cream-and-sugar service, and a selection of cookies.

I try to wave her off, but she hands me a teacup, the little minx. She's no dummy. She wants her mom and me to break bread, make peace. I'm not ready just yet, but I take the teacup anyway, for Syl's sake.

Our fingers brush, and at her touch, it's like a spark jumps between us. It cools my anger even as it ignites my longing for her. Her grey eyes meet mine, and I see my longing reflected back. We are two kindred souls trying to break free of our pasts to find a future. I want to grab hold of her, fight with her, forge our future… Together.

My eyes are burning again, but not with anger. I look down, not wanting to scare her with my intensity. *You've got it so bad, Roue.*

Syl's mom doesn't miss the look between us, but she doesn't say anything. At least not yet. Instead, she glances at the poker by the door.

I shift and casually move my jacket back so she sees the glint of my black-handled knives.

She gets it. I get it. Someday, we'll probably kill each other, but for now…it's all tea and cookies.

"Now," Syl says, polishing off her first cookie. "Tell me, Mom."

Georgina hasn't eaten or drank anything either. She's looking at me with an uncomfortable sincerity. "I didn't know what I was when the fair Fae found me. I was…" She looks at Syl. "I was like you, Syl, young and unaware. And when I Awakened, I found out they were already watching me. People who I had thought were normal—the postman, my old sixth grade teacher, the crazy lady on the corner—they revealed their true selves. Fair Fae who were sent to watch me."

"Because you were a sleeper-princess?" Syl stops, her teacup halfway to her lips. Is she wondering who else in her life might be a Fae?

Yeah, me too.

As far as I know, I'm the only one. A bolt of jealousy seizes me. I want to be the only one.

Certainly I'm the only dark Fae.

So bad, Rouen, you've got it so, so bad.

Georgina fiddles with her full teacup. "The point is…they used me. They sent me into UnderHollow. They told me if I touched the hearthstone—simply touched it—I would save thousands of lives. I'd be…" Her voice catches and she clears her throat. "A hero."

I hear the pain that word causes her. It's how I felt when my father condemned me to be the Huntress.

"Do you know what that's like?" she continues, her voice soft. "Being told you're a hero only to find out you've done something terrible?" Her hands shake, and Syl touches her knee.

Despite myself, I'm feeling pangs of sympathy. Maybe she really didn't know. After all, I've never trusted those fair Fae.

Syl shifts uncomfortably on the love seat, her hand halfway to claiming another cookie. "But I thought the fair Fae were good, and the dark Fae…" She looks at me, her voice trailing off.

Bloody bones, I know what she's thought. "It's not like that. The fair Fae aren't necessarily good, not in the way mortals think of good. A fair Fae will still gut you like a trout just because you stepped on her foot at the *ceilidh.*"

She looks shocked.

"Our morality isn't like human morality."

"But *you're* different," she says, and her faith in me burns hotter than the Moribund in my hand.

Am I? I've done terrible things too. All those sleeper-princesses…

To my surprise, Georgina gets me off the hook. "Euphoria's more...hospitable than the others because she's royalty. She's the daughter of the dark Fae king, princess of the Winter Court."

Syl looks confused. "Don't you mean the daughter of the dark Fae king *and* queen?"

"My mother was the king's consort, not a queen," I clarify, hating that it's all true. "There never has been queen of the dark Fae." Perhaps that's why Father had less of a problem giving me up to Agravaine. If I had been a boy—

Whatever. One day there may be a dark Fae queen. It may even be me.

One day, but today...today I have to concentrate on making sure we live past next month.

Agravaine knows we're together now. He'll be after us as soon as he recovers.

Syl bites her bottom lip. "But if..." She glances at her mom. "If you poisoned the dark Fae hearthstone, then...why aren't they after you?"

Crap. I was hoping she wouldn't put this together, but my girl is smart. Still, I don't relish the pain the answer will cause her. "Maybe you should get more tea."

But Georgina stops me. "No, it's fine, Euphoria." She chafes her hands. "I renounced my power."

"You..." Syl's grey eyes light up—with hope? "How?"

"I..."

Now it's my turn to save Georgina. "She simply said, 'I don't want to be a sleeper-princess anymore,' and the power left her."

Syl raises an eyebrow like I'm trying to put one over on her. Mortals always have a hard time with the simpler rules of magic, and Syl, in particular, is a bit of a skeptic.

"Um...okay?" she says.

"And dark Fae don't go after mortals." I lean forward to reach for the teacup. "There are a few exceptions, but once your mother became mortal, she was beyond our grasp."

And she does seem really sorry. My fingers brush the handle. I suppose it wouldn't hurt to break bread—or cookies—with her.

And that's when our alliance shatters.

She leans forward, meeting Syl's gaze. "You could do that too, Syl."

"Do what?" Syl asks. She's so innocent.

Georgina drops it like a bomb. "Renounce your power. Now that you're on the verge of Awakening, you can choose. Become mortal. Stop being a sleeper-princess."

CHAPTER SEVENTEEN
SYL

Many powers of Faerie
Work by will
A sleeper-princess must want to be a sleeper-princess
- Glamma's Grimm

"You can renounce being a sleeper-princess."

Mom's words hit me like a ton of bricks. I feel like Euphoria must feel—wrecked. It's never occurred to me to look for a way out.

"You could have a normal life, Syl." Mom's really warming to the idea, and I can't lie. After a night of terror and running and screaming Jurassic Park-style, *normal* sounds pretty good right now. "That's what you've always wanted, isn't it? To be normal?"

"You mean boring." Euphoria huffs and pushes away the teacup she'd been reaching for.

Darn it all. There goes my play for peace between them.

"Don't," Mom snaps, glaring at Euphoria sharp as knives. "Don't fill her head with nonsense."

"I would never tell her nonsense." Euphoria's eyes fairly glow, the golden rings burning like circles of fire through the blue. "Only the truth."

"It's too dangerous, Syl." Mom looks at me, and I see the mom-worry piled up from all those years spilling over. All the years she and Glamma protected me.

Maybe she's right. Maybe I should...be normal. After all, it's all I ever wanted. To fit in, to be popular, to have friends. It's hard enough just getting through sophomore year, never mind being a total pariah, a sleeper-princess chased and hunted.

"The dark Fae will be after you," Mom prods. I know she's doing it for my own good, and a healthy dose of daughter-guilt floods me. "You'll be running for the rest of your life. They're relentless. And once the Hunt has your scent, it won't stop."

Euphoria snorts through her nose. "Way to scare the crap out of her." But the way she folds her arms, all defensive-like, tells me Mom's not too far off the mark.

Mom sighs. "I'm not doing this to scare you, Syl, but...you have to think of these things. Things that she isn't going to tell you."

"Me?" Euphoria says, giving my mom the dark Fae version of stink eye. "What about you, Little Miss I Poisoned the Hearthstone but Conveniently Forgot to Tell You?"

Mom blushes, and like me, her fair complexion carries it from her cheeks to her neck. "At least I'll protect her for real."

"And I won't?" Euphoria sits up straight like she's going to go full-on supervillain and launch at my mom. "Are you calling me a liar?"

"I'm calling you a dark Fae."

Euphoria stands up. My mom stands up.

For a long, tense moment, they have this epic staring contest, Euphoria all statuesque and Mom, shorter, still fierce as any Irish warrioress. And it's more than staring. They're sizing each other up, looking for a weakness. The first one to flinch loses.

Euphoria's face is flushed, her blue eyes glowing and intense. I can feel the fury coming off her in waves, and her scent hits me—the crisp dead leaves of autumn, amber, and bourbon-vanilla. *Like you even know what bourbon smells like, Syl.* Oooh, but I can imagine. Clad in leather, she's just about the coolest, hottest thing I've ever seen. Everything about her attracts me—her look, her scent, her heat.

A huge part of me wants to go through with this for her.

To be with her.

Even the thought makes my stomach flutter and my heart pound. But no. *Cool your jets, Syl.* I'm not making a decision based on a girl—no matter how attractive she is.

This is real life, not some kind of Disney fairy tale where the girl gives up everything just to be with her man.

Are you crazy? the part of me that is one hundred percent a roiling ball of teenage hormones whispers. *Attractive is one thing. Euphoria is scorching-like-the-sun hot.*

I look at her. Yeah, she is. But no. "I'm not doing it for you." My voice comes out soft, as gentle as I can make it, but really, how can you make something like that sound...gentle?

Euphoria doesn't move, but a thread of pain flashes in those blue eyes. Whatever she was expecting, that wasn't it. She looks hurt, and I can't stand that she might take it as a rejection.

"I'm... Look, I like you a lot," I say, blushing as red as my hair. I hate saying this in front of my mom. I mean, seriously? It measures like a thousand on the embarrassment scale. "But I can't make my decision based on liking you."

I let out a heavy breath, hoping she'll understand, terrified she won't. I mean, isn't this the part in the teen-angst drama where the guy storms out all angry, knickers in a twist?

But Euphoria's not that guy.

She only nods. I can tell she's upset, but she channels it into rebellion, sitting back down and propping her New Rock boots on the table, daring my mom with a glare to say anything.

Mom's too busy gloating. "Good." She nods. "I can tell you exactly what to do to renounce your power."

Her words hang heavy in the air. I could do it. Renounce my power, go back to being the old me, get my old friends back, my old life back. Maybe Fiann and I could even patch things up.

But then what? Glamma sacrificed herself to save me. Do I throw that away? I have to think she knew what she was doing, that she protected me for a reason—because I was meant to do this. Whatever *this* is.

And Euphoria...

This thing—this connection—I have with her, it goes beyond just attraction. With her, at school, at the Nanci, fighting hell-hounds... I've never been more terrified, more exhilarated, more *alive*.

I've felt more like the real me than I have in a long time. Maybe ever.

I can't give that up. I won't.

And while I don't one hundred percent know what I'm doing, I have to try.

I square my shoulders. "I'm not renouncing my power."

"Ha!" Euphoria lounges back, a satisfied smirk on her face.

Now Mom looks devastated. How can I make her see that this is the right choice, the only choice?

She opens her mouth to speak, but I stop her.

"Please, hear me out." I take a deep breath and choose my words with care. This is important. I want to get it right. "I have to at least try to become the sleeper-princess, to Awaken and learn to use my power. To help people. It's what Glamma would've wanted. It's what I want. It's who I want to be."

I'm not there yet, and I know it. That's scary, but...

I glance at Euphoria. Her gaze is intense. It makes my heart beat faster. I'm not choosing this *for* her, but my heart tells me I can only do this *with* her. Together. "The old me just went along with the crowd, blind and unthinking, but now the crowd..." I think of Agravaine's motorcycle club, all the kids at school infected with that indigo-black gunk. "They're heading down a dark path, and I can only stop it if I stand up and do something about it. And that means, I have to Awaken as the sleeper-princess."

No matter how hard it is.

Mom sighs, runs a hand though her ginger hair. "Are you sure? This is a big sacrifice, and those girls... They haven't been very nice to you."

No, they haven't. But this isn't about them. It's about me. It's about becoming the kind of person I want to become.

I want to be honest, be the real me, and claim my power.

Even if I don't know the way. Even if I'm terrified.

"I'm sure, Mom. I'm sure as heck gonna try." I raise my chin, the feeling that this is the right thing to do the only thing keeping me from freaking out right now. I just promised to become something more than human, to learn powers I have no idea how to control, to fight an über-powerful dark Fae maniac.

I'm scared out of my mind right now.

"I have to try to save them and stop Agravaine. You and Glamma always taught me to try my best. And I will."

Even though I don't really have a clue as to *how* to Awaken.

Euphoria stands and crosses the living room to me. Drawn to her, I meet her halfway. She takes my hands, and my heart darn near leaps out of my chest at her touch—one hand gloved, the other not. "I'm proud of you. And I will protect you. With my life. Or if need be, my death."

Oh. Oh, wow. Did she just get even hotter? Answer: Yes. Yes, she did. Suddenly, I'm burning up, so hot I'm sweating. Her solemn vow shakes me to the core. "No one is going to die. Except maybe Agravaine." I look at Mom, hoping my brave words sway her.

She seems to deflate as she lets out a breath, her aura the washed-out blue of sorrow, and I see the worry and love in her eyes. I'm her little girl, the one she's protected all this time. Tears fill her eyes.

I pull away from Euphoria, my hands lingering as they leave hers, and go to my mom's side. "Mom, you've protected me all this time, all these years. Let me protect you."

If Agravaine has his way, the whole city will be infected with that black ick. I don't know what he intends to do once that happens, but whatever it is, I'm officially filing it under So Not Good and Not on My Watch.

I look at Euphoria, meet her gaze. Correction: Not on *Our* Watch.

"Syl...I..." My mom clears her throat, dabs at her eyes.

The show of emotion breaks me up inside. I throw myself into her arms. "I love you, Mom. I 'm sorry. I don't want to disappoint you."

"Hey…" She holds me at an arm's length. "You could never disappoint me. I'm proud of you, bug, my brave girl."

A few tears slip down her cheeks, and I pull away, wiping at my eyes. I always cry when my mom cries, and I can't afford this turning into an ugly cryfest.

I stand up and clear my throat. "All right. Agravaine. We have to stop him."

Euphoria nods gravely as she retakes her seat. She still hasn't touched her tea or the cookies, but at least she and Mom aren't going to murderface each other. Hopefully. "He's been killing sleeper-princesses. He claims their blood powers the hearthstone, giving it longer life, but I have reason to believe he's lying. It's like… he doesn't want to save us."

"It doesn't make sense," I agree, glad to have something to focus on aside from my very real lack of Awakening. Agravaine, the Wild Hunt, his hell-hounds, Euphoria. "Everyone is either his slave or servant. Why wouldn't he want to keep a deal like that going? Unless…" My pulse picks up, beating against my ribs like a metronome. "Unless everyone *isn't.*"

Euphoria and my mom exchange a puzzled look, but I rush on. "What is he in your world? Agravaine, I mean. Is he important?"

"I…guess." Euphoria shrugs one shoulder. It's clear she doesn't like the guy. "He used to be a blacksmith, respected but lowborn. When the opportunity arose, he took up the mantle of the Huntsman, the Master of the Wild Hunt. He thought it'd bring him more prestige, even though it made him a sluagh."

Sluagh. I've seen the word in Glamma's Grimm. *Sluagh, the Unforgiven, dead to their own people.* It hits me. "So he's not a prince."

Euphoria snorts, folds her arms. "Hell and hue, no. He doesn't have one drop of royal blood. He's been trying to get close to my father for years. First as the Huntsman and then…" She squirms a bit in her seat. Euphoria…*squirming*?

"What is it?" I prod, but I already have a good idea what she's going to say. I saw the way he looked at her, like she was already his, whether she wanted it or not.

"He wants to be my mate." She snorts again, and anger flashes in her eyes. "But fat chance on that."

Okay, now I really want to ruin Agravaine's day. I struggle with the first bout of real jealousy I've ever felt. It's like a slick, sick ball of anger and fear and hatred all tangled, tying me up in knots. "Tell me everything."

Euphoria sighs heavily, glancing at my mom. For a second, I think she isn't going to tell us, and then she spills. "My father and the arch-Eld put their trust in him to save the hearthstone and our world. I spoke against it, and they bound me to him with a Con-tract of Bone and Blood. After that, all it took was—" Her voice catches and she clears her throat roughly. "I made a mistake, and they let him infect me with the Moribund. He's been experiment-ing with it—the dark, killing magic in technology. He thinks he can remake our world with its power."

She clenches her right fist on her knee. The glove... Is that why she wears it? My Fae-sight kicks in, and I see the murky aura around her hand. It's violet instead of indigo, but it has that heavy, inky-gross look to it.

How could anything that poisonous remake anythi—

"No," I say as a shiver claws my spine, bringing dark thoughts. "That's not what he wants." Agravaine's not so different from Fiann, from me, from any teenager. He just wants to be popular. "Why save your world where he's nothing more than a Huntsman when he can use the Moribund to create his own dark Fae realm, right here in Richmond? With the student body as his subjects."

I take a breath and then drop the bomb. "He doesn't want to be prince. He wants to be king."

Realization pales Euphoria's face. "Weal and woe, Syl," she breathes. "You're right."

"Okay, then we have to get me to the hearthstone first." I start pacing then stop. "You can take me there, right?" I gesture all around us. "Faerie-land is everywhere, right? Glamma always said it was kind of…kitty-corner to the mortal realm, that you step sideways on a special magical path and there you are."

"It's just Faerie, not Faerie-land," Euphoria corrects me gently. "And that's mostly true, but…" She glances again at my mom. "I don't think it's a good idea."

"Why not?" I look at Mom, but she's also shaking her head. What is this, some kind of conspiracy? "What aren't you telling me?"

"You don't have control yet, Syl," Mom says, all grim. "If you touch the hearthstone, you'll just do what I did—you'll poison it with just a touch."

"But—"

"She's right." Euphoria looks a bit annoyed to be agreeing with Mom, but she stands firm. "I can't take you to UnderHollow until you learn control."

"Control? We don't have time for that. Agravaine's looking for us, probably right now even! And we might know his endgame, but we don't know what his actual *plan* is."

Euphoria levels that luminous, stomach-fluttering gaze on me. "I can teach you, but we need time."

Mom stands up. "I can help with that."

Euphoria looks at her warily. Mom has no magic left. She renounced it, so yeah… I'm also curious to see what she has up her sleeve. Earlier tonight, it was a hand cannon. What-all else does she have up there?

"I can mask the two of you, make you look like different people. You could go back to school under different identities, go under-cover, and find out Agravaine's plan."

That is so James Bond. Excitement rushes through me, but… "Isn't that risky? Won't he know it's us?"

"Not once I cast a Grimmacle."

"Wait, a what?"

Euphoria shoots to her feet. "How are you going to cast a Grimmacle?"

"With Glamma Gentry's help." Mom explains it all calm-like.

My heart jolts. I have no idea what a Grimmacle is, but Mom's got her super-serious face on. For a hot second, I fear she's lost it. She's always been emotional about Glamma's passing. "Mom... isn't Glamma...?"

"Yes," she says. "But she left me a last-ditch protection, in case things went south."

Of course she did. Glamma wasn't just a sassy old bird. She was cunning as a fox.

Euphoria looks dubious, but Mom goes to the hall closet and pulls down a hatbox. I recognize the floral pattern immediately. Glamma's Sunday best. Mom pops the top off the hatbox, and from among all the foofy ribbons, fake flowers, and dyed feathers, she pulls a slender wooden hat pin. It's cleverly made, carven with knotwork, what Glamma would call "cunnin.'" Mom twists and the thing comes apart, revealing a glimmering vial.

It has something in it. Glitter?

I look dubiously at my mom. I swear, if that's fairy dust, I'm going to lose my darn mind. *I don't believe in faeries, I don't believe in faeries...*

Mom turns. "It's—"

"Fae-flaunt." Euphoria's voice is filled with wonder. "It's very rare. When activated, it casts a powerful Glamoury, one that's permanent. Well..." She considers. "At least until dispelled."

I've got my Doubting Thomasina face on again, so Euphoria continues. "The permanency, that's what turns a Glamoury into a Grimmacle." She levels a gaze on my mom. "You're sure?"

Mom nods, tilting the vial so the glittery substance catches the living room lights. Tiny diamond-like grains shine and glisten in all different colors, too many to catch all at once.

"How does it work?" I ask, sensing that I'm missing part of the equation here.

"Making a Glamoury permanent is against our nature." Euphoria shifts, looks uncomfortable. "It requires a focus that is also against our nature." She raises an eyebrow. "It has to be cast on iron."

My heart seizes. "My leg...the shrapnel..."

Mom's watching me like a hawk. "After Glamma cast her Glamoury to hide you, she sprinkled Fae-flaunt on the shard of iron in your leg. It turned the Glamoury into a Grimmacle, putting your powers back to sleep. That's why it was so strong, and how it kept the dark Fae from tracking you even though the train tracks were destroyed."

"So wait…" I try to reason it out. "You're going to sprinkle fairy dust on my leg to make us look like someone else?"

"Yes," Mom says, and suddenly, she's giving Euphoria the stink eye. "For it to work on both of you, you'll have to stay in close proximity, or the Grimmacle will auto-dispel. That'll mean the same classes, the same schedule."

"I can work that out," I say, still trying to wrap my mind around Glamma, Glamouries, and Grimmacles. This real-world problem seems like nothing compared to that. "Lennon works in the admin office. She can switch us around. But we'll have to tell her."

Euphoria puts her foot down. "I don't like it."

I knew she wouldn't. "Lennon can keep a secret."

She gives me the raised eyebrow stink eye. "If Fiann finds out… We still don't know what part she has to play in all this."

"It'll be fine. Lennon will keep our secret, and we'll sneak round in our fake IDs and figure out Agravaine's plan, including Fiann's part in all this is." Yeah, I'm making it sound easy, but there's a crazy-psycho dark Fae Huntsman after us… We have to do something.

"And what about when Agravaine tracks Syl back here?" Euphoria asks my mom.

"I'll take care of that," Mom says matter-of-factly, and when Euphoria opens her mouth, Mom gives her the mom-glare from hell. "I can keep the apartment hidden as part of the Grimmacle."

Euphoria looks like she wants to say something, and then she lets it go and just shrugs. "Your funeral."

Wait, what?

Mom brings me back to the matter at hand. "When do you want me to cast it?"

"Right now," I say. "No time like the present." And then I stop. "No, wait."

I raise my teacup and prod them to pick up theirs. "We are going to break bread together." That's right. There's going to be peace between my mom and my… girlfriend? I don't know what Euphoria is. I don't even know what I am, never mind what *we* are.

I'll figure it out. In the meantime, I raise my teacup. "Come on, come on. After all the things you've kept from me, you both owe me one."

Mom looks like she'd rather eat those mud pies I made when I was four, but she lifts her cup. Euphoria is the last to pick hers up, her pretty face tense. I stand between them, two once-enemies brought together by a common cause to kick Agravaine's sorry patootie back to the Stone Age—or the dark Faerie realm. Whichever is farthest away.

"To finding friends among enemies."

We clink teacups, and everyone sips, Mom and Euphoria looking warily over their rims. I ignore it. It's a start. "Now let's crush this plate of cookies and fire up that Grimmacle. We've got to get to bed. It's been a rough night, tomorrow's Sunday, and then Monday, it's showtime."

For the rest of the night as we go over the plan and cast the Grimmacle, we're all in total agreement. The Trifecta of Patootie-Kicking.

Yeah, we got this. I hope.

CHAPTER EIGHTEEN
ROUEN

Close to you
This high school facade
Brings me close to you
Why must we play so hard?
- Euphoria, "Close"

The plan still buzzing in my brain, Sunday passes in a blur of sleep and recovering. I'm simply wrecked from all that energy I burned fighting Agravaine's Command and the hounds of the Hunt. Protecting Syl, obtruding without my body.

Yeah, there's only so much stress a girl's body can take.

Even a dark Fae princess.

Syl's pretty destroyed too. She's on the cusp of transforming from a sleeper-princess into a true princess of the fair Fae, her long-hidden Fae blood sending signals to her body to transform, to become, to Awaken.

The two of us sleep most of the day away, waking up only to eat and use the bathroom before going right back to bed— Well, me? I go to couch.

I hate being so vulnerable in the house of my old enemy, but now that the Grimmacle's been cast, Georgina eases up on the toxic glare-fest.

We're on the same page as far as protecting Syl is concerned. And she knows I'm in a better position to do just that.

Late Sunday evening, I wake up to find Syl gone. She's not in the kitchen, not in the bathroom, not in her room. I'm just about to call in reinforcements (aka wake Georgina up) when a breeze lifts the hair from my neck.

The window's open. A fire escape beyond. And there, huddled on the top landing is Syl, knees to her chest, chin on her knees.

I move to the sill and lean out. "Room for one more?"

She looks up, pleasantly startled, blushing adorably. "Uh, oh! Yeah." She scooches over as I climb out the window. I sit on the metal slats, stretching my legs down the rusty steps, vaguely glad the fire escape is steel and not iron.

I've had enough of iron to last me forever.

Syl stretches her legs out too, wincing a bit. I've noticed she favors that right leg of hers, and when it brushes my thigh, I feel the iron lodged there, even through her jeans, her skin.

Instinct screams at me to jerk away, but she's warm, and I like the way she leans against me, all subtle and yet not so subtle.

She sneaks a shy look at me as if to say, *Is this okay?*

I don't move an inch. Hells yes, it's okay. I could become addicted to her touch. I smile reassuringly at her.

Long moments pass with us sitting there in the cool night air, the heat from her leg making me burn and burn and burn... I don't speak. I don't want to push her. Besides, any number of things could be bothering her—her status as a sleeper-princess, trying to Awaken, the Grimmacle, the crazypants plan we've concocted to spy on Agravaine, all of the above...

She shifts so more of her leg is against mine. The iron makes me a bit swoony. If I don't move away soon, I'll start to feel sick, but I love the feel of her more than I hate what iron does to me.

"Rouen?"

I'm so startled that she calls me by my real name I nearly fall off the fire escape. It takes me a sec to regain my bearings. "Yes?" I know it sounds eager, and I don't really care.

I've never felt so connected to another person before. In her presence, I feel alive.

"I talked a good game the other night." She nods at the window, and I know she's referring to the talk with her mom. She looks down at her hands. "But I…I don't really know what I'm doing. I don't know how"—she meets my gaze, those grey eyes so honest and open it makes my black heart ache—"how to Awaken."

Now, Dark Fae are not known for having a softer side. My people are tough as nails, stoic and unmoving as mountains. We don't coddle and we don't comfort.

That means one thing: I'm going to blame this on the iron.

I clear my throat. "I was born Awakened to my power. I can't imagine what you're going through."

She slumps her shoulders, defeated.

Way to go, Rouen. Stubbornly, I press on. "But I do know what it's like to second-guess yourself." Throwing caution to the wind, I slip my arm around her shoulders, draw her in close to me. "To be unsure of what you're doing." Like right now. My heart is jackhammering against my ribs. My throat's gone dry, and I'm trembling at the feel of her in my arms.

But she doesn't pull away. In fact, she edges closer to me, looking up, innocent, vulnerable. "I feel like…like everyone's expecting me to be a certain way, to be the old Syl. Fiann wants the old Syl who followed along and never talked back. My mom wants the old Syl who didn't know what she was and was content to be protected." She sighs heavily.

"What do you want?" I ask her.

Her eyes swim with misery. "I don't know." She slumps into me, and I hold her. Even though I'm the one in the protective pose, I feel vulnerable, exposed.

Wild thoughts career in my mind. *I'm so blaming this on the iron.*

The words tumble softly from my lips. "As a child, I was expected to suck it up and push on. On my own. For most of my youth and into my teen years, I was alone. A symbol to my people—the dark Fae princess, untouched and untouchable. At least…that's the old Rouen."

Syl looks up at me, longing in her eyes. "And what about the new Rouen?"

"No one's ever asked me that before." But, looking at Syl, I realize…I don't want to be the old Rouen anymore, swallowing my feelings, hiding every emotion.

I don't want to be alone. I want to feel, to live, to love.

I want to be the Rouen that laughs at a joke, that flirts, that fights fang and claw against the darkness. I want to be the Rouen I am when I'm with her.

A new Rouen.

But I'm still a dark Fae, and no amount of iron can pull those words out of me. At least, not yet. Instead, I ask, "What about the new Syl?"

She smiles, so bright it nearly blinds me, but she's shy as she says, "Maybe new Syl and new Rouen can find out…together?"

She holds out her hand.

I take it, interlacing our fingers, squeezing hers. "Together."

It sounds like a vow, and when she squeezes my fingers back, I know she makes it too.

Monday morning, I'm woken from a sound sleep by a horrible screeching wail like a *bain sidhe* caught in a spin cycle. It rings in my eardrums, and I'm up like a shot, kicking aside the blankets and *My Little Pony* coverlet of my makeshift bed. My heart is a riot of pounding, my hands itching for my knives, my violin—some kind of weapon.

Agravaine? Hell-hounds? Dark Fae—who?

Syl's soft chuckle brings me back down to planet Earth. "It's okay." She hits a small white box near her bedside table.

The alarm, of course. I take a few deep breaths, trying to play it off. No, I didn't just jump out of my skin because of a Wal-Mart Special alarm. Nope. Not me. I'm cool, super-cool, cucumber-cool. *And trying way too hard, Roue.*

Then I realize…it's six a.m. A groan works its way all the way up from my toes.

I forgot. Syl actually goes to school on time, whereas I…I usually sashay my way in around noonish. Fee, the old buzzard, never says a peep. Agravaine told him not to pay any attention to our comings and goings.

I'm sure my new identity—what was it again…Minnie Maven? By the Hunt's hounds, I sound like a comic book supervillain—won't get such special treatment.

I guess we'll see.

"Are you okay?" Syl asks, and I realize I've been spacing out, all emo again.

"Yeah. Of course." I try to lean against the wall and shove my hands into my pockets, but I slowly realize with that creeping dread you sometimes have in dreams… I'm not wearing pants.

My hands travel up to my face to feel the scorching-hot blush there. My pants practically wink at me where they're draped over Syl's chair, my boots stacked neatly nearby. I'm wearing my torn Throwing Muses band tee, my boyshorts, and nothing else.

And…Syl is staring.

We lock eyes across her bedroom, the Goth-band posters on the walls the only witnesses to our mutual checking each other out. She's wearing a tank top and cute red bikini-bottom undies.

My heart seizes, and all other thoughts fly right out of my mind. I force my gaze to her face.

Those grey eyes like a storm at sea. I'm a goner.

Being apart from her was hard. Being close to her is even harder.

You're still half-naked, Roue, that oh-so-helpful part of my brain nudges. But I hide my sudden shyness like a pro, stalking my way over to my pants and pulling them on.

"Wait, ummm..." Syl clears her throat, looking anywhere but at me.

I stop, one leg awkwardly in my pants, one leg out. "What?"

Her own blush creeps up her neck. "Do you want to shower? Mom's probably getting breakfast ready, so you have time."

"What about you?"

She shrugs one shoulder. "I showered last night after..." She blushes. "After we talked."

Officially still blaming that on the iron. I share her blush, and we're super awkward for a second until I get my act together. "Ummm...yeah...a shower." I look down at my ragged band tee. I do not want to risk an experimental sniff. "Probably a good idea. Thanks."

"Great." She smiles, and it lights her face up so my heart aches and that heat between us flushes through my entire body. Suddenly, a cold shower sounds like the perfect thing.

She opens the door and pads down the hall. I shadow her.

Her apartment is small, but it's a damn sight better than the hotel rooms Agravaine and I were holed up in. Those were convenient, close to the ley lines, but they weren't as...warm as Syl's place. It's small and cramped, a bit cluttered, but there's a hominess to it.

Well, maybe if she took all the iron nails out of the windows.

"We'll have to get you some different clothes, but for now..." She shyly presses a T-shirt into my hands. "You'll need pants 'cause mine are all too short for you, but at least my shirts should fit. Even with the Glamoury, you can't go around wearing the same thing."

She stops and jerks her thumb at the bathroom. "There you go. You can use anything in the white container. That's all my stuff."

I nod, standing there like a dork until she leaves me, smiling shyly. Girl is seriously adorable.

Unofficially, I regret nothing about last night.

I go in and close the door behind me. The T-shirt in my hands is soft, and I bring it to my cheek, feeling the soft cotton, smelling the feminine vanilla scent of her. I slump against the wall, heaving a sigh. *You've got it bad, Roue.*

Pushing that thought away, I look around. The bathroom is small—toilet, sink, shower stall. It, too, smells like Syl, and I inhale deeply. *Really bad.* Thinking about using her bodywash, her shampoo, her shirt... It sends a shiver down my spine. The idea of wrapping myself in her scent makes me warm and fuzzy inside.

I look at myself in the mirror—fangs, pointed ears, glowing eyes.

I am not a warm and fuzzy girl.

I use the toilet and then skin off my clothes and shower. Washing the grit and dried blood from my body, my hair, is a blessed relief. Why didn't I last night or the night before? Georgina's Grimmacle took it out of me after the fight with the hell-hounds, the chase, resisting Agravaine's Command... I passed out as soon as my head hit my borrowed pillow. And yesterday was a total blur.

I step out of the shower, my skin steaming, smelling like Syl.

I tense as a clattering comes from the kitchen, then chide myself. *Relax, Roue. It's only breakfast.*

The sounds of plates clinking and silverware, and the smell of flavored coffee—it's all so alien to me. It hits me. *Syl grew up like this. We're so very different.* And then the scent of buttery waffles wafts through the door. My stomach growls, blotting out my other thoughts.

This is alien and different, but that's not a bad thing.

And if there's one thing I love, it's human food.

Agravaine hates it. But what does he know?

I mean, who hates waffles?

An idiot, that's who.

He's gotta be losing his mind by now, thinking we got away scot-free. We did. I smirk. And now we're going back, right under his nose. At least I won't have to worry about him ogling me anymore.

Syl's theory floats in my mind as I towel off. *He doesn't want to be prince. He wants to be king, to create his own realm right here in Richmond.* A dark Fae realm on Earth, with all the mortals as his Moribund-infected servants.

Even now, the black circuits in my hand stretch and pull. I yank my glove on so I don't have to look at it.

The Grimmacle will keep him from sensing our true forms, and Georgina claims she's strong enough to sustain it. I guess we'll see. The first time he lays eyes on us, that'll be the true test.

I pull Syl's T-shirt on, wrapping myself in her scent and trying not to feel too guilty or weird about it. I mean, I needed a fresh tee, and at least this one's got a logo of a sassy unicorn with the words, *I will stab you* in crimson over its head. I finish dressing and use a little gel to tousle my thick, dark hair. I like the messy look.

Stepping out, I let the delicious smells of waffles and coffee guide me. I feel odd, like an intruder walking into their kitchen nook. My own family setup was very different—a lot of secret family meetings across dark, polished tables; Mother and Father talking of ruling, of kingcraft and matters of the Winter Court. Never a needless word, never an easy word.

From time to time, my mother would squeeze my hand under the table. That was the extent of their overt kindness, but I know she loved me. I miss her so much.

"Good morning." Georgina looks wary but hopeful.

I force a smile, but it comes out wrong. Then I catch Syl's eye, and the smile breaks through, stretching my lips into a goofy grin. Here I go again.

One minute serious, the next I'm acting like a fool. As emo as Kylo Ren.

Syl slides a plate across the bar top. Their breakfast nook is tiny, a small stove and cabinets and a teeny island opposite with two barstools.

Syl's mom gestures, her voice gruff. "Eat. It's just frozen waffles and dollar-store whipped cream, but at least it'll fill you up."

"Mom took the day off," Syl says. "In case anything…wonky happens." She and her mom share a nod. I can feel the love between them, and my stomach clenches.

I look at the plate and swallow hard.

Syl touches my shoulder. "Don't worry," she says, misinterpreting my dire look. "We'll be fine. The Glamoury will hold." Her hand is soft and warm, and her cheerfulness dispels the gloom within me.

I feel like I can do anything, as long as she is with me.

She plunks down next to me, her knee touching mine, casual and yet absurdly intimate. *Should've taken that cold shower.*

Syl starts shoveling waffles into her mouth. "Oh!" She covers her mouth as she finishes her bite. "Do you want tea instead of coffee? I have some caramel crème brûlée in the pot."

"Please and thank you." I say it formally since I'm taking food at her table. Dark Fae take sharing meals seriously. It's like a covenant of trust.

She pours me the tea, and the rich caramel smell is wonderful, the taste heavenly. I take a bite of waffle, and Dollar Store or not, the buttery goodness and creamy sweetness burst on my tongue. By the Wild Hunt, I could eat this every morning and never get tired. I dig in and shovel food in my face just as fast as Syl.

She giggles and touches my cheek, wiping away a bit of cream. She licks her finger, and I almost pass out on my barstool.

Who knew something that simple could seem so...intimate?

Georgina clears her throat. "Bentos are in the fridge, girls. Now, let's go over the plan again."

Oh, right, the plan.

I remember it foggily from late Saturday night. I listen as Syl details it.

We're transfers students from Richmond Public High. Syl's going undercover at the school newspaper as a junior photographer, and I'll be the nerdy violinist for band.

In the wee hours of the morning, this plan sounded great, but now in the light of day, with some caffeine and calories in me, I'm totally doubting it. I lick the cream off my fork. "It's not going to work."

Syl looks at me, her fork halfway to her mouth. "Why not?"

"It sounds crazy. I mean, we're basically going in as ourselves, with different names—"

"The Grimmacle will hold," Georgina says. "It's Glamma's custom-made *seeming*. Not only will everyone who sees it believe it, they won't even think to ask questions. Your presence there will be one hundred-percent natural."

I raise an eyebrow, giving her the dark Fae glare, but she counters with disapproving-mom stare. I'm thinking Agravaine's lucky that Georgie isn't coming with us. But no…she has her own part to play—worried mom waiting for her little girl to come home. After all, Syl and Euphoria are just going to vanish for a while.

We'll be Minnie Maven and Susan Scurry.

Syl smiles at me. "And under the Grimmacle, I'll use my hall 'press pass' to spy on Agravaine, and, Euphoria, if we need to, you can cover me with your personal magic."

"Right." My gramarye. If we get in trouble, I can spell everyone with euphoria. They'll be so blitzed out, they won't care what's going on, or likely even remember. "Except…it won't be as powerful without my violin." I left it behind in the fight. I hate to think of it lying on the tracks, abandoned. Agravaine probably smashed the crap out of it once it was clear Syl and I had joined forces and escaped.

Syl gestures behind me, and I look.

It's not my violin sitting on the threadbare couch, but it's *a* violin. "Where did you…?"

Georgina takes a sip of her coffee. "This morning I went around to one of the schools I clean. Their band didn't get funded this year, so the violin was just sitting there with all the other instruments. I thought you might be able to use it."

I go over and pick it up reverently. The body is battered and scarred, but intact; the strings need replacing, but I can do that easily enough. The bow is a bit ragged. I pull some of the horsehair off to streamline it. "Thank you," I say, and I mean it.

It's a thoughtful gift. Even if she is playing it off.

"Consider it a peace offering."

"I didn't get you anything," I crack the joke—playing it off with her is safer—but I mean it. Georgina's kind of…okay, I guess. After all, if she didn't give up her sleeper-princess power, I might not have ever met Syl.

I look at Syl. And yeah. I'm super-glad I met her.

Syl clears the plates and put them in the sink. "We'll clean up when we get home." And then she takes out two small boxes from the fridge. "Mom made us bentos." The pride in her voice is evident. "I showed her how."

"Nice. I'm a sucker for those mini hot dog octopi." I'm playing it off again, but a weird feeling lairs in my guts. And it's not from the thought of hot dog octopi.

My mom was a woman of steel and surety, consort to my father, his moral compass. She had winter running through her veins. She never made lunches or breakfasts or saw me off in the morning. I don't know what-all that means in relation to Georgina.

Right now, I don't want to know.

Syl packs our stuff and hands me a beat-up backpack. "Sorry," she says. "You'll have to use mine."

I look at it, covering the fact that I'm touched—touched as hell—with snark. "Friendship is magic?" I read the inscription and give her the raised eyebrow. "Seriously?"

"Yes, friendship is super-serious." She meets my gaze, and I catch that she's referring to our talk last night.

Hell and hue, she's adorable. I can't resist teasing her gently. "Well, since you insist."

She gives it right back. "I do."

I hitch up the backpack and cradle the violin. "Ready, princess?"

She gives me that sweet half-smile of hers. "As ready as I'll ever be."

"Whatever happens, I'll be there for you." It just slips out, in front of her mom and everything, but I don't care. Things are about to get serious all around.

"I know," Syl says shyly, looking down. She reaches out and touches my left hand. "Whatever happens, we'll face it. Together."

Hells yes, we will.

We bid Georgina farewell, and I try not to see the worried look on her face. *I'll protect her,* I try to project with my every breath, my every action.

She gets it. Yeah, we understand each other.

I turn to the door. We're so doing this, and we are going to kick some serous ass. *Get ready, Agravaine. It's on like Donkey Kong.*

CHAPTER NINETEEN
SYL

A Grimmacle is a Glamoury of great power
Even the denizens of Faerie cannot
See through it
But there is always a price...
- Glamma's Grimm

With every step back into Richmond Elite Academy, I become more and more confident. Euphoria's totally styling in her Glamoury. She's got her usual long black hair, and chunky-black nerd glasses perched on her nose. Her eyes are a deep midnight, toned down from her dark Fae sapphire ringed with gold, but still plenty blue enough to lose myself in. She's Glamouried on a black dress and boots, and looks like an older, sexier version of Wednesday Addams crossed with Emily the Strange.

Me? I've lost a lot of my Irish to the Glamoury. I'm now a chestnut-brown brunette with grey eyes. I chose a cute minidress with skulls and death's-head moths all over it and my favorite Docs, along with a pair of leggings that make black patterns swirl up my legs. Even though the Glamoury covers our clothes, our styles, hair, everything… I guess I wanted Euphoria to see me looking extra cute.

After all, we can see through the Glamoury since it's cast on us.

People stare, some turn their heads. Others pass us by without a second glance. The main thing is…no one recognizes us.

Euphoria and I are totally incognito. Everyone's buying our geek-girl personae. Score! I mean, to be honest, it's not that different than my actual persona. So, there's that.

The best lie has a grain of the truth in it, right?

We waltz into Principal Fee's office like we own the place. I'm forgetting that we're supposed to be shy and not know the school layout. Whatever. It feels good to strut our stuff a little.

Lennon's at the desk as usual. She wants to be a high school principal, and she gets college credit for helping the administrators. Rumor has it she and Fiann are on the outs lately, and Lennon's been looking for a way to dismount—probably to avoid any scandal.

I'm betting she'll help us.

Or at least keep her mouth shut.

"Hi, Lennon."

She gives a little jolt. "Do I…know you?"

I lean on the counter, super-close, and lower my voice. "It's me. Syl."

"Did Fiann put you up to this?" She takes a step back, giving me the stink eye. "I don't know you, but—"

"When we were thirteen, we tried to sneak into the Nanci. The owner caught us and called my mom. We never told your parents because they would've skinned you alive."

The whole time I'm saying this, Lennon's eyes are getting wider and wider. When I'm done, she leans heavily on the counter. "Syl? Holy cats!" She looks me over and then Euphoria, and I see her doing the math. "Why the disguises? They're amazing, by the way, but why?"

With a quick nod to Euphoria, I give Lennon the super-quick, need-to-know, no-Fae version in whispers, including me and Euphoria needing identical schedules.

I don't lay out our master plan with the Grimmacle, but Lennon's a smart girl. She's top of our class, and she didn't get there by being a slouch. "This has to do with Fiann, doesn't it?"

I nod. It's not a lie. Not really. Fiann and Agravaine are in cahoots. We've just got to figure out how. We already know the why. Fiann's turned into a crazy person.

A sly smile breaks Lennon's usual shyness. "Okay," she says. "I'm in." She takes our fake school IDs and goes to her computer. Her manicured fingers fly over the keys like the doves on her Lolita skirt.

"We'll need passes, too, so we can skip homeroom this morning," I tell her, glancing at Euphoria. "Got some biz to take care of."

"Okay." Lennon doesn't miss a beat. In short order, two schedules pop out of the printer, and she hands them to us along with two hall passes that she totally forges with our homeroom teachers' names.

Note to self: if I ever start a criminal organization, hire Lennon.

"This is so awesome," she whispers, and then straightens as a group of freshman comes into the room "There you are, Miss Minnie Maven and Miss Susan Scurry."

"Great, thanks!" I take our schedules and lower my voice. "You can't say anything to anyone. Okay?"

She makes an X motion over her heart and nods.

I wave good-bye as Euphoria and I head out into the hallway for first bell. So far, so good. "Stage One complete."

"The possum is in the toolbox," Euphoria says in her best super-spy/detective voice.

I stop her, a laugh on my lips. "Wait, what?"

She shrugs one shoulder, totally unashamed. "I heard it on TV."

Holy— How does she manage to be so dorky and yet so darn sexy at the same time? Of course, I tease her. "Okay, *Miami Vice*, but maybe you should lay off those old-school cop shows."

She half smirks. "I'll have you know, those old-school cop shows are retro-cool. Come on, Miss Smarty Pants, on to Stage Two."

I get my game face on.

Stage Two is the riskiest part of the plan. The part where Euphoria and I split up. She's an M and I'm an S, so we have different homerooms. Besides, she needs to check in with the band teacher, and I need to check in with whoever's running the school paper.

We have an hour. Each Grimmacle has a limit, a weakness, and that's our Grimmacle's—we can be apart for only an hour at a time or the spell will break.

I look at my empty wrist. "Shall we synchronize watches?"

"Now who's going all *Miami Vice*?" She nudges me in a friendly way, and my heart soars.

"If I start wearing slacks and loafers with no socks, please shoot me."

"Deal."

I watch as she saunters away, my Fae-sight picking up the Grimmacle's aura around her. It blurs her image, like someone spread Vaseline on a camera lens. Blurry or not, I can't stop looking at her, each of her footfalls timed to the pulse of my heart.

When she turns the corner, I head to my new locker—Susan Scurry's locker—and stow my stuff, grab my new notebook. I take out my DSL camera, my baby. *Stupid Fiann and her shaving cream.* It cost me two weeks' pay to get it professionally cleaned. I wanted to put the money toward rent, but Mom insisted. I slam my locker a wee bit hard and head to the newspaper's HQ near the library.

My heart is suddenly pounding, and I wipe sweaty palms on my skirt.

What if the Grimmacle doesn't work? What if Miss Jardin sees me? Out of everyone, she's the teacher that knows me best. And so far, I haven't run into Fiann or anyone I've actually hung out with, except Lennon.

It worked well enough on her, Syl.

The idea that Glamma's Grimmacle keeps them from realizing the obvious—Syl Skye and Susan Scurry are the same person—seems absurd. But I trust Glamma. She was a wily old bird. She often said people don't question things that appear right, even when those things are dancing a jig under their noses.

I hope you're right, Glamma.

I turn and run smack-dab into a wall of a chest. "Oof!" I stagger back, rubbing my sore nose. My notebook's fallen. I bend to pick it up. "Are you all ri—?" I look up into the face of whoever just nearly ran me over. "Never mind."

Agravaine.

He's staring at me, those shark-black eyes searching my face.

He doesn't recognize me. Even so, my mind unhelpfully hurtles me back to Saturday night, him striding over the hill, all wild white hair and muscles and a thousand-percent terrifying, Commanding Euphoria to bring me to him.

A thread of fear coils inside me, but anger sweeps it away. *This time, we're coming for you, pal.*

He holds my gaze for a moment. "Do I know you?" He's turning on the charm, but the rich baritone of his voice slides over me with a creep factor of, like, a zillion. The bruised indigo aura around his left shoulder warps the air. The Moribund.

He knows I'm not infected. One of the few who isn't.

"Know me? Nope. Don't think so. I'm new here." I sidestep him, and he stands there a bit stunned. I'm probably the first girl to resist his "charms."

Gross. Dark Fae King on Earth. Ha! He won't be but a footnote once we're done with him. *But first things first, Syl.* Time to secure a permanent hall pass, and the best way to do that? Join the school paper.

I turn the corner and head into the paper's HQ. I've taken pictures for them since I was a lowly freshman, but I've never really gotten involved in the day-to-day goings-on.

Even so, I'm pretty sure the place isn't supposed to look like a hurricane hit it.

Desks are overturned, papers on the floor, the daily mock-ups torn down from the corkboard. A few kids rummage through stuff, picking up papers and trying to clean up the mess. The trash cans are already full, and they haven't even made a dent.

"Can I help you?"

Justice, the paper's editor in chief, strides up. He's a senior and way taller than me, super-thin and lanky. He's also varsity baseball, and I hear he once pitched a no-hitter. His face is tinged red under his dark complexion, and despite his athlete status, he's practically vibrating with some serious nerd rage.

I don't blame him.

Someone trashed the paper. But who?

"Hi, I'm—"

And then I see it...my old desk. It's in the center of the destruction, turned over, all the contents dumped out. My tiny cubbyhole gutted, my old scarf and the umbrella Mom always made me bring broken on the floor.

They trashed my desk. *Agravaine.* Dread drags cold fingers down my spine. He's looking for me, for any indication of where I might have gone. After all, Syl Skye and Euphoria simply vanished into thin air. Even the apartment's vanished, if Mom's claim about being able to hide it is true.

"Hey, you okay?" Justice looks concerned now. He reaches out awkwardly to steady me.

"I...uh..." *Get it together, Syl.* I snap myself out of it. "I'm Susan Scurry, the new junior photographer for the paper." I hold up my DSL. "I'm a transfer from Richmond Public."

I feel absurdly like I'm reciting lines from a bad play.

Justice fidgets, twisting his long fingers together in a way that looks painful. He takes a deep breath and seems to calm down a notch. "Okay, yeah, we could use some help. Someone turned the place upside down. Grab a broom."

"Okay." Relieved to be out of the spotlight, I go to the closet and grab a broom. Justice turns back to directing the troops—and by "troops," I mean the five or so geeky students moping around the mess.

I join them, just as geeky and awkward.

"Hi," I say to the girl next to me. She's got dyed blue-green hair like a mermaid. It looks great with her olive-tone skin. She's curvy, like I imagine a mermaid would be too. Her name is...Prudence something-or-other. I forget. I'm terrible with names.

"Hi," she half-says, half-grumbles. "Can you believe that someone trashed the school paper? I mean, who does that?"

"A total monster," I say, and her face breaks into a smile. The icebreaker warms me a bit, and we laugh together.

"I wouldn't be laughing if I were you nerds. This place is a disaster."

Ugh, Fiann. I'd recognize her voice anywhere, but seriously? Both her *and* Agravaine? It's been like ten minutes since I got here, and both of them have been all up in my ladybusiness.

Fiann stands by the door and whistles, her princess posse arrayed behind her like an intimidating wall of cotton candy. Everyone freezes. Fiann can get downright nasty, and no one wants to end up in Principal Fee's office.

"Tough break, freaks and geeks." She sweeps into the HQ like she owns the place. "My friend Syl said I should pick up her camera. Any idea where it is?"

What a dirty little liar! I cover my anger by sweeping extra hard with the broom. Agravaine put her up to this. There's no way on Gaea's green Earth that Fiann Fee would lower herself to come down to the nerdy school paper. Unless there was something in it for her.

But what? Why does she want my camera?

To find out where you've been. Again, those cold fingers press against my spine.

Justice points. "Her cubby's over there, but I didn't see a camera." *Nope, got it right here, buddy.* "Someone must've stolen it. Probably whoever trashed the place."

Fiann purses her lips. She's caught there. If she says the camera's missing and not stolen, then all the "freaks and geeks" will want to know how she knows that.

I mean, they're nerdy, but they're also the smartest kids in school.

I lean on my broom and smirk. Next to me, Prudence is grabbing something from her desk. I see an old-school mini tape recorder.

Fiann tosses her blonde ponytail like she's the Queen of England. "Whatever. If you find it, let me know. She really wants it."

She turns, but Prudence brushes past me and does the reporter bull-rush toward Fiann, firing questions as she goes. "Where is Syl? Have you seen her? Did you know she's been missing since Saturday night? Rumor has it she ran away. Was it because you and your friends bullied her?" Prudence holds the tape recorder out. "Can you comment on her status, Miss Fee?"

Fiann snarls and knocks Prudence's hand away. "Get that out of my face, troll hips." She's flustered by Prudence's questions, though, and everyone knows it. Fiann struggles to save her cool. "Just...clean this mess up. And you!" She points.

"Me?" I act all innocent, looking around like she could possibly mean anyone else.

"Yes, you, *new girl.*" She points at the camera hanging off my shoulder.

Crap. She recognizes it.

"Make sure you're at cheer practice today to get some shots. The big game is this weekend, and we've gotta create some buzz, people! Report on the real news, why don't you?" She sneers all mean at Prudence, and I relax.

Dodged that bullet.

To her credit, Prudence just puts her hands on her hips and gives Fiann the stink eye.

With a cartoonish *humph!* Fiann turns and flounces out, her princess posse trailing after her.

I look at Prudence. "That was tense."

She shrugs. "Only if you care what Fiann Fee thinks." She walks to the editor's desk and rifles through the mess, coming up with what looks like a key card. "Here's your temporary hall pass so you can cover special events. I'll order you the permanent one today. And remember..." Her grin grows wider. "With great power comes great responsibility."

I return her smile. "I promise to only use my powers for good."

The week goes by, Euphoria and I tromping from class to class every day. We're together for most of the day, except she uses her study hall for band practice, and I use it to run around the school under the pretense of taking pictures. It's the week after Homecoming, and Fee's extended Spirit Week, making it two actual weeks instead of one. People are trying to forget what-all went down at the Nanci Raygun by throwing themselves into cheesy decorations and pep rallies.

I'm supposed to be taking pictures, but really, I'm tailing Fiann and Agravaine around the school. Other than some illicit smoke breaks—Fiann—and secret meetings with his motorcycle fight club—Agravaine—and asking everything with a pulse about Syl Skye, the two of them are pretty boring.

Color me shocked.

But more and more as I run around, I'm reading those dark indigo auras on the student body. Agravaine's got a lot of the guys into motorcycle racing—infecting them with Moribund circuits built right into the bikes themselves, and even though Euphoria's not playing any more, the mics she tossed off the stage had dozens of Moribund circuits in them—enough to infect whichever girl caught it and all her friends.

But Fiann and Agravaine are pretty quiet.

Maybe they're laying low after the events of the weekend, after trashing the school newspaper and coming up empty. Planning, plotting... Euphoria and I should do the same.

That, and there's something else I've been wanting to ask her. Friday, I decide to bite the bullet, just do it—pick your inspirational slogan.

We meet up at lunch, hunching over our trays of lukewarm school pizza, soggy fries, and wilted green beans. We're the new girls, so we're alone at our table, and beneath the hustle and bustle of five hundred kids crammed into one small cafeteria, I drop the bomb. "I want you to train me."

"Train you...? In what?" She shoots me the dark Fae side-eye.

In return, I give her my best raised eyebrow. "You know what." I lift my soda can to my lips to mask my words. "My powers."

She leans back, folding her arms across her chest. It's her power stance, and I feel the *no* even before she says it. "It's not a good idea."

"What?" I struggle to keep my voice down. "Why not? What happened to all that 'together' stuff we talked about?"

She levels that intense sapphire-blue gaze on me. "No dark Fae has ever trained a fair Fae. It's against the rules."

"Rules schmules." Is she kidding? Is this another challenge? Indignation bubbles up inside me, and I can't help but respond to the gauntlet she's thrown. "You think I can't handle it, don't you? Well, I handled you just fine back at the tracks."

She snorts and toys with a limp French fry. "You got lucky, princess."

I hear the concern beneath the edge in her voice, but I gesture to where Agravaine and Fiann are living it up with a bunch of popular girls and jocks. More than half the student body, and all of them reeking of that sicky indigo aura, of the Moribund.

"We need an edge against them," I say, and it's true. "They've got popularity. But we've got power. Sleeper-princess power." That gets to her. I can see she's waffling, so I push. "I'll do whatever you say, no questions asked. Just train me."

She pins me with that dark Fae side-eye. "Whatever I say?"

Danger, danger! Dark Fae! I should so not agree to this. But I want to learn who I am, *what* I am. And the bonus of spending more time with Euphoria is a bright lure. I swallow it whole. "Whatever you say."

I am so going to regret this.

CHAPTER TWENTY
ROUEN

What use is good
In a world gone bad?
Can one act of good
Stand against all the hate and darkness?
- Euphoria, "World Gone Bad"

"Are you nuts?" Syl's voice reaches that girly high pitch that lets me know she's not bluffing anymore. She's really scared. Worse. *She doesn't believe.*

She stands at the edge of Richmond's tallest skyscraper, looking way, way down at the nighttime city streets. Twenty-nine stories below, the few cars zoom around like tiny ants on the wet black ribbon of asphalt cutting through the city center.

The wind whips around us, turning Syl's hair into a crimson halo around her head. Even afraid, she's beautiful, and I can see the fierceness that lies beneath her fear.

She's got this, Roue. Trust in her. Belief will come.

I hope so because I am breaking every rule in the dark Fae handbook, training her like this. No dark Fae has ever trained a fair Fae, never mind a sleeper-princess.

But that was what I wanted, wasn't it? That was my master plan way back when.

And I meant it when I told her we'd find new Syl and new Rouen together.

So I take a deep breath and meet her on the edge.

Syl's face is paler than normal as she studies the bank building across the vast, gut-wrenching gap of Main Street. It's a smaller skyscraper, lower than the one we stand on. I see her working out the math in her head—how far it is, how much lower the other building; she factoring in the wind, how fast she'll have to run to get up speed...

"I..." Her hands shake, and she clears her throat.

I want to comfort her, to wrap my arms around her and tell her she doesn't have to do this. But I can't. *Becoming* Fae is painful, terrifying, wonderful.

She needs to experience all three to fully Awaken. And the best way I can help her is to be hard on her.

So when she gives me the soulful, pleading eyes, I raise my chin and tuck my hood tighter around my face. My heart aches, but I stare at the empty buildings around us, trying to hollow myself out. Soft emotions won't help either of us right now.

She asked me to do this, to train her, and I said I would.

I have to be strong for her. *Tough love, Roue.*

She won't Awaken to her full potential if I coddle her. Besides... I steal a glance at her. I suspect Syl's more powerful than she realizes. Time to put my suspicions to the test.

I jerk my chin at the building across the gap. "Quit stalling, princess." My voice comes out gentler than I want. "Jump."

But Syl only hears the words—me ordering her to do the insanely impossible.

"No. No way." She steps back from the edge, her face a pasty white, her breath heaving in short gasps. I feel bad for bringing her up here, for springing Sleeper-Princess Level 50 on her when she just barely asked me to train.

But Agravaine's up to something. He's infected all the popular kids at school. It won't be long before he infects everyone, makes them his little Moribund minions.

The Moribund in my hand stretches and tightens painfully. It calls to him.

Luckily, the Grimmacle masks that call, but it won't forever.

We don't have the luxury of time.

The wind picks up, stealing my hood and whipping my raven-dark hair into my face. I leave it. Best if she can't see the regret in my eyes.

I make my voice hard—for her. "You asked to train, so here we are. Training Day One."

She gives me her patented Syl side-eye. "Are you crazy-bananapants?" She looks at the gap then at me. "This is Day One?"

I fold my arms across my chest and deadpan, "Wait 'til you see Day Two."

Disbelief pours off her in waves. "I can't jump that! It must be a hundred feet."

"A hundred and fifty," I correct her and watch her face go a sick shade of Gollum green. I keep my expression as deadpan as my voice, but inside I'm cursing the fact that I have to be her mentor in this.

Seriously. Me, a mentor? I'm no Obi-Wan Kenobi.

"I…" She bites her lip. "No. No way. Look, I don't mind hard, but this…" She points at the deadly drop. "This is *crazy*. I'm only human, Euphoria."

"You're really not," I tell her.

Nervous sweat slicks her face. She wipes it away, her hand trembling. "Can't we just go to a park and, like, start with a climbing wall or some parallel bars?"

I sigh heavily. Nope, not Obi-Wan. More like Kylo Ren—all dark and emo and seething just beneath the surface.

It's time for the tough love.

I lean against the rooftop HVAC and examine my fingernails. I let her paint them black last night. Even now, I remember the feel of her hand on mine, her touch gentle, her skin silky-soft, and the heat between us burning, burning, burning…

Focus, Rouen.

I keep my voice casual. "Do you think Agravaine and Fiann are spending their time on kid stuff like that? No. They're kicking ass and taking names."

Her face flushes, that Irish complexion awash in red.

Yes, get angry. That's it. Channel that anger.

She walks to the edge again and looks down.

I see the wheels turning in her mind. She remembers that night by the train tracks. She nearly outran me and the hounds of the Hunt. She was scared then just like she's scared now. But that night, she didn't have time to think.

Here, she's letting the fear get to her.

I know she won't for long. My girl's no whiner. She just needs a little nudge.

I pitch my voice low to calm her, but I keep my words all business. "Remember, breathe deep into your diaphragm. You're still Awakening, but your body knows what to do. You just need to give it a little push."

"This is your idea of a little?"

I heave an exaggerated sigh and pretend to let her off the hook. "Okay. We can go to your lame-o park. Come on, princess." I turn, but throw the coup de grace over my shoulder. "And bring your whiny-baby training wheels with you."

"Whiny... *Training wheels?*" Her temper's up now, her grey eyes sparking with fury.

Good. Use it.

Clenching and unclenching her fists, she takes a few steps back from the edge. And then a few steps more.

Yes, trust yourself. Believe.

You can do this. I know it.

"Screw your training wheels." She takes off at a run, her face set in grim determination, her eyes focused on the building a hundred and fifty feet away.

Her boots pound the rooftop. *Pound, pound, pound!* At the edge, she pushes off, her face ashy with fear and the rush of adrenaline as her body catapults her across the space.

She kind of panics a little midair and doesn't know what to do with her limbs, arms and legs going every which way, her expression caught somewhere between freaking out and total exhilaration.

And then she tucks her limbs in tight, soaring toward the building.

"Wooohoooo!" Her wild cry echoes back to me, filled with triumph.

She lands on the other side, stumbling and going to a knee. It's graceless, but she made it.

My breath comes out and my guts unclench. Effortlessly, I leap across after her.

I try not to show off, but I was born a dark Fae, and I have years of experience at this. I land way easier than she does; I alight, my boots slamming down on the rooftop as I stick the landing.

"Roue!" All adrenaline-flushed, she hurtles into me, wrapping her arms around my waist and laughing. "I did it! I did it!"

"You did!" *And you called me by my name.*

I blush hard, her joy contagious. I hug her back, and the next thing I know, we are face to face, her breath coming in short little gasps against my lips.

So warm, so soft.

So...*kissable.*

I thought I knew was burning was, but by all that is unholy, I am *on fire* for her. Our gazes meet, then we both freeze and jerk away fast. She stumbles, not yet used to her newfound strength or agility. I catch her by the arm and steady her. It only makes the heat between us go hotter, wilder.

What in all the hells is happening? My heart is pounding so hard, and I *ache* for her.

Stop it, Roue. I look awkwardly away, at the buildings, the skyline, the moon, anything. *You almost kissed her. What were you thinking?* My conscience scolds me like a schoolteacher.

But my heart answers quietly, from a place deep inside. *That she's amazing and wonderful and smart and pretty. That I feel more myself when I am with her than when I'm with anyone else...*

That I wanted to. I wanted to kiss a sleeper-princess. But she's not asleep anymore. Syl is Awakening for real, and this is proof. And once this is over, she'll become part of the fair Fae, and I am a dark Fae, I...

I will be her enemy.

Syl gives a shy little laugh that makes the ache in my heart wedge open wider. She steps back and looks down, her face still red. "That was pretty intense—the jump, I mean."

Yes, it was. And it's only just beginning.

We have more nights ahead of us. I plan to make the most of them.

I step to the edge, scanning the city line skyscape. All those buildings. My heart yearns to run across them—to run, with her—so I make a lesson of it. "Catch me if you can."

She looks surprised, and then I see the fire in those grey eyes as she warms to my challenge.

I leap off the roof, and she leaps after, chasing me.

The bell for study hall rings, and I slide from my seat with a wink at Syl.

She looks a bit tired, but her eyes are bright. All our late-night training sessions are starting to wear her out, but she stubbornly tackles any challenge I throw at her.

It's been two weeks, and it's only a matter of days before October comes to an end. We're no closer to uncovering Agravaine and Fiann's plan, and it's only a matter of time before they put two and two together and figure out Minnie Maven and Susan Scurry are really Rouen Rivoche and Syl Skye.

Syl's training is coming along, but she still has a long way to go.

She still hasn't caught me, even though our chase has led us all over the rooftops of Richmond. She gets stronger and more confident with every step she takes.

I know she doesn't believe yet. She doesn't see the changes in herself. How she shines. She has an inner glow now, that part of her that is Fae burning so brightly. And then there are the physical changes—her body stronger, fitter, her hair the lustrous red-gold of autumn leaves, her grey eyes glowing like sun on a stormy sea.

She's slowly coming into her own, *Becoming* fair Fae, testing out the summer in her blood, and everything about her draws me in, a moth to a blazing white flame.

So emo, Roue. So very emo.

I snort at myself for losing my train of thought. Kids are moving around us as we stare at each other, and I hear Danette whisper, "Lezzies" under her breath.

I only shake my head. I've heard she's kissed more girls than Brad Pitt. At least I wouldn't have to be in "party mode" to do it.

That is…if I ever did kiss a girl.

I haven't. I look at Syl. But I want to.

Maybe when she catches me, I'll get up the courage.

Stop it, Roue. This isn't about kissing her. It's about survival. A blush scalds my cheeks. I shake off the teen-angst drama.

Everything hinges on Syl's Awakening and her learning to use her powers— stopping Agravaine, healing the hearthstone, saving my people.

Yeah. Just about a dozen things more important than a kiss.

And yet…I can't shake the feeling that the kiss is, somehow, still vital. For both of us.

Syl smiles at me, and her smile lights up my whole world.

Focus up, Roue. I smile back and slip into the hall.

It's been two weeks, and nothing yet. Syl's been running around the school with her press pass, and I've been using my personal Glamoury to come and go as I please—as much as the Grimmacle will allow us to be apart.

We test it and push it. Being apart lets us feel the spell stretch like a rubber band between us, the tension increasing in our minds as the minutes tick by.

We can always sense when it's about to snap.

An hour is about all we can be apart. And then the Grimmacle has to rest and recharge for two. One for every two. It gives us plenty of time to roam around the school, for her to tail Fiann and for me to check up on Agravaine.

They've stolen Syl's file—another attempt to track her down. It won't work. Georgina's claim that the Grimmacle hides the apartment holds true.

Syl and I have been safe there. Safe, at least, from dark Fae-terference.

It's been…a little weird living with her.

I tried sleeping on an air mattress on her bedroom floor. But since the night we nearly kissed, I've been crashing on her couch, my dark Fae blood keeping me awake and restless.

And wanting her.

I can't risk being too close to her. With every passing day, my control frays like a knot pulled too tight. I need to blow off some steam, but my usual pastime of running across the rooftops has turned into a tense, angsty chase between me and her.

She chases me, but I am the real pursuer.

I'm afraid that one of these nights I'm going to let her catch me.

I turn the corner, heading toward the band room. A pack of freshmen dodges me, shouting "Band geeks!" and "This one time at band camp!" into the band room, and I give them a withering stare.

Even in my nerdy Minnie Maven identity, I make them back off a step.

"Freaky chick," one of them mutters as they scurry down the hall.

That's right, pal. Keep walking.

I enter the room, and the band is there, getting out and tuning up their instruments. All of them have beautiful gear—shiny cellos and horns and drums—and I feel a little self-conscious about my battered violin. No one's said anything yet, and they probably won't. The band really are a bunch of geeks, super-shy and…nice.

I haven't spent much time around nice people before. I kind of like it.

I set my backpack down and pull out my violin.

We're supposed to play the big game on Thanksgiving weekend. We have half the halftime show, and the cheerleaders are already saying how we're going to "lose" to them.

Leave it to Fiann and her minions to make a competition out of it.

Whatever. We're going to beat the spankies off those cheerleaders...

Once I figure out how.

Truth is, the band is good separately, but together? We're a hot mess.

Nazira, the lead cellist, is flat, and Octavia is a speed demon on drums. Marcus can't hear anything over the blatting of his tuba, and Chuck's too busy fiddly-farting on his keytar to pay any attention to the rest of us.

As we're keying up to murderface a selection from *Wicked*, Miss Hawklin steps into the room. She's all prim and arch, like the cat that not only ate the canary but burned down his house. "I'm afraid I have some bad news. Mr Carmen fell down some stairs this morning and broke his leg. He's going to be out for at least nine weeks."

"Nine weeks?" Nazira gasps. "But...but our halftime show is only four weeks away."

Miss Hawklin shrugs, but it's clear she doesn't give a hot damn. "Do your best?" She sidles out of the room.

It takes two seconds for the band to self-destruct, everyone talking at once, Nazira arguing with Marcus, Chuck playing a funeral dirge while Octavia tells him to shut it, the rest of the band freaking out, losing their minds until the whole thing devolves into total chaos.

"See? I told you they're a mess." Fiann flounces in as if on cue.

Seriously, what is this? A *Buffy* episode? It's like Joss Whedon is waiting in the wings, giving her stage cues. *Or she's causing it, Roue.*

I narrow my eyes at Little Miss Perfect.

Her princess posse spreads out—Jazz, Danette, Maggie, and a half-dozen other girls wearing green-and-gold cheerleading uniforms. They all look down their plastic-surgery-perfect noses at us band geeks.

Fiann primps. "You should just give us the other half of your spot in the halftime show."

That shuts everyone up. Fast.

"Why would we do that?" Nazira touches her hijab, her dark eyes serious.

"Because you're only going to make fools of yourselves."

Fiann's kind of right—we're super-unpracticed and the band is a hot mess—but they're *my* hot mess. I stand up. "We're not giving up anything. And..." I look around, steeling my bandmates with my confidence. "Our halftime show is going to kick your halftime show's sorry butt."

Fiann blushes purple. "Who the hell are you?"

"Minnie Maven," I say, putting my hands on my hips. *Can't see through the Glamoury, can you, sweetie?* "I'm the girl who's going to kick your butt." I smile, showing some fangs that she can't see.

She seems to get my intention, though.

"We'll see about that." She sniffs and turns on her heel. "Your funeral. See you on the field, geeks!"

I can see why Syl hates her.

With the cheerleaders gone, the entire band turns to me.

"Great job," Octavia says, twirling a drumstick. "We're going to get killed out there."

"Yeah. Why'd you have to open your big mouth?" Marcus sits down heavily, resting his tuba in his lap. He takes out a small green fidget spinner from his pocket and starts clicking away.

"Listen," I say. "We're all good. All we need is to get in sync. That's all."

"And who's going to help us do that?" Octavia won't let up. "Mr Carmen's out for nine weeks."

Chuck looks up from the keys. "Yeah, who?"

I look at my fellow band geeks. I know Fiann and her cronies have something planned for the Thanksgiving game. Next to Homecoming, it's got the biggest turnout—or so Syl tells me. Something also tells me Fiann and Agravaine have been laying low so they can make their move.

Well, I'm making a move of my own.

"Me. I'm going to teach us. And we are going to kick some cheerleader butt."

CHAPTER TWENTY-ONE
SYL

Only through strife, fear,
And the wonder of discovery
Can a sleeper-princess
Truly Awaken
- Glamma's Grimm

Two weeks. It's been two weeks, and I still can't catch her. Seriously, I'm losing my mind. Every single time, just as I'm about to grab her, she tosses me that cheeky half-smirk and puts on a burst of speed, and bam! She leaves me in the dust.

Ugh. Just thinking about it makes me—

"Miss Scurry."

Mrs Wright's voice cuts through my daydreaming, and the snickers and giggling of the class slam me back to reality. I realize I've scribbled so hard on my notebook that I've put the pen right through it.

Sheepishly, I lift my hand. The pen self-destructs, and ink oozes out all over my fingers, the desk, and dribbles to the floor in split-splats.

Rad.

Everyone is looking at me like I'm some kind of weirdo freak. Except Mrs Wright. She's got blue-bloody murder on her face. She has the shortest fuse of all my teachers. Ugh. Of all the classes to lose my cool...

I glance at Euphoria, but she only gives me that sexy, teasing half-smirk that makes the butterflies in my stomach do the cha-cha. If she calls this a "learning moment," I swear I'm going to smack her one.

Mrs Wright slaps a red card down on my desk. "This is for you," she says sweetly, like she's giving me an early birthday present. "Give Principal Fee my regards."

Double rad. Thanks to Fiann, I've become one of Richmond E's "special cases" who reports directly to the principal instead of to an administrator. Ever since I stood up to her in the paper's HQ, she's made it her special mission to torment me.

Some days, I think she really can see through Glamma's Grimmacle.

Or maybe she's just super-mean to everyone who doesn't fit her idea of cool or beautiful or popular. Whatever.

The long and short of it is she's a huge Jerky McJerkface.

Mrs Wright looms over me, all five-foot-one of her. "Are you waiting for an engraved invitation?"

"I know, I know." I sigh and shove up from my desk. "Go directly to the principal's office. Do not pass Go. Do not collect two hundred dollars."

"Now, Miss Scurry."

I grab the card and crumple it without realizing my strength. More giggles and chuckling erupt from the kids around me. *Game face, Syl.* I breathe out and loosen my grip. Euphoria's been teaching me control, but when I get upset or excited or afraid, I still kind of lose it a little.

Becoming new Syl is a whole lotta work, I tell ya.

Euphoria gives me an encouraging nod from the back of the class, and I take some comfort in that.

And at least Mom can't ground me for this when I get home. I mean, I'm a sleeper-princess. I should totally be above grounding, right?

God, I hope so.

Mom's pretty much a stickler for rules. And she carries a gun, so...it's anybody's game.

I slip into the empty hallway and drag my sorry butt in the direction of Fee's office. With the next breath, I blow out the last of my whining. Glamma's counting on me. All my friends are counting on me. *Euphoria's counting on me. Suck it up, buttercup.*

I'll go to Fee's office and take whatever punishment—detention, in-school suspension, I'll write *"I will not crush my pen until it explodes like a pimple"* on the board a thousand times. Whatever. None of that matters, really.

What matters is that I master my powers so Euphoria and I can beat the stuffing out of Fiann and Agravaine. *Easier said than done.*

I've been kind of...sucking. And they've been super-secretive and hard to pin down.

It's like they're laying low because we're laying low. I almost want to break the Grimmacle and just have everything out in the open. All this sneaking around is killing my nerves... Euphoria acts like it's all cool, but I can sense something else going on with her—something tense between us when I chase her, when I almost catch her.

It's like...she wants to be caught, and yet she's afraid.

Of what, me? She's a kickass dark Fae. I don't think she's afraid of anythi—

A flash of blonde ponytail catches my eye as I round the corner. *Fiann!*

I duck back around the corner and peer around in time to see the side door closing. *She's just going out for an illegal smoke break. Relax.*

But something tells me that's not it.

Fiann's alone, and that's weird. If she wanted to smoke, she'd make sure a dozen girls saw her doing it. Since that's "totally cool" and all...

My heart pounding hard, I tiptoe to the door. Just as I'm about to crack it open, I hear voices from the other side.

Crap! I look for any kind of escape. The girls' room!

I duck in and run into a stall. My heart is pounding. *Holy cats, holy cats, holy cats.* I'm freaking, but adrenaline is giving me a crazy rush. I do that thing where you close the door and stand on the toilet. It always works in movies, right?

And I am determined to be the final girl in this picture.

The *click-clack* of Fiann's heels—the ones she's not supposed to wear because, hello...dress code—are followed by the heavy *clomp-clomp* of motorcycle boots.

My heart jumps into my throat. *Agravaine?*

"What's our progress, Fi?" His deep baritone leaves no doubt.

There's crack between the stall's side and the door. Through it, I see a sliver of Fiann lounging against the sinks. She bends her blonde head and, with a popping flare of her lighter, lights a cigarette.

Smoke fills the air. Gross. I put my hand over my nose and mouth and try not to make a sound.

"It's done. Daddy's all filled up with circuits."

A chill crawls down my spine. *Principal Fee...her own father?* I remember that creepy look on her face at the Nanci—that night Agravaine sent Euphoria after me, the night the hell-hounds attacked.

The night Fiann totally lost her mind.

I peer through the crack. Yup. My Fae-sight picks up the heavy indigo aura wafting around her like a nightmare shroud, and she's got this insane-o light in those green eyes. Oh, yeah. She's gone around the bend, crazypants, a few sandwiches short of a picnic.

Agravaine plucks the cigarette from her lips. "And the trolley restoration?"

Restoration? I rack my brain. It doesn't make sense. Yeah, the old trolley tracks from the 1940s are being dug up, repaired, and restored all around Richmond, as part of some citywide historical restoration plan. But what does that have to do with anything?

I thought the Fae didn't like iron.

"It's on schedule to be done before the Winter Formal. Just like you wanted." Fiann eyes him as he turns the cigarette over in his fingers.

What are they up to? Are they trying to create a circle of protection like Glamma did for me? But what for? Hmmm... Euphoria mentioned something about the Winter Formal being on the same night as the winter solstice, the night dark Fae power is at its strongest. I'm betting this trolley thing ties into that somehow...

"Give me my cigarette." Fiann tosses her ponytail, but Agravaine flicks the butt into the sink. Clearly, he's not having any of her flirty crap.

Fiann's pretty face turns an interesting shade of purple, but she only takes another cig out of her pack, lights up, and blows smoke in his face. "You're a real jerk, you know that?"

A dark chuckle rumbles from his throat. "Make sure the restoration stays on target."

"Don't get your panties in a bunch." Fiann flicks ashes into the sink and takes another drag. "Daddy's got the mayor wrapped around his little finger. Those black-magic circuits don't hurt, either."

"Good. Now we only have one more problem." Agravaine's deep baritone rumble seems to suck all the air out the room.

He turns and meets my gaze through the door.

Oh, this is so not good.

"Perfect," Fiann is rattling on. "The trolley should be fully up and running all around the city by the time we're picking dresses for the Winter Formal, and—"

"We're not alone."

My blood freezes, and my fight-or-flight response kicks up to DEFCON 1.

Fiann follows his gaze, and her eyes meet mine through the crack in the door.

Crappity, crap, crap, crap. "What in the holy hell?" In two strides, she's at the door. She yanks it open. "You!"

"Me." I wave. "Hi."

"What are you doing in there?"

"Ummm…peeing?"

She gives me the stink eye. "Get your butt out here."

I step out of the stall. Out of the frying pan and into the fryer.

Agravaine looks at me curiously. The Grimmacle is holding. *Thank you, God, Buddha, and all you cosmic nice guys.*

I stare back at him. "You know you're in the girls' bathroom, right?"

He only shrugs, that arrogant, amused look on his face, but Fiann nearly loses her mind. "She knows. She *heard*, Agravaine."

"So?" He smirks at her, the way a shark smirks at his supper. Then he turns that super-intense look my way, and my Fae-sight blurs as his aura grows deeper, darker, stretching out like a shadow over me.

Ruh-roh. What is he doing? I see his Glamoury falling over me, shrouding me.

It does…nothing.

He speaks with some serious intent, and I recognize the tone he used to Command Euphoria. "You'll forget what you heard here today. You'll go back to class and forget."

Ummm…no, I won't. But I can't really say that, so I pull from all those vampire teen-angst shows that Euphoria likes to watch late at night when she thinks I'm asleep. I speak in a monotone, like I'm totally under his spell or whatever. "I'll go back to class and forget what I heard here today."

I hold my breath.

"Good."

He buys it. *Idiot.*

Fiann breathes out. "Whoa. Can you do that…to anyone? Make anyone do what you want?"

I look blankly back and forth between them, faking that I'm under his control.

"Yes. Why?" He looks suspiciously at her.

An evil smirk comes over her face. "Tell her to come to my Halloween party tonight. And bring her girlfriend."

Euphoria? But no, with the Grimmacle shielding us, Fiann can't know Euphoria's *actually* Euphoria. What could Fiann want with Minnie?

Agravaine gives me the order, and I repeat it like an automaton. I feel like a complete tool, but they swallow it hook, line, and sinker.

They let me go, and I wander out and back to class like I've been "ordered." I'll get another red card the second I walk in, but it's worth it to sell the drama.

I can't wait to tell Euphoria. We're going to a Halloween party.

"Why are we doing this again?" Euphoria grumbles, lying across my bed with an arm thrown over her eyes. Her legs are so long they hang off the end. "I can't believe I have to go to a high school Halloween party."

"You're *in* high school, you dork," I tease, but she only groans some more. "Don't let your broody emo-ness suck all the fun out of it."

"I thought you liked my broody emo-ness." She gives me the raised eyebrow and that sexy half-smirk. "Isn't that why you have my band poster on your wall?"

Note to self: take that incriminating thing down. Just as soon as I can breathe. Our snarky tease-flirting has my poor heart racing like a rabbit. There's been a lot of that witty banter between us since she started training me.

It's been part flirty and all tough love. But even when she's being tough, I can see the concern in her blue eyes. And the heat between us is off the charts. I let out a breath. *Get a grip, Syl.*

I've already told Euphoria about the trolley restoration/Winter Formal/winter solstice connection, but we're still racking our brains to figure out their endgame. "Anyway, Fiann's planning something for tonight." I go to my closet and start rifling through to see what I have for costumes.

"Tonight is Samhain." Euphoria pronounces it kinda like *sow-hen.*

I dig deeper into my closet, my voice muffled. "I remember that from Glamma's old stories. Samhain, the Irish feast of the dead, when the year turns from summer to winter." I pull out an old Red Queen costume, then thrust it back. *Nah.*

Euphoria watches me. "Fae power is tied to the seasons—the fair Fae to summer and the dark Fae to winter. So at midnight on Samhain, tonight, when summer gives way to winter, the power of Faerie will shift to favoring the dark Fae over the fair Fae." Her tone is thoughtful, calculating. "Considering the trolley restoration's on track for completion by the winter solstice..."

I catch her eye. "Seems like Agravaine and Fiann might be waiting for a night of power. But why not tonight?"

Euphoria cocks her head, thinking. "The power shifts to the dark Fae tonight, but it might not be enough."

"The winter solstice-slash-Winter Formal, then?"

She meets my gaze fully. "Bingo." Her blue eyes are super intense.

I feel a blush crawling up my neck to my cheeks. *Keep your head in the game, Syl.* "First, we've gotta get through tonight."

"Agreed." She bites her bottom lip, and I nearly pass out from all the sexy.

I turn back to my closet. "Tonight, Fiann'll probably have Agravaine try to mind-zap you like he did to me." I press an old cheerleading outfit to my body. *Ugh. No.*

I look her in the eye. "Why wasn't he able to use his mind-wooj on me?"

"You're immune to personal gramarye. Mine, his...everyone's." She pulls the arm from her face and meets my gaze, all seriouslike. "You're the strongest sleeper-princess I've ever seen."

I blush. I love it when she gets all intense like that, but sometimes it's *too* intense. "What about you?"

Her eyes lose some of that fire. "It's different. I'm bound to him. If he Commands me—even without knowing I'm really Rouen— I'll have to do his bidding."

"Can you fight it like you did last time?"

Euphoria raises an eyebrow, and I can tell from her look it's like I just asked, *Oh hey, can you lift that eighteen-wheeler in an adrenal-fueled feat of superhuman strength, and can you, like, eat a cheeseburger and juggle a chainsaw while doing it?*

"Oh. Sorry."

It's quiet between us, and I throw the cheerleading outfit aside. "Maybe we shouldn't go. It's too late to find costumes, anyway." I try to hide the disappointment in my voice.

I know it's dumb, but I kind of wanted to show up at Fiann's party—show up and show off a little, prove to her she doesn't scare me or Susan Scurry.

The bed squeaks as Euphoria gets up. She comes over to me, and I see our reflections in the mirror, how well she complements me—her bronze skin and sapphire-blue eyes, my pale skin and red hair.

We're like night and day. I like it.

"You don't need a costume," she says, putting her hands on my shoulders. "You can make your own."

"How?" I meet her gaze in the mirror, so heated I think I'm going to burn up right here.

She leans in, her breath warm on my ear. "With your personal Glamoury."

"But I don't have that. Only Fae—"

"You are," she says, and a flicker of pain goes through her blue eyes. "You're a fair Fae, Syl, and you'll soon be fully Awakened."

Oh. There's that. "Aren't...?" The question catches in my throat, but I ask it anyway. "Aren't the fair Fae and the dark Fae enemies?"

"Yes," she says quietly, and that pain in her eyes intensifies. "The Summer Court has long been at war with the Winter Court."

I turn to face her. "So...will we—?"

Her finger touches my lips, and all thought, all breath goes out of me at that soft caress. I look into her eyes, lose myself in them.

"Let me show you." She steps back and breathes out. With her breath, her appearance *changes*. She becomes shorter, blonde, then taller and red-haired, with ebony skin. She gestures, and her leathers vanish into a ball gown. She turns, and the ball gown becomes a pair of jeans and a ragged concert tee.

A thousand of the best Disney animators couldn't make it look cooler, more seamless. It's like she *flows* from one appearance to another.

My own breath goes out. "Holy…" I mean, I knew she could do that, but I've never actually *seen* her do it.

"It's called *seeming*. You can use your Glamoury to seem like someone else." She turns me toward the mirror. "Your turn."

I straighten. I don't care that this is a learning moment. That power is totally awesome and I want to master it.

"Breathe in and hold it," she tells me, and I do. "Now imagine how you want to look."

I make a picture in my mind—I want to look like her, all cool and sleek in black leathers and a motorcycle jacket. I feel the breath held in my lungs begin to burn, but I shove the pain aside and concentrate.

Her voice is hypnotic. "Imagine it. Down to the last detail."

The scuff mark on the jacket's right arm, the metal on her boots…

"Breathe out and *will* it."

I breathe out. For a moment, nothing happens, and then a sensation begins at the top of my head. My hair prickles and my Glamoury slides over me like silk, shimmering as it comes, leaving me encased in black leather.

A rush of excitement flashes through me, and my skin tingles. "Whoa…"

The wonder of it makes me giddy and excited. I don't care what tonight holds—Fiann, Agravaine. I'm high on sleeper-princess power.

I turn to her, still giddy. "I have an idea for our costumes."

CHAPTER TWENTY-TWO
ROUEN

Fall into the spell
Of my Glamour
Of my Glamour
My Glamour girl
- Euphoria, "Glamour"

It's dark by the time we put the finishing touches on our costumes and head out, just Minnie Maven and Susan Scurry, out for an innocent high school Halloween party.

Nothing to see here, folks.

The streets in Fiann's rich neighborhood—Syl tells me it's called "the Fan" because the streets spread out like a literal fan—are jam-packed with kids in costumes. Pirates and witches, Disney princesses and ninjas, zombies and the occasional vampire. I spot a girl in gauzy faerie wings.

Well, damn. That's ironic. I could've gone as myself this Halloween. A dark Fae would have gone completely unnoticed in this mob. Just another freak among freaks. Only, my freakiness is real. I don't get to take it off at the end of the night.

But who wants to be ordinary, anyway?

As it is, our costumes are part real—ball gowns and zombie makeup—and part Glamoury layered over it to make us look even more intense and scary.

It's a good combination, if the kids running away screaming are any indication.

I slowly guide my Harley—in the Glamoury, it looks like a scooter, my poor bike!—around a group of creepy killer clowns with their glowing jack-o'-lantern flashlights. Ahead, Hanover Avenue is all hazy streetlamps and the glimmering lights from crazy over-the-top house decorations. From here, I catch a glimpse of a giant pirate ship, its prow sweeping up over the top of the house. Next door is an Alice in Wonderland house, complete with suit-card "guards" and a giant inflatable White Rabbit.

And that's just for starters. Every house is decked out to the nines. It's like *A Nightmare before Christmas* threw up out here. Everything seems magical and hazy and unreal.

For one night in this mortal realm, I might actually fit in.

And that's just it… I glance over my shoulder at Syl.

With her, I always feel like I fit in. No matter where I am.

The ache blossoms inside my chest like a poisonous flower. A… what? *Bloody bones.* Looks like new Rouen is going to be as emo as old Rouen. *Gah!*

I maneuver the Harley into a tiny spot between two cars and put down the kickstand. "We'll have to park here."

The entire street is blocked off by police so the kids can do their trick-or-treating. I slip my leg off the Harley, a bit glad to get off the bike, considering the ball gown and all its many layers. How did I let her talk me into this again?

Oh, right. She's adorable. And I'm a total sucker for her.

Syl gathers her own skirts, and I give her a hand getting off the bike. As soon as her fingers brush mine, I realize it's all worth it. Wearing a ball gown, getting "dressed up" in our

Glamoury, going to Fiann's party, even risking Agravaine Commanding me.

It's all worth it because I'm with her.

Plus, it'll give us a chance to scope out Villain Headquarters.

Fiann's a total control freak, so I'm sure we'll find some kind of evidence in her house—something to clue us in to what their next move is.

Syl takes my hand. "So we don't get lost," she says, but I know it's mostly an excuse. I can tell by the flush on her cheeks and the way her pulse beats in her wrist.

It's okay. I like holding her hand too. "Ready?" she asks me as we stand on the edge of Hanover Avenue.

"Tell me again how to get the free candy."

She laughs as we enter the throng of costumed kids and parents, and indicates our own gown-and-Glamoury, zombie-and-prom gown costumes. "I guess if we're skipping training tonight, you deserve some free candy."

"Who said we're skipping training?" I deadpan, cocking an eyebrow at her.

"You're…impossible."

"And yet, still amazing."

She snickers at my not-so-serious self-assessment and tucks her head close to me so only I can hear. "I can't believe that I'm taking *Euphoria* to a Halloween party, and I can't even tell anyone about it."

"Don't you mean you can't believe you're taking a *dark Fae* to a Halloween party and you can't tell anyone about it?"

Syl's face falls. "The fair Fae really hate the dark Fae, don't they?"

I blow out a breath. That is a seriously loaded question, way too complicated to explain in the short time it'll take us to get to Fiann's house. I answer simply, "Yes."

She stops in the middle of the street, trick-or-treaters swarming around us. "So we're going to end up enemies?"

No! My heart cries out against that thought. I step in and take her face in my hands carefully, so as not to ruin her makeup. She looks up at me, those grey eyes piercing my soul, making me ache to the core of my being.

I want to kiss her right here in the middle of the street, sweep her up in my arms and show her that I could never, ever be her enemy…

And then two little boys dressed as Ninja Turtles bump into us and break us apart. They turn, take one look at our zombie faces, and run screaming into the crowd.

I meet Syl's gaze across the space separating us. She's chuckling, a pretty blush on her face, and I laugh with her.

She takes my hand again, and we continue walking, our laughter subsiding.

In the awkward silence between us, I say, "The only ones that can decide if we become enemies is us."

"I won't be your enemy." Syl's face is grave as she says it, and then she smiles radiantly. "Besides, we're too good a team." Her gaze is heated, her voice teasing. "After all, I actually got a dark Fae to wear a gown instead of black leathers and motorcycle boots. I mean, if that's not testament to my sleeper-princess powers, I don't know what is."

Her teasing breaks the seriousness. In answer, I hike my dress up a few inches to show her my New Rocks. "Still wearing the motorcycle boots, princess, but yeah, I don't get into a gown for just anyone."

She smiles, all cat that got the cream. "I know."

Of course she does. I'm totally into her, and no Glamoury could ever hide it. I'm only dark Fae. And she's gorgeous—even in zombie makeup.

"That one's Fiann's, right there," she says, pointing to a huge mansion with about a gazillion carved pumpkins out front.

By the Hunt, all those candles must be a fire hazard. Then again, given that Fiann's family is old money, her dad probably owns the fire department.

I sigh and try to look at the bright side. "At least they'll have full-size candy bars. None of that snack-size nonsense."

We enter the gauntlet of scarecrows, hay and fallen leaves crunching under our feet, and I get a sudden whiff of autumn—that dead-leaf, earthy-clean smell of dying things. It strikes me how short-lived everything is in the mortal world.

A blink of an eye to a dark Fae, and soon, to Syl too. Once she fully Awakens, once she becomes fair Fae.

They'll come for her, Roue.

I tighten my grip. Maybe. No one's seen a fair Fae in a hundred years. With their sleeper-princesses mostly dead, they've lost a lot of power. Maybe they've gone into the fair Fae version of Winter's Sleep, like my people.

Syl tugs on my hand, jolting me out of my distraction. "Fiann's loaded, so we'll probably bob for apples and eat donuts on strings and stuff like that."

I force a smile to my face. "Well, if there are donuts, I guess I can put up with Miss Fancy Feast."

She grins, dragging me through a small crowd of preschoolers and parents and onto the giant porch to ring the doorbell.

Fiann's dad, aka Principal Fee, answers the door, holding a bowl of—yup. Full-size Snickers bars. He's wearing a Dad-cula outfit with a bathrobe and fake fangs, and when he sees the two of us, Minnie Maven and Sue Scurry, two geeks standing on his doorstep, he falters a bit.

"Fiann? Fi baby," he calls back over his shoulder.

I help myself to a Snickers bar and pass one to Syl. Fi baby? Wow, that's just bloody awful. I shove the candy bar in my face to keep from making a snarky comment. Instantly, the sweet, blessed chocolate gives me a bit of a sugar high. Good. I'll need it to survive this night.

Downstairs, I hear a door open, and music blares out.

"It's fine, Daddy!" Fiann's voice floats up from the basement. How does she even know it's us? Cameras in the pumpkins? I look accusingly back at the scarecrow.

That's it. No brains for you, buddy-boy.

"Come in, come in." Principal Fee ushers us through the house, into a huge kitchen that would put Martha Stewart to shame. He's got the sallow-eyed, hollow look of a mortal infected with the Moribund.

I give a side-glance at Syl, and she nods almost imperceptibly. Her Fae-sight is showing her that, yup, he's infected all right.

A pang of guilt spears me. He doesn't seem like too bad a guy. I almost regret coming here solely to spy on his daughter.

Almost.

"Go on down," he says, and I usher Syl ahead of me.

I know one of the reasons Fiann got Agravaine to make Syl bring me— Well, to make Susan bring Minnie. Fiann wants Agravaine to Glamour me into throwing the half-time show at Thanksgiving. She wants the band to screw up so she and her cheerleader cronies can win the day.

Fat chance.

I've got a few tricks up my sleeve too.

"Go on." I wink at Syl. "I'll catch up in a sec."

"Ooookaaaay." Syl gives me a suspicious look, and I respond by putting on my most innocent face.

Well, as innocent as a dark Fae dressed up as a zombie can look.

"I don't want to know, do I?" she says, biting into her Snickers, her voice adorably muffled.

"Nope. Shoo." I wave her away teasingly.

Shaking her head, she goes down into the basement.

I turn to Principal Fee. "So, I hear there are some boys who are going to show up?"

"Boys?" A frown creases his face. I mean, what self-respecting dad wants boys at his teenage daughter's party? "Well, there aren't any yet, but Fiann said that a few might show up."

I step in, look him in the eyes, and hit him with a double dose of Glamoury. "You don't want any boys coming to this party. Any boys at all."

"Any boys at all." His intonation is correct, but given that a) he's infected with Moribund and harder to Glamoury, and b) my clever girl pulled a fast one on Agravaine this afternoon, I check Fee's eyes. Yup. They're all dilated. Black as night.

"You'll send them away."

"I'll send them away."

Good. Agravaine won't cause a scene. He doesn't get anything out of helping Fiann win the halftime show. And without him here, we'll be able to scope the place out, look for clues. "Thanks." I pat Fee's shoulder. "You're the best." I snag another Snickers out of the bowl and head down stairs.

Goth music floats up from the basement, and I hear the familiar strains of my violin in "Breathtaken." Well, at least Fiann's got good taste in music.

I barely hit the bottom step when I see Fiann. She and her minions have Syl cornered. My protective instincts go on high alert, but I tone it down. No need to snap any necks. They're just teen girls.

Which means their evil level is just somewhere south of Darth Vader.

Fiann's dressed like some kind of sexy...cat, I guess—kitty ears and kitty paws and a black tail bobbing from her backside. Her makeup's on point, though, and it looks like a stylist did her face and hair. Danette and Maggie and Jazz flounce up. They're wearing mice costumes with dark glasses.

"Rats on parade!" Syl guesses, and I can tell she's messing with them.

"No." Danette fluffs her already fluffy hair. "We're three blind mice. What the hell are you?" She looks over her two-hundred-dollar Ray-Bans at Syl.

I take her cue to swoop in and put my arm around Syl, flaunting the torn ball gowns, the blood, and the zombie-ness of our outfits. "We're Deadutantes."

Syl smiles at me, and it's all worth it, wearing this silly ball gown, just to see her smile and all of them stunned to silence for like a half second.

Fiann's gaze roams over the fake blood and white zombie makeup, our ripped-up ball gowns. "Okay, whatever. Just come on." She sighs like she's just so put upon.

Syl and I sneak grins at each other.

I mouth the words, *Best party evar* and roll my eyes, and she giggles.

But I have to admit, the place looks pretty swank. The basement is all decked out in purple Christmas lights and tiny bobbing orange jack-o'-lanterns. Blacklights and mirrors distort the room and make it look bigger. Cobwebs and fake bloody curtains hang everywhere, and there's just a touch of fake fog rolling in.

Mostly the guests are cheerleaders with a few popular-girl exceptions like Lennon and Jazz. Lennon waves at Syl from the snack table. Syl and I head over.

"Hey, Lennon." Syl hugs her.

Lennon's decked out like a marionette, complete with top hat and cute Lolita-style skirt and bodice. Her makeup accentuates her doll-like features, and she has her usual giant glowing cat-ear headphones atop her head. "Hi," she says breathlessly.

While they chat, I take stock of the snack table. It's like the junk-food version of a *Game of Thrones* feast. "Catered?" I throw the question out there.

"Of course." Fiann flounces by. "What do we look—poor?"

I just snort. Catered. Good. That means no one in this house prepared this food. Which also means, eating it is not the same as breaking bread with them. Ha! I snag a handful of Cheezy Bitz and munch away, wondering just how long we have to stay before we can bail.

Syl glances at me, and I give her an arch look.

"No donuts. That's it, I'm outta here." I turn in mock outrage to leave (i.e., find an excuse to roam about the house unattended), but Fiann's there.

"We're going to play Truth or Dare," she announces. "Come on, girls."

Everyone gathers around Fiann on the floor. "Everyone," she emphasizes, and Syl and I get reluctantly dragged in.

"Okay," Fiann says. "I'll start." She looks around, clearly loving it as everyone squirms. "Dani, truth or dare?"

Danette squeals, and the girls around her giggle. "Truth!" she says amid the good-natured groans and teasing.

Fiann looks like she's thinking. "Okay, if you could date any guy in school, who would it be?"

I roll my eyes, and Syl giggles.

Dani milks her moment in the spotlight. "Oh, I guess it'd be Mikhail Despres."

The quarterback. Duh.

I tune out as the girls go around. Syl seems kind of interested, but I know it's more about being included than anything else.

When her turn comes, she calls truth.

"If you could kiss any girl here, who would it be?" Maggie asks.

Syl turns a pretty shade of red. She glances up at me. She's lovely—even through the zombie makeup and fake blood. "Minnie," she whispers.

Her admission is an arrow to my heart.

She wants to...kiss me?

I've felt it every night, the connection between us growing stronger, stronger, the heat between us wild and scorching, the number of times we've almost kissed on the rooftops, or that time in the alleyway, or that time in the street like two seconds ago—

"Truth or dare, Minnie?"

Fiann's voice jolts me out of my thoughts.

She looks at me and waves a hand in front of my face. "Hello, Earth to Miss Maven. Truth or dare?"

"Dare."

The girls erupt into giggles and excitement.

"Fine." Fiann's eyes are bright with malice. She looks at Syl. "Kiss me."

My stomach drops out. *Ugh.* Of course Miss Mean Girl Extraordinaire would choose that. I just cock an eyebrow at her. I could Glamoury her right here, but the other girls would notice.

"You chose dare." Fiann clearly senses I'm reluctant.

Yeah, if *reluctant* is the word for *no friggin' way.*

Syl's tense. She's wringing her hands.

I look Fiann in the eye. "I'm not kissing you."

Fiann turns purple. "You have to! It's the game."

I stand up. There's no way I'm hurting Syl. Not for a game. Not for anything. "No thanks."

Fiann jumps up with me, and the next thing I know we're all on our feet, Fiann in my face. "You have to. It's my party, and I said that's your dare."

Hunts' hounds, she just doesn't get it, does she?

Syl steps in. "Look, she doesn't want to, okay?"

"No." Fiann says. "It's not okay." She grabs Danette's Diet Coke and throws it in Syl's face.

Everything stops.

The music is still bass booming, but there's a tension in the air as the amber liquid drips down Syl's cheeks, her chin, her neck. It's all over her costume, "staining" the Glamoury. Her makeup's running. She looks mortified. Tears well up in her eyes. I want to grab her and hold her, protect her, and guilt swells up in me.

You were standing right there, Roue.

I didn't think Fiann would—

That's the problem. You underestimated the Homecoming queen.

Syl takes off, running upstairs. I follow her, but at the top, she ducks into the bathroom, slamming the door.

I give Fiann a murderous look and then go after Syl.

I knock softly on the door. "Syl...? Can I come in?"

"Go away!" Her voice is muffled, but I still hear the tears.

Damn it. Damn Fiann. Damn me. "Please. I have something to show you."

I wait for what feels like an hour out there. I'm tempted to just use my dark Fae strength to kick the door in, but again, announcing who we really are is a Very Bad Idea.

Finally, I hear her get up and walk to the door. The door opens a crack and her tear-stained face appears. "I've ruined everything."

My heart aches for her, and in that moment, I don't care about Fiann or Agravaine or finding out their stupid plan. I just care about Syl. "Please let me in."

She opens the door wider, and I step in.

In a flash, she's in my arms. I close the door behind us and lean on it, holding her. "I'm sorry," I whisper into her hair. "I should have stopped her."

"You didn't know." She snuffles. I know she hates crying. Her complexion makes her wear it all day.

"Let me have a look." I try to push her gently away, but she resists.

"I don't want you to see me like this."

"Like what?" I push a little more firmly so I can see her. Even with the makeup and mascara running, she's beautiful. "It's not so bad." I brush her sweaty hair from her face and turn her toward the mirror.

She's a bit of a wreck, and her face crumples when she finally looks. "I'm a total mess. Look at me. Coke all over my dress, my face, my makeup."

She was so proud of the Deadutantes, and now it's ruined. But there's something she doesn't know. I take a washcloth from the rung. I run it under warm water and slowly wipe the makeup and Coke from her face.

"Our costumes are ruined," she says.

"No." It's time for another learning moment. She normally hates when I do this, but maybe she won't mind this time. "Remember earlier when you put the Glamoury on to make us look scarier?"

It was just little things—to make the blood look more real, to make our eyes wider, deader looking, to make our flesh look like it was really peeling instead of crappy latex makeup.

"It only stains the Glamoury because you *think* it should. Because you let it." I lean in. "Don't let it."

She looks up at me hopefully.

"Close your eyes."

"Roue—"

"Do it, princess."

"Fine. You're impossible."

"But still amazing. Now do it. Trust me."

I see her take a deep breath and gather herself. Her chest hitches a few times as she calms her crying, and when she breathes out, her Glamoury shimmers over her. Her gown looks freshly torn and bloody and her makeup is even scarier. Picture perfect.

"Open your eyes."

She does, and her expression transforms. "Rouen," she breathes. "It's perfect. Thank you!"

She throws her arms around me for the second time tonight, and I don't care that she actually does have Diet Coke all over her dress. I hug her back, and again we're close, so close that her breath is warm on my face. I can smell her feminine vanilla scent, and my head starts to swim a little.

This time, there's no iron to blame for my softer side, but I don't care. I'm really starting to like new Rouen.

A knock on the door brings us out of our embrace. "Syl?" Lennon's voice. "Are you okay?"

I turn to Syl and hold my hand out. "Are you ready?"

She nods firmly. I see the resolve in her eyes. "I'm ready. Let's go show Fiann how a sleeper-princess deals with bullying."

CHAPTER TWENTY-THREE
SYL

With the Fae
There is always more
Than meets the eye
- Glamma's Grimm

I'm fuming and fired up by the time we open that bathroom door.
My Glamoury is perfect, not a hair out of place. My zombie makeup's twice as terrifying, and Euphoria's right next to me. At first
I was disappointed that no one knew it was her on my arm, but
now, you know what?

I know. And that's all that matters.

This is part of me becoming my new self. The new Syl. Taking
no crap—only names.

Okay, Fiann. Time to pay the piper.

I strut my stuff back down into the basement, my hand lightly
holding Euphoria's. I glance back at her, and her face—creepy with
the zombie Glamoury on—softens with a smile.

Go on, that smile says. *You got this.*

I do. I've *so* got this.

Fiann's jaw drops when she sees me fresh as a daisy and looking more boss than ever. I smile sweetly at her and walk over to her iPhone. I know what she listens to. She was my best friend since kindergarten—before me and Mom moved out of the Fan.

I pull up one of Euphoria's songs, "Heartbroken," and the synthy-rich violin and bass throbs through Fiann's million-dollar bluetooth speakers into the basement. While Fiann's catching flies with her mouth open, I take Euphoria's hand and pull her into the center of the room.

There's no dance floor in Fiann's basement, but you know what? I don't care. We make our own dance floor.

The song is half-slow, half-fast, because at the last second I might chicken out a bit, at least as far as Euphoria goes.

But as always, she seems to know exactly what I want, what I need. She steps in. "May I have this dance?"

I nod, my mouth suddenly dry.

Euphoria takes me in her arms, and I relax for the first time tonight. This, this is where I belong. It's a crazy thought, but it's been a crazy night. I go with it. We sway and dance while Fiann looks on, Grinch-green with envy.

Maybe a part of her can actually see—or maybe feel—through the Glamoury.

I almost wish she could.

And then the music winds up faster, and Euphoria spins me around. We break apart, still dancing. I'm laughing and she's smiling, that giddy heat between us building, and the whole world seems to just go away, seared in the flames.

There's nothing but me and Euphoria.

My heart swells, the feeling within me both strange and sweet.

Euphoria is lovely, and I'm glad I can see beneath the makeup to see the real her.

But is it the real her, Syl? She's a dark Fae, the enemy.

My stomach clenches with a fear that's rooted down deep into my soul. I push it away. No. I won't be afraid of her. I won't buy into whatever war and bad blood that's caused fair Fae to hate dark Fae and dark Fae to hate fair Fae.

Looking up into Euphoria's eyes, I vow. We will find another way.

A different way. A way that is ours.

New Syl and new Rouen. Together.

Drawn to her, I place a hand on her heart. My own heart is pounding so hard I feel like I'll pass out. *Yeah, that'd be rad, Syl.* She touches my hand with her left; her skin is soft and warm.

A spark jumps between us, like her heart shooting a bolt of energy into mine. It's too much. My heart swells and stretches, my head spinning, giddy. It's too big for me not to share, not to breathe it out in the world, as Glamma used to say. I breathe out, letting my feelings of bliss expand and fill the air around me.

In a burst of movement, Lennon joins us, dragging Maggie, and then Danette and Jazz are dancing with us, jumping up and down in excitement as the music cranks up to a fevered pitch of violins and dark synthwave.

I breathe out again, and the other cheerleaders jump in, and we're surrounded by girls singing and laughing and pogoing like crazy.

The energy in the room is intense, alive and positive.

I'm glad the night's turned around.

The only one that stands apart is Fiann. She glares at me, and then her face glazes over and she steps into the dance with us.

Wait, what...?

I give Euphoria a questioning glance.

She bends, her soft dark hair brushing my cheek, and whispers in my ear, "Look." And I see.

My Fae-sight picks up all the warm, bright pinks and purples of everyone dancing, enjoying themselves, their faces stamped with a blissful expression. No, not blissful.

Euphoric.

I'm... I start in Euphoria's arms. "How? Did you...?"

"No," she whispers simply. "You did."

Me, but how? That power is Euphoria's. How did I just use it? *The spark, Syl. When you touched her...*

Realization hits me like a ton of bricks. "Will they remember?" All bright and pink, purple and euphoric, caught up in my personal magic.

My gramarye. *Mine and Euphoria's.*

"They'll remember we danced and they felt at peace, euphoric." Euphoria's studying me like she's seeing me for the first time. "It'll seem like a dream to them."

Am I weirding her out? Holy cats, I hope not.

I mean...I didn't melt anyone's brain, and after what Fiann did, I consider us even. "Will it stop?"

"It fades," she says. "Naturally."

"Good." I nudge her. "Let's get while the getting's good."

She takes my hand, and we slip from the party. As we leave the basement, Fiann gives me an evil glare. She's locked in the gramarye, but unlike the others, she knows she is.

Crap. Fiann was the only other person to resist Euphoria's gramarye on Homecoming night...the night everything changed. *Was she faking it? Could she have seen us? Through the Glamoury and Grimmacle?*

And then Euphoria's pulling me back onto the street among the thinning crowds—it's late now—and exhaustion hits me. It's like a tidal wave of tired slams into me.

I slump to the sidewalk, Euphoria at my side. "Whoa, I feel a little..."

"Just sit." She's so nice it kind of kills me. "Relax and take some deep breaths." She straightens, looking back at the house. "I'll be right back."

"Wait, where are you going?"

Determination sets her jaw. "To scope out the house like we planned."

"But..."

"I'll just knock on the door and tell Fee I forgot my jacket."

With everyone spelled, Euphoria should be able to case the place pretty fast, but... "You shouldn't go alone."

Euphoria smiles gently, touches my cheek, and then she puts her mentor face on. "Training starts now, and I say you need to take a breather. I'll be right back."

I'm about to argue with her, but bam! She's gone in a flash.

Ughhhh... I hate it when she does that. With no other choice, I chill on the sidewalk for what feels like an eternity, catching my breath and wondering what the heck happened back there.

A gust of wind announces Euphoria's return. I can tell by the look on her face. "Didn't find anything?"

"Well, she has a giant collection of Urban Decay, and under her bed could use a good vacuuming, but otherwise, nope. Nada." She sighs heavily and sits next to me. "You okay?"

"Yeah. What happened back there?" I search her face. "I mean, I took..." One minute I was touching her, feeling her heart pound beneath my fingers. The next, that odd pulse of energy, and then...

Then I was using her power!

Euphoria's blue eyes are all serious. "You tapped into my power, Syl. You tapped in and used it."

"But how...?" I can't even fathom that.

She shakes her head. "I don't know. I've never known a sleeper-princess who fully Awakened."

"Because..." I swallow hard. "Because they were all killed by Agravaine?"

"By Agravaine." She winces a bit. I see the pain in her blue eyes. "I helped him, Syl. I..." She tugs at her hem, her gown pooling around her, hiding her giant boots. "I'm not proud of that."

"Agravaine made you do those things. I know. I understand. It's not your fault. But you're not helping him anymore." I lean in to study her face. "Are you?"

"No, of course not. I'm with you."

With me. Her answer gives me a sudden giddy burst. I feel like I can do anything, as long as she's with me. I take a deep breath and stand. "Well, there's only one way to find out how I did that."

"How's that?"

"I've gotta do it again." I hold out my hand. "Come on, training's begun for the night, and this is a learning moment."

She doesn't miss a beat. "You're impossible."

"But still amazing," I return, the both of us chuckling.

"Okay," she says, standing up. "But first we need to get out of these ball gowns."

I cock an eyebrow at her. "If you think that'll help your cause."

"Oh really?" She straightens to her full five-foot-eight.

I step in so as not to be intimidated and look up into those blue eyes. Energy crackles all around us as we warm to the challenge, and to each other.

"Yeah, really. Tonight I'm going to catch you, Rouen Rivoche."

Two hours later I'm a sweaty mess, and she's kicking my sorry butt around the rooftops of Richmond. I'm so regretting my bold words.

I still can't come close to her, never mind actually catch her.

I take a break on top of Richmond City Hall, leaning over to catch my breath. She alights next to me, all power and grace. If I wasn't super into her, I'd kind of hate her guts.

"Tired already, princess?" she teases.

Okay, I'd hate her a lot.

"I'm not tired. You're tired." I grab for her, but she dances quickly out of my reach.

That smirk on her face is infuriating and intoxicating. As always when we play this game, I want to kill her and I want to kiss her.

I see it in her eyes. She wants the same.

We lock gazes, and the tension between us ramps up so high my body practically *ignites*. There's fire in her eyes, and in the next second both of us are stepping in, silently daring each other to make the first move.

She touches my cheek, leans down so her dark hair brushes my cheek. My heart stops. And then a smirk curves those perfect lips of hers.

"Catch me if you can, sleeper-princess."

And she races to the edge of the building and jumps off.

Gah! How many times am I going to fall for that?

Probably as many times as she pulls it.

I chase after her, and we race across the rooftops, jumping HVACs and dodging flocks of startled pigeons. One gap between buildings is too far, but I jump anyway, trusting to my Awakening body.

My breath goes out, and for a few gut-wrenching seconds, it's just me and the wind and gravity, and then bam! I slam into the fire escape on the other side and catch hold. My hands sting from grabbing the rusty metal railing, and if I were still one hundred-percent normal, I'd have probably knocked myself cold. Ugh, I'm so glad this sleeper-princess gig comes with super-toughness.

I pull myself up in time to see Euphoria.

Without stopping, she races to the edge and swan-dives off the building. She always makes it look so easy.

But tonight I'm going to catch her.

I push my Awakening body, and it responds, giving me the speed and dexterity I need to make up some of the distance. Even when I miss a landing, my body recovers. I stumble only to roll up into a stand and keep running.

Soon, I won't be a sleeper-princess anymore. Soon, I'll be…

What will I be?

Euphoria leaps from the next building, and I lose sight of her. I lengthen my stride as I reach the edge, and push off.

For a second I'm soaring above the entire city, the buildings below me carving up the night with their lights. Then I plummet, letting my body relax.

I land hard, my Docs pounding down on the rooftop the way I've seen her do a million times now. I stick the landing.

I want Euphoria to see, but she doesn't stop. She pelts to the edge of the building and is off like a shot. I follow, pushing myself to keep up, to catch up.

The chase continues until the buildings get shorter and shorter, and soon, we're racing across Shockoe Bottom, the old section of town by the flood wall. I can smell thick fishiness of the canal and the savory greasiness of Bottoms Up Pizza.

Maybe I can talk her into stopping for a slice. *Where is she going anyway?*

We're almost to Rockett's Landing before she stops on a condo building, crouching low, as though she doesn't want to be seen.

I make the final leap to join her, crouching beside her.

Below us, the silhouettes of cranes and other construction vehicles rear their ugly heads against the night sky. A huge section of the street is torn up, asphalt and old cobblestones strewn into a pile next to rows upon rows of shiny new tracks waiting to be laid and glinting in the streetlights.

A trolley construction site.

I know why we're here. Agravaine's plan involves the trolley reconstruction, the winter solstice, and draining the entire student body of Richmond E dry. Though…I still don't know how all those things connect or what he hopes to accomplish.

"Euphoria?"

But she lays a finger to her lips, and I hush.

Minutes tick by, the two of us hunched there like gargoyles looking over the city. And then I hear it…the blat and whine of motorcycles.

Two seconds later, a group of bikers hauls butt into the construction site, peeling out and spitting gravel. The leader stops and pulls off his helmet. Long white hair cascades down around a handsome, angular face.

My heart seizes against my ribs. Agravaine.

Several of the other bikers pull off their helmets. I recognize them as the popular guys in school, the jocks and rich kids. Each one of them looks hollow-eyed and sickly, but they surround Agravaine, looking at him like he's some kind of god. They hang on his every word, all faestruck. My Fae-sight picks up the inky indigo staining their auras.

Faestruck *and* Moribund infected!

Euphoria and I exchange a knowing glance. Even though we've figured out the trolley/winter solstice connection, it doesn't really make sense. The restoration project is unearthing the old iron tracks and extending them.

No dark Fae in his right mind would want to mess with iron. So why is Agravaine so interested?

How does this help him create a dark Fae kingdom on Earth?

We sit there in silence, hoping to find out, but Agravaine and his cronies only ride around the construction site, pulling wheelies and jumping over the rails, fiddly-farting around with their bikes and talking smack.

I roll my eyes. Every reason I don't want to date guys? Yeah, it's right there on display.

At one point, while the other guys are busy racing, Agravaine gets off his bike and walks over to the pile of new tracks. He shrugs off his motorcycle jacket and flexes his shoulders.

I slap my hand over my mouth to stifle my gasp. The Moribund eats up the entire left side of his body, flesh spliced into black circuitry. Indigo lightning wisps off each individual circuit, making it look like there's a storm captured in his skin.

He lays a hand on the rails.

The circuits ripple and undulate like a wave, flowing from his fingertips to the rails. They race into the metal, infecting it, turning every inch into glowing black circuitry.

A chill grips my guts. This is *so* not good.

Euphoria's white as a ghost, watching Agravaine push more and more power into the rails. His hand shakes, and he grits his fangs. The Moribund rippling up the left side of him darkens, zapping with indigo lightning. He gasps in pain as it twists farther up his side, eating up his skin to his collarbone and then up over it.

He's becoming even more machine than man.

Euphoria backs up from the edge of the building and waves me away too. In silence, we race back the way we came. We don't stop until we're safely at home.

We climb into my bedroom window, and I shut it behind us.

My breath comes in gasps like someone's squeezing my lungs. I can't get the image of Agravaine, the Moribund consuming his flesh, out of my mind. "He's... What's happening to him?"

Euphoria paces, biting her bottom lip so hard I'm afraid she'll draw blood. "There are consequences to all Fae power—a price that must be paid—and the Moribund is no different. In fact, it's worse." She clenches her right hand, and even through the glove, I see the Moribund glittering. "The more you use it, the more it corrupts you." Her sapphire-blue eyes meet mine. "Until there's nothing left of you but a soulless machine. A dark *contrivance.*"

Her words strike fear into the very heart of me. My legs tremble, and I feel rooted to the spot. But I make myself move. I go to her and take her hands—both of them, even though she tries to pull her Moribund hand from my grasp.

I don't let her.

I can feel the weirdness of circuitry and flesh beneath my fingers, but I don't flinch. "That won't happen to you," I vow. I see my own fear reflected in her eyes, and I caress the back of her hand. "I won't let it."

She swallows hard, and a vulnerable smile cracks her usual super-cool demeanor. "Thank you, princess." She bows her head. Her dark hair brushes my cheek.

In this moment, I'm hyperaware of everything Rouen—her touch, her sultry scent, the way her body is angled toward mine, her lips parted. Her breath is warm on my cheek, her lips so utterly kissable.

I want... I need...

I can't. New Syl is still a work in progress. Besides, we can't afford to get distracted. We're so close to figuring out Agravaine's master plan.

With effort, I step back, get my head in the game. "He's...infecting the tracks. Why? It's iron, and—ohhhhh..." It hits me like a hammer between the eyes. "Does he have Fae-flaunt?"

Euphoria snaps out of our mutual flirty trance-fest. "I'd know if he did."

"Then he can't cast—"

"—a Grimmacle," we both finish.

"But he's going to try, isn't he?" That's it. I can feel it in my bones. Agravaine's setting up the trolley tracks as a focus for a Grimmacle. It has to be cast on iron, and the tracks are full of it. I still don't see how iron tracks + Grimmacle = dark Fae kingdom on Earth, but there's a more pressing issue… "How is he going to get past the need for Fae-flaunt?"

She shakes her head, pacing. "I don't know. But one thing is for sure, Syl." She turns to me, that serious look in her blue eyes. "We have to find out."

CHAPTER TWENTY-FOUR
ROUEN

Restless
My soul is restless without you
Restless
I can't breathe in your world
And you'd suffocate in mine
- Euphoria, "Restless"

Try as we might, we don't figure out Agravaine's endgame. After his stunt at the trolley site, he goes around to similar sites and infects them too. It drives me wild watching him, night after night, pushing more poison into the city. He doesn't have the Fae-flaunt, so casting a Grimmacle is out, unless he finds another fair Fae power source...

Where is he going to get that kind of power?

Syl, my mind whispers unhelpfully.

I vow with every beat of my heart that's not going to happen. Not on my watch.

But I can't confront him. He'd only Command me to subdue Syl and hand her over to him.

Our best bet is to wait until the winter solstice when he reveals his endgame, when dark Fae power is at its peak and I have the best chance of resisting the Contract that binds me to his will.

Until then, Syl and I wait, and we watch.

Halloween passes, and November comes. It's almost Thanksgiving, Syl and I sneak around, tailing him around the city by night and tracking him and Fiann around school by day.

They keep pushing their dark plot—infecting the trolley sites, infecting the student body.

Did I mention I hate standing by and doing nothing? I do, but until we know Agravaine's endgame—what he plans to do with the trolley tracks and how the infected students figure in—we can't risk exposure. Syl's not fully Awakened yet, and as for me…

The Contract of Bone and Blood hangs over me like a sword ready to fall.

Even Georgina agrees that we're in a holding pattern until we can figure out his endgame and a solid way to stop it.

So we spend our days at school and our nights racing across the city rooftops, training like superheroes. Even though Syl's powers are growing, even though I'm certain, from my experience with the hearthstone, that she can heal the Moribund with her white flame, it's too risky. She doesn't have control, and we can't risk any mistakes. Once someone is infected, it's a whole lot harder to Glamoury them.

So until then…we wait, and we spy on him and Fiann.

The Trolley Restoration Project continues on, laying more and more tracks in a circuit around the city. Mayor Tranh announces that it'll be complete by the winter solstice—what the dark Fae call Midwinter Night—the same night the school is holding the Winter Formal.

And something is happening with the Moribund, something beyond Agravaine infecting the tracks, turning iron and steel into ensorcelled circuitry.

The Moribund in my hand is restless. It burns with a cold-blue light, the same hue as the ley lines, late at night when I'm trying to sleep. I grit my teeth and keep my hand beneath the covers so Syl and her mom don't see the blue burn purling off the circuits in my flesh.

The Moribund, the ley lines… How are they connected?

Everything's coming to a head.

I can feel it in my blood, in my bones. Agravaine's plan is coming full circle. We have to figure it out. Before everything goes to hell in a hand basket.

And speaking of hell…

In the middle of all this, I have to survive a family Thanksgiving with Syl and her mom.

"Rouen… *Rouen!*"

Bloody bones, it's zero-dark-thirty, and someone's shaking my shoulder. Grumbling, I push back my protective blanket cocoon enough to see Syl's mom through my slitted eyes. *Ugh.* Georgina Gentry is not who I want to see first thing in the morning.

It's like waking up to the boogieman cheerfully eating your Cheerios.

I groan and roll over on the couch, tucking my long legs under me, using the blanket as a shield. "Go 'way…"

I'm tired. Last night Syl nearly caught me. She's coming into her own, that girl. She still can't summon the white flame without almost burning my face off, but it's no longer so easy to stay ahead of her and you know…make it look easy.

And then there's our mutual teasing. I tell myself it's to help her believe in herself, but really, I love flirting with her. Her snarky responses, that raised eyebrow, the fire in those storm-grey eyes. Some nights, I think the heat between us is more dangerous than any white flame sleeper-princess power.

I really need to keep my cool around her. Becoming new Rouen is hard work. And for that, I need me a solid eight hours of sleep.

So I give Georgina the seven-yard dark Fae stare.

"That doesn't work on me," she says, looming like a gargoyle.

"No? I'll try again later." I pull the covers back over my head.

She's having none of my cheek. I can just see her standing there, hands on her hips. Her voice rings out with authority. "Rouen Rivoche, you get up off that couch this instant."

Yup. That gets me up. The combination of Mom voice and my true-name is like a bucket of cold water in my face. Somewhere down the hallway, I hear Syl dragging her butt out of bed.

At least I'm not alone in my misery.

"Ugh…" I give Georgina a baleful look. "I thought today was a holiday for you people." I mean, seriously, hasn't she ever heard of sleeping in?

"It is a holiday," she tells me matter-of-factly, "but holidays take preparation."

"Of course they do." A yawn kills the awesome glarefest I'm having with her.

Round one goes to Georgina.

And she knows it. "Get cleaned up, and then the two of you meet me in the kitchen. Go on now. Shoo."

I shoo, wondering why I'm obeying her when all I want is to snuggle back down on the couch. I've never had the kind of mom who'd kick my butt out of bed to spend time with her.

It feels…weirdly good.

But I'm not telling her that. Oh, hells no.

I pad barefoot to the bathroom. Syl and I meet at the door, almost running smack into each other.

"Morning," she says a bit shyly, her red hair charmingly rumpled. She smooths it down in that self-conscious way that makes my heart ache.

"Good morning," I say, trying not to notice the form-fitting cami and short-shorts she's wearing. *You're noticing, Roue.* By the Hunt, she's… Wow. Just wow. I gesture while I try to catch my breath. "You can go first."

She smiles. "We can brush together if you want."

My return smile is shy, so unlike me. "Okay."

She goes into the tiny bathroom, and I squeeze in after her. We're elbow-to-elbow in the cramped space, trying not to bump each other as we reach for our toothbrushes.

She bumps me and grins. "Sorry," and I forgive her instantly.

I like her touch, her nearness.

And as much as it feels odd to be *brushing my teeth* next to a sleeper-princess of the fair Fae, everything about this feels easy and strangely...intimate. We maneuver around each other in the teeny bathroom like it's natural, brushing and then spitting into the sink.

We grin shyly at each other in the mirror, both of us lingering, and I get a glimpse of how new Syl and new Rouen would fit together.

Perfectly.

"You..." I catch myself blushing. *What the hell, Roue?* "You can shower first."

She shakes her head. "You're the guest."

"You just want to escape your mom for ten more minutes," I say, getting my cool back a bit.

She gives a cute little start like I've caught her, then chuckles. "You got me."

"I know all your tricks, princess."

"Not *all* my tricks." The fire is back in those grey eyes, and she leaves me standing there, floored, snickering as she steps out. "Enjoy your shower."

Uhhhh... My cheeks are burning furnace-hot. *She got you good, Roue.* Shaking my head, I strip out of my boyshorts and tank top, then turn the hot water on. Steam fills the small space, and I mentally prep myself for a day of holiday cheer.

Joyful and triumphant. Blurrgggggg...

A moment later, Syl's voice comes muffled through the door. "It's snowing!"

Snowing... A sense of comfort sinks into me at the thought of soft, fluffy snow covering everything, cocooning the world in blankets of white. Like being protected.

I like winter. The cold, the snow, the biting wind that makes you feel alive and hyperalert. Plus, it's a time of power for our people.

Agravaine's out there right now, watching the snow, waiting for Midwinter Night. He'll make his play then, his attempt to create a dark Fae kingdom on Earth and rule, with everyone his Moribund slaves.

It'll all go down between us that night, for good or bad, and then we'll see who wins out. Old Rouen would have dreaded it, but this new Rouen I'm becoming?

She can't wait to confront Agravaine, to break the Contract of Bone and Blood and stop his villainous plan. Once and for all.

Or die trying.

I shampoo my hair vigorously, washing out all the sweat and grime from running around near the trolley tracks. We've checked out ten sites so far, tracking Agravaine's "infection trail" and training Syl as we go. Ten sites, and all of them infected with the Moribund.

He's surrounding the city, but what for?

Unused, the Moribund infecting the students and the trolley tracks will run its course. That's bad news for its living hosts, sure, but even killing off an entire school full of students doesn't get him any closer to creating his dark Fae paradise on Earth. And he doesn't have the power to reach out, tap the Moribund circuitry, and blow the fuses on such a big area. The backlash would kill him outright.

He's waiting. He's going to make a play for Syl.

I clench my right hand into a fist. Over my dead body.

It just might come to that, Roue. I can feel us racing headlong toward some brutal clashing.

With every passing day, I am more and more restless. The hearthstone weakens. I feel it like a second heartbeat, flagging, failing. It's dying in the darkness of UnderHollow, and that's not just me being all emo. It's for real. And Syl... She's growing every day, learning her powers, experimenting, Awakening.

But she's not ready.

Not ready to have the fate of all UnderHollow placed on her shoulders.

She couldn't stand the strain. It would cripple her. Maybe even kill her.

Stop it. None of that's even happened yet, and I'm already stressing about it. *That's a new level of emo, Roue. Even for you.*

I let out some deep breaths as I rinse out my hair and will all my anxiety to go down the drain with the shampoo.

Focus on what you can control.

High school. The band. Beating the pants off Fiann and her cheerleading cronies. As much as I've turned my nose up at this mean-girl nonsense, I really want to teach her a lesson.

Call it the dark Fae in me.

And the band's been practicing hard every day. Under my mentoring—Kylo Ren or not—they've gotten better. Like exponentially better. After a month of practice and me getting them each in line, showing them what they can do as a team, they're pulling together.

Our sound is tight and clean, if I do say so myself.

Syl's on board with the school paper. She and Prudence are going to video us performing and then post it to YouTube. We'll show everyone the Richmond E band doesn't back down—not to cheerleaders or jocks, not to anyone.

Everything's coming to a head.

Agravaine and Fiann. Me and Syl. Old Rouen and new Rouen.

But first I have to survive Thanksgiving.

I finish my shower and get out, dry off, and get dressed.

Syl high-fives me at the door like I'm about to run a gauntlet. "Good luck!"

Yeah, I'll need it.

I drag my butt to the kitchen, drawn by the smells of coffee, toast, and eggs.

Of course it's a trap.

Georgina stands in the small kitchen nook, and the sheer amount of food prep laid out—frozen turkey, boxes of stuffing, potatoes and veggies, cans of cranberry sauce, pie fixings... Holy crap. It *is* a gauntlet.

A cooking gauntlet.

I'm badass. But I'd rather fight a dozen hell-hounds.

I freeze like a deer in the headlights.

Syl's mom hands me a cup of hazelnut-flavored coffee and a bag of red potatoes. "Start with these."

I set the coffee down and look at the taters. Unless I'm going to use them as projectile weapons, I've got no clue.

She chuckles softly, but it's in a good-natured mom way. Grabbing a peeler, she starts the first one. "Peel them like this and then cut them up into small pieces." She slides a pan over from the terrifyingly huge stack she's got going on there. "Put them in the pan when you're done."

I eyeball the potatoes. Me, the princess of the dark Fae and the Winter Court...peeling potatoes?

I cock an eyebrow at her, but she doesn't back down one bit.

"In this house, if you want to eat Thanksgiving dinner, young lady, you have to help prepare it."

Young lady? I nearly choke on that. "You better be a good cook."

She only shakes her head and turns on an old battered radio. Showtunes fill the kitchen, and I have to admit, the music makes the work go by faster. There's something...oddly satisfying about such a simple act as peeling potatoes, and by the time Syl appears in the kitchen, looking cute with her wet red hair, the pan is filled and I'm toeing the floor, looking at Georgina like maybe I want my next assignment.

Maybe.

"Wow," Syl says. "This is a lot of food."

She towels off her hair and comes to help us. Just like in the bathroom, we move around each other, seeming to know what the other will do before she does it. A few times, we misjudge and come up short before colliding, breathless grins on our faces.

It's silly, but it makes my heart pound like no tomorrow.

In between singing showtunes—okay, so I like showtunes—Syl's mom gives us assignments: make the stuffing, stuff the bird, cut the carrots, peel the apples for the pie, roll out the crust...

Soon enough, the turkey's in the oven and the entire kitchen is cocooned in toasty warmness while the snow falls outside. It doesn't even matter that by tomorrow it'll all be melted. We work in unison, in comfortable silence. And then "For Good" from *Wicked* comes on, and Syl starts singing.

She has a lovely voice, untrained but strong and true. I join in, taking the Elphaba part. I mean, hey, if anyone in this relationship is the Wicked Witch, it's me.

With a jolt, I realize the song really is us—a good girl and a bad girl becoming friends, kicking ass, and taking names.

And then…becoming enemies.

A tiny bit of melancholy tinges Syl's voice as we finish.

"That's going to happen to us, isn't it?" she asks softly, looking at me.

"What is?" I look down, though I know exactly what she's talking about. We're breaking all the rules, fair Fae and dark Fae, and eventually, someone's going to make us pay the consequences.

But Georgina's having none of it. "All right." She wipes her hands off on dish towel and hands it to me. "Enough prep for now. Let's take a break, girls. Let's talk strategy."

We wipe our hands and follow her into the living room. She sits on the beat-up love seat and takes out the maps again. We've been filling her in on the trolley sites, and she's updated our map. I suspect Georgina's done some digging on her own too. Lady is resourceful.

She shows us trolley tracks she's already marked and takes a red pen. "Last night, you saw new sites here and here." She draws the two lines on the map.

The circle of trolley tracks is nearly complete.

"Agravaine's surrounding the city with Moribund," I say, voicing my earlier frustration. "But why? He can't power all that without Fae-flaunt and he can't stretch his gramarye that far. He'll need an extraneous power source."

Georgina looks at Syl.

I meet her gaze. "I won't let him take Syl."

"Hey now." Syl eases her hand over mine. "It's okay. He doesn't know that Minnie Maven is you or that I'm Sue Scurry. As long as the Grimmacle holds, we'll be fine."

I look at Georgina. "Is the Grimmacle holding?"

"It will hold," she says confidently. "And this trolley stuff is all prepwork. We need to wait, be patient, until they make their move."

She's right, but I can tell Syl hates it as much as I do.

We sit for a few long minutes in silence, looking at all those red lines. Outside, the snow's tapering off, just tiny fluffy flakes failing to the ground. Soon, it'll be gone.

Will there be another snow before all this goes down?

Georgina stands up, wiping her hands on her jeans. "Come on, you girls can help me baste the turkey."

Glad to have something to do, we head into the kitchen. My mind's whirling. The air of holiday cheer seems broken, but Syl's mom turns the radio up and pours us each a glass of sparkling cider.

"What shall we toast to?" She looks at me, urging me with her gaze. "Rouen?"

I get it. If things go south, this will be her last Thanksgiving with her daughter. Maybe her last Thanksgiving period.

I raise my glass. "To whatever happens. May we face it together."

Syl's smile breaks the clouds of our dark mood. "Whatever happens." She clinks her mom's glass and then mine, her gaze steady on me. "We face it together."

We drink, and then "Popular" comes on the radio. Syl starts singing, and I join in and Syl's mom too, and we sing showtunes and make a Thanksgiving meal that even Gordon Ramsay couldn't diss. The cheery air comes back in full force, and for a second, I'm convinced Syl's grabbed my power again and is using it on us, but that's not it. This is real.

When I look at her, it's real.

No amount of Glamoury could make me feel this way.

And I will protect her to my last breath.

She sees my troubled look and takes my hand. "We can do anything," she says to me. "You and me together. We got this."

I look at our entwined fingers. "New Syl and new Rouen?"

"You betcha." Her smile is radiant.

I can't help smiling back. She's infectious.

The day passes in a flurry of cooking and baking until finally, the fruits of our labor are ready for tasting. Like a well-oiled machine, Syl and I set the table. Georgina plates the food. And by the time we sit at the table, it feels right.

It feels like...

"Family," I say, clinking glasses with each of them.

They're not my blood and they're not perfect, but it's okay.

Families never are.

CHAPTER TWENTY-FIVE
SYL

A sleeper-princess's power
Comes from belief
In herself
- Glamma's Grimm

The day of the big game comes, and before I know what's what, I'm on the sidelines with my DSL, and Prudence is right there next to me with her GoPro. Everyone must be recovered from their post-turkey haze because the stands are packed, and like a million people are cheering and shouting as our team tries to bring home the bacon.

Or touchdowns. Or whatever. I've barely paid attention through the first half.

Now, it's nearly halftime. I have no idea what the score is or how many touchdowns we have versus field goals versus safeties versus who knows what else.

Sportsball just isn't my jam.

I do know that a lot of the bench is playing today because Agravaine's popular-boy posse is too strung out on Moribund to perform worth a dime.

These guys don't get to play very often, so I've been running my butt off on the sidelines, getting some action shots for the yearbook and the newspaper. It's only fair. They're playing their hearts out and all, and the crowds in the stands seem to think they're doing a good job.

Besides, everyone deserves to have a cool pic in the yearbook, right?

Finally the whistle blows, announcing halftime, and I back off the field, climbing into the stands, me and Prudence. She gives me the side-eye and then nudges me.

Prudence knows I'd rather be down in the locker room with Euphoria.

She left a little under an hour before me just to get the band together, warm up, and go over last-minute details. My girl's not leaving anything to chance.

My girl... A blush crawls over my cheeks. The idea that Euphoria could actually belong to anyone, even me, is odd.

I want to go to her, but there's really no time. The band is up first, the cheerleaders second. Euphoria's been super-secretive about their performance, and I don't want to spoil the surprise.

So I wait, bundled up in the stands against the chilly November afternoon. I'm all jitters even though I'm not the one playing in front of a stadium full of people. Euphoria's probably as cool as a cucumber. I guess all those stage performances have prepared her for this.

Something like a high school halftime show should be a breeze.

Still, I know she's worked hard with the band. I know it means a lot to her—maybe even more than she understands. These past weeks, she's played it all stoic and cool, but I see the truth.

She cares about them. About me.

The thought sends shivers of pleasure up my spine.

And yet, a bit of dread coils there too. Eventually, I will fully Awaken, and if we defeat Agravaine, I'll go with Euphoria into the dark Fae realm. UnderHollow, she calls it. I'll go and I'll heal the hearthstone.

I'll pull the white flame out of it and undo the damage my mother did when she poisoned it with her touch. That won't change the fact that the dark Fae have hated my kind since the dawn of time.

Once the hearthstone is healed… I mean, then what?

Is it too much to hope that new Syl and new Rouen can just ride off into the sunset?

There's a blare of fanfare, and Principal Fee walks out into the field and announces the band. There's a smattering of cheers—mostly band parents. My mom's among them, hitting the air horn even though the people around her look annoyed.

I know I'm supposed to think my mom is uncool, but you know what? She's pretty awesome.

All right… Showtime.

The band comes marching out, looking smart in their green-and-gold colors, and I fairly stare at Euphoria. I've only ever seen her dressed in leathers and motorcycle boots, in the starkest black. In her band uniform, she looks…different.

Less severe, almost normal, except, yeah, she's unearthly pretty.

With my Fae-sight, I can see through her Glamoury, both the Minnie Maven disguise and the one she layers over her real self—Euphoria over Rouen. Beneath all that, she's got fangs and pointed ears, bronze skin, raven-dark hair, and luminous eyes, blue ringed in gold. She's stunning and scary.

I mean, she doesn't scare me, but she should.

I think my feelings for her scare me more.

The band plays the usual opening number, the school anthem, as they march onto the field. It's kind of…boring, I have to admit, but at least they're all together.

They march in formation, left-right, left-right, Euphoria leading like a real-life Pied Piper. I check out the stands and see the spectators yawning and shifting. Several break from their seats to get coffee from the food trucks.

A flash of a blonde ponytail catches my eye.

Fiann's waiting in the wings. From here, she looks supremely satisfied, like the band being boring is just what she wants. Of course it is.

Jerk.

I turn back to watch. I just know my girl's got something up her sleeve.

Come on, Euphoria. Come on…

The band comes to a stop, and Euphoria steps out. She lifts her bow to her beat-up violin and begins playing one of Bach's violin concertos. It's beautiful, lilting and sweet, but the crowd decides right then to have none of it.

Boos and jeers echo over the stands. Someone flings a tub of popcorn at the field, and it lands at her feet. Behind her, the band turns their backs. She finishes the last note, letting it linger. It hangs in the air.

I'm on pins and needles. Why doesn't my girl just use her power?

Because it wouldn't be fair, my mind whispers. She wants to beat Fiann fair and square.

That last note is swallowed by the booing and someone shouts, "You suck!"

On cue, Euphoria draws her bow along the strings, the band coming in low beneath that shimmering note. I almost recognize the song, but I can't place it… And then Euphoria raises her bow once more, and when she brings it down, the entire band opens up, slamming into "You Shook Me All Night Long" by AC/DC.

The crowd shuts up, stunned.

The band begins a march, but it's unlike anything I've ever seen. Octavia is slinging her drum around, hitting it back and forth, and Nazira's got a bass guitar instead of her standup bass, and she jams out on it. Chuck rocks out on his keytar, and the horn section stomps and swings their trumpets like some kick-butt jazz band, the brass flashing in the sun.

Euphoria's grinning like a loon over her violin. They're supposed to be playing the National Anthem, but clearly she's gone off book.

Slowly, people in the stands begin swaying and a few stomp their feet, a low thunder beginning from the top of the stands and rolling all the way down.

Following Euphoria's lead, the band rocks out, turning AC/DC's power ballad into "Don't Stop Believing" by Journey. It's a page right out *Glee*, but darn it, it works. This time, Euphoria sings, and her voice carries strong and proud over the stands.

She's not even using her power, but soon enough, the stands are rocking, and everyone's singing along, even some of the cheerleaders.

The recruiters in the stands are on their feet. The parents are on their feet. A million cell phones are raised, and everyone's taking pictures and videos. Prudence is on point, getting every angle while I snap pic after pic of my girl and her band.

Finally, Euphoria steps forward and brings the song home, rocking out hard, madly sawing away at her violin. With the final note sent shimmering into the air, the crowd roars its approval and pours onto the field, singing and clapping.

The band kids go crazy, hugging one another as the stands empty onto the field. They hoist Euphoria—Minnie—onto their shoulders and run her around the field as everyone cheers for them.

I catch Euphoria's eye and wink at her. She winks back.

Fiann's on the field, shouting at her dad. I can hear her even from here. "We've only got fifteen minutes! Get them back in their seats, Daddy!"

But when Principal Fee lifts his mic, nothing comes out.

Prudence sidles up to me, holding a ginormous power cord. "Whoops. I must've accidentally unplugged something with my 'troll hips.'"

I cover my mouth to stifle the giggles.

Fee does his best, enlisting the coaches to help him get people back into the stands. But by the time everyone's finally in their seats, the cheerleaders have like five minutes to do their routine.

No one really watches. Everyone's too busy uploading their band videos and talking about my girl's amazing performance.

I tip an imaginary hat to Fiann, grinning when she turns a hilarious shade of purple, and then I head down to meet Euphoria at the locker room. I get there first and high-five the band as they pass—Octavia, then Nazira, then Chuck, and the jazz players.

"Awesome job, guys!"

Euphoria comes after them, her tall frame filling up the hallway. She's backlit, and all I can see is her silhouette. She steps into the locker room like she's stepping out of light and shadow. For a moment, a chill rakes my spine—that part of me that is fair Fae knee-jerking in fear at the dark Fae-ness of her. *Danger, danger, danger.*

I squelch it down, and fast.

Laughing, she grabs me, shattering the weirdness, and swings me around. I smile back, slinging my DSL over my shoulder so it doesn't bump her.

When she sets me on my feet, we're so close I can feel her breath on my cheek. My stomach lurches like it's full of butterflies doing the cha-cha. I look at her lips then meet her gaze.

Shivers run down my spine, and not from the chill November air.

Just barely, I keep from doing something stupid. Something awesome but stupid. "Minnie Maven"—I hold out an invisible mic—"you've just won the halftime show, what are you going to do?"

"Go to Disney World?" she asks skeptically, playing along.

"Don't think this gets you off the hook," I lean in to tell her softly. "Your triumph will be short-lived when I catch you tonight."

"Ha," she says, her eyes brightening with challenge. "You haven't caught me yet."

Something in her tone invites me to flirt more. I go for it before I lose my nerve. "Maybe you should make it worth my while?" I step back into her warmth against the bite of the air.

"Oh?" She raises an eyebrow and put her arms around me. She lowers her voice so only I can hear. "And what does my sleeper-princess want as a reward for catching me?"

My sleeper-princess. The way she says those words, sultry smooth, undoes me. "I…"

She continues to tease. "Bragging rights?"

I'm tempted to say yes, to get myself off this hook I've cheerfully jumped on, but my teenage hormones won't let me. "For starters."

"Hmmm…" She pretends to think, but really, she's practically reading my mind. "At the party, you said you wanted to kiss m—Minnie." Her smile is a little breathless, and a flush crawls over her cheeks. "How about that?"

"Not quite." My heart is racing. *Be bold, Syl. Be brave.* "If—when I catch you, *you* have to kiss *me*."

The challenge hangs between us like a glass ornament. One wrong word or move and it'll shatter.

But Euphoria only smiles gently, blushing prettily. "Deal. But I warn you, I don't just play hard to get. I *am* hard to get."

"I wouldn't have it any other way."

I come close that night, and the night after that and the night after that and the night… Ugh. You get the picture.

November passes, and December comes, bringing chill winds and Christmas decorations. After Euphoria's triumph at the game, Fiann leaves off with her teasing and plotting. She and Agravaine go back to their old faithful routine. The Trolley Restoration Project plods on.

All around school, posters for the Winter Formal go up.

I've never been one for dances, but when Euphoria asks me, I am as giddy as any schoolgirl. I tell myself she has a dual reason to ask me—business and because she likes me.

But if she likes me, then why does she try so hard to keep away from me?

One of these nights, I'll catch her and find out.

In the meantime, we get ready for the Winter Formal, where it'll all happen. The major showdown.

I'm aware how cliché it is, how much like a *Buffy* episode, but there's a reason *Buffy* rang true to a lot of people—because they got it right.

On Midwinter Night, Agravaine will have no choice but to put all his cards on the table.

The formal falls on December 21st, the winter solstice, the shortest day and longest night, the night of peak power for the dark Fae. Until then, we're just playing a waiting game.

Meanwhile, I launch myself into my training, pushing my Awakening body harder and faster each night. And each night, I try like hell to summon the white flame, but it dies as fast as it comes. I can't sustain the heat. A part of me is afraid.

The part of me that clings to old Syl, safe Syl.

But December plods on, cold and Christmassy.

Until one night, just two days before the Winter Formal, I chase Euphoria to the viaduct at the edge of Shockoe Bottom and toward the outskirts of town. There are still a few trolley sites we have to check out.

Tonight, she heads straight for the train. I can hear it now, the nine p.m. from Harrisburg, blaring out in the darkness...

Flashes of that night assault me—the train, the storm of violet lightning, the sounds of tearing metal, the crash... In a breath, I'm shaking in my Docs. I jerk to a stop at the edge of a condo building. I'm old Syl all over again.

She looks back as though she knows I'm freaking out. The train horn blares out again, but Euphoria only gives me that tough-love nod, urging me onward.

Ugh. She's always saying how Awakening is painful. Painful, terrifying, wonderful.

This is definitely in the painful and terrifying camp.

"What's wrong?" she calls from two rooftops down. "Scared you can't catch me, princess?"

I swear, I'm going to kill her.

I could quit right here. Walk away. Chase her another night.

It's my choice, and she lets me make it.

My guts are churning as I stand at the edge of the building, watching as she takes off, leaping with ease to the next rooftop.

Beyond…the viaduct, the train tracks. And the train is coming.

The horn is blaring, my skin is crawling. I feel like I'm going to hurl.

She leaps to the lower overpass, looking back over her shoulder. Her face is grim, set in that tough-love expression I've come to know so well, but her eyes are soft.

She believes in me.

I believe in her, if not myself.

I leap off the building and onto the overpass. Dodging cars on the interstate is the easiest thing. Just Glamoury myself so they don't see. Those few people who are partway Awake might see a flash of shadow like a ghost, but they won't see Syl Skye.

And then I'm on the edge, the viaduct below me, the train racing toward us like a huge mechanical dragon belching smoke. Euphoria doesn't wait. She jumps to the train, making it look easy as she lands on top of the engine car. It flashes by me, every car rattling on the tracks as it thunders past.

Its horn is blaring, deafening, the stink of diesel choking me, threatening to catapult me back to that night. Lightning on the tracks, the tracks heaving… My mouth is dry and my hands are clammy. The images have their way with me, and I—

Forget that. I stop the images. Full stop. *I'm in control here. Not my memories. I'm not that girl anymore.*

I leap.

For a moment, I'm in free fall, and then I slam into the side of the train, scrabbling for a rail, an oh-crap handle—anything. My hand catches a side rail, and my legs swing back and forth, the tracks rushing past me at breakneck speed.

Euphoria leans over the side, her eyes glowing. "Climb up. You can make it."

She could offer me a hand. I see she wants to do it, but it has to be me. I can't rely on her all the time, and I know it. We have to be equals.

I want to be her equal.

Equally strong, equally capable, equally everything.

My arms are screaming, but I'm stubborn. Inch by inch, I pull myself up and roll over on the top of the train, gasping.

She dashes off, and I'm up and off like a shot after her.

This time, I'll catch her.

Our feet pound the train cars as we leap over and among them, the massive metal beast rolling and lurching. Below us, a trolley site comes into view. We should check it out. Euphoria motions to me, a satisfied smirk on her face. We've agreed that, during our chases, the trolleys sites are "ghouls"—the dark Fae word for "home base." If she reaches it before me, the chase is over. She'll have won.

I pour on a burst of speed. Nearly there, nearly there...and as the train turns the corner, I throw myself into a flying tackle.

My body connects with hers. *Yes!* And we tumble down, down, down. She rolls midair, cushioning me with her body as we land crushingly hard in the middle of the construction site—an impact that would have broken mortal bones.

We roll to a stop, me on top of her, our legs tangled.

"Caught you," I say triumphantly.

"You did." Her eyes darken into deep sapphire blue.

"Take it off," I say and then blush. *Who are you and what have you done with shy Syl Skye?*

"Take what off?" Her voice is husky, sultry, and my heart races against my ribs.

"Your Glamoury. All of it. I want to see you when you..." *When you kiss me,* I want to say, but I can't. My pounding heart makes the words jam in my throat.

Euphoria nods, but I can tell she's uneasy, maybe a little afraid.

Does she think I'll reject her?

Slowly, the Glamoury shimmers, and the real Rouen Rivoche lies before me— Well, *beneath* me. All bronze skin and smirky-smile and blue eyes ringed in glowing gold. She smiles around her fangs. I reach out and touch the tip of her pointed ear. She shudders.

Her body is warm against mine.

"Shall I kiss you now?" she whispers, and her voice cracks a bit. She's trembling. And I'm trembling with her.

"Yes," I breathe the word across her lips.

My stomach is in knots. I can imagine the softness of her lips, the taste of her. I am shaking to my core. After this, everything will change between us.

Our own personal Awakening. I can't wait to see what we will become.

New Syl, new Rouen.

She leans down, her lips almost brushing mine—

And that's when I hear the growling of the hell-hounds.

CHAPTER TWENTY-SIX
ROUEN

We're in deep
You and me
Never gonna be free
Till the sky falls down
Around us
- Euphoria, "Deep"

Syl is warm and soft, lying on top of me. Her eyes, that impossible shade of storm-grey look into mine. Suddenly, I am shaking. Me, Rouen Rivoche, dark Fae princess. Shaking in the hands of a mortal girl.

But Syl is not mortal.

She is the last sleeper-princess of the fair Fae. I am her guardian.

Drawn to each other, we both lean in. Her breath is warm and sweet, her bottom lip trembling. I want to bite it and kiss the sting away.

My heart is pounding. Our lips barely brush—

And then, guttural growls rumble through the construction site.

Seriously? I mean, can I have, like, a moment *here?*

The growling gets louder, fiercer, rattling the piles of trolley tracks. Fear spikes down my spine—not for me, but for Syl.

I know with sudden certainty. The Wild Hunt is back. And they're here for her.

And now I can hear their great padded feet bringing them closer, from out of the darkness.

Her body tenses on top of mine. Our gazes meet, and I flick mine to the right and then to the left. She gets my unspoken command. Slowly, we look in opposite directions. Her heart is hammering against mine. All my desire for her turns into fight response, my adrenaline kicking in full force as I see them.

Hulking and wolflike, their hackles raised in spiky tufts of black. Their furnacing green eyes glow, their jaws slavering. *Cú sluagh.* Agravaine's hell-hounds. "Five on my side," I whisper.

Predators, they are wary, confused by the way we lie still. They stalk in for the kill with mincing steps, their Moribund-infected paws scraping the ground.

"Four over here," Syl whispers. She meets my gaze once more.

"Wait for my signal."

She nods. She's a bundle of nervous energy against me. I shift, trying to ignore the rising warmth between us. *Focus, Rouen.* But I can't help my body's response. I'm excited by the prospect of a fight, by her closeness, by her.

The hell-hounds creep closer, crouching low, their bellies touching the ground, tongues lolling and dripping with venom-green saliva. Their growls echo across the construction site. They creep closer, closer…

My heart rate kicks up a notch. *Come on in.*

They grow bolder. *Come on…*

The lead hound inches closer. I feel the blast of hot breath on my face.

Sucker.

In the bat of an eyelash, I'm up like a shot, shoving Syl behind me. Snarls erupt all around us. The lead hell-hound pounces first.

He doesn't count on my speed. *Silly puppy.*

His jaws snatch empty air.

A second later, all the others dogpile in on him, snarling and growling just like in the cartoons. Until they realize...we're not there.

I back me and Syl up toward one of those huge yellow bulldozers. The hounds won't fall for that again.

If only I had my violin. I could take out all nine hell-hounds. I flex my Moribund hand, and realization hits me. If I use my power—any power at all—Agravaine will know. The Moribund will alert him. Is that why he sent the *cú sluagh*? To flush us out?

My skin goes clammy-cold.

If I use my lightning gramarye... If Syl uses her white flame...

He'll know.

She's behind me, ready for a fight.

"Strength and speed only," I toss back over my shoulder. "No powers. None of that white flame stuff."

Her face falls. "Why not?"

Of course she wants to try using her powers again. That's my girl. But still...

"Agravaine." I want to give her more of an explanation, but the hell-hounds are not the most patient of monsters.

The lead *cú sluagh* leaps, all fangs and frothing green saliva. I meet it full-force, slamming it back to the earth. The ground shakes, and it lurches back up, swaying. It comes in again.

I dodge its snapping teeth and grab a handful of its wiry scruff.

With a grunt, I toss it into the rails, sending them rolling away with sharp *pinks* and *plops* and *pangs*.

It rights itself, eyes furnacing a hideous green. It lifts its head, and the howl that bays from its throat sends shivers down my spine. The other hell-hounds surround us, all low growls and snapping teeth.

This is so not good.

Another howl, and they attack.

One snaps for my face and I dodge, grinning madly. *That's it. Come on!*

A second hell-hound lashes out for my legs, and I kick it in the face, staying in front of Syl. She's looking for an opening, nervous but ready to test out her Awakening body.

A third attacks, and I sidestep, but the fourth and fifth crash into me, using their combined weight to being me down. My head smacks the ground. I see stars for a second.

Not my finest moment.

Teeth flash before my face, and I grab the beast's muzzle, squeezing hard. Green saliva drips on my collar, searing it, the sizzling of leather sending my adrenaline into overdrive. I kick the hell-hound off over my head and then grapple with the other on my chest.

Its weight feels like a Mack truck crushing me, its ozone-tainted breath blasting in my face.

And then Syl is there, hauling it off, red hair flying. She's strong and capable. She tosses the dog into the side of the bulldozer, upending the massive construction vehicle. The *cú sluagh* scrabbles to get clear, but the bulldozer pitches and tilts and finally crashes down on it, crushing it.

Black circuitry scatters from beneath the fallen truck.

"That's one for me," Syl calls, a challenge in her voice. I'm seriously impressed, but I can't let her know that.

"One?" I tease. "That's a start not a score, princess." I lunge, striking the nearest *cú sluagh* square in the throat. It explodes into black circuitry. I step away as the Moribund jerks and jiggers on the ground.

"Now we're even," I tell her.

She sticks out her tongue at me and then dodges a hell-hound's bite.

We're in the thick of it now.

And you need to step up your game, Rouen, before that sleeper-princess shows you up. At least making a game of it keeps me from freaking out worrying about her.

The nearest *cú sluagh* snaps at me and tears my sleeve.

"You...ruined my jacket." I grab it around the neck, avoiding the snapping jaws. Heaving hard, I slam it into the huge bulldozer wheels, and it shatters into a million fragments. Black circuits flip and flick on the ground.

It's creepy, the entire site crawling with Moribund. But no worries. Without a host, they'll die soon enough.

I glance back over my shoulder. "Syl!"

We've gotten separated. They're backing her up to the tracks, her face white but set in determined lines. She's not used to this. I've been training her to be fast and quick, to be accurate but not to fight.

My bad. Seriously my bad. I'm kicking myself as I scramble to my feet and race toward her. "Syl!"

One of the hell-hounds lunges for her, its teeth spearing in for her throat. She ducks and punches it, screaming. Her fist goes right through it, and the beast crumbles into flying circuits around her.

Bloody bones. On second thought, I'm glad she's on my side.

Another one leaps at her, and she slams it to the ground so hard the very earth shakes. Her hand crushes it, and the black circuits race up her arm. She slaps them away, and then she's fighting hard, spinning this way around one hell-hound, whirling that way. Punching, kicking. She steps on one hound and flips forward, kicking another in the teeth.

Dark glittering circuits go flying.

And then there's one behind her.

She doesn't see it.

"Syl!" I throw my body out and flying tackle the hell-hound. We go down. I pound at the thing until circuits fly.

"What is that—like six to three?" Syl says, smirking through labored breaths. "You're kind of sucking, E."

I get up, brushing myself off. "Go ahead, princess, get cocky."

As soon as I say it, I wish I hadn't.

The black circuits on the ground begin to twitter and flick back and forth, agitated. One by one, they race together, piling up, teeming over one another like bugs, leaping, jiggering.

The pile grows and grows, tilting and revolving, becoming… something. Something massive, even more dark and sinister.

Licks of green lightning burn from the circuits as they come together, fusing into the biggest, baddest hell-hound I have ever seen. The circuits form a carapace, armoring the massive beast from head to paws, and a tangle of tentacles bursts from its shoulders, lashing out.

As Syl would say, *Crappity crap crap crap.*

Warily, I step back, pushing Syl behind me. She places a small hand on my back, and I feel her warmth through my leathers.

"What is it?"

"A barghest," I whisper. *Agravaine's really stepping up his game,* I think sourly. *The jerk.* Commanding the *cú sluagh* to Megazord into a bigger, badder beast is next-level mastery of the Hunt.

The barghest rises up, howling, huge and black and teeming with circuits that crackle with green lighting. It opens its jaws, the green glow brightening.

So not good.

"Syl…look out!"

It snaps its massive jaws and green lightning lashes from its teeth. We dive, Syl going to one side, me the other. The lightning strikes a backhoe, tearing a shrieking scar right down the center. The vehicle collapses, split in two, smoking.

I crouch, giving what I hope is an encouraging nod at Syl.

My girl's scared but brave and determined.

We got this. I think.

The barghest wheels about. I expect it to be clumsy, unwieldy, but no such luck. Thing's damn fast. It snaps at me, and I barely duck its gnashing teeth. Its tentacles lash out, and I dodge, feeling the wind as they blow past me, smashing the construction site to smithereens.

The circuits light up, all electric green, and the stench of ozone hits the air. *Not again.*

"Look out!"

I try to get to Syl, but a swipe of the beast's paw sends me crashing back into the rails. I shove them away, gritting my teeth.

All right, buddy-boy. Now I'm mad.

"Hold him for me," I growl. "No one makes me look bad."

Then again…

As I rush the thing, its tentacles lash out again. I dodge one, two, three…

The fourth, fifth, and sixth hit me like mule-kicks, wrapping me up tighter than a Christmas present. They squeeze and lift me. Baring my fangs, I grab hold of them, snapping them away, but more and more come, wrapping tight around my midsection, lashing my arms, my legs, my vision cut with inky blackness.

Below, I see Syl rushing in, determined to help me.

No, Syl…don't.

She raises her left hand.

The barghest laughs deep in its throat as it turns toward her. She's so small beneath it.

"Syl!" I fight like the nastiest woman scorned and wedge my torso and arms from its grip. I grab its head, wrenching the beast off balance. Its tentacles miss Syl as she dives…closer. *Why is she getting closer?*

Gah! Girl is going to be the death of me.

The barghest smashes its free tentacles down on her, but she's no longer there, her Awakening strength and speed keeping her alive.

And then, lucky me, the barghest remembers it has me in its grip. It lifts me high, crushing me. My world becomes pain and black tentacles, green eyes glowing, snarls like burbling laughter. Grey spots dance in front of my eyes.

Somewhere dimly, Syl is screaming my name.

I can't speak, so I can't sing, can't use my gramarye. *No choice*, I think grimly. I lift my right hand, calling on my Moribund. Circuit Fae gramarye lights up the night. Violet electricity pours off my fist, and the Moribund splices deeper into my hand. But the barghest only wraps me tighter, trying to smother my violet lightning with its green. The ozone stench stings my nostrils, tentacle after tentacle wrapping me tighter, tighter, crushing me...

"Rouen!" Syl's cry seems torn from her throat.

No, Syl, please.

Sheets of pure white flame leap from her hand, flaring, washing the entire construction site in brightness. Like daylight striking.

The barghest howls and then whines, its body bathed in the light. It lashes out, trying to use me to bludgeon her. I brace my feet against its hide and haul hard on it again. It staggers off balance.

Syl flicks her wrist, and flares of white fire strike it, washing over the black of the barghest, tiny white flames licking at the darkling circuits, consuming them one by one.

The Moribund beast howls and turns in on itself, revolving inside its skin in a desperate attempt to get away, but Syl pours on the heat, both hands lit up in blinding-hot white. It hurts my eyes. The Moribund in my hand cries out.

The tentacles loosen and fall away. I stagger to the ground and shield my eyes as the flames light up the beast, a brilliant funeral pyre consuming the Moribund, leaving nothing behind—no smoke, no circuitry, nothing.

The barghest is gone, and only Syl remains—beautiful, haloed in power. Beautiful and terrible.

A beacon of white flame. The sleeper-princess of the Summer Court Awakening.

But as soon as it comes, the power is gone. The flames die down, and Syl collapses. I dive to catch her, easing her to the ground. Her hands are smoking. I avoid touching them.

Every instinct screams for me to get away from her, from that white flame.

Look what she did to the barghest. She could do that to you. How'd you like to have only one hand, Rouen?

But I don't listen. I cradle her in my arms, my heart pounding in fear for her. The output of power... Agravaine will have seen.

Staggering, I lift her up. I have to get her out of here.

She reaches out to touch my cheek. "Are you all right? Roue…?"

"Yes," I say, pressing my lips to her temple. "I'm fine, princess."

"Good," she says, and then passes out in my arms.

An hour later, I'm taking her shoes off and laying her gently on her bed. Finally, she stirs as I pull the blankets up.

Her grey eyes open and pin me where I sit. "I messed up, didn't I?"

Gingerly, I touch my sore ribs. "That thing almost killed me." I hate admitting it, but I hate seeing her doubt herself more. And she did save my life, the little minx.

She smiles tiredly. "How many points was that last one worth?"

"All the points." I brush the red hair from her face. "Rest now."

"But, Roue… What about school tomorrow?" Her face is grim. She knows the truth. She lit up like a white beacon. There's no way Agravaine would have missed that.

Still, I try to stay positive. For her. "He knows we didn't run away, but he doesn't know we're still at school." I lean over and turn her vanity mirror. "See? The Grimmacle's holding up. Nothing to worry about."

Even as I say that, I know it's not true.

We still don't know Agravaine's endgame. I suspect he wants Syl, the last sleeper-princess. But we still have to wait until he makes a move. And if he's drawing us out, we have no choice.

Her friends, my people, my entire world—everything is riding on us.

We have to stop him.

She knows it too. I see it in her eyes.

"So we go to school tomorrow," she says, reaching out to touch my hand. "Business as usual."

I squeeze her hand. "Business as usual."

She smiles tiredly, and her eyes close in exhaustion. Business is how this all began. The business of freeing myself from Agravaine's Contract, of saving the hearthstone and my people. But now...

I fix a stray lock of red hair and lean down. Gently, I brush my lips across her temple. It's not business anymore.

I will do anything to protect her.

I clench my Moribund hand, wincing as the newly grown circuitry pulls at my flesh.

I only hope that will be enough.

CHAPTER TWENTY-SEVEN
SYL

Control will always
Be the hardest
For the most powerful
- Glamma's Grimm

After last night's crazy white-flame powerfest, I'm shocked to make it through first and second periods, all the way to lunch without so much as a side-eye from Fiann or Agravaine. Euphoria and I even pass them in the hallway on the way to our lockers.

Nothing.

Not even a second glance.

I breathe a sigh of relief. Lucky for us, the Grimmacle is holding. Even despite my stunt last night.

I lost control.

I slam my locker overly hard, and Euphoria gives me a side-long glance. She's worried about me. I mean, I did collapse like a total dork. When I think of the way she carried me all the way back home, to my room, to my bed, her arms around me... The butterflies in my stomach start twerking like they're trying out for *Dancing with the Stars.*

She wants to ask me if I'm okay. I can see it in her eyes. But she doesn't. Truth is, she asked me like a dozen times on our way into school, and now that it's clear that Fiann and Agravaine aren't on to us…things should go back to normal, right?

I smile at her, trying to look convincing, and heave my backpack onto my shoulder.

She squeezes my hand for a sec. "Let's go."

We make our way through students pushing and rushing to get to their after-lunch classes.

I lost control last night. But what could I do? Euphoria was in danger. That thing nearly killed her. I couldn't just stand by. I had to do something. The sight of her being crushed in the barghest's tentacles… It messed me up a little.

The idea of losing her…

A shudder goes through me, and I shake it off as we walk down the hall, dodging other kids. People get out of the way for Euphoria without even knowing it's her. As for me, I make myself small against the crowd. *Just me, Susan Scurry. Nothing to see here.*

My body is still sore from pushing so much power.

So much… It built up and built up in my chest until I couldn't breathe, until I thought I'd explode. I hadn't felt it since Homecoming night. That white-flame power inside me, building, burning, blazing in my heart. It was too much.

I had to release it. Besides, Euphoria needed me.

And I killed the barghest, didn't I?

It's got nothing to do with the fact that I'm super into her.

Nope. Nothing at all, I tell myself as we walk into geometry class.

Mr Barney is already at the board, writing equations and formulas. I swear, the guy has to be at least fifty, and he's got more energy than me. "Good afternoon, class." He turns, trusty laser pointer ready to go. His aura is all bright and bushy-tailed.

Ugh. Another class of boring lectures—all angles and formulas and fractals.

I'd rather be back in bio class dissecting frogs, even though it makes Euphoria squeamish. I glance at her as she sits. I think it's hella cute that my girl is a badass dark Fae but gets squeamish about the idea of frog guts.

Don't worry, E. I'll protect you from frog guts and barghests. All in a day's work for your friendly neighborhood sleeper-princess.

Now if only I could fully Awaken already.

I sigh heavily as I slump in my seat, the rest of the class coming in all noisy and tired. Seriously, the class after lunch is always the worst. Just when you think you can relax a bit—bam!—it's right back to work, work, work.

Fiann passes by me, flipping her high ponytail over her shoulder. She looks back and winks at me, a gleam in her eye.

It's that gleam that's been there since Euphoria and I started this whole Minnie Maven/Susan Scurry thing. The gleam that makes me wonder... *Can she see the real me?*

Euphoria said Fiann could see through layer one of her Glamoury, but a Grimmacle is so much stronger. Not even the Wakeful can see through a Grimmacle.

But ever since last night, I've had a bad feeling in my gut. Revealing myself like that. Euphoria said I lit up like a white beacon. Ugh. Looking at Fiann, I'm sure she knows. I can feel it in my bones.

Relax, Syl. If she knows, why hasn't she done anything about it?

She sits behind me, and I feel her gaze drilling into my back. She leans in and her voice is soft, sinister. "Have a nice night?"

Panic prickles down my spine. Next to me, Euphoria shifts in her seat. She heard it too, but she's playing it cool. I should too. I turn around and look Fiann right in the face. I hope my shrug is casual enough. "Just some studying. You?"

She leans back and throws Mikhail Despres a heated look across the room. Gross. "Oh yeah... I had a great night." She's all making goo-goo eyes at him.

Relax, Syl. She's just showing off. She just wants someone to brag to. "Yeah, uh, that's great." *So gross.* "Really great." *Like pukefest.* I relax and then give Euphoria a sneaky thumbs-up under my book.

We're still secret. Whew! I slump back into my chair as Mr Barney begins his lecture, laser pointer whipping around like one of those will-o-the-wisps in the pages of Glamma's Grimm.

Yeah, we dodged that bullet. Like *The Matrix.*

Just call me Neo. Whoosh. See all the bullets flying past me?

I'm feeling pretty smug about putting one over on Fiann and Agravaine when the devil himself comes to the door. I see him through the tiny slice of window, Agravaine in all his uppity masculine beauty. His white hair covers half his face. *Dude, that style went out with the 80s, and it is so not coming back.* He taps the glass to get Fiann's attention. She raises her hand.

"Mr Barney?" Her tone gets all wheedling. "Can I please go to the bathroom?"

Ol' Barn fixes Fiann with an eagle's stare, but then waves her out the door. Fiann flounces out without a backward glance at Mikhail. It's not like a mortal dude can compete with a dark Fae stud, anyway. I mean, if you're into that thing.

I think about it for a hot second. Nope. Not in the slightest.

The door closes behind Fiann with a soft *whump.*

Euphoria slides me a note. *Now's our chance!*

She's right. I nod, and my heart is hammering like thunder as I slide from my seat. I made sure to have Lennon give Susan Scurry an IEP. She's—I'm—allowed to just leave class to walk up and down the halls when I'm feeling "tense" or "anxious." It feels weird taking advantage of the system, but we have to find out what they're up to.

Are they finally making their move?

We previously decided, Euphoria and me, that I'd be the one to follow the Villainous Duo because Agravaine doesn't have any power over me—not the way he does over Euphoria. If he finds her out, he could control her, make her do his bidding.

And that would be sooooo not good.

But me? I'm immune to his woojy-woo.

Barney gives me the nod. I slip out the door into the empty hallway with one last look back at Euphoria. Suddenly, dread hits me hard. Like I'm never going to see her again.

Quit it. You're being ridiculous.

I force myself to turn away. *Head in the game, Syl.*

I slink down the hall, my Docs quiet on the tiles—quiet as a cat on little fog feet, Glamma would say. I stick close to the wall, hugging the lockers. Ahead of me, a door opens into the hallway. I catch a flash of blonde ponytail, and I duck into an empty bio room, my heart kicking like a jackrabbit.

Crap!

I hear footsteps approaching, two sets—one a pair of clack-clack heels and the other, stompy boots. I look around for anywhere to hide. The supply closet hangs open. Ugh, could it get any more lame and obvious?

The door to the room opens, and I practically dive for the closet. Lame, it is.

I barely get the supply closet door closed before they saunter into the room. Fiann takes up position near the black-tiled sinks and plays with one of the stray dissecting kits.

Agravaine leans on the counter, his presence huge and looming, seeming to suck all the air out of the room.

My heart is still going a mile a minute. *Seriously?* It's so loud I'm sure they can hear it. I swallow hard and try to calm my breathing. A broom handle pokes me in the back, but I stay still. It would really suck to knock something over and get found out.

Then again… *So what?* I tell myself. If I get caught, I'll just make something up. Agravaine will try his woojy power on me, and that'll be that. They can't see through the Grimmacle.

Last night proved that—and today.

If they didn't jump me earlier, then they don't know it's really me. Right?

I peer through a crack in the door.

Agravaine seems agitated. He paces a bit, running a hand through his white hair. "Are you through playing your silly games now?" His deep, rumbling voice oozes like slime through the room.

I'm not sure what-all he means, but Fiann's having none of it. She tosses her ponytail. "Whatever. Just lay out the plans already and tell me what you want me to do."

With a disdainful snort, Agravaine takes out a folded-up piece of paper and opens it on the lab table. He pushes the dissecting kits aside and spreads it out. I'm practically looking over his shoulder at a map of the City of Richmond crisscrossed with red and blue lines.

Agravaine traces the red lines with his index finger. "The trolley tracks are nearly done. On the night of the Winter Formal, they'll surround the whole city."

Okay, we knew that, but what are the blue lines? They seem to travel *inside* the red ones, making a smaller circle…

Fiann shrugs one shoulder like she could not care less. "We've been over this, Ag. Bored already. Let's just get to it."

"We wait," he rumbles, absently tracing the blue lines, his shark-black eyes intent. "Until the winter solstice, the perfect time." He seems to be almost talking to himself.

Creepy.

Fiann puts a hand on her hip and pushes. "Why does it have to be the same night as the Formal? Can't you cast your spell or whatever on another night?"

He gives her the stink eye. "My…spell? Is that what you would call it?"

"Isn't it? I mean, you're basically creating a dark Fae paradise on Earth. With magic."

My breath freezes in my throat. We were right. That *is* what they're up to. *Holy—*

Fiann tosses her head as though they're talking about the latest fashions. Like creating a dark Fae realm on Earth is nothing more serious than getting a new wardrobe at Bloomingdale's. "But seriously, can't it be some other night?"

Agravaine looks like he wants to smack her one. "No. It cannot be some other night. I need the power of the solstice, and I need all of the infected present."

Okay, the students and the solstice. And a night of peak dark Fae power.

But how does solstice + Moribund students + trolley tracks = dark Fae paradise on Earth?

I run it over in my mind again: infected students, the Moribund, the solstice, the tracks, the night when the dark Fae are most powerful, a night when the... Dread jolts through me.

When the ley lines are the most powerful.

Euphoria told me all about the ley lines and how they power the gates and Snickleways to UnderHollow, how they tie the entire dark Fae realm to Earth. If they were shattered...

A cold sweat breaks out across my skin. The trolley tracks in red. They're made of iron and Moribund. Those blue lines he's tracing...

The ley lines.

This is so not good.

He's using the iron and the Moribund in the trolley tracks to corral the ley lines, to shape them into a circle. I'm no expert on dark Fae magic, but I know from watching a gazillion movies that when bad guys start making a circle of power around the city it's a bad thing.

A very, very not good, nasty-bad thing indeed.

I take a shaky breath. I've gotta get back to Euphoria and tell her, but... I can't exactly move right now.

Fiann sniffs. "I still don't know how you're going to push that kind of power through all the infected students and out into the city?" She tips a skeptical look his way.

Agravaine's look is shark-sly. "That's for me to worry about."

"Fine." She tosses her blonde ponytail. "As long as you make me the dark Fae queen."

Whaaaaaaaat? I nearly choke. Fiann? The dark Fae queen?

Fat chance.

If anyone's going to be the dark Fae queen, it's Euphoria.

"You'll get your reward, no matter what happens," he rumbles, and I hear the warning in his voice even though she clearly doesn't. Ugh. What an idiot. "Now there's just one more thing we need to do."

"And what is that?" She's sure snotty to him, especially for a girl who wants to be crowned his queen.

"Just a few loose ends." He turns around and meets my gaze dead-on through the crack in the door. "Isn't that right, Syl?"

Oh, crap. Crappity crap crap crap.

For a hot second, I think about running. I could *maybe* get away, from them, from the school, but Euphoria's still here, and Agravaine's smart. If he knows about me, he knows about her.

He might already have some sicko plan to hurt her.

Old Syl might've run, but new Syl? No way, buster.

I push the door open and step out of the closet. Maybe I can get him to monologue. I mean, all villains like to monologue, right? "How'd you know it was me?"

Agravaine holds out his right hand, and his flesh teems with black Moribund circuits, twisting and turning, forming a fist then knotted, outstretched fingers. "I'm tied to every circuit of the Moribund. The instant you destroyed my barghest, I felt your power. Your white-flame power."

Yay, monologue!

He stalks toward me now. "I think it's time to break that little Grimmacle of yours. It's been fun and all, watching you and Rouen these past weeks." He closes his hand into an anvil-like fist. "But the fun is over."

I back up toward the door, still baiting him. "Why? Why wait to break the Grimmacle?"

His eyes get even blacker, his aura all dark menace and Moribund. The sickness of it makes me feel nauseous.

He smiles, a shark closing in on its prey. "Because, Syl, I wanted you at the height of your power."

I take another step back. "Then you should totally wait, because I'm not really there yet. Like...maybe in a few weeks? I'll let you know. We'll do lunch." My hand fumbles on the doorknob. Even new Syl might be okay with running at this point.

The better part of valor, and all that.

"I don't think so." He's smug, the jerk—a tomcat who got the cream. "Besides, I can't wait to see the backlash of the Grimmacle on the one who cast it."

The one who— Mom! "What...what's it going to do to her?"

His smile is jagged and wide, something the Cheshire Cat would envy. "Only kill her."

Rage sweeps through me. My punch takes him by surprise, and I knock him back about three paces. His smile turns vicious, and he's on me.

Fiann screams as he grabs me, lifting me up and slamming me down on the lab table. My breath goes out in a whoosh. Moribund circuits crawl off his hand, winding around my throat, choking me. More bands of it jigger and twist, binding my wrists and ankles to the table, fusing into the tiles where they touch.

I fight, struggling to Awaken the power inside me—*Come on, white flame!*—but the Moribund smothers it.

If ever I needed to Awaken, now's the time. *Please, let me Awaken.*

The pressure is so huge and hot and powerful in my chest, I think I will explode. *Mom. They're going after Mom.* I breathe out, trying to release the power, to burn away the circuitry holding me down, but his fist slams into my cheek.

Pain rockets through my skull.

"I could have the Moribund infect you," he says, his shark-black eyes drilling into mine. "But I think I'll settle for settling for something a little more…bloody."

He holds out his hand. "Get me that scalpel."

"Wh-wh-wh…" Fiann is breathless, white and trembling, but she hands it to him.

Seriously, girl?

He touches the scalpel to my leg, tracing the shape of the iron shard beneath the skin. "Here's the source of the Grimmacle. The focus. Very smart…" His lips pull back from white fangs. "Hold still. I wouldn't want to hit an artery."

"Screw you." I don't hold still.

I struggle and fight, and then I feel the kiss of the knife slicing into my skin. I reach for my power, but it's smothered beneath the Moribund.

Euphoria… Euphoria!

But there is only pain and then blackness.

CHAPTER TWENTY-EIGHT
ROUEN

Inside-out
The heartbreak in me
Whispers to the heartbreak in you
Inside-out, we'll never be the same
- "Inside-Out," Euphoria

I'm in class, waiting on pins and needles for Syl to come back, to text me, chat me, call me—anything. It's been twenty minutes now, and I'm starting to worry. Yeah, despite my cool exterior, dark Fae can worry. I scribble at my notebook, trying to make it look like I'm doing the geometry formula Mr Barney is teaching. But really, I may as well be drawing hearts and *Rouen & Syl 4-Eva* on my notebook.

I can't concentrate.

You never should have let her go alone, Rouen.

I sigh heavily. I'm just about on the 4 part of *4-Eva—bloody bones, Roue, you're really drawing that?—*when I feel it.

The Grimmacle shatters.

Like a tether between me and Syl—like that silver cord that keeps your spirit from floating off into the afterlife—it snaps. Suddenly, I'm adrift. I'm alone. I'm...

Euphoria.

Hells and hue. My Minnie Maven disguise melts away like butter in the hot sun, leaving me—Euphoria, glam-Goth star—sitting there in the middle of a sophomore geometry class.

One by one, heads start to turn, whispers rippling, growing louder by the second. I guess it's not every day that a Goth star materializes in a geometry class around here.

But that's the least of my worries. My heart stops. *Syl.*

I stand up, my chair scraping back obscenely loud, and as the whispers turn to shouts and pointing, I dash from the room. The door slams behind me, the safety glass shattering. I hear Mr Barney above the din, trying to calm the class, to get them back into their seats.

Good. That chaos will keep him too busy to follow me, or worse, call it in to administration.

Not like I'd care. Syl's in danger.

Syl! I summon my fairy wind, and in a chill burst, it swirls around me, giving me a burst of speed. Did they catch her? Did they hurt her? A thousand scenarios go through my mind— Agravaine torturing her, taking her away, using her blood to power his Grimmacle, to destroy the hearthstone, killing her—

No. Don't think like that, Roue. Just find her.

I fly classroom to classroom, looking in, throwing open doors, disrupting lectures. I barely hear the angry shouts of teachers, the shocked cries of students. My blood is rushing in my ears, making it hard to breathe. I turn the corner and see the door to a bio lab jammed open. A few stray Moribund circuits flip and flop on the floor, beckoning me like jigging fingers.

I crush them beneath my boots, nearly taking the door off the hinges as I plow through into the lab. And stop dead in my tracks.

A bloody scalpel lies on the floor, crimson dripping onto white tiles. And lying there on the matte-black lab table— The light goes out of my heart.

Syl. My sweet Summer princess...

She lies unconscious, her face a sickly ashy color. Her right leg is a mess of blood, her pant leg torn and stained bloody, the skin beneath... My heart goes out, and anger and rage fill me, sweeping me away for a moment while everything turns red.

Agravaine did this.

And then as swiftly as the anger comes, it goes, leaving me with only my concern for my girl. I dash to her side and cradle her head. She's still breathing, still alive but in pain.

I pick her up, cradling her to my chest, willing her body to Awaken, to heal her. We have to get out of here before Agravaine comes back, before anyone finds out.

Agravaine...

I clench my Moribund hand into a fist. All the evils he's committed. Binding me to that Contract, Commanding me, and now this. Injury to insult. This is the bloodiest evil, and the worst.

I swear, I will make you pay, Agravaine. If it's the last thing I do.

Syl moans and stirs in my arms. "Roue..." Damn, now I know she's really hurt. She rarely ever calls me by my real name.

"It's okay. I've got you." I move carefully through the door and into the hallway. Glamma's Grimmacle might be broken, but my personal gramarye still works just fine.

I throw up a don't-see-me Glamoury, and we slip past all the kids milling in the hall, the teachers trying to get them back into their classrooms.

"Rouen..."

The massive amount of noise masks Syl's voice, but I hear her loud and clear. "Don't speak. I'll get you home. Just—"

"No. Rouen..." She opens her eyes, and I see the effort of will it takes her. "They're after my mom." Her voice shakes, and tears stream from her eyes. It breaks my heart, and another, fiercer feeling pounds there too.

Georgina Gentry and I were enemies once. But now... Now... I mean, bloody bones, I sang show tunes, I made *turkey* with the woman.

I nod. "I'll take you." *And ancestors help Agravaine if he's done anything to Georgina.*

I race out of the school and into the parking lot. The Grimmacle on my bike broke too, my sleek Harley sitting where Minnie Maven's crappy Vespa earlier. But even with a Harley, I'd have to obey traffic laws. I glance up at the tops of the school buildings.

It's over a mile to Syl's apartment, but it'll be easier to run.

I summon my fairy wind, but Syl grabs my arm. "Let me down, Rouen."

"Syl, I don't think—"

"She's my *mom*," she says, and that hits me with the force of a brick between the eyes.

I get it. I let her down and watch her warily.

She limps a bit like a bird with a broken wing. Blood spatters the asphalt. She bites her lip, straightens. My girl's brow furrows. She's in pain and trying to control powers she's never used before.

And then I see the flesh beginning to knit together. It's slow, but at least it's happening.

By the time my fairy wind is fully summoned, swirling around me like a personal vortex, she can at least stand upright. It'll take her days to fully heal, but we don't have days.

We might not even have minutes.

"Are you ready?"

I don't care that at this point we're standing on the school grounds, in Miss Jardin's rose garden to be exact. She sees me and Syl through the window—dead-nuts *sees us*, like through the Glamoury—but she only nods.

Note to self: investigate Miss Jardin. Later.

For now, I swirl my fairy wind around me and Syl, and take us to the rooftops. Syl keeps pace with me, and we rush over the rooftops toward Jackson Ward, toward her apartment complex. We don't speak. We just push ourselves, harder, faster. In the places where the buildings are spread out, we hit the streets, ducking and zipping along the sidewalks.

I keep stealing glances at her. I can't help myself.

Her face is white in worry, and I just want to scoop her up and hold her and tell her everything's going to be okay.

But I can't. And it might not be.

Genevieve Iseult Eldredge

Finally, finally, we reach the tenement. We dash into the back alley. I know what Syl's thinking. If the Grimmacle on us shattered, then it shattered on the apartment. And Agravaine has a twenty-minute head start on us.

We rush up the fire escape, making all kinds of noise—*pang, pang, pang, pang* on the metal steps. So much for a surprise attack. But then again, I don't want to ambush Agravaine. I want to meet him head-on, full force, with all my fury. I'm not thinking straight. Instead I'm all dark Fae woman scorned.

We didn't leave Syl's window open, so I grab it, cranking it up with my strength. The pane cracks, and I shove the bits of glass aside with my gloved hand.

"I'll go first." I can't risk her. Not if Agravaine is still here.

I swing my leg over the sill and fold my tall frame through the window.

Her room is destroyed. Her bed overturned, the stuffing ripped out of the pillows, her vanity mirror smashed, her closet torn into, makeup scattered.

Syl climbs into the room, and then she's off like a shot.

"Mom!"

"Syl, no!"

I catch up to her in the living room, my heart practically seizing in my chest. If Agravaine is still lying in wait, we are so screwed.

Syl's stopped in the door to the living room. Her pale hand grips the doorjamb so hard the wood creaks and groans. Beyond her, the living room is a mess. The battered couch is torn in half, one side limp and bleeding stuffing, the other crumpled by the wall. Huge, long claw marks scar the doorways, the walls. The lamps are overturned, and broken glass peppers everything like deadly glitter.

Georgina's gun lies on the floor. And a few feet away.

No...

Georgina lies, pale and unconscious.

The sound that tears from Syl's throat shatters something inside me, and I'm right there beside her, the two of us cradling her mom,

Syl feeling for a pulse. "She's alive." She runs to the landline. Thank the ancestors it still works.

She talks, her voice eerie calm, to the first responders as I look over her mom.

Georgina Gentry, my old enemy. Ever since we made the promise to stick together over Thanksgiving turkey, she's been friendly to me. She invited me in, cooked for me, did my laundry, nagged me about homework.

She's been like...like a mom to me.

I grit my fangs and clench my fists. I look at the bruises on her face. She fought back. "Good girl." I brush her hair away from her forehead.

She's breathing, but it's shallow.

The backlash of the Grimmacle breaking along with Agravaine's attack has taken a brutal toll on her, body and mind and spirit.

Syl comes back to me, tears streaming down her face. My Fae hearing picks up sirens wailing in the distance.

I reach for Syl's hand. "She'll be all right. She's a fighter, Syl."

Syl plops down, hands in her red hair, destroyed. "This is my fault."

My heart sinks. "No. It wasn't your fault." With nothing else to do but wait, I rise up and pace. "This wasn't you. It was Agravaine."

"He knew it was us. He's known for a while." Syl gets up with me. She kicks the shredded couch, and it slams into the wall. "So stupid! I knew it. We should have been more careful. I was an idiot."

"No, Syl, you're—"

"It's my *fault*! It's my fault I dragged her into this. It's my fault I *became* this. I can't even fully Awaken, Rouen. When my own mother needed me, I couldn't..." Her words choke off into a sob, and she flumps down heavily. "I'm stuck. Stuck being old Syl."

I know exactly how she feels, like she'll never escape her past, but I give her a minute—a minute I spend grabbing Georgina's gun and stowing it away—and then I go to her, wrapping her in my arms, my heart aching for her, for Georgina, for me. Because the truth of the matter is, I'd started to like Georgie. She *was* like a mom to me, and over these past weeks, we'd almost become a family.

When I think of no more holidays, no more early morning wakeup calls, no more stern Mom looks…it breaks my heart. I hold Syl tight and stroke her back until the EMTs come.

They're careful and kind but efficient. They load Georgina onto a stretcher, and Syl goes with her. I want to go, too, but only blood relatives get to ride in the ambulance. The police arrive, and they're nice enough to give me a ride. I answer whatever questions the officer puts to me. No, I don't know what happened; no, no one is after us; no, there hasn't been anyone suspicious lurking around.

It takes all my self-control to grit my teeth and get through the questioning.

There's no mortal law that's going to make Agravaine pay. I'll make him pay. For Syl. And for me.

We get to the hospital. I find Syl, and then it's all a waiting game. They take Georgina in, and we pace the spotless, blinding-white floor in a spotless, blinding-white room, bludgeoned by intercom calls and depressing machine dings. We pace and then I sit with Syl and keep an arm across her shoulders. Not even delicious, bad-for-us vending machine food and coffee can cheer her or me up.

It's hours and hours. They move Georgina into surgery for broken ribs and a ruptured spleen. It sounds bad. Georgie's no sleeper-princess anymore. She's just a normal human woman. Syl's as white as a sheet.

Finally, finally, the doc comes out. We lie and say we're both Georgina's daughters. It doesn't feel like a lie to me. It feels like I'd knock this doctor into next week if she tried to keep me out of that hospital room.

And then we're standing at Georgina's bedside. She's breathing evenly now; at least the machine that breathes for her does. Syl lets out a heartbreaking sob and rushes to her mom. She holds Georgina's hand and stares bleakly.

And everything inside me splinters into sharp edges and anger. I can't just sit here.

I want blood and vengeance. I'm a dark Fae. That is our way. I lay a hand on Syl's shoulder and say softly, "Stay here, okay?"

She looks up, those grey eyes swimming with tears. "Where are you going?"

"To track down Agravaine."

Syl sees the grim look on my face. She stands up and faces me. "You shouldn't. That's reckless."

"Syl—"

"No. I nearly lost my mom today. I could still…" She chokes on the rest, and more tears slip down her face. She throws her arms around me. "I don't want to lose you too."

The gentle impact of her body, her arms against mine, her sobs…it all threatens to undo me. A part of me just wants to hold her, to comfort her.

But that's not realistic. Agravaine is out there. He and Fiann are plotting. They're coming for us. I have to get to them first.

"I'll just go look. I won't engage. I can't stand here and see her and do nothing."

Syl sniffles and looks up. "You promise? No heroics?"

"I promise." It's the second lie I've told tonight, and I hate telling it—especially to her. But I know myself. When I see Agravaine, I might break that promise. No one hurts my girl and the people she loves.

No one.

CHAPTER TWENTY-NINE
SYL

Once, there were dozens of sleeper-princesses
Mortal girls with unAwakened fair Fae blood—
Until the dark Fae began killing them
For their own foul means
- Glamma's Grimm

It's late by the time the nurses finally kick me out of Mom's hospital room. They've let me stay long past visiting hours, and in truth, they'd let me stay longer. But the charge nurse gives it to me straight—the best thing for Mom right now is total quiet and rest. My mind understands, but my heart just wants me to stay with her, holding her hand, wishing she'd heal, wishing she'd wake up.

But I'm not a kid anymore. I shouldn't believe in wishes.

So I slog my butt out of the ICU, down to Emergency, and out into the parking lot, where I turn on my crappy TracFone. Nothing. No message from Euphoria yet.

Worry shoots through me. It's late. Past midnight. Where could she be? And what's our plan? I didn't really think past getting Mom here and keeping her safe. The apartment's a mess, it's definitely not safe, but where else can we go?

I shoot a text out to Euphoria. *U ok?*

Minutes pass. Nothing…nothing… Then my phone vibrates. *Sure.*

Sure? What the heck does that mean? I text back. *Where r u?*

Her text comes back immediately, like it crossed mine in cyberspace. *Meet me at apartment.*

My fingers fly over the phone. *Kk.*

A moment later, her answer comes. *C u soon.*

A shiver spikes my spine. *That doesn't sound like Euphoria.* She relentlessly spells out *everything* in text. My tired brain goes into anxiety overdrive. What if it's not her? What if it's someone else using her phone to get me to the apartment? What if it's Fiann, or worse, Agravaine?

Chills flash over my skin, leaving me a sweaty, clammy mess. *Think, Syl. Think!*

Okay. The chances of it being Agravaine are slim. Euphoria said she wasn't going to engage. She wouldn't have risked getting close to him, getting Commanded, and if she *had* been Commanded, she'd have written everything out in text, like she always does.

Unless…

Unless she's trying to send me a warning.

More chills leave me shivering, my teeth chattering. *They're at the apartment waiting for me.* This is so not good.

But what choice do I have? I only have Euphoria. I won't lose her to Agravaine. I'll figure out a way to save her. Maybe if I can get her alone… Maybe we can find a way to break the Command. She resisted it before.

I'll help her.

All right. No more stalling.

I take a deep breath and let it out, trying my hardest to summon a fairy wind like I've seen Euphoria do a gazillion times. She makes it look so easy. A gentle breeze kicks up, a tiny dervish that picks up a gum wrapper and a crushed pack of cigarettes. It winds and whirls and then dies.

Crap.

I have to admit to myself that I'm exhausted. I look at myself in the reflection of the glass-front doors of the ED. I look like death warmed over. My red hair a frizzy mess, dark circles under my eyes. I've seen better days.

Okay, so...running it is.

I blow out a breath. And run.

Running feels good, even though my leg still throbs. The pain drives my adrenaline up a notch. My limbs are fatigued and burning, but it feels good to push myself, to push my exhaustion to the back of my mind. I am still Awakening, I tell myself. I can't summon even half the power Euphoria has.

I'm not new Syl. Not yet. Not by a long shot. But I have to try.

I push myself, racing over the rooftops and down dark and narrow alleys. The hospital is about six miles from home, and I use the last of my energy getting there.

I'm a ninja, a shadow, my speed hiding me from passersby. Oh, they might look twice, but then they convince themselves I'm just a figment of their imaginations. *Nothing to see here. Just your friendly neighborhood sleeper-princess.*

I'm lucky. I don't run across any of the Wakeful. I can cast a basic personal Glamoury, but I don't have Euphoria's ability to keep it going. Not yet. Will I ever fully Awaken?

You have bigger problems right now Syl. Yeah, like my girlfriend being kidnapped by a complete jackwagon. My...girlfriend? Is Euphoria...? Are we...?

Holy cats, Syl, focus!

I'm home. I come to a stop in the alleyway. A sharp winter wind blows, scattering the trash there. A tuxedo cat, sleek with glowing white paws and belly, lurks in the alleyway, swaggering about like she owns the place. She sees me and promptly pauses to lick herself. Her whiskers twitch, those glowing eyes drilling into me. And then she bolts off with a loud *mroworrr.*

Glamma always said tuxedos were the smartest cats, witches' familiars and all that. *Glamma, I wish you were here.* I shake off sudden chills and put my foot on the fire escape.

This time, I'm wary. I creep up the metal stairs, the soft *pangs* beneath my boots freaking me out a little. I look one more time at my phone. Euphoria's last message glares up at me accusingly.

It's not her, Syl.

I jam the phone into my pocket and wipe my sweaty hands on my torn school uniform pants. My window is open. My room is still a mess, everything everywhere. I slip inside, trying not to step on broken glass and porcelain from an antique doll Glamma gave me. Like the tuxedo cat, the doll's eyes seem to follow me.

You're really freaking out, Syl. I shake off the creeps and steel myself. My door is open, and a thin light from the living room shines in across my walls, making jagged shadows.

Every pool of darkness a hiding place for bogeymen.

Fear crawls over my skin, but I shove it down deep. If Agravaine is here, he'll pay for what he did to my mom. I square my shoulders.

I walk through the living room, my Docs crunch, crunch, crunching on the broken glass. The shadows are warped and weird here, the overturned lamp casting light weirdly along the wall while keeping the main sections of the room in darkness.

In a dark corner, the shadows undulate.

My breath goes out as a tall figure steps from the darkness. "Euphoria!"

I want to run to her, but my instincts scream a warning. She's standing there with her head down, her raven-dark hair like a curtain across her face.

Still, I take a step, drawn to her. "Euphoria."

"Syl." It sounds like she's choking my name through a throat full of razorblades.

I try to catch her eye. A shiver slides up my spine. Her bronze skin is all ashy, and when my Fae-sight kicks in, I see a warped indigo shadow suffocating her aura.

No. Oh no, no, no, no...

"Euphoria...?"

Blood trickles from her nose.

"Syl...run..."

The light goes out of my heart. "Euphoria!" I run to her, taking her hands. I don't know what I mean to do, how I mean to save her…

"Run!" She pushes me, but I am back at her side in an instant.

"I won't! I want to help you."

"You can't." Her voice is desperate now, and she lifts her head so she can look me in the eye. I see that same wildness in her as that night when Agravaine first Commanded her to attack me. Her sapphire-blue eyes darken to indigo, and her whole body trembles. Even now, she's fighting the Command. "Go, princess. Please, you don't have much ti—"

"Syl."

The deep baritone shakes the room to its very bones. Agravaine steps out of the darkness. Fiann cowers behind him.

"So good of you to join us." He holds up Euphoria's cell phone and then drops it. His boot comes down on it, and the crush and crunch of it under his heel is stupidly loud in the small space of my apartment. Fiann has that crazy Joker smile on her face, like she might scream in triumph or puke her guts out or both. Either way, seems like this is more than she bargained for.

I still want to punch her in the face. "What do you want?"

"To kill you, of course." He says it mildly, but the shark's gleam in his eyes tells me he's hungered for this moment. "The last sleeper-princess. The last one who might have the power to stop me."

"Will," I tell him. "I *will* stop you."

"I don't think so." His smile curves, showing all his sharp teeth. "Once you're dead, I'll have Rouen here."

I snort in disgust. "And what? You'll force her to marry you? She already told me that's not how it works, not even among you dark Fae." I cock an eyebrow at him. "Besides, no means no, dude."

A muscle ticks in his jaw. "Oh, she told you, did she?"

The jealousy is super-evident in his voice, and that gives me an idea. I played him before. Maybe I can play him again, get him to monologue. Like a good little villain. "She told me lots of things."

"Really?" He draws the word out, his tone all sugar and syrup, but his smile is pure rat poison.

"We know about your plan with the Moribund and the tracks and your stupid circle of power." I play it cool, but really my brain's working double-time. *Keep him talking.* "It'll never work. You don't have the juice to power it."

"Well, you've certainly got it all figured out, don't you?" He doesn't seem fazed at all, which is so not good. I keep my best sarcastic look stamped to my face, but I'm starting to sweat.

Agravaine slings an arm across Euphoria's shoulders, and I have sudden fantasies of breaking that arm, stomping the Moribund circuits out like the embers of a dying fire. "Well, Syl, truth is...I do have the 'juice' to power it." He brushes Euphoria's hair from her shoulder. "Don't I, Rouen?"

My guts drop out. *It's not me he's after.* We got it all wrong. This whole time, we've been protecting *me*...

"Syl..." Euphoria looks at me, misery swimming in her blue eyes. I see her disgust, the way she jerks, wanting to push his arm off. She can't. Not with him Commanding her. "Please. Please run."

But I don't. I can't just leave her. Whatever Agravaine's got planned for her, it's not good. Does he want to somehow use her to power his Grimmacle? But how? I poke at him. "Whatever stupid plan you have, it's not going to work."

He laughs, all deep in his chest like I've just told the funniest joke in the world.

Ha, ha. Jerk. God, I want to punch his lights out.

"Oh, it'll work." His eyes gleam black, hungry. "Rouen here is connected to the hearthstone, and when I use the Moribund within her, when I blow those circuits, they'll consume her...and when she dies, she'll take the hearthstone with her. And I'll consume all that power. I'll have all the juice I need."

My heart seizes, leaving me breathless. That's it. His endgame. And it's so much worse than anything I'd ever imagined. Any smart-aleck comment I might have dies on my lips.

He crosses the room in three strides, looming over me. "Sadly, all of that will kill poor Rouen, but you won't have to worry about that, Syl."

I don't back down. "Why is that?"

"You'll already be dead."

His threat makes my guts clench in dread, but he doesn't make a move. Instead, he looks back over his shoulder. *Creep.* I hear the Command in his voice as he looks to Rouen. "Kill her. Meet me at the high school after you've taken care of her."

Euphoria jerks toward me and then stops herself. She fights. The trickle of blood becomes a gush from her nose.

A vein pops out in Agravaine's temple. "I said kill her."

She jerks forward. "Syl...run."

I can't. I don't want to. I want to help.

"Run." She steps in, taking Agravaine's place looming over me. She lowers her voice. "I need you *to run.*"

To run... Her hint slams into me. To run, to get away from Agravaine. Of course!

I run.

Instantly, I feel her behind me, chasing me. I haul butt through the front door and down the old beaten steps. I hear her coming after me, her boots pounding warped wood. I jump the last landing. She's right behind me.

Crap, crap, crap.... But if I can get her away from Agravaine, we might have a chance.

We speed out onto the street. It's empty except for a homeless man sleeping in the gutter. She's after me, and my heart is pounding wildly. The game has changed. I'm not chasing her anymore. She's chasing me.

To hurt me, to kill me.

At Agravaine's Command.

My anger spurs me on. I run despite the tears in my eyes. I have to lead her away from him. I have to save her.

We race into the city, and at the nearest tall building, I leap up. Yeah, in a single bound. But I don't waste time happy-dancing. She's faster and she's coming. I hear her strides lengthen, and I know what's coming next.

She leaps...

The impact of her body crushes my breath out. We land hard and roll on the very tip-top of the skyscraper, wrestling, her trying to hold me down, me fighting to get free. We roll to the edge. *Oh crap.*

Crappity crap crap crap.

We tilt off the side, and of course, now all my efforts actually work. At the worst possible second, I fight free—only to plummet off the edge.

She grabs me. I grab back.

My heart is rabbiting in my chest, and we're holding on, Euphoria dangling me over twenty-nine stories. If she drops me, I'm going straight down, down, down to my death.

But the Command to kill me is strong. Her grip loosens. Blood rushes down her face. I see her eyes, confused, conflicted. She fights with everything she has.

It's killing her.

Her or me.

Below, the few cars on the streets streak and flash by like the matchbox cars I always played with at Glamma's house.

I squeeze her hand. I can't let her do this. "Rouen...I...." I can't let her sacrifice herself for me. Not again.

This time I'll save myself. "Rouen, it's okay."

It strikes her visibly, like a note from her violin.

"Syl..." For a moment, she's herself again—my Euphoria, concern lighting her blue eyes.

I let go.

"Syl!"

Her scream chases me as I plummet, down, down, down...

CHAPTER THIRTY
ROUEN

What is life without you?
Part of my heart, part of my soul
Can't breathe, can't live
Without you. Without you
- "Without You," Euphoria

I run. From the city, from the building, from my last image of Syl...falling...down, down, down... My heart clenches and aches, and tears blur my vision. *Bloody bones, Syl!*

She did it to save me.

And I am totally, one thousand-percent unworthy.

And now she's gone.

Tears streak down my face. I've gone totally emo dark Fae, and I can't find the strength to care.

I will my fairy wind to take me as far as fast as I can, Agravaine's Command lacing my body with obedience. I should stop fighting it. I should let it take me fully. That way, I won't have to think, won't have to feel.

Who'd have thought? Who'd have thought I could ever fall for a sleeper-princess?

Syl...

My heart aches as though an iron spike has been thrust through it. Looking down at myself, I'm surprised I don't see blood staining my black tank top. *Syl...* Guilt and grief threaten to overwhelm me. I want to sink down in the middle of the street and sob, but no.

I am the princess of the dark Fae and the Winter Court. I will see this out.

No matter how bleak, no matter how grim my chances.

Even now, the Moribund circuits in my hand stretch and tug; they pull against my flesh, making me ache inside and out.

How much of that ache is physical and how much is because I love Syl? It hits me with the force of a Mack truck. I love her. *But you couldn't save her,* an accusing part of me whispers. *Not this time.*

Regret weighs on me, dragging me down. I will regret that for the rest of my life—whatever is left of it. Oh, I'll fight to the end and all, but without her, I don't care much for my own survival. My people. I must think of them now. A true princess puts her people first.

Agravaine's plan for me is grim. He'll call upon the Moribund inside me. He'll blow those circuits wide and consume my gramarye, my power, my very life-force, not to mention the hearthstone bound to me. All to power the Grimmacle, to create his dark Fae realm on Earth—with him installed as king. He never had any intention of saving the hearthstone, saving my people.

He was just using us all. To remake himself as king.

The Moribund in my hand stabs agony into me. There's nothing I can do. I must obey his Command. Even now, it burns in my brain. *"Meet me at the high school after you've taken care of her."*

Taken care of her... The words twist and wrench in my guts.

The last sleeper-princess is dead, and with her, the hopes for the hearthstone. The hopes to save my people. Agravaine never wanted to save them. It was always about him, about amassing power. Now the hearthstone will die in the darkness, the ley lines will collapse, taking the gates and Snickleways with them, and the vaults of UnderHollow, once held up by our dark Fae magic, will crumble. Everything will collapse and fall to ruin as the darkness closes over it. My people, my homeland, the Winter Court, all lost to the Harrowing.

Father, I have failed you.

No, he failed when he and the arch-Eld set Agravaine above you, when they put their faith in him as the leader and allowed him to Contract you into slavery. You can do nothing, that soothing part of me whispers. It would be so easy to accept it.

But I can't. Syl would have kept fighting, and so will I.

I hope, at least, to take Agravaine out with me.

I leap off the last tall building. My boots hit the sidewalk, and I'm off running, the Command returning me to Agravaine like I'm some kind of drone he's calling back. Still, it's a relief to let my body go for a moment. The pain and agony of resisting flows out of me. I wipe dried blood from my nose. I won't give him the satisfaction of seeing me bleed.

I dash down the streets and then up the long drive to the school and into the parking lot. It's empty, the lights a dim, gross yellow.

Beneath them, near Miss Jardin's runaway rose garden, Fiann lounges against the wall. She's got one leg kicked over the other, her designer jeans and designer shoes, her babydoll top so perfect, not a hair out of place. "Euphoria." She practically purrs my name, looking down her nose at me in a gesture I think she thinks is… sexy?

Ugh, really?

I'm emo, but nowhere near emo enough to self-destruct by falling to Fiann's charms.

"You look tired, E." She examines her fingernails, all coy.

On my one to ten barf-o-meter, she's a twelve. I cringe inwardly, thinking that's exactly something Syl would say, and my anger flares. Fiann thinks that just because Syl is gone, I'll suddenly be into her? She's well and truly cracked. I glare at her, and she skips the rest of her grade-school seduction attempts.

She jerks her thumb at the gym. "He's waiting for you."

"Of course he is."

Stiff-backed, I walk to the back door of the gym and wrench it open. Screws patter to the ground as I step across the threshold into the gloom. Shadows and silhouettes hunch and soar all around me. The Winter Formal committee has already been here, doing their decorating. The ice castle and fake icicle banners glimmer and gleam in the dimness. A slight breeze blows the curtains, and a spatter of blue glitter breaks from above and falls.

Syl... I take a deep breath and steel myself. Syl would be brave. So must I. An image comes of the Euphoria posters in her room.

If I was half the hero she thought I was...

But without her, I have no hope of that. I am only old Rouen, come to pay the final price for all my crimes.

Agravaine stands on the stage, where fake ice columns soar up to a fake ice balcony made of crepe paper and foam. It's surreal, seeing his dark form against something so bright. His back is to me, and I see the slight straightening of his spine.

He speaks without turning. "Join me."

He doesn't Command me, so I stand there, defiant, in the middle of the gym floor.

Agravaine turns and glares. *"Join me, Rouen."*

The Command means I have no choice, but whatever. I want to get close to him anyway. I move to the stage, propelled by the Contract that binds me. The Moribund in my hand responds to his proximity, rushing with heat and cold at the same time. It flashes through me like a fever, like knives through my skin, my heart.

But I won't show him any weakness. I can't afford to.

Despite myself, tears well in my eyes. I try to blink them back.

He takes one look at my face. "It's done, then?"

I can only nod. My tears shame me at first, and then hot defiance boils through my blood. *To the hells with that.* I straighten. Let him see my tears flowing. I'm not ashamed of loving Syl, emo or not. I don't care.

He shakes his head and lays a hand on my shoulder like he's going to console me.

You know that last straw that broke the camel's back?

Yeah, that was it.

I snap my hip as I punch, throwing my bodyweight behind it. The satisfying crunch of his nose echoes across the gym, and I follow up with a quick one-two to his ribs. He doubles over in shock and pain, and I grab him by the hair, slamming him into the floor.

"Olé!" I yell like a bullfighter.

He hits the stage hard with an "oof!" and I swear the wood groans and buckles.

Chump.

I laugh wildly, showing my fangs, and grab him by the back of his jacket.

But Agravaine is fast. He whips around, throwing me off and doing a quick kippup to his feet. He barrels in at me. He's strong, but I'm fast. I avoid most of his blows, dodging and ducking, kicking him in the chest and once more across the cheek.

The satisfying *smack, crack* is sweet, sweet music.

He staggers back, wiping his bloody lip.

A low growl echoes across the stage. It's me. *Go ahead. Call me emo dark Fae one more time...*

"Rouen, stop!" The Command infuses his tone, but I fight, struggling against my own body. He comes in, and I hit him again. And again.

He takes the blows, his body shuddering as he says the Command again. "Stop hitting me."

A low growl rumbles from my throat. "Screw you." He'll have to Command me to do *anything* he wants. I swear, even if he said *breathe*, I'd resist him.

His eyes gleam shark-black. "I'm warning yo—"

Smack! My fist connects with his cheek, sending him sprawling. "You're what?" I hold my hand to my ear like I can't hear him. "Speak up."

He gets to his feet, his jacket hanging off his left side. The Moribund glints, sinister, and he throws a hand up. In a flash of chimerical black, the Moribund circuits leap off his hand and shoot toward me like dark tentacles.

I dodge them, one, two, three—

The fourth and fifth ones wrap my arms, binding me tight. More bands of Moribund tighten around my legs, my waist. He gestures, and I hurtle back, slamming into the ice castle so hard a nearby column falls over with a *whump*, casting a spate of icy glitter.

I struggle, but I am bound tight, pinned to the fake castle by writhing circuitry. My right hand goes numb, the strength gone out of it, sapping me.

Agravaine saunters toward me. The blood makes him look wild, his white hair a mane about his face. "You're the final piece of my plan, Rouen."

He walks heavily, the left side of him burdened by the Moribund. Even now, I see the tiny bursts of indigo lightning licking across his flesh. He's using it too much, and it's spreading, eating away at him, slowly consuming him, turning him from man to machine. His eyes are full-on black now, inhuman and inhumane. He shrugs as if sloughing off his injuries.

How can he feel anything with that junk inside him anyway?

All I know is, I'll see him dead. For my people. For Syl.

"I need you," he says, and I expect more of his man-baby whining about him being the Huntsman and me, his fated Huntress mate, but instead he shocks me. "You're tied to the hearthstone."

"So what?"

"So, once I infect you fully with the Moribund, then I can blow the circuits. The resulting shockwave of your death will reverberate down the bond you have with the hearthstone and destroy it, and the resulting backlash will not only send UnderHollow into the Harrowing, it will—"

"Allow you to power your Grimmacle," I finish for him, my guts churning. It was one thing to suspect it. To hear it from his own lips is another. He's never wanted to help my people. He only wants to help himself.

I fight, struggling against the black bindings, but they hold me tight.

"I'll create UnderHollow on Earth, but it will be a new Under-Hollow." He paces before me. "For those of us who have been downtrodden." His face grows somber. "I always thought you, of all people, would be with me, Rouen."

"Me?" I want to smack that look right off his face. "I'd never stand by and watch you collapse the Snickleways and trap our people in the darkness."

"Our people?" He spits the words like poison. "They're not our people, Rouen. The entire Winter Court hates us for being sluagh. Your own father abandoned you to this fate. Why stay loyal to him, to them, when you could rule with me? At my feet."

Bloody bones. He's got a point. Of all the arch-Eld, my own father should have believed in me. But full-on betrayal is not my style. And *at his feet*? Seriously? This guy just doesn't get it. "Are you deaf or just stupid?" I fix him with my dark Fae death glare. "I don't want to rule with you."

He chuckles darkly. "A shame."

"And what of these people?" I gesture with my chin out into the gym. Tomorrow night is the Winter Formal. Tomorrow night, this place will be packed with mortals. "What about them?"

He shrugs his Moribund shoulder, and I swear, I hear the circuits hum. "They will fall in line or be consumed." He amends, "Eventually they'll all be consumed anyway."

Clearly he feels no fear at telling me his entire plan. Now that he knows I'm his captive and not going anywhere. I prompt him more. "And when you run out of power?"

He closes the distance between us. He's so close I can smell the ozone of the Moribund. "You'll be a long time dying, Rouen. A living battery."

Shivers run down my spine, but I raise my chin, defiant. "Go ahead, then." I am prepared for it. Prepared to die. Will I see Syl on the other side? Is there a heaven that allows dark Fae and fair Fae both?

Agravaine shakes his head, tsking. "So impatient. But not yet. Tomorrow night, at the mortals' silly Winter Formal dance, when the moon is high and the solstice is at its peak. Midwinter Night. It must be then."

"The ley lines," I say sourly. Like the ocean tides, ley lines respond to the moon cycles, flooding with energy during the full moon. He needs the ley lines to fuel his dark plot, to add power and permanency to his Grimmacle.

"Yes."

I glance across the stage. Fiann is craning her neck to see what we're doing.

"What about her?"

His eyes glint shark-black. "I will keep my promise to her. She will become the new dark Fae queen at my side."

I snort in disgust. "Turning a mortal Fae?"

It's an old trick, a powerful and painful trick—one normally reserved mortals who despise us. To turn them into that which they hate. In Fiann's case, though, she's worshipped us since the first time she saw me take the stage.

It's a dream come true for her.

Except for the part where she'll be Agravaine's little slave, to do with as he pleases. She won't be a queen. She'll be a puppet. At his feet.

"I'm sure she'll enjoy her life as your trophy."

He shrugs that black shoulder, circuits humming. "It is a fate she chose." He studies me, and I see him working out the angles. Can I escape? Can I twist his Commands? Can I break the Contract?

All the answers come. No, no, no.

I am well and truly screwed.

And he knows it.

He turns to walk away, leaving me bound to the wall, bound by the Moribund. He has nothing to fear. No one will find me here. And just to make sure... Ugh.

The creep steps back and casts a Glamoury over me. His smile is all sharky edges. "Tomorrow night, at moonrise, I'll be coming for you. Make your peace."

His boots clomp heavily on the stage as he walks away, and now I let go and let the tears come. Make my peace? I want to be brave. I try to be brave.

But how can I when I've lost Syl and all hope with her?

CHAPTER THIRTY-ONE
SYL

Awakening is the key
Disbelief is the enemy
- Glamma's Grimm

Twenty-nine stories. Holy cats, this is high! The wind whips past me, the coldness cutting through my clothes, making every breath hurt as I hang by my fingernails from the window-washer's scaffolding. *Lucky it was here, Syl.* Another gust blasts me, buffeting me one way, then the other.

Euphoria is long gone.

Still, I'm hanging by that scaffold, four stories below the top. Still a long, long way to fall. The fairy wind I summoned—go, me—to save my bacon when I let go of Euphoria, now it sputters like a car low on gas.

Hang on, hang on.

I've counted four minutes since Euphoria left, since I watched her leap from the building and streak off toward Richmond Elite High. I wait another full sixty seconds to make it an even five.

Then I heave my leg over the railing of the rickety scaffold and crawl to safety.

My heart is pounding in my ears, in my throat—everywhere but where it should. My breath is a hacking rasp, my sweat both clammy cold and stifling hot as I lie there shaking. For a second, I think I could kiss the cleaning-chemical-stained boards, but then reality sets back in.

I'll pass.

Instead, I take some deep breaths, trying to get my poor heart to come down from DEFCON 1. As it does, I lie on my back, looking at the city lights, and take stock of exactly how crappy and impossible my situation is.

Euphoria's gone. She's controlled by Agravaine. Tomorrow night is the Winter Formal, and Agravaine's Moribund-laced trolley tracks surround the entire city. He's got Euphoria, Fiann, the infected student body, *and* an iron circle of power.

Everything he needs to cast a Grimmacle.

Rad. Now I know why Han Solo says, "Never tell me the odds."

Because the odds? Yeah, they're terrible. The world vs. Syl Skye, sleeper-princess, not yet fully Awakened. My power is unpredictable at best. And I'm all alone now.

What can one unAwakened sleeper-princess do?

Nothing.

Ugh. Of course, the part of me that doubts and despairs, that disbelieves—old Syl—that part of me is fully awake. Figures. *Euphoria thinks I'm dead. Euphoria…*

Agravaine's going to hurt her, going to infect her with even more Moribund, and when the solstice strikes, he'll harness the power of Midwinter and the Moribund and use her body as a living conduit. He'll blow the circuitry within her to power his damn circle and cast his Grimmacle over the entire city.

That's why he ordered her to kill me.

Because you can stop him, Syl.

Don't be silly, the disbeliever in me whispers. *You're not even Awakened.* Agravaine holds all the cards. He's got Euphoria, Fiann, the solstice tomorrow night, and a circle of power just raring to go.

But I have to try. He's going to hurt Euphoria. No way am I going to stand for that.

But I can't just go in there all guns a-blazing.

I try to think. What would Mom do?

She'd go in there all guns a-blazing. Gah! So not helpful. I can't even fire a gun much less hit anything. How am I supposed to—?

Unless guns aren't all she's keeping secret. She did pull that Fae-flaunt dust out from Glamma's old hat box. What else could she have been hiding in that closet? In the apartment?

A shudder goes through me. It's such a long shot, and though I feel in my bones that I'm right, I don't want to go back there. No way. No how.

But it's the last place they'd look for you, Syl.

That devious little part of me is right, the cheeky monkey. It *would* be completely stupid and desperate to go back there.

Well, I'm not stupid, but I am desperate, and fifty percent of a plan is better than no plan at all. I decide to risk it.

I look down at the street below. My fairy wind's totally given up, so it looks like I'll be running. Again.

I swear, if we get out of this alive, I'm making Euphoria teach me how to summon a fairy wind and keep it around.

With a sigh, I clamber back atop the building and make the jump across Main Street. My boots slam down, and I'm running across rooftops. My body is bruised, but my heart pounds hard, keeping me going. I'm Euphoria's last hope, the last hope of her people, and now mine too.

I make it back home in record time, and I don't bother with stealth. Agravaine and Fiann are probably long gone, probably at Richmond E, twirling their mustaches and muwahaha-ing in anticipation of tomorrow night. My heart aches, thinking about Euphoria. I should be busting into the school to save her. But at this point, I'd only get myself captured.

I have fifty percent of a plan, but I need more.

I slam through the bottom door and nearly jump out of my skin as a streak of black and white cuts across my path with a loud *mrrowwworrrr!*

Tuxedo kitty?

"What are you doing out here in the hallway?" I bend down to scritch her stubbly ears. She drops into motorboat-loud purring, winding through my legs and rubbing against me. I stand and try to take another step.

Mrrowwworrrr!

Her little kitty-hackles are raised as she tries to block me, with all her six pounds, from heading upstairs.

"Come on, kitty." I sigh and go to pick her up, but she darts away. Little minx. I roll my eyes, refusing to believe I've entered that part of the story where a sentient cat is trying to tell me something. Glamma once made me watch *Lassie* reruns, and I thought I would literally die of boredom. That Timmy kid was the worst. The. Worst.

My mind goes a little crazy, though, when tuxedo kitty blocks me again.

Tux-Kitty, did Timmy fall down the well?

"What is your problem?" I stage-whisper, and yeah, now I'm talking to a cat.

"She doesn't want you to go up there," a familiar voice says.

I have a moment of total culture-shock when I see *Miss Jardin* standing on the landing. I've never seen her outside of school. She still looks like a sexy-evil anime librarian, dressed in a pencil skirt and blazer, her green shirt and red hair too bright in the crappy dim hallway. Her spectacles—yeah, that's the only thing you can call those half-moon jobs—sit perched on her nose. I smell the fresh sweetness of roses and—

"Hello, Syl." And is that the smell of habanero peppers stinging my nose?

"Wait, what...?" I stumble over the obvious question and look around as though I'm getting trolled or something. "What are you doing here?"

"I live here." She steps to the side, and I see the initials on the door. "I'm J.J.—Jessamine Jardin."

"Uh..." Nose still tingling, I look around the hallway, trying to act all cool, like my entire apartment up there hasn't been totally destroyed by evil dark Fae. "I'm...a little busy."

She follows my glance up the stairs. "Do you"—she looks over her spectacles—"need some help?" For a second, I swear she...gets bigger somehow, like she swells up with power, and her shadow gets all weird and distorted on the wall.

It's like something huge and dark and sinister revolves inside her skin. "I can help," she says quietly, her voice all freaky, raspy razorblades.

The stinging scent of habaneros ramps up in the hallway, and my eyes start to water.

A chill runs down my spine, and I try like hell not to see her aura, all warpy and red as hellfire. "N-no," I manage to get out. "It's..." I clear my throat. "You should stay out of it."

"I see." Suddenly, that dark energy is gone, and she's standing there all prim and proper, adjusting her spectacles. She calls the cat—"Miss Hillary!"—and the little tuxedo obeys, just as prim and proper as her mistress. Miss Jardin steps back into her apartment. "If you need me, just call my name."

She closes the door quietly, but it's like all the air rushes back into the hallway, dispelling the Hotty McHotness of chili peppers.

Whoa... What in holy heck was that?

And then I shake it off. I've got a dark Fae girlfriend to save.

Who said she's your girlfriend, Syl?

Ugh. I swat my teen angst away and rush up the stairs.

The door is busted off the hinges, and the couches are all still torn up, glass on the floor, everything broken, and that stupid lamp is still on. I step over shattered glass, trying to be quiet even though there's no one around.

Please tell me there's no one around...

I go straight to the closet, to where Mom pulled down Glamma's hatbox. It's buried behind a ton of junk, so I dive in, cursing as old Rollerblades and some ancient school art projects, most notably a papier-mâché T-Rex, fall around me. The T-Rex bops me on the head, and I pull back, yanking all the garbage—T-Rex, some old clothes, and a spill of battered board games, Clue, Sorry, Parcheesi—with me. Crap goes everywhere.

But I have the hatbox in my hot little hands.

I sit down in the pile of junk and open it, trembling. Just an old pillbox hat and veil. The damp stink of mothballs nearly makes me choke on my own breath. I pull it out. Nothing.

"Looking for something?"

That voice, cold and cruel, shoots down my spine like a spike of ice. I straighten and turn, dread making me all edgy.

Fiann.

She stands there, looking out of place in her designer jeans and Jimmy Choos. Her heels *click-clack-crunch* on the glass as she walks toward me, that crazed Joker Homecoming-queen grin on her face.

"Fiann?" I put the hatbox behind me, but of course she sees it. She's bananapants, not blind. "What are you doing here?" I swallow the rest: *Shouldn't you be scheming your glorious world takeover with what's-his-bucket?*

"I knew you weren't dead." Her eyes look right through me, unblinking, obsessed. She pulls a black dagger from behind her.

Okay, where exactly was she stashing that thing?

It's stupidly huge, like something you'd see in *Final Fantasy,* but that's where the stupid ends. Because it's made of Moribund circuits: dead black, the whole thing—hilt, handle, blade—teeming and jiggering.

"But it's better that you survived." Fiann keeps up having diarrhea of the plan. "Because I'd rather see you alive and on your knees."

Wait, what? I back up, still holding the hatbox. "Fiann, we used to be friends."

Her laugh is madness splintering. "I don't want friends." She comes closer, her teeth bared in a predatory grin. "I want *subjects.*"

So that's what her crazy is all about. I snort. "He'll never make you queen." I back up and up until my back fetches against the wall. "Agravaine's not the kind of guy who shares power. You'll be his hench-wench, at best. Not exactly what I call relationship goals."

"Oh, Syl…you'll see. Once you're infected too."

Crap. I jerk toward the door, but she cuts me off, swiping the dagger down. Barely, I avoid getting nicked. That's all it'll take.

"Fiann, listen—"

"No, you listen!" Her voice rises all shrill, school girl on the edge. "I've had it with being in your shadow, watching you get everything I want, watching you be *special*." She spits the last word venomously, and a toxic laugh rolls out of her. "But now…now you'll be just one of my subjects, your power drained, your lifeforce taken." Her green eyes glitter evilly. "On your knees as my slave."

Yeah. Fat chance, Miss Crazypants.

She lunges for me, and I deck her one. It's satisfying, feeling her nose crunch beneath my fist. *Bam!* I expect a girly scream, but no. Fiann's in full-on bee-yotches-be-crazy mode. Like a killer in a slasher flick, she keeps coming, her nose bloody, her teeth smeared red.

Holy—! I shove the hatbox at her, saving my breath, though I want to laugh when she goes tuckus over teakettle. In a flash, I'm in the hall at the top of the stairs. Home free!

Not.

A sharp pain pierces my shoulder, stopping me cold. I reach back, frantic and freaking, but the knife only breaks, releasing its black circuits to swarm my shoulder, my arm, my hand, the Moribund enveloping the right side of me.

I feel the corruption of it entering my system. I fall to the landing, trying to scream but unable to. I can't breathe, can't think.

Fiann's shadow falls over me. She looms in, her grin all Joker cheerleader on crack. "I'll see you tomorrow night, slave, when the Moribund calls you to Agravaine's ritual."

She steps over me like I'm a sack of potatoes. Her heels *click-clack* on the stairs.

I only hope she breaks one on the cobblestones outside. My mind whirls wildly, my vision going dark, and I grasp for anything before the darkness takes me.

I grasp for anything, and Miss Jardin's voice answers, *"If you need me, just call my name."*

I do it.

My head throbs and swims. My vision blurs as I open my eyes. "Wha...?"

My body hurts, but I am lying on something soft, and there is a purring, motorboat-loud next to my ear. I try to lift my right arm to rub my eyes but can't. I can't feel it.

I try my left and that works. I rub away the blurriness.

I'm on a couch, and Miss Hillary is snuggled up next to my head, purring like mad.

"You're awake." Miss Jardin bustles into the room, bringing her prim and proper air and the spicy smell of chili peppers with her.

Her apartment, it dawns on me. *That's where I am.*

And even though I'm tempted to check out all her 70s disco-retro decor I have waaaaaay more important things to deal with: Euphoria being captured, Agravaine, Fiann, the Moribund dagger—

The fact that I only barely whispered her name before I passed out. How in the holy heck did she hear me?

I sit up awkwardly, my right side numb and oddly heavy at the same time. Steeling myself, I look. *Oh, God. Oh, God, no.* I squeeze my eyes shut. This can't be happening.

Miss Jardin's voice brings me out of my denial. "The blade didn't contain enough circuits to infect you fully, but..."

I look at her, trying not to see the black circuitry spliced into my right arm and shoulder, the Moribund infecting me. "But?"

"But it will continue to spread, like any infection."

Panic settles into me, but I push it down. "There has to be a way to stop it."

"There is." She sits on the love seat across from me.

I blow out a breath of relief. "Great! What is it?"

"The power of an Awakened sleeper-princess."

Not great.

Not to mention… I shoot to my feet. "What time is it?"

"Nine p.m."

Nine…p.m.? That doesn't make sense. I got back home after midnight. *Oh, crap. Crappity crap crap crap.* "I was out the whole day?"

"I'm afraid so."

"So the Formal is going on right now?" I feel like I'm losing my mind here.

"Yes." She looks a little frazzled too. "Syl…"

"What?" I pace, getting used to my right side feeling numb, heavy, useless like a limb that's been put under anesthesia.

"The wound has closed up…" Miss Jardin meets my gaze. "But, Syl, the Moribund is inside you now, and that will speed the infection."

Dread grips me. "How long do I have before it takes me over?"

"An hour, maybe less." She stands. "I'm sorry, Syl. I've failed you."

I look at her. I've no time to sort out what she means, but one thing is for certain. "You haven't failed me. But I have to go. Euphoria needs me."

"You can't go there like that." Miss Jardin's speaks calmly, but Miss Hillary leaps into her lap, lashing tail punctuating Miss J's next words. "Agravaine will sense you. He will kill you."

I shake my head. "If I don't stop him, he'll kill Euphoria, he'll take over the city. There won't be anything to live *for*."

I take a deep breath and steel myself. "I'm going." Tonight is the night.

And no matter what comes, Euphoria and I must face it together.

CHAPTER THIRTY-TWO
ROUEN

Alone, I wait for you
Twisting in misery
I am nothing
Without you
- "Alone," Euphoria

Once Agravaine sets the Moribund free, once it swarms me, the initial shock and agony subside into a spreading numbness, my body thrashing on the column like a leaf buffeted by the wind.

I pass in and out of consciousness as I am infected.

One time, I come to and find Agravaine standing too close, his hand on my heart. His touch is cold, more poisonous than all the Moribund put together. And then comes the pain. White-hot and freezing cold, it feels like he is trying to pierce me through. The agony makes my body bow off the column. It leaves me breathless, staring at him in hatred.

He leans in, his lips nearly brushing my ear and whispers, *"In the end, you'll destroy everything anyway, Rouen."*

I want to tell him to stick it, that I'd die before harming my people.

But I only grey out again, back into the numbness. I am glad of it. I don't want to feel anything.

Syl is…gone. I can't bring myself to say *dead*, even in my mind.

Emo to the end, Roue.

Struggling is no use. I've been struggling through the night and into the day, the Moribund slowly eating away, infecting me, the sounds of the empty school echoing lonely around me—until finally Agravaine and Fiann come, and bring with them the hellhounds of the Hunt. Savage, pitiful beasts. Their circuitry claws clack and scrape the lacquered wood as Agravaine Commands them into place around the stage.

They'll watch and wait. In case anyone tries to stop him or tries to save me.

Wishful thinking, Roue.

As I watch, Agravaine casts a Glamoury on the stage, enveloping me and the hounds in an illusion. I look like a statue at the center of the ice castle, and they become columns of shimmering ice.

I'm on my own now. Over these past twenty-four hours, I've never felt so alone.

Syl…

It won't be long before I join her—assuming that dark Fae and sleeper-princesses have some kind of common afterlife.

Ooh, grimdark *and* emo? I'm such an overachiever.

Even now, the Moribund circuits spliced into my flesh spark and flare as they drain me, indigo lightning spasming across their circuitry as they devour my strength, my gramarye, the winter in my blood. My very life-force.

Every part of me that is Rouen Rivoche being siphoned away.

It doesn't hurt. Much.

If I'm lucky, when it's through I'll be like those Moribund hounds—husks of empty machinery, dark contrivances bent to Agravaine's will. Disguised, they lurk on the stage, the Wild Hunt ready to savage any who might try to stop Agravaine and his dark plot.

Will I become one of them?

But I know deep in my wounded heart, that's not my end.

Against all hope, I still see myself with Syl.

New Syl and new Rouen.

Her hand is in mine, and we are at the top of a building in Richmond center, laughing. I'm pushing her. Another tough-love lesson, and she's giving me crap as always, but our connection's strong, the heat between us rising, and there's that gleam in her—

The Moribund glints and gleams a bruised blue-purple as a flash of energy surges from me. Dimly, I become aware of other noises in the gym—people talking, laughing, a few bro-dudes shouting.

The Formal's starting.

And then, all around me, the music swells as the band strikes up. Somehow, being drained is less painful than watching Fiann take my place on stage. She lifts my violin—my actual violin, not the borrowed one—the glassy surface shining under the stage lights. She begins to play.

The violin glimmers with foul indigo power, and the pain in my hand stretches and pulls all the way up my arm and into my shoulder, like cords of energy being plucked. She's pulling the gramarye right out of me, using the violin as a conduit.

Agravaine smirks my way. This is his doing.

All right, *now* it hurts. Now it feels like the essence of me is being torn away, torn through my skin, leaving me gasping, captured in the Moribund.

I give Fiann the stink eye. *I swear by rue and wrath, before this is done I'm going to slap the crap out of you, Moribund Barbie.*

The music swells outward in ripples of serenity, bliss, *euphoria.* I am immune. It's still my power, even though she's stealing it. The students, though… They stop their mad dancing and begin to sway in a wave, just like that night I met Syl. They sway as one, their eyes going glassy, and Fiann shouts with triumph, her song turning into a mockery of mine, dark and sinister, and promising blood and retribution.

Syl...if only you were here with me.

I block out the music, let it swim around me. I conserve my strength. Syl wouldn't give up, and neither can I. I only need a break, a chance, a distraction. Anything.

Another jolt of pain racks through me as the Moribund drains me slowly, so slowly. It's not solstice-time yet. How do I know? Because Agravaine so helpfully carved a skylight out of the ceiling directly over center-stage and yours truly. *Jerk.* Through the ragged hole I see darkness and stars, the glimmer of moonlight, but the moon's not at its peak. The ley lines aren't fully charged yet, and so Agravaine hasn't begun draining the student body.

But soon...

I feel it in my blood. In my bones, the hearthstone cries out, weakening.

Tonight it will die.

Unless I do something. But I cannot get free. I must wait. Choose my moment.

Hours pass, the music flowing and fading, the moon creeping closer until I see the very edge of it through the hole in the ceiling. Once it's directly overhead, framed by the makeshift skylight, that's when he'll start.

That's when people will start to die.

On stage, Fiann keeps sawing away at my violin. She seems to never get tired. Agravaine must not have told her... It's dangerous, the gramarye. Her fingers bleed on the strings, but she's caught up in her first experience with Fae magic. Personal gramarye takes years and years to learn to control.

She'll likely play until her fingers are ragged, bloody stumps.

Boo. Hoo. After what she did to Syl and me, I feel exactly zero sympathy for her.

Syl... I want to struggle, to cry out, but no one will hear me beneath the Glamoury that Agravaine has cast on me. They see only the centerpiece of the scenery, a statue in the courtyard of an ice castle.

The irony is not lost on me.

Bloody bones, I'm going to die as a set piece in Frozen.

My situation is eye-rollingly bad. Even if I could get free, there are the hell-hounds to consider…

A better time will come, Rouen, I tell myself. *A better time.*

But my time seems short. Like, scary-short.

I'm not sure how much passes before a shadow falls over me. Agravaine stands there, all picture-perfect in his black leather jacket, black jeans, and jackboots. His face is pallid white, his eyes shark-black, and beneath the leather, Moribund teems across his flesh, tiny licks of indigo lightning sparking and flaring. It's almost taken him over completely now—his chest, his abdomen, shoulders…every part of him glittering and black as though he's grown some gross bug carapace.

I bare my fangs at him. "I'm glad to see your exterior finally matches the ugliness inside."

His face twists in a mockery of sympathy. "Oh, Rouen." With a Moribund-infested hand, he pushes my sweaty black hair from my face. He leans close so I can hear him over the music. "Rouen, Rouen, it didn't have to end like this."

He looks like one of those romance-book heroes, but I know the truth of him. Liar, murderer, usurper. The dark Fae didn't make him a prince in UnderHollow, so he wants to make his own realm and be king.

"We could have been allies in this," he says, and now there is a note of regret in his voice.

Seriously? I summon a laugh from deep inside. "Who the hell are you kidding, buddy-boy?" My body shivers and racks as the Moribund festers within me. It's been a slow process this past twenty-four hours, and I see in his eyes, he means to speed it up. "You enslaved me, tried to turn me against my own people—*our* people."

"They were never my people!" Rage stains his cheeks, his face the only part of him that isn't Moribund-black. "I had no choice.

They never saw me as anything but the Huntsman, an errand-boy sent to chase down their prey."

"The sleeper-princesses…" How many of them did I help him kill? Even at this late hour, I find the strength to struggle. "You used them for your own purpose, drained them of their blood and their power."

"Yes." He paces, his hobnails *clunk-clunking* on the wooden stage. "The sleeper-princesses gave me the strength I needed to exist outside UnderHollow." He fixes me with a baleful eye. "I am not a royal dark Fae, Rouen. Away from UnderHollow, I have very little innate power and needed all the help I could get. Their summer blood did nicely." He checks my Moribund bonds, testing each, his biceps flexing with black circuitry. "And now, once I drain the hearthstone power through you, once I fuel the Moribund in the trolley circle, I will create a permanent, solid Glamoury. My own Grimmacle. UnderHollow right here on Earth. My kingdom."

I want to spit in his face, but my mouth is dry, the Moribund's drain dehydrating me. I settle for snark. "You might be king, but you're still a loser." I cough, the Moribund spasming through me. "King of Losers."

The strike comes as anticipated, and my head rocks back.

I laugh, tasting blood. "Kind of proving my point, guy."

His fangs are huge and white as he snarls. "You would do well to respect me, and I might end you quickly."

Ha. Fat chance. I remember his words in the throes of his gloating. *"You will be a long time dying, Rouen."* I snort. "Spare me the lies, pal." I struggle again. "You're going to look awfully foolish when I get out of this."

It's his turn to laugh now. "Oh?" He arches a perfectly white brow and shakes out his perfectly white hair. "You don't understand, do you, Rouen? Let me spell it out for you." He gets in my face, all bad boy and spite. "I hold all the cards. I Command you. I have the city encircled with Moribund tracks. Once the moon hits its crest, I'll blow those circuits in you and all these students"—he gestures at the teeming crowd below the stage—"and the energy from the hearthstone will surge through you. I'll steal it as you're dying, run it along the trolley tracks, and divert the ley lines into creating my circle of power. Your life-force will power my Grimmacle, create my paradise on Earth and—"

"Blah, blah, blah…" I roll my eyes and manage a chuckle despite the pain.

And just then, the first beams of moonlight strike down on me.

Damn it. There goes my gloating.

With the cruelest smile imaginable, Agravaine steps back. "Good-bye, Rouen." He clenches a fist, and by his will alone, the Moribund inside me increase their draining, surging my strength out of me. In horrific answer, I feel the hearthstone in my chest. Like a second heart, it beats, labored and failing. The hearthstone gutters in my mind's eye, beginning to break, taxed to its limit. It pitches and shakes. Cracks rip across its dark surface.

Agravaine is pulling the power through me, out of me, and I can do nothing to stop it.

My body racks, and I fight, screaming through bared teeth.

And then the doors to the gymnasium crash open.

Brilliant light spills into the Winter Formal, casting all the decorations into a blaze of white.

No, it can't be. My heart seizes, and my breath freezes in my throat. I can't hope. I shouldn't hope. But I do.

Dear ancestors, I do.

A figure steps into the light, short and lithe, confident.

The music stops, Agravaine gesturing, Fiann lowering my violin, her fingertips dripping blood.

Syl.

Bloody bones. I've broken all the emo barriers, and I'm straight-up hallucinating.

But no. It's really her.

She stands in the open doorway, my sweet Summer girl at the edge of winter, all badass, dressed in jeans, a graphic tee, and my leather jacket. It's big on her, but it looks good. Fitting. My body responds with a different kind of heat. She takes a step into the room, and the entire student body parts for her, darkness parting to let in the light.

I feel her presence calling to me. I see her trying not to look at me. I sense she wants to. I want her to, but something tells me I must not distract her.

She focuses on Agravaine, her grey eyes filled with disgust and amusement. And then her voice echoes across the gym. "Did someone order a steaming pile of whoop-ass?"

CHAPTER THIRTY-THREE
SYL

Before the light of Awakening
Comes the darkness of doubt
- Glamma's Grimm

After mic-dropping my snarky threat on Agravaine, I get my inner Buffy on by swaggering into the gym in Euphoria's leather jacket like I own the place. Yeah, just call me the Belle of the Brawl.

I touch my shoulder gingerly. I only hope the Glamoury I just cast holds. It's one of my first, and it's meant to trick the Moribund into thinking I'm not a Happy Meal. *Nothing like starting the video game on Level Fifty.*

The student body parts in a wave. They're all glassy eyes and hollow cheeks, their mouths open, catching flies. On stage, I see Fiann lowering Euphoria's violin, and I want to slap the sick look of triumph clean off her face.

But first things first.

Agravaine. He's got my girl bound to a column in the middle of the stage. I try not to meet her gaze for fear I'll totally lose my mind and rush in like an amateur. *Keep your head in the game, Syl. Focus.*

I mean, yeah, I'm gonna rush in. My fifty percent of a plan kind of demands it. But when I rush in, I want to be more Wonder Woman and less love-struck sophomore engaging in Bad Idea Theatre. I take my time crossing the gym, like I have all the time in the world. Like I'm savoring the moment before I kick Agravaine's sorry Moribund-infected patootie. No matter what happens, I swear I'm going to punch him square in the face at least once.

No one hurts my girl and gets away with it.

My girl... For the first time it feels right. Mine. Because if we get out of this, I'm going to tell her how I really feel.

Somehow, the idea of that is scarier than taking on Agravaine all alone.

All right. Enough teen angst for two seconds. Let's get to the butt-kicking!

If the Glamoury holds...

If it keeps the Moribund from seeing me as...me. The sleeper-princess. Confused, the dark circuitry revolves in on itself, forming a protective knot in my shoulder, refusing to infect the rest of my body because it can't sense tasty sleeper-princess flesh. It can't sense anything. Convinced it's in a hostile environment, it's curled into a ball.

But I'm not fully Awakened, and the Glamoury is so not perfect. It has flaws and imperfections. It's only a matter of time before the Moribund, like a rat in a cage, tests the limits of it Glamouried prison and finds one of the walls weaker.

Only a matter of time before it breaks through.

Until then... I look up at Agravaine on the stage. Until then, I have this jerk to take care of.

I'm not yet Awakened. But hey, this is the part where the plucky heroine saves the day, right?

I swallow hard. I hope.

"Syl." Agravaine plays the part of jerky bad guy to a T, coming to the edge of the stage to taunt me.

Keep it up, pal.

He leans over, studying me as I saunter up through a parting wave of students. He cocks his head. "You're supposed to be dead."

"I got better."

"Hmmm…so it appears." A dark chuckle rumbles from his chest. He's not wearing a shirt beneath his motorcycle jacket, and all I can see is the chittering expanse of Moribund circuitry that's taken over his flesh. Gross. Agravaine looks at me and grins evilly. "Here to beat me up, little girl?"

"You know it."

He straightens to his full six-foot-two and cracks his neck. "You can certainly try."

"Try, nothing." I can't wait to punch his face in. "I'm gonna kick your sorry butt back to UnderHollow. I know it. You know it. All these people know it. It's gonna be legend."

"Legend." He smirks. "Speaking of legend…" He gestures at the dark half of the stage—"Kill her"—and the shadows leap up like eager…hounds.

Crap.

I'm still about twenty feet from the stage, and it's only now that I notice them. *Too busy checking out the cute girl, Syl?*

Ummm…guilty.

Disguised as ice columns flanking the giant fake ice castle, the hell-hounds of the Hunt lift their heads and howl, their furnacing green eyes burning through the gloom and fake fog.

Ugh. Of course Cheaty McCheaterface is going to use his minions.

They prowl toward me, their black circuitry coats glistening, hackles raised. Within me, the Moribund lurches. I push back with the Glamoury.

Please hold. It has to.

I'm not done yet.

As one, the hell-hounds attack. I dodge one as it flies off the stage, all teeth and howling. Instinctively, the students move away from the snarling hell-hounds, their eyes glassy. A few of them begin to shake off Fiann's stolen Euphoria spell.

Agravaine snaps at the Queen of Mean. "Play! Now!"

Fiann jolts, a deer in the headlights, then lifts the violin to her chin and draws the bow across the strings. Her fingers drip blood, and her face wears a plastic expression of triumph, confusion, pain, pleasure—all mixed up into some gross tangle, like that whacked-out grin she wore on Homecoming night.

Note to self: Fae magic is some creepy stuff. Like Euphoria said, there's always a price.

Also, I will never understand Fiann.

I never want to.

Whatever. Time to kick some dark Fae butt.

I charge in, dodging two more hell-hounds on my race to the stage. I might only be partway Awakened, but I can still pull off some pretty fancy moves. Three more steps, and I do a forward flip onto the stage.

"Agravaine!" I swing, slamming him in the chest, but my fist *pangs* off the circuitry armor he's got going. Looks like one hit won't do it.

Fine. Dude deserves a beating.

I wade in. He backs way up, that annoying smirk on his snotty face, and the biggest hell-hound leaps in my way. I lash out with a kick that sends it sprawling. In a flash, the others leap to their alpha's defense, charging the stage—and yours truly. One latches on to my arm, and I punch it in the muzzle. With a yelp, it lets go. Luckily, Euphoria's leather jacket protects me.

Still, the Moribund in the hell-hound calls to the Moribund inside me.

The Glamoury begins to crack.

Hang on. I will it to hold. *Hang on.*

The other hell-hounds pace around me, all slavering jaws and green-glowing eyes as the music swells and the student body sways on the floor below. Fiann picks up the pace, really winding up with Euphoria's gramarye.

She turns to me with that crazed Joker grin. "Having fun, Syl?"

"Loads," I assure her. Without waiting, I lunge, striking one of the hell-hounds in the head with a hammer-fist. I follow up with a kick to its ribs and an elbow uppercut that Ronda Rousey would be envious of. The thing explodes in a shower of jiggering Moribund circuits, raining down over the stage.

And then it's on.

I'm a blur as I move through the hell-hounds, dodging teeth and claws, lucky as hell that Euphoria's jacket keeps me from getting too torn up. Power sings through my veins as I destroy hell-hound after hell-hound, the explosion of Moribund circuits around me making my skin tingle, prickle…

The Glamoury cracking and cracking…

Only three hell-hounds left. *Hang in there, Glamoury!*

The first hell-hound leaps in, and I meet it, my punch entering its throat and tearing out the back of its head in a shower of black circuits.

Cool—gross! I'm not sure which…

The second and third attack me together, leaping on me, bringing me down with their weight. I land hard on the stage, the hell-hounds snapping at my face. I throw my leather-clad arm into the left one's mouth and turn aside. The right one gets a mouthful of stage. I roll with the left hound, smashing it with my free fist until it lets go.

One more punch sends it to hell-hound heaven, and I turn to face the other one. Two down. One to go.

I don't wait. I attack, faking a kick and then driving down with both fists onto the top of its head. It collapses, shattering into Moribund circuits.

And then it's just me standing on the stage, the Moribund circuits chittering and jiggering around me. My Glamoury is seriously cracked but holding. Euphoria's still alive. We might actually get out of this.

I might actually win this thing.

I face Agravaine. "Where were we?"

He chin-nods, a *look behind you* gesture, and laughs.

"Seriously, guy? Do you think I'm going to fall for tha—?"

And that's when the lightning hits me.

Black as night, it tears across my body in great lashes, searing through the leather jacket and into my skin, making me feel like I'll never breathe anything but burning-hot ozone ever again. I jerk and writhe, caught in the electrical current.

Deep inside me, the Moribund awakens.

It pushes against the Glamoury I've constructed, cracking it even more, and my house of cards begins to topple.

Cackling like Witch Hazel in a Bugs Bunny cartoon, Fiann hits me again, black lightning lashing over me in jolting tendrils. My knees buckle, and I crash to the stage. In a moment, Agravaine is there. I sit up, but his boot slams me down.

The Glamoury is breaking, shattering. I hold on to it for dear life. If my Glamoury fails, the Moribund will overrun my body.

He leans down, and now the Moribund circuits jitter across the floor. "Come to me." And they do. They leap at his command and bind me up like they did that day in the lab, like they did to Euphoria. Even now, she is fighting, screaming my name. I can barely hear her through my own struggles, my labored breath, the beating of my heart fast and crazed.

"You failed." Agravaine's words are hot in my ear, sowing the poisonous seeds of doubt, and on the heels of it, he tries to gaslight me. "You're not a sleeper-princess. You're just a little girl. You failed to save your mother, and now you'll fail Rouen, too. Aren't you tired of failing, Syl? Aren't you tired of fighting? Just give up. Give in."

"No!" I struggle, but the Moribund binds me tight, threading around my arms, my legs, pinning me to the stage. Worse, the Moribund inside me surges like nobody's business.

More of the Glamoury breaks and breaks, collapsing.

"Why fight it, only to fail again?" Agravaine's voice is rumbling, soothing. I struggle and strain, but he presses down, the Moribund binding me tighter. "Just let go, give in. It'll be so much easier."

I fight on, struggling, but the Moribund ignites like a fever, and for a second, his words make a twisted kind of sense.

And then, the Glamoury shatters.

My skin tingles, becoming numb as the Moribund within me breaks free and begins to infect me. Immediately, I feel my strength ebb, the Moribund splicing into me from the inside out, taking me over cell by cell.

All my doubts grow stronger, darker, and my strength rushes out. My partly Awakened body grows tired and heavy, the black circuitry racing through my skin, rewriting me into a creature of despair and darkness.

"That's it, Syl. Good girl." Agravaine's words come from far away now. "Give up. Give in. Rest."

I've fought the good fight. I tried to Awaken, tried so hard to become the sleeper-princess, the new Syl. I deserve to rest now, don't I?

He echoes the thoughts poisoning my mind. "Stop fighting, and I will show you mercy. I'll let you and Euphoria be together. I'll send you to your end together."

That sounds...nice. The Moribund steals my anger, steals my pain. Everything is going numb and blissful. I should be immune to the gramarye Fiann is pumping out, but the Moribund opens me up to it. Steals my immunity the way Fiann stole Euphoria's gramarye.

"You didn't think you could actually beat me, did you?" He looms over me, his weight like having a house on my chest. "A little girl like you. You're not even Awakened."

He's right. I'm not even Awakened. I'm not the sleeper-princess. I'm just the old Syl. My heart cries out for Mom, for Euphoria, for anyone to help me.

I can't do it alone. What's the point of doing it all alone?

"That's it. Give in. You're nothing. Become nothing..."

I want to fight. My heart cries out, but my body, drained by the Moribund, can't fathom how to fight. My eyes are closing, my body relaxing, the Moribund eating through my cells at an alarming rate. In a few moments, it'll all be over. I am ready to let go.

Only a tiny part of me remains, a tiny flicker inside.

I claw at the stage, my heart not allowing me to let go even though my mind is sluggish and my body aches. The agony will only continue.

I guess I will die in agony then.

Euphoria... My heart beats hard. *Euphoria... I cannot give up. I will not.*

The agony bears down, and my world lights up in darkness and doubt and pain.

CHAPTER THIRTY-FOUR
ROUEN

Standing at the finish line
Not knowing if we win or lose
As long as we're together
There's a chance
- "Endgame," Euphoria

Syl...Syl! All my excitement at seeing her stride like a total badass into the gym, all my pride in seeing her fight, destroying the hellhounds and standing up to Agravaine, goes up in smoke as he slams her to the floor and begins binding her with Moribund circuits.

Her cries are blotted out by the music, and she fights, but he is too strong. The Moribund is too strong. Something else hinders her, too, but I cannot put my finger on it.

I want with every fiber of my dark Fae being to help her, but I've got troubles of my own to deal with first.

Pinned to a fake ice castle, the Moribund poisoning my strength, draining my life-force away in tiny ebbs like a tide pulling out to sea.

I've stopped fighting. For now. The Moribund binds me too tightly anyway, and I'm saving my strength for one last surge to break free. I'll have to deal with Agravaine and his Command over me, that blasted Contract, but seriously?

I'll burn that bridge when I come to it.

For now, I wait, fighting my every instinct as the Moribund drains and drains me. It knows I want to escape. It knows my heart goes out to Syl, and it locks down, trying to crush my body, my spirit.

"S—" It steals my breath, and I cannot even cry out to her.

My chest constricts and then expands painfully, and I feel the hearthstone inside me like a second heart, cracking and breaking from the strain. At any moment, Agravaine will force me to tap into its power.

More and more moonbeams shine down upon me. It's only moments before the moon hits its zenith, only moments before the solstice occurs. He'll Command me then, force me to pull the remaining power from the hearthstone for his own dark purposes—to ignite the ley lines and bend them to his will, encasing Richmond in a citywide Glamoury. He'll Command me to use the last energy of the hearthstone to make it real, to turn it into a Grimmacle.

UnderHollow come to Earth with him installed as king, dictator, tyrant.

The thought of it is bad enough, but Syl…

She lies on the stage, thrashing in agony, and now it hits me like a hammer to my head. The Moribund. They've infected her. I can tell from Agravaine's triumphant smirk, from Fiann's creepy grin.

They're like a crappy pair of James Bond villains. *I can't wait to kick both your asses.*

But maybe that's a little…ambitious.

Syl and I aren't in any condition to kick much of anything.

Except the bucket, the grimdark part of my mind nudges me, and I tamp down on it with gritted fangs.

But it does look bad. And I'm not even being emo about it.

Not one little bit.

The Moribund infects her body. I smell it, the sickly-sweet ozone of it filling my nostrils even at a distance. Somehow, Agravaine and Fiann bypassed what should have been her natural sleeper-princess immunity and infected her.

And it's getting worse. It ripples and writhes beneath her skin. Her cries are lost in the sounds of Fiann sawing away at my violin, but I hear her. It strikes a chord in me, rumbling in my chest.

I have to help her.

I have only one chance to break free.

And then what?

Agravaine will only Command me, and I'll be right back at square one. There has to be another way...

I have only seconds. Even now, the moon is almost framed in the makeshift skylight. Any second now, any breath, it will move into position, and the moment of the solstice will come. The ley lines will fire. They'll be ripe for the bending, the plucking, and then Agravaine will Command me to tap into the hearthstone. He'll blow the Moribund circuits in all of us—me, Syl, the students—and our deaths will power his dark scheme.

Dark scheme? That is so emo, Roue.

Whatever. I save my strength. I want so much to break free, but I'll never get to Syl in time.

Agravaine stands over her, but his shark-black gaze turns to me, bathed in the moonlight. *He knows he's got us. Creep.* Below, on the floor, the student body still sways, captive to Fiann's spell, my stolen gramarye. When the solstice falls, he'll call upon the Moribund in their bodies before he ignites it down the lines and blows their fuses, devouring their life-forces as the Moribund rips them apart from the inside out.

He's waiting—we all are—for the solstice.

More moonbeams pierce the skylight. Agravaine jerks his chin toward the dance floor. I want to keep giving him my death-glare, but I look.

Damn it all.

The ley lines! Seven glowing blue lines cutting laser-like through the fake fog rolling onto the dance floor. They come from seven different directions, each making a beeline for me. I am the center of the spell, of Agravaine's mass Glamoury. The ley lines will converge on this spot, the center of his circle of power, and then the solstice will energize it, the hearthstone will augment it, and we will all die.

And Syl...

Agravaine stands over her, berating her. "You're nothing, Syl. You can't save anyone. You can't even save yourself."

I grit my fangs so hard I'm surprised they don't splinter. *Don't listen to him, Syl! Don't listen!* But I can't call out, can't scream.

Inside me, the hearthstone is breaking. I've reserved my strength for this, for one final push to break out. I can make it. I can save myself.

Or I can save Syl.

I don't have the strength for both.

The ley lines glow brighter as they carve through the fog, racing up and then onto the stage. They are coming for me. If I am to break free, I have to do it now.

Do it! Break free! Run!

My every instinct ramps up into flight mode, and I let it, let the strength build up inside me. I grit my teeth, and a cry forces itself up from deep inside—filled with rage and power and all that is Rouen Rivoche, princess of the dark Fae and the Winter Court.

My muscles flex, forcing the Moribund in my body to obey, and with a monumental surge, I rip free of the black circuitry bonds. Moribund circuits scatter about me, pattering to the stage like scarabs falling.

Go, run! Go! My instincts drive me to flee, but my heart...

Syl...

All my love for her fills me up, overflows, and keeps me here. *Oh, hell. Emo to the end, then.*

I brush the remnants of clinging circuits from my shoulder and deliberately boot the ice castle column. Hard. The thing teeters, totters, and then falls with a crash between Fiann and Agravaine.

I smirk, showing just enough fang to really get his goat—"Oh, yoo-hoo!"—and as he looks up, I flying-kick him over the column, hitting him right in the kisser. *Pow! Zowie!* Down he goes—boom!—and away from Syl.

I'm on him in a murder's moment, grinning wickedly, my raven-dark hair flying wild as I punch him in the jaw and then the cheekbone. A smattering of blood flies, and while he's dazed, I glance back over my shoulder.

"Syl!" I find my voice and shout for her. She's nearly taken over now, Moribund circuits crawling over her flesh. She struggles to rise at my voice and then collapses back to the stage, the circuits like insects feasting on her flesh, turning her into a creature of dark machinery.

Keep your head in the fight, Roue!

I turn back… Right into Agravaine's fist.

Not my best moment.

His punch slams me backward, staggering, seeing stars. I shake off the pain, catch my balance in time to see him leap. *Crap. Crap. Crap.* Midair, he thrusts his fist out, and the Moribund circuits rush down his arm, making a black blade, sharp and glinting in the stage lights.

Barely, I dodge it and it slices into the stage, kicking up wood and splinters in the spot where I just was. My heart is throbbing in my chest, the hearthstone failing, threatening to drag me down with it. "Syl! Fight!"

She's our last chance. If only she could see it. If only she believed, she could Awaken. This has been her problem all along. In every one of our training sessions.

She doesn't believe in herself.

Agravaine strides toward me. The Moribund expands along his chest, forming a thicker black carapace-armor over his body. Spikes thrust upward at his shoulders, jagged planes that glint razor-sharp. He lifts his blade-arm as he bears down on me. "Dumb move, Rouen."

He slashes, and I dodge. The columns next to me tilt and shear off in the middle, their tops crashing down to the stage. Still, Fiann and the band play on. Still, Syl fights.

"Syl!"

Behind me, a blue glow ignites the fog, lighting up the room, the ley lines gleaming like diamond spiderweb strands as they all come to a point.

A bright flash, and a column of blue energy surges upward through the ceiling to the sky. The solstice, the ley lines... Everything is ready. His Grimmacle needs only one more thing.

Me.

He steps in, swiping at me with his blade, backing me up. "You're going into that column."

"Screw you, buddy-boy." But I can't help moving back before the swipes of his huge blade.

His black eyes gleam, and his voice grows heavy with Command. "Step into the column of light, Rouen."

The Command slams into me harder than his fist. I fight back. "Screw. You." Immediately, a rush of pain stabs into my head, lighting up my body in agony. Blood rushes from my nose, but I fight.

No way am I going down like a chump.

He extends his finger, and a blade shoots out, all Terminator-like. He aims it at Syl, but before I can react, he pulls back an inch from her throat. The Moribund holds her there, his captive, her throat exposed.

"The column, Rouen, or she dies."

"You won't kill her." *Damn it all to the Harrowing, he will.* He doesn't need her any more. He's got me, the Moribund, the trolley circle, the ley lines. Syl is...icing on the cake.

And that icing is about to get bloody.

He watches me figure it out and raises one perfect white eyebrow.

Seriously. I hate losing to this guy, but what choice do I have? Eventually, I'll lose against his Command, and he'll have my power anyway.

At least with Syl alive...

I stop struggling. At least with her alive, we have a chance in hell. Okay, it's a *snowball's* chance in hell, but I'll take it.

I step into the column of blue light. Instantly, it numbs me, and my body seizes. The drain and draw from the Moribund was nothing compared to this. I feel the power of winter solstice slicing into me, as though the column is a blade of light. It cuts deep, to the heart of the hearthstone.

My heartbeat riots, hard and fast, and for a moment, the hearthstone hangs in my mind's eye, a cracked and imperfect jewel.

And then, the cracks light up with guttering, glowing darkness, the infections and flaws running over it like rivulets of water, creaking, cracking, opening the faults into gaps.

I fall to my knees, racked with pain, all my strength fleeing.

Instead of fighting, I use my last breath before the breaking. I use it to call out to her.

"Syl, I believe in you."

And then in the darkness of UnderHollow, the hearthstone shatters.

CHAPTER THIRTY-FIVE
SYL

Clap if you believe in fairies
-Glamma's Grimm

It's over.

I want to keep fighting, but the Moribund takes me over. It drains me of my strength, my will, everything. I feel Agravaine looming over me, see his hobnailed boots on either side of my head. His words are cutting, cutting deep into my soul.

"You can't save anyone. You can't even save yourself. Sleeper-princess—ha! Who do you think you are? You're nothing special. No one."

Is he right? Have I failed?

The Moribund infecting me whispers, *Yes. Just let go, let it all end in peaceful numbness.*

I don't want to, but holding on seems so hard, and in the next moment, I am falling, failing. The music becomes a low, dim throb, the Moribund within me, pulsing, growing stronger as it eats away at me.

From the corner of my eye, I see the glowing blue lines. The ley lines have all intersected on the stage, making a seven-pointed star. A column of light stands in the middle, so crazy-bright my vision blurs and I have to look away. I know all this is important, but for the life of me I can't remember why.

Euphoria told you, my tired mind pokes me. *Euphoria. Remember her?*

Agravaine's laughter is vicious and somehow soothing. "It will all be over in a moment, and you can die as plain old Syl Skye."

Old Syl. Is that who I am? Every cell, every pore, every nerve ending is on fire, aching, hurting. I know in my heart I have to fight, but my body is breaking, becoming Moribund.

In my mind, I hear Glamma Gentry, her voice sharp and commanding. *Syl. Syl, get up. Stand up. Don't give up.*

Glamma, it's so hard...

Don't be whiny-pants, Syl. Don't give in.

A tiny flame ignites within me.

There are still people who love you, who need you.

Really, Glamma. Who? I know there is someone, but the Moribund won't let me remember.

And then from far off. "I believe in you, Syl. I believe in you."

That voice... It can't be. *Euphoria?*

Euphoria! She is nearby and she needs me. I look up, struggling to see through the black circuits that clog my vision like scales, that try hard to turn me into a dark Moribund machine. My Fae-sight stutters. *Come on, come on!*

I fight, give it a vicious push, and the world lights up in auras. Oranges and reds and yellows, blues and greys. I see Agravaine surrounded by indigo-black ick—more machine than man, not even half of him warm, living flesh. Fiann all red and bleeding, the students a cold grey, washed out and caught in the gramarye of her stolen magic.

And Euphoria.

I see her in the column of light now, her aura suffocated in a growing black shroud, the ley lines a muted blue all around her.

She is racking and jerking, her strength pulled from her veins by the Moribund.

Our gazes meet, her blue eyes ringed in gold, glowing wildly, and then that glow, that fight fades. A sad smile curves her full lips.

"I believe in you, Syl."

And then she is lost to her agony.

I believe in you.

Euphoria believes, but did I ever? It all flashes before me—the train, the accident, my struggles to Awaken. I never believed I was anything but ordinary Syl Skye. On top of the building, I'd argued with Euphoria. *"This is crazy. I'm only human,"* were my exact words to her.

But you're not. For the first time, the sleeper-princess in me whispers. *You're extraordinary, Syl, and it's time to embrace it.*

Time to embrace it. Time to embrace the new Syl. Like you promised. New Syl and new Rouen. Together.

I take a deep breath. I steel myself.

I believe in you, Syl.

I breathe out. And believe.

Instantly, the power within me sparks to fiery life, summer's heat fanned to flame. It swells inside my chest, blistering, burning, burning away all my fear and doubt—a massive sheet of fire about to sweep down upon me and ignite me, body and soul. I'm caught up in the power, in the terror and exhilaration, all wrapped up in my belief.

And my love for Euphoria. That is there, too, blazing in my heart.

I have denied it for too long—all of it.

No more. No more being whiny-pants.

This time, instead of shying away from my power, my love for her, I dive in. I dive into the deep end.

New Syl and new Rouen.

Summer's heat bursts inside me, hot and wild, a runaway bonfire blazing in my heart and soul. With my next breath, I am filled with fire and purest sunlight, with power and newfound strength. I slough off the Moribund circuits, a dark snake shedding its skin.

The circuits ignite at my touch, burning away in white-hot flame. My entire body is on fire, with power, with…*Awakening.*

I stand before my enemies, Syl Skye reborn.

My belief, my love for Euphoria makes me powerful, a force to be reckoned with. In fury and anger I turn to Agravaine. His eyes are wide, wild. He sees his precious plans going to crap all around him. He strides toward me, his white hair flowing like a movie villain's, his arm elongating into a wickedly curved Moribund blade the size of a steel girder.

"You really think that's going to help you?" I smirk, all drunk with power. "You're so done, pal."

"You won't stop me. You can't!" He lunges at me, throwing his arm out, that Moribund blade sweeping in to make me a head shorter.

As if. I lift my hand, contort it.

White flame burns from my fingertips, cutting through the stage smoke. And when the blade touches my fingers, it scorches away like paper in the wind. Cinders, ash—that is what the Moribund becomes—and Agravaine staggers away, my white flame eating down that blade, down his arm.

Now who's the Happy Meal, jerk?

And yeah, now that it's had a taste, my sleeper-princess power ignites even brighter, hungry for more. Can't stop, won't stop, it consumes the Moribund down his arm to the shoulder before he finally makes a second blade with his good arm and chops off the first.

Whoa. Now that is next-level crazy.

His severed arm falls to the stage, bursting into ashes as my white flames eat up the rest of it. Like Glamma always said, *What goes around comes around.*

And hoo-boy, it's coming around.

Agravaine shakes his white mane, his face screwed up in pain. "No," he growls, and I know he's going to say something totally villainesque like, *Oh my beautiful wickedness!* or some such nonsense.

Ridiculous to the end, he totally does. "You can't win. You're nothing. You're no one. No one!"

"Wrong," I tell him, straightening to my full five-foot-six. "I'm Syl Skye, the last sleeper-princess."

And with that, the final barrier breaks. I Awaken in all my power and glory. White fire lights me up inside and out. I am burning, but I am unharmed.

I am on fire. I *am* the fire. The white flame.

Hell yeah.

I stride toward him, and he backs up fast, panic on his face as he calls to all his little Moribund circuits—the ones I haven't totally burned to blackness. The circuits that lie on the floor jigger and jerk and leap to him, building and rebuilding his arm, stacking up until his blade arm and shoulder are a black map of teeming circuitry and jagged spikes.

He turns to me, leering. "See if you can defeat me now, sleeper-princess."

I snort. "You should really quit while you're ahead." My hands ignite in white flame. He comes on, spikes and spears of Moribund slicing in to pierce me. I stand there, and as they wing in, with a small gesture, my white-flame power burns them all. Black Moribund goes up in smoke.

Ashes rain down. The stench of ozone ripples in the air, and through all the smoke, I can barely see the stage, the floor, the students. Somewhere, Fiann is sawing wildly at the bow, freaking out because she literally can't stop. Euphoria is somewhere behind me, the ley lines lighting her up in a blare of blue.

Euphoria! I turn to go to her, but Agravaine gets in my way, rebuilding himself again.

"You're not saving her," he snarls, doubling down on his stupidity.

Seriously? I've got no more time for this clown.

I step forward. "It's time, Agravaine." I barely recognize my own voice. The sleeper-princess in me sleeps no more. I am fully Awakened, all the fire and fury of summer pulsing through my limbs. In one last-ditch effort, he charges. He strikes and strikes at me, but the white flame burns and burns and burns.

Finally, I clench my fist and dim my fire.

His body a smoking ruin, Agravaine lies there on the stage. I stride toward him all casual-like, and he scooches back on his butt like a washed-up comic-book villain. I keep coming, white flame trailing a garland in my wake.

Fear swallows his smugness, but Jerky McJerkface has more tricks up his sleeve. "What about Rouen?" he asks. "She has only a few more moments before the Moribund consumes her."

He gestures, and finally some of the smoke clears. I turn to see her racked with pain, spasming inside the seven-star ley lines. "Euphoria!" I take a step, but I feel him loom up, a Moribund blade like the one Fiann used on me in his hot little hand.

I whip around and grab his wrist, the sound of my hand slapping on his like a gunshot. He struggles to dagger me, the knife an inch from my face. But I'm stronger than him now, fully Awakened.

I hold him easily.

"That's...impossible!" he grits out, totally losing whatever cool he had left.

I can't help smirking in his face. "It's not impossible if you believe. And I do."

Okay, I might just said I believe in fairies, but whatever.

Alarm and panic flicker in his eyes, and I kind of love it. *Yeah, you got this coming, pal.* He throws another punch, and I catch that hand too. I'm like Jet Li and Jackie Chan all rolled into one badass chick. I hold him there, by both his wrists.

"You can't..." He struggles, trying his best to pull away, but I have him.

"Agravaine..." I hold his wrists and then slam his hands together again and again. "Clap if you believe in fairies." I keep him there for a sec, making him clap like a baby harp seal, and then I slam my forehead into his nose.

Blood gushes, and he falls to the stage in a heap. *Jerk.*

I turn and rush to Euphoria.

She's burning up in blue. I go to reach for her, but as soon as my hand gets close, the white flame ignites on my fingers like brilliant fireflies. An alarm screams in my mind. *Don't! You'll kill her.*

It's true. I know by instinct that the summer fire in my blood would strike at the winter chill in hers. I can't even touch her—not with Awakened sleeper-princess power. *No. No, no, no, no.* I pace before her, freaking out. There has to be a way. We've come so far.

"Euphoria! Fight it!" *I'll save you. I'll find a way.*

I have to. She's my love. My life.

My love…

"Rouen…" Her real name feels strange on my lips—strange but also right. It fits. We fit. Together. "Rouen Rivoche, I love you."

CHAPTER THIRTY-SIX
ROUEN

My angel I hear you from the heavens
My angel, I dwell in hell
My angel
My white-flame angel
- "Angel," Euphoria

"Euphoria! Fight it!" Barely, I hear Syl's voice coming through the haze of agony and pain. How long have I stood here, helpless? Hells and Harrowing, I've become the damsel in distress.

Totally emo, Roue.

Fact is, though, right now? I might need a little saving. And if anyone's going to do it, it might as well my girl. *My Syl.* Even through the pain, the thought warms me, brings me at least the promise of relief.

"Rouen!"

Now I know it's serious. She never uses my real name. Her hand passes close to me. The white flame sears into my eyes, my heart.

It sears me with fear. If she so much as touches me with that Summer power...

I'll die, and not only that. I'll cease to exist, my very soul scorched to cinders.

Why not? Let her touch me. The hearthstone is shattered. In my mind, I feel the slow, crushing collapse—the gates and passages, all the Snickleways to UnderHollow breaking down in the wake of the hearthstone's demise, the vaults buckling, the castle crumbling as the ley lines are pulled off course from their natural arcs. There will be no way to get home. No way to save my people.

They will slumber, trapped in Winter's Sleep, in the collapsing darkness. Forever.

I've failed.

A failure as a princess.

But Syl... She is anything but a failure. She's Awakened, a full fair Fae princess in all her bright glory.

She'll defeat Agravaine, and I will be but nothing more than a casualty.

Ooh, that's even more emo!

She wants to touch me, to save me. I can see that in her eyes. I want to be with her too, but we are as we are—me, a dark Fae princess, and her, a princess of the fair Fae. Awakened. Burning with white flame that will poison me, kill me, burn me out of existence.

I am not the hearthstone. I could not survive the barest brush of her fingers.

"Syl..." I manage, not caring that the entire world is a raging Dumpster fire. Fiann still playing, and Agravaine is down, but not dead. I have to warn her, have to tell her to kill him.

"Syl..."

She tries to shush me. "Rouen Rivoche, I love you."

Everything stops.

The world, the Moribund, my heart.

She...*loves* me?

317

A dark shadow falls on her. Agravaine!

My heart swells with fear and love. In that moment, my strength returns.

"Syl!" In a Herculean effort, I tear free and throw myself at him, tackling him to the stage. He fights, punching at me with his one good fist, and the blows that come, that rain down on me feel like penance—all I've done wrong returning to remind me of old Rouen and all her crimes.

I roll to my back, Agravaine snarling. *"Take her,"* he snarls. *"Take her now."*

His Command laces my bones and blood with obedience, and though I fight, I am exhausted, spent. My body obeys him, dragging me up to stand before her.

The last sleeper-princess.

Syl faces me, shining in an aura of white flame.

If I so much as touch her, I will be killed, consumed…

At least I will die with her.

Take her, Agravaine's Command sears into my brain. *Take her, take her, take her…*

I fill myself with all the love I have for her, tears welling in my eyes. Yeah, it's emo, but here, at the end, I don't really care.

"Take her now!"

I stand before Syl, and she looks up at me with those storm-grey eyes. A deep breath. I reach out to her, to take her as Agravaine Commands, and to die in her arms.

She remains still, unafraid. "I believe in you too, Rouen."

And in that moment, the blazing heat between us—the heat that I've felt from the very moment we met—ignites, and all the love I feel for her rushes into fire and flame inside me.

I take her…in a kiss.

The first brush of her lips against mine is a balm to my soul, my heart, my body. I've wanted this forever. Every part of me wants her, needs her. I fall into her—into her arms, into her kiss, into everything that is Syl.

The white flame washes over me.

"Rouen," she whispers into our kiss. My body relaxes, all the agony pouring out like liquid from a vessel. I am home. I am with her. No more fighting, no more pain. Just bliss.

The fire intensifies, purifying me inside and out, burning the Moribund and my old self away, ashes falling as our kiss deepens. Her hands are in my hair, mine around her waist. I pull her close, her body blazing-hot against mine.

She is burning me, but I am not consumed.

We blaze and we burn. Together.

Summer and Winter occupying the same space.

Take her, take her, take her! Agravaine's Command blares in my mind, but our combined heat sweeps through me, firing through my veins like cables of electricity igniting. The Command in my mind glows red-hot and then burns away, and with it burns the Contract—my body, my blood purged in the pure white flame of the sleeper-princess.

And when she finally, gently breaks our kiss, I take what feels like my first real breath, and we stand together, hand in hand.

New Syl and new Rouen.

She steps back from me, holding me at arm's length. "There, now. No more reason to be emo."

I cock an eyebrow, trying hard to keep my cool. "There's always a reason to be emo." But I crack on the last word. "Syl, I..."

"I know." She lays a hand on mine. "It's okay."

"It's not okay—not by a long shot," a deep growl rumbles from behind her.

Agravaine. He pushes himself to his feet, his arm a raggedy stump up to his shoulder. Blood spurts from beneath the fingers of his good hand as he grips it tight. His face is as white as his hair, blood running from his mouth.

"Do it," he snarls. I brace, but he throws the Command over his shoulder—at Fiann. "Do it now!"

Fiann hits a shrill note, and black lighting arcs from my violin across the room. It strikes through the students, piercing them through one by one, wrapping them in chain-lightning, linking them all together.

Hell and hue, this is not good. So not good.

The ley lines ignite in fiery blue energy, and Agravaine steps into the column of moonlight. He raises a hand, calling on the power of winter solstice, calling it into him, channeling it through the sorry remains of his Moribund circuitry.

Fiann saws away with bloody fingers at the violin, and as the black lightning strikes through the last student, it comes back to her. She redirects it, lashing it toward Agravaine.

It hits him solid, and he staggers, but the lightning isn't piercing him. He's consuming it, consuming all the energy from the students infected by his Moribund. One by one, they begin collapsing like broken marionettes.

He's blowing their circuits—igniting the Moribund within them and then siphoning it off. He'll devour their energy and use it to heal his injuries.

His plot with the trolley circle and the Grimmacle might be totally ruined, but if he succeeds in this, he'll be whole and hale, ready to fight, ready to try again.

"Syl." I reach for her hand and take it.

"You two," Agravaine says, laughing as the power pours into him. "Wait right there. We have unfinished business." And the entire gym lights up as the power rushes from the students into him.

Another wave of them topples over. Part by part, circuit by cell, Agravaine is being remade, the Moribund circuits on the stage leaping into his body, stitching him back together like some horrid dark contrivance.

Crap, crap, crap, crap, crap. I tug Syl's hand, but she stays firm.

She meets my gaze. "I have an idea. Trust me?"

I do. My gaze is steady on hers. But I have to give her a hard time. "You have a plan, princess?"

She shrugs one shoulder. "Fifty percent of a plan."

I nod sagely. "Good enough for me."

She takes my hand, and with fifty percent of a plan, we face the end together.

CHAPTER THIRTY-SEVEN
SYL

Don't piss off the fairies
- Glamma's Grimm

I really don't know what-all I intend to do, but I am filled with power, so much it feels like my body will burst with it, burst and burn like a supernova. One thing's for sure—I'm through denying who I am, what I am.

I'm Syl Skye, fair Fae princess of the Summer Court, and I am ready to kick some serious butt.

I look at Euphoria.

Correction—*we* are about to kick some serious butt. It's always been about me and Euphoria. The dark Fae princess and the fair Fae princess. Mortal enemies.

Now we are brought together. In love.

I grab Euphoria's hand, and that fifty percent of a plan inside my brain blooms into about seventy percent. *Ha! Better than nothing.*

Instead of racing toward Agravaine, I rush at Fiann.

Fiann's the key.

She stands on the edge of the stage, her face locked in that crazy Harley Quinn grin. Hoo-boy, I am going to enjoy wiping that off her face. And by wiping it off, I mean smacking it off.

She's playing and playing, caught up in the gramarye she's stolen from my girl. It's dangerous—Fae power—if you don't know how to control it. Clearly Fiann has zero clue.

She's one of the Wakeful, she might even be becoming Fae, but right now, she's nothing more than a pale imitation. An imitation sleeper-princess. A wannabe.

And I am so about to burst her little bubble.

She sees me coming, and even though she's faestruck by the gramarye, she's got enough sense to attack. The first slash of the bow sends a lash of black lightning at me. Euphoria and I dodge. The bolt strikes the ice castle, splitting it into a smoking ruin.

It collapses between us, and I duck as Fiann lashes out again. Dark lightning zaps past my head. *Whoa. That was waaaay too close.* Crouching, I skirt around the destroyed ice castle, but Fiann spots me and lashes out again and again.

I run, barely keeping ahead of the bolts. "Euphoria!"

She meets me on the other side, and as we come together, Fiann lashes out at both of us, indigo bolts shearing through the air. We're caught.

Instinctively, I throw my hand up…

…and a shield of white flame flares into being.

The black bolts crack off it.

"Use your gramarye!" I urge Euphoria, but she looks at me like I've got ten heads.

"I can't. I'm not powerful enough without my violin." She ducks against me as Fiann pours on the insane-o villainess act, dark lightning crackling and spitting off my shield.

If we step one foot wrong, we'll get fried for sure. I nudge Euphoria. "You've got to. We have no other choice."

"This is your fifty-percent plan, princess?" She cocks an eyebrow at me as we're washed in the sinister light of indigo electricity.

"Yup." I pour all my power into my shield. "It's your turn to Awaken."

She gives me the stink eye. "I'm no sleeper-princess. I can't Awaken."

"I know. I'm just trying to get you to"—and now I know how she felt standing on that skyscraper with me denying all my powers, all my potential—"to use your power in a way you haven't yet." Like her, I know my girl has it in her. I've just gotta show her.

Another lesson of tough love.

But this time I'm the teacher.

I shove her out from behind the shield.

"Syl!" She glares. "That's it! We're breaking u—"

Too late! Fiann looses a zap of black lightning at her.

Euphoria instinctively throws a hand up, and she absorbs it. She *absorbs* it! After all, it's her power Fiann's using.

I whoop and do a little happy dance.

Euphoria takes just enough time to give me a dirty look, and then she strides forward, absorbing every single one of Fiann's blasts. She's so badass, but she is weak from being drained by the Moribund.

And Fiann is all caught up in her stolen power, crazed and faestruck.

Euphoria gets three steps from her, but the barrage of lightning keeps her at bay.

It's time to do this together.

I step out from behind my shield, waving it away into white smoke, and come to stand shoulder to shoulder with Euphoria. "Ready?"

She looks aside at me. "Always."

"So, you're not breaking up with me?" I ask cheekily.

She smirks. "We'll see, princess."

A simple gesture, and I send a sheet of white flame at Fiann, melding it with Euphoria's as she sends a bolt of violet lightning lashing from her hand.

Our combined power—dark Fae/fair Fae—strikes Fiann, cutting through her own lightning, and taking her down to her knees. That Joker grin of hers turns ugly, and just like Agravaine, I know she's going to resort to some TV movie villain threat.

"You'll never win!" She grits her teeth, blood pouring from her torn-up fingers.

I don't even justify that with a comeback. I just step in and punch her in the face. She goes down like a ton of bricks, dropping Euphoria's violin, and I shake out my hand with a sigh. "Shut up already."

And then I scoop up the violin and thrust it into Euphoria's hands. All around us the students are collapsing, their life-forces sucked away into Agravaine. He is seconds from reviving, his Moribund spikes growing, growing, sweeping in to pierce us.

Maybe I should've paid more attention to him. But, in my defense, it was only fifty percent of a plan.

Time for the rest of it. I look at Euphoria, and she gets me. She knows what I mean to do.

Like the pro she is, Euphoria hoists the violin, and with the first stroke of her bow, she sends violet lightning scorching through the air. I lend my white-flame power to it.

We don't target Agravaine.

We target the kids.

The bands of violet and pure white flame strike the students, piercing through them just as Fiann's gramarye did, but this time, instead of draining them, the power burns away the circuitry, purifying them, stopping the energy transfer to Agravaine.

He howls from his place in the moonlight, and Euphoria and I both turn as one, unleashing our combined might on him. We strike Agravaine, white flame and violet lightning piercing him, and the stolen energy bleeds out of him, his Moribund circuitry melting like black butter.

Pulling back on our power, we reverse the stream, pulling out of him and back into the students. Giving them back their stolen life-force, purging them, reviving them.

Fiann screams from where she lies on the stage, the pain finally reaching her now that the gramarye has let her go. A pang of sympathy strikes me, but I need my head in the game.

Agravaine steps from the light.

He raises his hand, the Moribund dripping off him, melting as he comes.

"I will kill you!" He lunges at me, wild, savage.

I try to step back, but he's quicker.

He grabs me.

And then he begins to burn.

There's no big moment, no time for a witty retort or taunt. One minute, he's got me in his grasp, and the next, he's on fire, the white flame leaping from me to him, purging him, purifying him.

Now is not a good time to be made of Moribund.

He snarls, gritting his teeth, his leather jacket rippling like he's caught in a high wind. He tries to push through my power, the Moribund staring to rebuild even as it's eaten away.

I pour on the white flame, wrestling with him, his fingers gripping my throat. I hear Euphoria cry out my name. And then the white flame flares over him, igniting his clothing, his skin, his hair.

In a flash, he's burnt black—a crispy critter. I break away from him, and he collapses into ashes. I want to say I regret him dying, but seriously? He enslaved Euphoria, attacked my mom, nearly killed me. Jerk had it coming.

I brush the remnants of him off Euphoria's jacket. "Guy really knows how to make an exit."

Euphoria checks me over and then walks over to the fire alarm. "Time to make our exit." She pulls it.

The blaring wail seems to wake everyone up. Just like that, the lights come up, students pick themselves up off the floor. No one notices us, cloaked by my Glamoury. They won't remember us passing through them; they won't remember us being here. I don't know how I know, but I do.

It's a shame that tomorrow I will go back to being ordinary Syl Skye.

I take Euphoria's hand in mine.

But no. Nothing could ever make me ordinary again. My white-flame power coils in my chest, warm, waiting for me to call on it again. I am Awakened.

I snatch the Winter Queen crown off the podium right before Fiann's eyes and put it on my girl's head.

She cocks an eyebrow and adjusts it. "What's this for?"

"You're my princess now."

"Oh really?"

"Well, I did finally catch you."

Her smile lights up the room. "So you did." And right there on the stage, in the midst of the destruction that was our Winter Formal, she grabs me around the waist and pulls me in. "And I've caught you back."

"So you did."

She kisses me under the archway, and the world goes away.

CHAPTER THIRTY-EIGHT
SYL & ROUEN

"Syl!" my mom calls as the nurse wheels her across the blinding white hospital lobby toward me and Euphoria. The wheelchair makes Mom look small, but the fierce look in her eyes is back. She's chopped most of her long red hair off—too much bed-head from being in a coma for weeks and weeks, she said—and she looks pixie-ish and mischievous.

Nothing keeps my mom down, that's for sure.

It's been months since Euphoria and I gave Agravaine the old smackdown, and in between school and work, I've spent every waking hour at Mom's bedside, hoping, just hoping she'd wake up. And then bam! One night, there she was, sitting up, asking for a Five Guys bacon cheeseburger.

Once she could stomach solid food again, I got her one every day. That was a month ago. Since then, it's been some serious therapy to get her back on track. She's coming home today.

I wave as the nurse brings her closer. It seems so unreal. My mom come back to life, practically. Suddenly, I've got something in my eye... I look away, try to think of something else.

Euphoria and I have spent the past month redoing the apartment, getting everything ready. Miss Jardin helped too. I guess it's nice having a helpful downstairs neighbor who knows what we are, even if I don't really know who—or what—she is.

The apartment smells like jalapeno peppers, but it's clean and the furniture's been repaired.

Anyway, later for that. Right now, I'm just psyched that Mom's going to be okay.

Euphoria gives me a little nudge, and I run to my mom and hug her. Thankfully, she has no real idea of what went down the night of the Winter Formal. The papers just said there was a "technical problem" with the sound equipment, and a lot of kids got treated for dehydration. Fiann got treated for malnutrition—probably from the Moribund—and her raw fingers—from being faestruck by the gramarye—and then she was sent to a rehab of sorts. Or at least, that's the official story.

I guess no one wants to say the words "mental health facility." Looks like her rich, privileged family would rather everyone think she was on drugs.

A part of me feels sorry for her, even after all she did to me, to my mom, Euphoria…

I mean, she fell to madness. And all for the sake of popularity? No thanks. I'd rather be a misfit geek forever.

At least, the danger's passed. Agravaine is dead. Fiann's no longer a threat. Without the Moribund, it's not like she can make good on her plans for world conquest. Guess she'll have to wait on that teenage dream of becoming the dark Fae queen.

Boo. Hoo.

I step back and take my mom's clothes and stuff from the nurse. "Ready?"

Mom nods. I see in her eyes and in her aura that she wants to ask me what happened that night, but she doesn't. I told her that everything was taken care of. Agravaine, the Moribund. Of course she heard about Fiann. Everyone did. I blame Prudence for that, the little minx.

Fiann'll have all she can do to pass this year and not get held back. Her parents are wealthy, though. I'm sure a hefty contribution to Richmond E will smooth things over. After all, no one knows that she was half of the plan behind killing the entire student body and turning them into batteries for Agravaine's dark plan, à la *The Matrix*.

Yeah, that girl's got some serious baggage.

The nurse wheels my mom to the door, where I've got our crappy soccer-mom SUV waiting. I fall in step and Euphoria trails behind.

As for the rest of the school… Winter's come and gone, and spring is in the air. Classes end in a week. Things are back to normal. I'm still on the school newspaper, me and Prudence with her GoPro. Nowadays, we use our hall passes as they were meant to be used—to take pics for the yearbook—not to spy on evil dark Circuit Fae. Prudence's even worked her way up to senior editor since Justice is graduating.

The Spring Formal's tonight. Euphoria and I are skipping it. We've had enough stuffy formals with dark Fae trying to take over the world to last a lifetime.

The gymnasium was repaired for minor damage. The cops cited a water main breakage. It's like nothing ever really happened there.

But Euphoria and I know.

We know the truth.

I hug my mom tight. I'll never forget as long as I live all the sacrifices she made for me; I'll never forget what Fiann tried, what Agravaine did. I'll never forget who I am.

"I love you, Mom."

"Love you too, bug." She eyes Euphoria over my shoulder.

Uh-oh. I can feel it like a prickle up my spine—the old enemy starefest thing is going to come back full force. I swear, the two of them. Glamma would say they're like two little old French ladies bickering.

But my mom only holds her hand out to Euphoria. "Come on, girls, let's go home."

We get back to Syl's place, after a side trek to Five Guys for bacon cheeseburgers—yum!—and I'm expecting Syl's mom to want to crash out on the couch and relax. Instead, she points at her daughter. "Syl, go grab a sheet from the hall closet."

Syl gives her a bit of a funny look but does it, and when she comes back, Georgina tosses me a hammer and a pack of nails. I catch them both, wondering if she meant to brain me with the hammer. That smirk on her face tells me she wouldn't have minded. Not like it can really hurt me, anyway. But I swear, lady likes to embarrass me.

"What gives, Mom?" Syl finally asks, standing there with a *Hello Kitty* sheet. It's kind of adorable.

Georgina starts stringing twine across the living room and gives me a look over her shoulder.

Uh-oh. I know that look. It's a *mess with my daughter at your peril* look. And suddenly I get what she's doing.

"If you're going to stay here, you can't very well stay on the couch or in Syl's room." She's rocking that Mom stare, the one that lets us know that she knows. About us.

I do my best not to blush. *Nope. Not gonna... Ah, crap.* At least I'm darker complexioned than Syl. She wears her blush like a badge of pink on both cheeks. I want to kiss those cheeks, but not with her mom staring at me like I'm some kind of stalker.

I only nod, bobbing my head like a dork and then helping her string the twine across a third of the living room. We hang the sheet, and I've got a little alcove of my own.

"We'll pick up a futon at the Scratch 'n' Dent this weekend," Georgina says. "And you'll be expected to chip in around here."

"Sure." I shrug one shoulder. I'm, like, a fancy glam-Goth star. "I'm happy to chip in for rent." No sweat.

"And chores and cooking." Georgina fixes me with that glare again.

I want to tell her I'd burn water, but my objection dies on my lips. It feels weirdly good to have a mom getting on my case. "I'll… uh…learn."

"Good." She puts her hands on her hips. "Now get out of here and let a lady get some rest."

"Wait, what?" Syl asks.

"Go." Her mom makes shoo fingers at us. "The Spring Formal is tonight. Don't think I don't know."

Syl looks at her. "But we don't have—"

"Your tickets are taped to the fridge."

Whoa. That is some next-level mom wizardry.

"But…" Syl splutters, trying to find an excuse, and somewhere in there, I get the sense that maybe she does want to go.

I step in to save her. "We can use the same dresses we bought for the Winter Formal." I wink at her, and she caves. I suspect she wanted to cave all along.

"Thanks," I say to Georgina as Syl scampers off to her room. I go to follow.

"Rouen." Georgina's voice stops me cold. "Have my daughter back by eleven. No fighting Moribund hell-hounds, no battles with dark Fae wannabe princes, and no funny business."

My face gets red at that last thing, and I have to throw a retort or I just wouldn't be me. "What are you, my mo—?" And then I stop, because yeah, she kind of is.

And I'm kind of okay with it.

Plus, I don't want to tell her that although Agravaine is dead and Fiann's out of commission, there's still the matter of UnderHollow and my people. With the hearthstone broken, the passages to UnderHollow are all caved in. The rest of the dark lands will follow, in a slow, collapsing decay, until my people are entombed in the vaults below the gloomy castle, entombed in Winter's Sleep. Forever.

I'll never stop looking for ways to free them.

And then there's Syl…Awakening as the fair Fae princess. The fair Fae haven't been seen in a hundred years, but then again, they've had no reason to resurface. Maybe with Syl Awakened and Agravaine gone, maybe they'll come to claim her.

And then who knows that'll happen? It's not like the fair Fae and the dark Fae are on friendly terms. Nope. Not at all. I'm sure there'll be some big throwdown when those fancypants fair Fae find out a dark Fae princess is dating their golden girl—the entire Summer Court with their panties in a bunch.

My gaze meets Georgina's, and I see it in her eyes—she knows all of this stuff is coming down the pipeline. When it does, we'll be ready.

For now, though, Syl and I can revel in being "ordinary" high school students going to a Spring Formal.

"Come on, E!" Syl's voice echoes from her bedroom.

Georgina nods, and I do what I always do.

I go chasing after Syl.

The End

The Adventure continues in *Ouroboros*,
Book 2 of the Circuit Fae

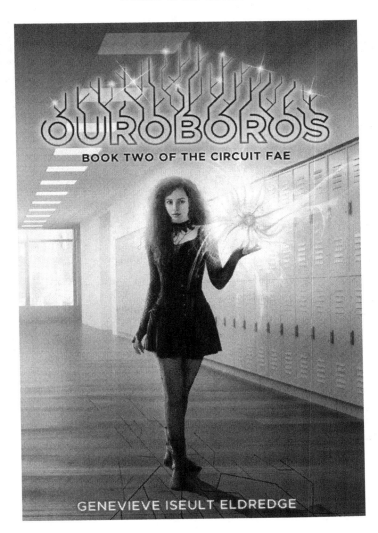

Also from Monster House Books
The shifter fairy tale, *Wolves & Roses*

Also from Monster House Books
The best selling paranormal romance series, *Angelbound*

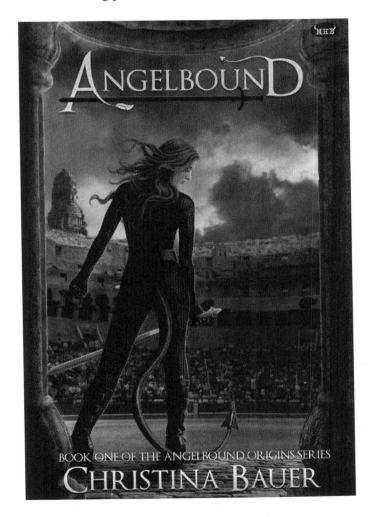

Also from Monster House Books
The dark fantasy romance series, *Beholder*

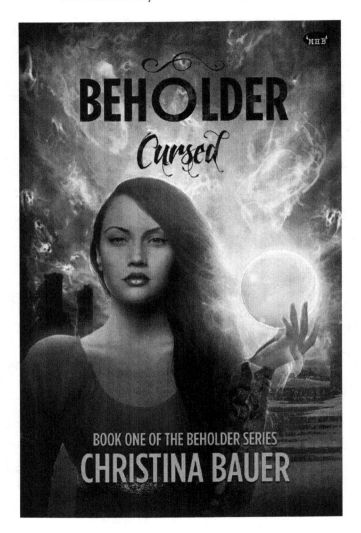

Also from Monster House Books
The snarky dystopian novel, *Dimension Drift*

Like Orwell's 1984, only Meimi Archer kicks ass and topples governments.

DIMENSION
DRIFT

PREQUEL 1
CHRISTINA BAUER

Genevieve Iseult Eldredge is an author and editor, an MFA grad from Seton Hill University, a martial artist, sapphist, a self-rescuing princess, and all-around strong female character. She's multi-published and in her role as an editor has helped hundreds of authors make their dream of being published a reality.

Born in the wrong century, GIE is more able to fix a chariot than a computer. Nevertheless, she forges ahead on her trusty laptop to bring her love of LGBT literature, urban fantasy, young adult fiction, and fairies together in her lesbian YA series, Circuit Fae.

She believes in fairies (in fact, she's clapping right now), true love (not "to blave"), and championing the often-unheard female voice. She might be using D&D figures to plot out an epic fight scene right now.